Bellies

Bellies

a novel

Nicola Dinan

HANOVER
SQUARE
PRESS

**HANOVER
SQUARE
PRESS™**

Recycling programs
for this product may
not exist in your area.

ISBN-13: 978-1-335-49088-9

Bellies

First published in 2023 in Great Britain by Transworld, an imprint of Penguin Random House UK.
This edition published in 2023.

Hanover Square Press
22 Adelaide St. West, 41st Floor
Toronto, Ontario M5H 4E3, Canada
HanoverSqPress.com
BookClubbish.com

Printed in U.S.A.

In memory of Dad

1

Bellies

I wore a dress on the night I first met Ming.

A crowd swarmed the union bar, and my shoulders jostled as boys dressed as girls and girls dressed as boys pushed in and out of the front line. A tightness seized my brain, a vacuum-pack seal over its folds. I looked up. Large paper flowers hung from the vaulted ceilings, tinsel streamers stretched from one corner of the long Victorian hall to the other, music blared through the double doors opposite the bar.

The ruffled bodice of the leopard-print dress hugged my chest. Everything else Sarah had was too small for me. The dress robbed me of full breaths. Rob had fastened me into it with his strong hands, wolf-whistling in my ear when he'd let go of the metal zip. A bulb of dread had flowered in the seat of my stomach as I saw my reflection in Sarah's mirror. I was lanky and looked as if I'd lost a dare. Sarah was behind me, standing like Supernanny even with her bare breasts duct-taped. Her voice rattled in my ear. Tonight will be good for you, Tom! Loosen up, otherwise in a room full of drag queens you'll look like an incel. Look at Rob. She'd pointed to Rob, tall and twirling in the corner of her room in a white linen dress, the lace hem dancing against his shins, his floppy brown hair bouncing on his forehead.

Sarah had a new monkish wisdom about all things queer, but with none of the monastic silence. She'd come out after I had, but in a few short months she'd acquired a buzz cut, found a new girlfriend called Lisa, and pretended to understand Judith Butler. It was as if we'd never dated. Can you even believe me and Tom were together? It was literally six months ago, Sarah.

I looked behind me, above the heads of the crowd at the bar. Sarah was at the other end of the room, hugging a boy in a platinum wig. A corset pinched his waist; his nipples were bare. He stood on stilty heels poking out from his black flares, towering over Sarah. He looked much better than I did. More pop starlet reclaiming her image, less Liza Minnelli in sensible black loafers.

I turned back to the bar and ordered three drinks from the pale and expressionless bartender. One for Sarah, one for me and an extra third. I held them with both hands as I moved out from the crowd, lifting the triangle of glasses to take a careful sip; it restored some lightness to my head. Sarah waved me over. I set the drinks on the low table in front of them.

"I'm Tom," I said.

"Ming," the boy said.

I reached my hand out towards him. He leaned in for a hug. The backs of my fingers met the steel bones of his corset, its lip pressing into my chest. We were the same height with his heels on. He fanned his arm along my back in a strangely familiar way, then lowered himself, landing on the sofa cushions. Sarah sat down next to him, and I on the adjacent armchair. The edge of my knee touched Ming's.

Up close I could see the mealy glue that held his real eyebrows down. Foundation had settled in the ridges of the laminated hairs. Two thin and inky arches took refuge above the ridge of his brow bone, framing his dark, long eyes. Thick contour disguised the round tip of his nose. Above and below the makeup was a handsome face. A delicate face.

"Ming's a friend of Lisa's," Sarah said. "We met after I got back from China."

Lisa's name aroused discomfort in me. Another reminder that Sarah was ahead, and I was behind. They had got together while teaching at a summer camp for wealthy children on the outskirts of Beijing. The last conversation between me and Sarah as a couple began to replay in my mind. This happened sometimes. The supercut spared me the minutiae and showed only the highlights, and for that I thanked the disintegrating touch of time and an active want to forget. The cringe still lingered on, though. It'd been after she'd got a place to teach at that camp. We'd sat on the bed, and she'd looked at me sternly. Why haven't you booked your flights to Beijing yet? I just can't. My Mandarin's fluent, Tom, how much easier do you need the trip to be? I can't come and visit you because I'm gay. What are you saying, Tom? I'm gay, and I think we should break up. And then my eyes had sputtered like taps onto her lap. I just don't want you to think I'm a bad person! Okay, Tom. I could still feel the cold stroke of her fingers over my hair.

"Ming and Lisa wrote a play together last year," Sarah added.

"What was it?"

"Gay Virgins," Ming said.

"What was it about?"

"Gay virgins."

Ming laughed. Sarah laughed with him. His smile widened, pushing a small dimple into his cheek. I imagined myself poking the fleshy dent. Boop! What the fuck are you doing? A quick panic flushed through me. I brought my legs closer together; the blobs of leopard print sagged as the fabric gathered. I held the rim of one of the drinks on the table and gave it to Sarah. I moved the third drink towards Ming.

"This was for Rob," I said. "Have it. I don't know where he's gone."

"Thank you."

His eyes lingered on me as I pulled my dress up and fished the flask out of my tights, taking my bag of tobacco out with it. I leaned forward, my knee pushing a little more into his. I twisted the cap and tipped some vodka into my own drink, then into Sarah's, and then held it over Ming's. His red lips curved into a smile, and I splashed some into his cup. The dress felt more natural sitting next to him.

"Cheers," Ming said.

Our eyes met as we sipped. Is this a vibe? Maybe it's just polite eye contact.

"Have either of you seen Lisa?" Sarah asked as we lowered our cups.

"I think she's in the main room," Ming said.

"Shall we head in?" she asked.

I held up the pouch of tobacco. Ming's eyes followed it.

"I can roll one for you?" I offered.

Ming smiled. I looked to Sarah, tilting my head, motioning for her to go ahead through the double doors. She left us. Ming hobbled along towards the exit. His heels restricted his gait, and so with each step I held for a moment longer at the balls of my feet.

"Sorry," he said, "I'm really slow in these."

"I didn't even notice."

Ming looked down at my shoes.

"What are those?" he asked. "They look orthopedic."

I stopped walking and twisted my feet inward, staring down at the plain black loafers.

"This is all I really had," I said. "I didn't want to buy anything new. Are they that bad?"

"For the occasion, yes. Don't worry." He held a hand over his eyes. "I'll block them out."

I laughed.

"How kind of you."

We kept on walking. I looked back before we stepped outside and saw Lisa and Sarah, already making out by the double doors. I think I like girls, Tom. It's so nice dating someone who isn't white and just gets it. In Sarah's eyes, bar the color of our hair, Lisa and I were as far apart as could be. I was a gangly white boy in his ex-girlfriend's dress. Lisa was a vegan who wore vintage leather and had an eyebrow piercing. And she was Asian. South, not East like Sarah, and only half, but still. They were also the same height. Perfectly matched. Seeing them made me feel lonely.

Ming led us towards the rail that snaked around the union building. It was dark and a bit quieter, away from the courtyard filled with smokers sitting on picnic tables, standing in clusters on the grass. Ming watched me as I rolled a cigarette. The cold wrapped around the joints of my fingers, and a small tremor began in my hands. Part nervousness, part frostbite. My rolling was slow. I wasn't a smoker; I just did it when I needed a time-out. I sealed the paper with my tongue and gave him my lighter, but he waited for me to roll one for myself. He then lit his own, and held the small flame in front of me. I dipped my head towards it, and once the fire had spread onto the cigarette he put the lighter back into my hand. He dangled the slim roll-up between his index and middle finger, taking deep drags, allowing a column of ash to grow at the tip.

"What does a play about gay virgins look like?" I asked.

"It was kind of, like, immersive theater," he said. "Each character was gay and thought they were a virgin. One was an older man who'd fucked loads of guys but had never slept with a woman. Another was a gay woman who had endometriosis and couldn't have penetrative sex. There was another man who grew up in a small town and was a virgin in every sense of the word, but especially to all things gay."

"That's interesting."

Ming let out an elongated meh.

"We thought it was groundbreaking. But it definitely wasn't. I think straight people liked it. Gay people thought it was boring."

He took another drag of his cigarette. I wondered what he thought about my enthusiasm for *Gay Virgins*. Wait, does he think I'm a gay virgin?

"I like your makeup," I said. "Did you do it yourself?"

He gasped.

"Rude! I'm not wearing any," he smirked. He swallowed a large mouthful of his drink, and I watched the gulp traverse his gullet. He looked at me from above the cup. "Leopard print suits you."

"Sarah lent it to me."

"Did she do your makeup, too?"

"She did."

Ming furrowed his brow. He scrutinized my face. My eyes drifted towards the grass. It was awkward being examined. I thought of Sarah holding my jaw in one hand. For God's sake, stop moving, Tom! The waxy pencil had glided above my Cupid's bow, and the small, flat brush colored the spaces in between, squishing my lips in short, aggressive strokes.

"She hasn't done you justice," Ming said.

A smile crept over my lips. My blushing cheeks stung against the cold. I looked down at my feet. Maybe he does want to get with me. Maybe I'm not stupid for thinking it.

"You kind of look like Liza Minnelli," he said.

"Oh."

I fucking knew it. Ming set his elbow on the rail as he squatted towards the grass.

"Are you cold?" I asked.

"Look at my nipples." He pointed at them, swollen like BB

pellets. "They could take an eye out. I just need to sit down for a second. My feet hurt."

I laughed, then sat down close to him on the grass, knees towards my chest. He shifted into me, allowing his elbow to rest on my thigh, the side of his hand grazing my knee. I drank what was left in my plastic cup. There were a million interesting things to say and I couldn't think of one of them.

"Did you meet Lisa through the play?" I asked, groaning inside.

"We were friends beforehand. She hadn't come out yet, though. She was the only gay virgin there."

I laughed again. I felt the weight of my body on the damp grass. The moisture in the soil climbed into Sarah's dress.

"You and Sarah dated, didn't you?" Ming asked.

"Yeah, a long time ago."

"It wasn't that long ago."

A flash of embarrassment thrummed through me. I tried to laugh it off.

"I know."

Ming ground the end of his cigarette onto the gravel.

"Was it hard?" he asked. "Like, being gay and dating a girl?"

It was hard. Sarah had been my first and only girlfriend, but towards the end of our relationship the thoughts I'd long avoided had spilled in, like drops of food coloring into water, green fluid expanding until the ink was all I could see. And then my stomach would warp from the closeness of her body to mine, unknotting only as I turned my back to her in bed; and the old discomfort that grabbed me when Sarah and I fucked had gained new meaning, and I could see that the threads that had sewn us together were spun from cowardice. It was one thing to feel that I didn't want something, and another thing to know it or to say it or to live it. My stomach twisted thinking about it again.

"It's not like I forced myself to do it," I said. "I just thought it's what I wanted, and then I realized it wasn't. Her too, I guess."

I set my cup back on the grass next to Ming's, then put my cigarette out. I reached for the flask and offered it to him. His long fingers coiled around the cap as he unscrewed it. He took a quick sip. His face scrunched at the taste. He passed it back to me, then kissed me on my cheek. It straightened my spine. My face went hot.

"Thank you," he said.

His warm breath sailed into my ear. I was hard. He spoke again before I could lean in towards him.

"It's good you guys figured it out, though."

I looked at him with a weak smile. My brain felt foggy; the tightness returned.

"I still feel slow to it all," I said.

"What do you mean?"

"I came out late, I guess."

I was oversharing, but he charmed the words out of me. People didn't ask about this stuff enough. Nobody wants to admit that people leave the closet but not the room.

I looked again to my left at the people in the courtyard. Rob had appeared across the patch of grass. There were pink dribbles of cranberry juice along the hem of his dress. He was speaking to a girl. She was beautiful, but rake-thin in a way that seemed to draw the youth from her face. The red rubber of her latex dress clung to her like a cherry peel. She wore matching gloves that went halfway up her arms. They stood beneath a yellow spotlight affixed to one of the building's walls. This was Rob's stage. He laughed as he gesticulated over her, arms moving across the narrow diameter of the beam of light, features large and expressive. I knew the sorts of things he said. Do you know Tom? He's my best friend. He's gay! The drinks are fucking expensive down south, right? Have you ever had a threesome?

It's such a natural way to fuck if you think about it, isn't it? The girl giggled. Rob never had to say much.

"Is that Rob?" Ming asked.

"Yeah, it is."

"That's my housemate, Cass. She thinks he's hot."

"He is."

"You're hotter, though," Ming said.

"No, I'm not."

"You are."

"No."

"Stop it," he said.

"What?"

"There's nothing more boring than a hot person who doesn't know it."

He squeezed my forearm. My dick moved against my tights. I mouthed a soundless thank you.

"Honestly," he said. "Also, you haven't left anything late. Try not to worry about it too much. Let's go back inside."

I felt a sudden defensiveness, even though I'd brought it up. Who says I'm worried? I'm not worried at all! I pushed myself off the grass. He tipped more of the flask into his mouth and held out his free hand. I pulled him up from the ground.

Inside, the crowd at the bar had thinned, and so Ming charged to the front and ordered two drinks for us. Sarah and Lisa hadn't moved. Sarah's back was still against the doorframe, knees bent slightly so that Lisa stood over her. My eyes fell to Sarah's hips; her pelvis tilted back and forth. Sarah ahead. Me behind. They didn't notice us as we walked past them towards the sound of the second room. I looked out for security and poured the last drips of the flask into our drinks.

A drag queen spun onstage in a skirt made of red plastic cups. Ming and I danced together in the crowd. My knuckles grazed his hip, and then my hand moved around to his back, my fingertips touching the narrowest part of his corset. We looked at each other as we swayed, first to the beat, but then not at all.

As Ming and I stared at each other, I felt that fear from the summer just past. The one I felt when I fucked that guy near my parents' house. He was staying with his gran and invited me over when she was out. There were pictures of their family everywhere, smiling approvingly as I plowed into him on the velvet couch. It was the same fear I tried to shoot into that ginger banker's throat, the one that I hoped he'd swallow but instead left inside me. He coughed, placed his hands on his hips, sat on his ankles and huffed. That was at least two grams of protein, kiddo! I nudged his shoulders away from me and he nearly fell over. Fucking creep!

Ming and I danced closer and closer until his smile touched my lips. The tips of our tongues shook hands. He pulled back a little, then put his mouth close to my ear.

"Do you want to go back to mine?"

Ming and I walked hand in hand towards his house. His grip was cold, disconnected from the heat of his body. I slowly rubbed the top of his hand with my thumb, transferring a little warmth. We took one of the main roads through town, lined with shop fronts shut for the night. A group of drunk men laughed at us from the pub across the street. They looked like they smashed chairs over each other's backs for fun. I'd forgotten what I was wearing. One of them stepped onto the road. His muscular thighs bulged in his tight jeans. He wore fake tan. Even in the dark I could see his boomerang eyebrows, the work of hot wax and an overzealous hand.

"Can I have a kiss, ladies?" he shouted.

I kept walking but Ming slowed down. He blew the man a kiss. The man laughed, and Ming laughed, and the men across the street laughed. I felt like the butt of the joke. We walked on.

"It's interesting, isn't it?" Ming said. "Like, he was in just as much drag as I was. It's the horseshoe theory for gender. They probably mix their drinks with Armani Code." He stopped walking. "Hold on a second. My feet." Ming put his hand on my shoulder and pulled his heels off one by one. "I'll walk barefoot," he said. "And if anyone fucks with you, I'll—" He raised a heel-wielding arm.

I chuckled. The walk felt easy again, and I stopped thinking about the makeup and leopard-print dress and the stupid shoes that didn't go. We turned off onto a side street and walked up the steps to his house. He led me up the dark stairs and into his room. The lights turned on. His room was simple. A desk by the window, a neat bed. A tall mirror, a chest of drawers and a standing rail along a wall. I saw a pile of clothes at the far side of the room, peeking out from behind the bed. I hated mess, but maybe there was a reasonable explanation. A fire alarm when he was about to put them away. A concussion.

I looked at the large, framed painting of an open pomegranate above his bed, each seed the size of my palm. Some of the pink pellets had untethered themselves from the white membrane and spilled out of the blushing shell.

He peeled off his wig to reveal a small mop of sweaty hair, dark and parted at the center like mine, but straighter. He reached into a desk drawer and took out a packet of face wipes.

"I lied," he said. "I am actually wearing makeup."

I laughed. I was doing a lot of laughing. The edges of my lips and the bottom of my cheeks felt strained. Stop laughing so much. Say something interesting. Nothing came to mind.

He pulled out some of the wipes and handed them to me. I watched him clean the makeup off. The wipe glided across the planes of skin that formed as he stretched and contorted his face. The lines he'd drawn on vanished, and his black and bushy eyebrows emerged from the dissolving glue. He pulled the sides of his eyes and scrubbed away the thick liner. The squareness of his jaw crawled out of the disappearing layers of pigment; his eyes were smaller on his face and his nose less delicate. The only thing that appeared unchanged were his pert lips. I wanted to kiss and touch him again, but I didn't move. Gay virgin behavior.

"How do I look?" he asked.

"Beautiful," I said.

I sat down on his bed and began to wipe. I scrubbed until I was sure the moist paper had stripped the color from my face. I looked up at Ming. He gestured towards the standing mirror by the desk. I stood up and saw my reflection. The dark eyeshadow had smeared around my eyes, the color of mature bruises. It'd spread as far as the edges of my cheekbones. The red lipstick enveloped the skin around my wide mouth. We laughed.

"Do it carefully," he said.

He gave me another sheet. I rubbed my shut eyes with it until the wipe was soiled. Red spots bloomed on my cheek and stung the surface of my skin.

"Much better," he smiled.

He took me to the bathroom on the landing and pumped a dollop of white fluid into his palm, and then onto mine. He massaged it into his cheeks and forehead. I did the same. I splashed water from the running tap onto my face, the droplets hitting my eyes. He wiped himself clean and gave the towel to me. I set my face into the damp patches that his had already touched. We went back into his bedroom, and I sat near the head of his bed, drawing triangles on the white sheet with my index finger. The silence between us was heavy. I should've kissed him in the bathroom.

"Do you have anything to drink?" I asked.

Ming gave me a surprised smile, which then melted into something kind and understanding. I felt a little stupid. Always kiss in the bathroom!

"I'll get us some beers," Ming said.

He slipped out of the door, returning with two cans and two

empty glasses before pouring our drinks. I took a sip of beer as he sat at the other end of the bed, taking in nothing but its foam hat, the mass dissolving into drops of fluid and gas, lingering at the top of my chest after I swallowed. I pointed to the painting behind me.

"Did you do that?" I asked. "It's beautiful."

"Yeah, over summer. When I was at home with my dad."

"Where's home?" I asked.

"Kuala Lumpur."

"You don't sound like you're from Malaysia."

"What does someone from Malaysia sound like?"

I chuckled into my glass. In that moment my world felt small and shameful.

"Are your parents still there?" I asked.

"My dad is," he said. "My mother died six years ago."

"I'm sorry."

He gave me a soft smile and nodded, lifting both his legs onto the bed to move closer to me. He hunched his shoulders over the glass he held between his thighs. His eyes drifted to the amber well in his lap.

"Would you ever move back?" I asked.

"No."

"Why not?"

"It's not so hot for the gays," he said. "I was insulated from the worst of it, but it's not like I could've, like, held a man's hand. It's nice living somewhere where I can."

My fingers stretched, and I extended my arm to reach for Ming's hand. Smooth. My thumb ran along his knuckles, over the skin that gathered on the top of bone. I set my beer on the bedside table to my right. I took his glass and set it on the table to my left, and then I moved towards him.

He lay on his back while we kissed. Our tongues grew forceful. He got up and turned away from me. He lifted his arms and asked me to loosen his corset. There were so many knots. I pulled at the mass of black string until the weave of laces began to dangle. The panels of his corset split with the tectonic slowness of continents, his back the mantle from which the world would open. He turned around and I unbuckled the hooks at the front. He let out a long sigh when it came off. His ribs expanded with his breath.

I drew my dress over my head, then pulled his velvet trousers off. I ran my mouth down his body; the point of his nipple slid down the groove between my two front teeth. It landed in my mouth. Ming grinned.

I was grinning for most of the time we fucked. The fumbling was more fun than clumsy, and when he elbowed my face by accident he cupped my jaw and kissed it better.

Afterwards, as I lay breathless on top of Ming, a feeling bubbled beneath the stupid smile on my face; the cousin of that fear from the summer and the dance floor with Ming. It was stronger than with the banker or that other boy, and I knew this time that it was more than the aching joints of a shame-filled youth. I didn't want any more bankers or boys on old ladies' couches. What if this is it? What if he doesn't want to see me again?

We cleaned up and lay down next to each other under the covers. He curved his spine perpendicular to mine and placed his head on my chest, sliding down from my ribs and onto my stomach.

"What are you doing?" I asked.

"You can hear everything," he said. "Not in a gross way, but it's soothing. I used to lie on my mother's stomach when I was younger. Try it."

He lifted his head and sat up. I placed my ear on his abdomen and listened to the low gurgles under his skin. The system beneath it seemed larger and more powerful than the belly of a boy. Ming stroked my hair, and his hand covered my ear. I shut my eyes. It was a dark and endless canyon. The deep deep sea, outer outer space.

"Do you think you'll do drag again?" he asked.

I lifted my head and lay down next to him.

"I don't know," I said. "I didn't like it. Will you?"

He shut his eyes and yawned, one hand holding mine and the other over his chest.

"Yeah," he said. "I feel more confident in my body when I do it."

"Do you not like your body normally?"

"Does anyone?"

I met this with silence. I didn't love my body, but to me my body was just that. A body. I thought of how Sarah used to stand at the mirror, pinching love handles and complaining about her short legs. I'd offer reassurances in the way I thought boyfriends were supposed to. You have lovely, long legs! Maybe even the longest legs I've ever seen? Please don't change!

"How about when you're in drag?" I asked.

He yawned again, drawing his thumb back and forth against mine.

"It sort of stops feeling like my body. Like, I don't feel as self-conscious."

"That's weird."

He stayed silent. His thumb went slack. I regretted my tone.

"You have a beautiful body," I said.

He opened his eyes and smiled at me. I kissed him. We held our faces close.

"Let's go to bed," he said.

His fingers gripped the switch of the lamp and clicked us into darkness. We shuffled deeper beneath the duvet and I fell into a dreamless sleep.

Ming shifted on the bed when I woke up the next morning. We weren't touching. The light of the room poked through my eyelids. I peeled them open. My head faced the wooden bedside table. I studied the chips in its coat of white paint. The

glass of beer I'd set down was still there. A hairline rim of bubbles ran along the edge of the beer's surface, neither popping
nor dissolving, held in stasis. A gust of wind blew through the
window and across my cheek. It hit the glass, and the bubbles
began to wobble.

2
Heart

When we left for Christmas break I worried we'd stop speaking, but we messaged every day. I'd wake up in the middle of the night to texts from Malaysia, and when we came back in January we picked up as normal.

I started to skip lectures for mornings with Ming, catching up using Rob's notes and then not at all. Ming never went to them anyway. He didn't care for much other than plays.

"I like to make people laugh," he'd told me. "And cry! Just feel stuff, you know. Maybe I like controlling the room. Sue me."

Ming reached over to me for my laptop on the bedside table. He typed in my password and opened the web browser.

"I've got a lecture in half an hour," I said.

"Tom." He looked at me, wide-eyed and mouth ajar. "Our days here are numbered. It's second year. Enjoy being a waste-man while you can. Bailing on your responsibilities gets depressing in a couple of years."

I pretended to sigh and shifted closer to him. Ming didn't
need to study. Sometimes when I went over to his I found him
doing things other students didn't. Reading out one of his scripts
while standing on his desk chair, rolling out fresh pasta, squatting over a large metal bowl and making kimchi.

Ming searched for a video. He usually got to pick. I'd once
made him watch a video essay about fully automated luxury
communism, but he'd fallen asleep halfway. I didn't really care
what we watched, I just liked that Ming wanted to show me
things. He put on one of Britney Spears's VMA performances
and placed the laptop in between us, one half on each of our
thighs. I put my arm around him. His eyes darted between the
screen and my face. He did this a lot. He was often nervous that
I wouldn't like the videos, and so when Britney Spears held a
snake behind her neck during her performance I gasped and
looked at him open-mouthed.

"Right?" he exclaimed.

We watched a couple more, and then he told me about the
vegan videos he liked. He wasn't a vegan. We clicked on to a
high-carb-low-fat vegan woman. She peeled the spotted skins
off two dozen bananas, blending them to eat in one sitting. She
had the body of a supermodel and the face of a leathery pen-
sioner. Apparently she was only thirty-five. His eyes were on
me as the motor whirred the yellow flesh into a pale, gloopy
drink on-screen. He reached for the laptop keys.

"I'm sorry," he said. "This is really dumb."

"No." I held his hand and pulled it back. "Let's finish it."

We lay still as the woman drank liters of the blended banana
juice. She slapped her ripped stomach hard to prove she wasn't
bloated. Ming shut the laptop afterwards and kissed me.

"I rolled a couple of joints yesterday," I said. "Do you want
to smoke one?"

Ming nodded. I wrapped a sock over the smoke detector
and sat on one of the old chairs by my bedroom window. I was

naked, my elbows wide, one knee up and one down. I lit the joint for us. Ming put some gloves on and wrapped himself in his coat, sitting on the other chair. His hands got too cold even when we were indoors. He was a shivering ball of fabric. I wanted to squeeze him tight. He held the spliff between his fingers, each fattened by a thick layer of black wool, the glowing end of the blunt approaching the stray fibers.

Time had never slipped away in the same way with Sarah, but I'd obviously never liked Sarah the way that I liked Ming. I hadn't ever liked anyone in the way that I liked Ming. I'd never wanted to give this much time to someone, and I was as anxious when I was apart from him as I was happy when I was with him. We passed the joint between us, staring out of the window of my and Rob's flat. It looked over a cobbled street. There was a large field behind it, and boys built like tractors played rugby at the far end. It always scared me how much those boys ate. A rotisserie chicken for each of breakfast, lunch and dinner. Their farts could kill a small child.

"Do you like boys like that?" I asked.

"No," he said. "I prefer yours."

"My what?"

"Your body."

Ming looked at me, giving my nakedness a quick up-down. I held my breath as he did. Sometimes I thought he read me too closely.

"Would you ever want to be that stacked?" he asked.

"I don't know. You?"

"No. Gross. I don't have the requisite daddy issues."

He set his gaze back out of the window, and something in his eyes switched from focused to unfocused. Tension in his eyebrows. A rise of his shoulders. He brought two fingers to his neck for a moment and held them there until his body seemed to relax. This wasn't the first time I'd seen him do this, and it wasn't the first time I'd stopped myself from asking about it. I passed the joint back to Ming.

"I used to be friends with boys like that at school," I said. "Not anymore, though."

"Why?"

"The friendships always felt superficial. And I kind of wanted to start fresh."

"Fresh and gay?"

"Yeah, maybe. Sort of, but me and Rob still made friends with a few guys like that in first year."

"Really?"

Ming raised his eyebrows as he puffed some smoke out of the corner of his mouth. It made him look older, already weary from my survey history of shitty friends.

"Yeah, me and Rob kind of split off, though. They were either posh twats or posh twats that pretended not to be, like saying they were from South London when they grew up in Surrey."

Ming cackled.

"What do you think drew you to Rob?" he asked.

"We have a lot in common," I said. "Music, I guess. We went to a Flying Lotus gig together the first week we met. And we both wanted to learn how to DJ."

Ming nodded. I kept talking.

"And then we put our money together and bought those decks in the living room, so that we could learn and play at student nights."

Ming nodded again, having heard a version of this before. It was much less impressive than it sounded, which wasn't impressive at all. The bar was low for house and techno because most clubs in town still played Cha-Cha Slide. Not everyone liked it. Each time we played, at least one Sloaney girl would ask us to play "Temperature" by Sean Paul, and I'd have to explain that wasn't how it worked, cringing as the words left my mouth.

"We also both went to state schools," I added.

"Eeerr," Ming made the noise of a wrong buzzer, tilting his head down, eyebrows raised. "Yours doesn't count."

"What?"

"It's one of the best in the country."

"How do you know that?"

"I looked it up," Ming laughed. He tapped the end of the joint with his index finger. Ash fell onto the tiles below. "All of this is, like, a very British charade. Or at least a middle-class one."

"You actually went to a private school, though," I said. "An international one."

"I don't pretend otherwise."

My face reddened. Fucking hell. I both knew and didn't know what I was doing, opting for form over substance, choosing a narrative that better served my self-image. Whether that was a human habit or a British one, I didn't know. I laughed through the embarrassment. I wanted to change the subject.

"How about you?" I asked. "Were you ever friends with boys like that?"

He took a final toke and coughed, pressing the end down on the ashtray on my windowsill. He brought his knees up on the chair and held them with his thick-coated arms.

"No," he said. "I followed my femme instincts and latched on to a group of popular girls for survival. I guess it's mostly still the same."

"What about Rob?" I asked. "He's your friend now."

"I'm just the gay best friend expansion pack."

I laughed. I was cold, so I got up from the chair and put on my clothes. They hung loose on my body. Ming's clothes had crisp lines and big price tags. I wore thick and heavy jeans from a vintage store, a suede jacket I'd bought from a charity shop near my parents' house, and beneath that a sweatshirt with a logo across the chest. It was delicate embroidery of a wood-pecker belonging to an ornithological society in Maine. People who didn't get it sometimes asked about the meaning. No, I'm not from Maine. Yes, it's a woodpecker. No, actually, I'm not super into birds. But this was the way I'd learned I should dress, how I'd observed I should find clothes, because if I did this, then people would think I looked good and relaxed and didn't care but cared enough. I sat on the end of the bed.

"Should we get some lunch?" he asked.

I nodded. I went to brush my teeth. In the bathroom, the white foam collected at the edges of my lips. I wiped it away, then plucked some stray hairs in between my eyebrows the way that Mum once told me to. A few years ago I'd found a pair of tweezers on my desk from her. I'm not saying you have to do it, Tom. I'm here to give you the tools, but I'm definitely not saying you have to. No shame either way, but just in case you wanted to. I often watched her maternal instincts and her therapist instincts negotiate in real time.

I rubbed the skin around my face like I was rolling dough. Ming had told me on one of our early dates that I looked like Anna Karina. When she was younger, and if she was a man, you know. It's your dark hair and wide, blue eyes and even wider lips. How your face can look a little mopey. Resting Anna Karina face. And Rob, too. Not Anna Karina, but Jean-Paul Belmondo. You could land a plane on his nose. And his lips would, like, keep him afloat if he ever fell off a boat. And that brown hair and long face. So luscious!

"Maybe that's why you spend so much time together," he'd said.

I'd feigned understanding at the time. Oh, yeah! I see that. When I'd popped to the pub loo, I'd sat in a cubicle and looked them up.

I came back into the room to find Ming changing into some of the clothes he'd left in my wardrobe. I observed the gentle beginnings of muscles on his back and thighs, defined but long, and how they vanished as he stepped into his trousers and emerged from the top of his shirt and jumper. He left the room to brush his teeth.

I returned to the window. I stared back out at the rugby boys and wondered if Ming was telling the truth when he said that he preferred my body. It was hard to know what people really wanted. I'd never been bulky, and I didn't know if I ever could be. Ming came back in, droplets of water on his cheeks and toothbrush in hand.

"You could leave a toothbrush." I cupped one hand in the other and scratched the tops of my fingers. "Just because you're spending a lot of time here, I guess."

"Wow, a toothbrush," Ming exclaimed, his face compressing into a forced seriousness. "I think we're moving a little fast."

I laughed.

"Are you sure Rob won't mind?" he asked.

"He wouldn't," I said. "And he wouldn't notice, anyway."

He returned to the bathroom and came back empty-handed. We put on layers upon layers and left my bedroom. As we approached the front door there were giggles from Rob's room to the left. Girl giggles.

"Cass?" I mouthed to Ming.

Ming nodded. Rob had started sleeping with his housemate, Cass. She was a strange girl. She quoted things from niche reality shows that nobody but Ming understood. She edited grainy selfies into Goya paintings and screencaps from *TOWIE*, overlaying them with Hemingway quotes, or sometimes just a Destiny's Child lyric. I wasn't sure if I needed any more of her in my life. Rob slept with a lot of girls, anyway, and it didn't take much to see she was more into it than he was. I wasn't sure why Ming hadn't said anything about Cass staying over sooner.

Ming took his phone out, smirking as he showed me a text from her.

Heading back to Rob's after drinks. Maybe see you there. He just asked me if I've heard of that book Sapiens. *Still into it. What's wrong with me?*

We walked to the chain restaurant down the road. My feet felt light on the ground, my head spaced out. We floated through the streets together. I was twenty, but moments like these felt like I was catching up on some of the levity absent from my teenage years. Back then, at parties, I would make drunk and idle conversation over kitchen islands while boys and girls hooked up in upstairs bedrooms, and helped clear empty cups and cans without being asked. Teachers said I was conscientious and sensible, because there wasn't room for me to be much else.

Two boys in Hollister jumpers walked past us. They were different shades of maroon. One was washed out, but they could've just been the same jumper in a technicolored wall.

"Stop judging people's clothes," Ming said, scratching the center of my palm with his finger.

"It's like being a walking billboard for a sweatshop."

Ming tutted.

"It's just taste, isn't it?" I said, knowing it sounded shallow. "And ethics."

"It's never just taste." Ming let go of my hand to gesticulate. "You're being very London. I take the sweatshop point, but not the taste one. Your taste hasn't formed around a dying high street in Coventry."

"Since when did you become an expert on the Coventry high street?"

"Even then! It's the way you said Coventry, like you were coughing up phlegm."

"I'm friends with Rob, Ming. He's not from London."

"I'm not a snob!" Ming mimicked, placing a hand to his chest. "My best friend's from Manchester!"

I sighed and rolled my eyes, laughing as he linked his arm in mine. There was an ease to these back-and-forths. Ming was quick to call out my ill-thought takes, but also quick to forgive, even if it wasn't his place to do so on behalf of Coventry. It was still embarrassing, another stamp in the passport of my Moët Marxism, but the tension that should've been there wasn't.

The restaurant was half-price for students if you ate there between twelve and six. We got there at half twelve. We sat on red pleather benches in a booth. They gave us some bread and we ordered two pizzas and a mac-and-cheese to share. We stared at one another, laughing at Ming's bloodshot eyes. Ming picked up a bottle of chili oil to drizzle over the bread, but the nozzle fell off, drowning the rounds of baguette in a cognac-colored slick.

"Fuck," he gasped at his oil-covered hands, then laughed. "Look at my fingers."

"Look at your bread."

Some of the oil had spilled onto the table. We grabbed napkins and wiped it all down before anyone could see it. The wood glistened where the oil had been. An old couple sat in the booth next to us and smiled. They looked like Claymation figures. Really crusty ones. Our food arrived.

Ming dug his fork into the pot of macaroni and pulled. The fork went up and up, but a stubborn shoelace of mozzarella stretched until it became hair-thin, still not breaking when Ming's arm was stretched all the way above him. He looked at me open-mouthed before giving it another tug. It snapped upward, and he caught the twirling end with his tongue. We both started laughing, first softly and then uncontrollably. The stares of the old couple next to us became scowls. We laughed more. Ming was crying, his back hunched, pulsing up and down. I wiped tears from my eyes. We picked slices of pizza up with our hands, elbows on the table.

"I love eating with my hands," Ming said.

"Me too."

As I chewed on one end of some leftover crust, my mother's voice ripped through my mind. I was eleven, and I'd teased Krish at school for eating with his hands, even though at that age I was throwing bits of Babybel cheese and Peperami into my mouth with dirty fingers. My parents were mortified when he told on me. Mum put me in the chair for her clients and sat across from me. She took a deep breath and spoke to me in her therapist-mother voice. Tom, please don't mock people for where they come from or for their cultural practices, because thoughtless comments last a lifetime in the minds of a victim, and calling someone a fist gobbler isn't half as smart or funny as you think it is. I don't think it even makes sense. If you can't stop saying things like that for yourself, then would you at least do it for us, because where else will people think you've picked these things up from? It's damaging for Dad and me, in the line of work we're in, because we're trying to help communities, not harm them. What if Dad's school found out? What if my clients found out? It could be very, very bad. Was it Peter Reynolds who came up with fist gobbler?

I decided to keep the memory to myself, feeling a hot prickle of shame on my cheeks and the back of my neck. I picked up another piece, catching two slices of pepperoni in one bite. Ming held a slice with two hands as he bit it, putting it down as he chewed. He brought his fingers to his neck again, and when he released them his oily fingers left a small sheen.

"What is that?" I asked.

"What?"

"That thing you did." I drew two fingers to my own neck. My heartbeat thumped onto my fingertips. "This."

"I'm checking my pulse."

"Why?"

He grew quiet for a moment, then put his forearms in front of him.

"I have OCD."

"What?"

He gave me a questioning look, like he was appraising my stupidity.

"Obsessive-compulsive disorder," he said.

"I know what OCD stands for," I said. "I just don't know why that's OCD, I guess. Sorry, I probably should know, with my mum and stuff."

"It's not like I arrange Oreos when I put them in a jar," he said, leaning back into the cushion of the bench. "I read this article about a twenty-four-year-old dying from a heart attack. Sometimes my heart feels like it's skipping a beat so I check my pulse. And then it beats hard. Kind of like when a judge hits their gavel, and then I panic." He brought his fingers to his neck. "And I have to keep them here until it goes back to normal." He stared at his plate. "And I know anxiety makes your heart funny anyway, but when it's happening it feels so real. Like, for a few seconds I really think I'm about to die, and I have to check my pulse to convince myself I'm not."

Worry sprang. I thought of Ming's fingers on his neck, and the unrippled stillness of his face as he did it. Three months to learn he was hiding thoughts of imminent death.

"How do you fix it?" I asked.

"Fuck knows," he said. "You've heard of CBT, right?"

"Cognitive behavioral therapy."

"I tried it, but I didn't finish it because I didn't like my therapist. He used to pick stuff out of his teeth with his pinky finger. It's fine, though. I'm managing. It's been much worse before. I check it less when I'm around you, anyway."

A pleasant warmth circled my chest. I reached over the small table to hold my fingers to his neck. My thumb rubbed his jaw. I could feel his heart slow. The thumps softened, and I felt like I held his life in my hands. After a moment, I let go and he picked up another slice of pizza before looking at the old couple again.

"What do you think their story is?" Ming asked.

"I don't know."

"Come on!" he said. "It's good practice."

"For what?"

"Writing."

I looked at them. They sat in silence as each of them held the menu with both hands. Matching chains dangled onto their chests from their tortoiseshell glasses. I rummaged through my brain for who they could be.

"Married early," I said. "They love antiques."

"And?"

I pursed my lips. I was flustered and frustrated at my imagination, shallow and dull. I thought of what I could borrow from life. I had an uncle who liked to collect random shit. Something came to me.

"She collects blown-glass cat ornaments but has never owned a cat. He once broke her favorite one. They don't talk about it."

Ming laughed.

"What was it?" he asked.

"A Sphynx cat."

"Doing what?"

"Um." I paused. "Meditating."

"Very good."

Sweet relief.

"What do you think their story is?" I asked.

"Longtime caravan swingers. He likes pegging. She likes ball gags, but she's allergic to silicone so they use one made of wood."

My neck went slack as I laughed through my nose. Next to Ming's, my own mind felt flat, a city highway and not a winding road with sharp loops and swerves. Ming's thoughts seemed an exciting place to be, a lucky thing to experience. I didn't have parents in far-off places, I didn't think of funny games or have the balls to perform and be seen. I'd once won a hundred pounds on a scratch card I'd found on the street. Another time, I'd seen Shia LaBeouf headbutt someone at a pub in New Cross. These were surface-level things. They said nothing about me as a person. It wasn't like Shia LaBeouf had headbutted me, although maybe I wished that he had.

Ming cleared his throat.

"Can I ask a personal question?" he said.

I nodded as I took a bite of a slice.

"How did sex with Sarah work?" he asked. "I don't really get how you got it up."

I coughed. The bit of pizza wouldn't go down. Ming's expression remained casual, patiently waiting for me to stop choking. We'd arrived at my repression. I set the slice on my plate, now a doughy trapezoid. I imagined myself slumped over Sarah, our synthetic moans competing in volume and deceit, the blood rushing away from my body and into my head as my mind ran loops.

"Why do you want to know?"

Ming shrugged his shoulders.

"It only just occurred to me. Like, I don't get how it could've worked. You don't have to answer."

"It's fine. You can ask whatever you like. I'm an open book." I coughed again into a clenched fist. "I didn't a lot of the time. If I went for a long run, then it wasn't as difficult. Also if I was hungover. Shutting my eyes, too, I guess."

"Shit."

My shoulders rose towards my ears. Ming released his hands from his lap and placed them in front of him on the table.

"I kind of thought I had erectile dysfunction," I said. "I changed my diet massively the year before last."

"How?"

"Well. Milk and cheese were bad foods because dairy products absorb the estrogen from cows. Tuna was good food. I started eating tins of it between meals, even on Christmas Day."

Ming opened his mouth in shock.

"You thought dairy made you gay?"

I told Ming about Mum's reaction when I took the garbage bag downstairs from my room. She was lifting Tesco groceries out of a Whole Foods burlap tote. It sounds like you're holding a bag full of cans, and you're holding a bag, so I can only assume it's filled with cans, Tom. It's tuna, Mum. Tuna? Empty tins of tuna. Her features—eyebrows, eyes, lips—separated from one another with consternation.

"Did it work?" he asked.

"Yeah. I'm straight now."

Both of us laughed. Ming pushed his plate a few inches forward. He'd only eaten five slices.

"How'd you stay friends with Sarah?" he asked.

"I don't know. She and Rob stayed friends, and it just sort of happened that way, I guess." I took a small bite out of the crust and chewed. "I'm glad we did, though. She's really funny, but she's also like the voice in your head that tells you the stuff you don't want to hear. It can be fucking annoying, but it comes from a place of love."

"Tough love," Ming said.

I finished my final slice of pizza and then had one of Ming's. After lunch the high had worn off, and threads of a headache elbowed their way across my cranium. It was a cloudless winter day, and so Ming suggested that we go to the botanical gardens. I texted Rob to ask him to join us. He responded with a yes, following up with an unrelated timestamped link to a Kaytranada set, something he often did.

Rob arrived before us, leaning against the wrought-iron entrance gates in an old shearling jacket and light jeans, his bike already on the racks. We walked through the gates and showed our student cards to the old man sitting in a small glass pavilion. He waved us through to the narrow path covered by a canopy of

evergreens. We reached a fork, and turned along a further narrow path flanked by bright yellow daffodils and purple crocus,
and dry bushes of desaturated greens, creams, reds and oranges.

"I didn't hear you guys in the morning," Rob said.

I wondered if Ming was about to mention the Girl Giggles,
or if he'd play it cool on behalf of Cass.

"We left quite early," Ming said. "You must've been asleep."

"Did you make it to your lecture?" I asked.

"Our lecture," Rob said. "And yes, just about."

Rob linked arms with Ming. I let myself fall a couple of steps
behind them, observing them as they chatted away. Ming took
long, slow and elegant steps. He put his hands in the pockets of
his bomber jacket, his elbows wide.

"How's your play going?" Rob asked.

"Yeah, it's all happening," Ming said. "It's showing next
month."

"Can you can say what it's about now?"

Ming smiled.

"A later-life lesbian called Dorothy who decides to marry her
gay friend as cover, but then leaves him at the altar."

"What's it called?"

"*A Friend of Dorothy.*"

"My nan used to say that!"

"Really? So it's a thing. Lisa came up with the title. I've been
skeptical."

"It's a thing," Rob said. "You're a friend of Dorothy, aren't
you?"

"Duh," Ming said. "Our mums were in Lamaze classes together."

Rob twisted his head back to me.

"And you, Tom?" he asked.

"Never heard of her."

They laughed. Ming turned back and looked at me, too, his
smile wide and sweet.

"Why does she leave him?" Rob asked. "Other than her being a lesbian?"

"I mean, that's all there is to it, really," Ming said. "The play's about how sublimating our true desires for banal conveniences is never sustainable. Dorothy just comes to it first."

"Do you find all of it hard?" Rob asked. "The play stuff."

"I think the idea's always the hardest part," he said. "You don't know if it'll come. But once that's there you can sort of trust that everything else will fall into place."

"That makes sense," he said. "It's cool you can do this kind of thing."

Ming leaned into Rob's shoulder. Rob kissed the top of his head. The sun fell on my face as I looked at a tussle of rust-colored stems, a nest of fingers pointing towards the sky. There were crowds of pansies along the winding path, sharing a border with some daphne shrubs that surrounded a meters-wide fountain, water trickling down from clusters of tiered basins at its center. Ming and Rob settled on a bench a few steps back from the water, and I joined them next to Ming. Rob yawned.

"Are there toilets anywhere?" Rob asked. "I really need to piss."

Ming gestured to a crowded bed of snowdrops. Rob laughed.

"We passed some loos a bit earlier," I said. "On the right."

"Yes, Dad."

He got up from the bench and walked back the way we'd come.

Ming held my hand.

"I'm glad you left your toothbrush at mine," I said.

"Are you?"

"You could leave other things."

"A douche?"

I laughed, and we relaxed back into the hard wood of the bench. We spoke about Lisa, how Ming was struggling to deal with her anxiety over the play. I asked if his OCD made him more or less sympathetic towards her.

"You'd think more," he chuckled. "But when you're convinced you're going to have a heart attack, a twenty-pound overspend on prop budget doesn't seem so bad. Worrying about it feels annoying."

"I can see that."

We fell into a comfortable silence. Ming broke it.

"Lisa's taught me this thing called the Meisner technique."

"What is it?"

"So, you sit in front of someone and just observe what the other person is doing. You say it out loud and then they repeat it. And then they do the same to you, whenever an observation comes. Let's try it. Stand in front of me."

I put my hands in my pockets and got up from the bench. I stood a meter in front of him. Gravel crunched under my shoes. His hands were in his lap. We stared at one another.

"You're smirking," he said. "Now say, I'm smirking."

"I'm smirking," I said.

"You're moving your weight between your feet."

"I'm moving my weight between my feet."

"Now observe something about me," he said.

"You're shivering," I said.

"I'm shivering. You look happy."

"I look happy."

I felt happy. The question I wanted to ask sat on the tip of my tongue. My heart began to pump fast, fear sailing through each artery, tingling my chest, rattling my toes. Ming started to talk.

"Some people go on forever," he said. "It takes you out of yourself and makes you tune in to the other person. Sometimes you just need to listen and be listened to. It keeps you responsive."

"Do you want to be my boyfriend?" I asked.

Ming's mouth opened wide, then curved into a smile. He

nodded. I bent my knees towards the bench, kissing him as he laughed. After a few moments we parted.

"Should we keep going?" Ming asked with a smile.

I nodded and stepped back again. He looked towards my feet.

"You're bouncing on your toes," he said.

"I'm bouncing on my toes. You're fiddling with your thumbs."

I heard footsteps behind us. I looked back and waved at Rob.

"I'm fiddling with my thumbs. You're looking behind you."

"I'm looking behind me. You're shifting your bum."

Rob sat back down and watched us, unquestioning, as if Ming and I describing each other to one another made perfect sense.

3
Control

The sound of retching woke me up. I looked at the clock. It was two a.m. My torso jolted upward. Ming stirred but didn't wake. I pulled the duvet away from me, tiptoeing around the sides of his bed towards the door. My fingers wrapped around the knob and turned it, pulling it open slowly to muffle the creaking wood. I stood still in the doorway. More retching, and the sound of a running tap. It was coming from the bathroom. It took a second to realize it was Cass. I thought she might be drunk, or ill, but she'd stayed in and seemed fine the night before. Then I remembered that Ming had dropped hints that she had issues with food. I wondered if this was what the issues looked like.

I stepped back from the door and shut it as gently as I could. I climbed back into bed with Ming. She gagged a couple more times after I shut my eyes. The sound looped in the back of my brain. I thought unfair thoughts.

★ ★ ★

Ming and I woke up at the same time in the morning. He stretched in bed with a cavernous yawn. I liked the sound he made when he flexed his jaw, the slobbery smack of his tongue separating from the pink of his cheeks and the roof of his mouth. Ming was otherwise a silent breather, his nose and mouth a frictionless road. The only sign of life was the rise and fall of his chest. I'd allowed myself to notice these things about him since he'd become my boyfriend.

Ming's arm landed on my bare stomach, and the bony protrusion on the inside of his elbow nestled in my belly button.

"What'd you dream about?" I asked.

"My dad, weirdly. He kept shouting Michael at me from inside our house in Malaysia, but I couldn't find him."

"Michael?"

"He calls me Michael."

"Why?"

"I was born Michael," he said. "Michael's on my birth certificate as my first name. That's what my dad wanted. Ming was my middle name, which is what my mother called me."

"Are you telling me it's taken me four months to learn your name?"

"I'm very mysterious."

I tickled him. He laughed, writhing around, the rustling covers creating white noise. His body crumpled onto mine when I stopped, his arm over my belly again and his head on my shoulder. Four months felt like a long time. I knew that small details slipped out when you got to know someone; that time pulled the accordion bellows, revealing the things scratched into the cardboard folds. But four months was a long time. Four months to learn my boyfriend's name, or other name, or old name. Four months wasn't a lie, but it made me anxious. This seemed entitled, so I buried it.

"Was it a cultural thing?" I asked.

He let out a thoughtful hum. The sound vibrated through my arm and neck.

"No, I don't think so. Maybe. I went by Michael until I was a teenager. It never felt like it fit me. When I think of Michael, I think of, like, an old, boisterous man."

"We'll all be old men someday."

There was silence. Ming's body shifted on the bed. He exhaled; the air slid along my sternum.

"I should've added, straight," he said. "But anyway, I changed my passport when my mother died."

Ming would sometimes ration out information about his mother, tiny parcels of detail and memory. She'd had long black hair, and in photos she smiled with her mouth stretched and teeth parted, as if she was mid-laugh. Ming smiled the same way. He'd inherited the wideness of her features. He rarely spoke about her; he spoke around her. Ming had told me he'd spent a lot of time in hospitals growing up, so much that the smell of disinfectant still made him gag. He knew the basics of a good mole and a bad mole. He'd told me how you should never move someone if they have a seizure. The death of his mother had become a star from which he mapped other things. His favorite place in Malaysia was the lake gardens in his mother's hometown, not far from where they'd spread her ashes. His dad had remarried two years after.

Ming got out of bed and pulled the roller blinds covering the sash window. The mechanism spurred to drown the room in light. I shielded my eyes with my hands. Ming climbed back into bed. I stared at the tree outside. Its branches tickled the glass. Ming pushed the right side of his face onto my chest. I could feel the slow beat of my heart on his cheek, and the beat of his on my rib, out of sync.

He dropped his head towards my belly. As his ear landed, my stomach roared with hunger. Both of us laughed. His head returned to my chest, and he placed his palm flat against my body.

"I think I heard Cass throwing up last night," I said. "I didn't know what to do."

Ming sat up, pushing off his palm and shifting his bum towards the wooden headboard. His face was pensive.

"Thanks for telling me."

"It was pretty gross."

Ming scrunched his eyebrows with his head towards me. I knew it was a stupid thing to have said.

"Gross? Christ, Tom. Are you sure your mother's a therapist?"

I was embarrassed. Mum's apparition floated behind Ming, massaging her temples as she shook her head.

"Sorry," I said. "How can I help, then?"

Ming exhaled through his nose, rounding his spine into the headboard.

"I don't know. Sometimes people just need you to be there."

"Okay," I said. "Sorry for calling it gross."

"It's fine." He kissed me on the cheek. "Don't tell anyone about it, okay?"

My arm sprawled behind him and across the bed. Ming lay back down on his side, resting his head on the inside of my elbow.

"I've been wanting to ask you something," he said.

"What is it?"

"Do you want to come to Malaysia this summer?" Ming asked. "My dad shits air miles. I think he'd let me use some of them. We could get flights for a bit cheaper."

A wobble in my chest radiated towards my stomach, a warm worry. The invitation made me as anxious as it did excited. It could've been an offer he made to lots of people. What if he doesn't mean it? Maybe he was just saying it in passing.

"I'd love to," I said. "Don't worry about the air miles, though."

How much are flights to Malaysia? I didn't know, but letting his family pay my way there felt weird to me. I had money saved up from working at the pub down the road from my parents' house last summer. If I was careful until after exams, then maybe that would cover it. We rolled onto our sides and lay parallel for a few moments.

"I'm going to be late," he said. "I need to shower."

He bounced off the mattress and out of the room. I turned around and buried my face in the pillow on his side of the bed. I heard his voice against the light trill of Cass's. The wood of Ming's bedroom door swallowed the words' definition, but I heard my name among the noise. I liked the way it fluttered between their mouths.

I could hear the sound of trickling water from the bathroom. When it stopped, he came back into the room in a towel, holding it under his armpits. He turned away from the mirror as he let the towel fall to the floor and reached for some clothes from the standing rail. His light-green shirt darkened from the water running off his back. His trousers sat high on his waist.

Ming checked his pulse before taking his bag from the chair and swinging it over his shoulder. He grabbed the long wool coat from the stand by his desk.

"I'll see you after *Friend of Dorothy* later," he said. "Can you let yourself out?"

I nodded. He kissed me before leaving. I rolled around for a little while longer before putting some clothes on. I made Ming's bed, then grabbed my bag and walked down the stairs. Cass was in the kitchen, standing with her phone pointed at her shoes. She turned round and smiled, her braids in a bun.

I hugged her. Her perfume overwhelmed me. She smelled of varnished wood. She always doused herself in it.

"What are you doing?" I asked.

"I'm taking pictures of my feet in old shoes." She stretched her leg again, hinging her torso back. "Sometimes I sell old shoes on eBay. It's a fetish thing for the buyers. My student loan's late."

I stood leaning on the doorframe, watching her as she snapped photos of herself with her heel stretched along the table, legs otherwise bare.

"Do they sell for much?"

"I just sold five ratty pairs for two hundred quid."

"What the fuck?"

"Honestly." She bit her lip. "Could you actually maybe help me take the pictures? I usually get Ming to. It just doesn't work from this angle."

She held the phone out to me and I paused. I didn't want to reach for it in a way that seemed eager. I wondered how it implicated me. Not in any legal kind of sense, but I didn't know if what Cass was doing was sex work. Is Cass a sex worker? What does that make me? I held the phone and squatted before her. I took a photo. She leaned over to see what I'd captured in the frame.

"O-kay," she said, lengthening the second syllable. "So you've captured the shoe. Like, we can really see the shoe in the photo."

"What did I do wrong?"

"These look like teddy bear legs," she said, circling her perfectly long legs on the screen with her finger. "Length sells. I want my legs to look like skyscrapers."

"Like the Gherkin?"

She laughed, handing the phone back to me.

"Absolutely not the Gherkin."

I took another few. She slipped the trainers off and told me to wait. A moment later, she came back with another pair. I began to take pictures again.

"How did you get into it?" I asked.

"By mistake. I thought I could get, like, a fiver for old shoes, but the bidding just kept going up. I couldn't figure it out, but then I started getting messages from people asking me to describe the smell, and then I clocked it."

I handed her back the phone. She flicked through the pictures.

"Why do you have so many?" I asked.

"I don't. Sometimes I just buy ones from charity shops and pat some dirt into them, or wear them for a day without socks."

I wanted to ask her more questions. Does it make you feel undignified? Maybe it was offensive to assume as much, but I still wanted to know.

"Do you ever feel ashamed?"

She looked at me with her mouth open, as if me saying shame had forced it into existence. I cringed at myself. Dick. She locked the phone and then stared at the shoes for a moment. When she looked back at me, her expression was resolute.

"Why would I feel ashamed?" she asked.

"I don't know. I'm sorry. It was a stupid thing to ask."

"My mum would beat me into the nineties," she said, softening. "But it's fine. The only thing I don't like is that sometimes you have to flirt. They'll ask me how dirty my feet are and stuff."

"What do you say?"

"That they're so dirty." She shook her head, then popped her hip and tilted her head downward, like she was about to scold me. "I'm a dirty girl with dirty feet."

I laughed.

"Anyway, it's a really sustainable use for old shoes," she said. "We're all so divorced from supply chains. It's nice to be adding something and selling it on."

"Dirt?"

"It's something, isn't it?"

I smiled. Sex work or not, Cass telling me about this like it was nothing, getting me to take the photos—these were the actions of someone who didn't give a shit. It wasn't just the shoes. Her garish clothes. Her makeup. It was all a symptom of not caring, comorbid with confidence. It was hard to reconcile this with the sounds from the night before. And then I thought of Ming. His heart, how the elegant bravado could vaporize under the threat of a worry, and how sometimes those two halves of being didn't make sense to me, either. For the first time I understood Ming and Cass as a pair. I wasn't sure how I felt about it.

"What are you up to today?" I asked.

"I'm seeing Lisa and Ming's play later," she said, her voice slightly lifted.

"Oh, me too."

"Rob mentioned," she said. "I think he's coming here after."

She smiled at me, but with an intensity in her eyes, like she was trying to locate Rob's private words on my face. Cass is fun, right? I hope she doesn't think it's going anywhere, though. Has Ming said anything? It's got nothing to do with her. She'd get that, right?

I felt bad for her, knowing and hearing what I had, but it wasn't Rob's fault she was so attached. I forced my voice into a flat register and said I'd see her later.

As I walked along the bridge and over the river towards my and Rob's flat, I noticed the sun reflected on the surface of the water, split and bent by gentle ripples like a particle into strings. The wind accelerated as I reached the other end of the bridge, forced through a tunnel formed by the narrow road and rows of wonky old houses. The air pushed into the skin of my face, and cool tendrils of wind crept beneath my jumper. Once I arrived home, I beeped my fob against the reader and climbed up the old stairs to the flat.

Inside, Rob was lying on the couch, his long body under a knitted blanket. The weak floor lamp behind the couch loomed over him. The colorful collar of one of his charity-shop shirts peeked out from his black sweatshirt. Cartoons moved within the rectangle of light from his laptop on the coffee table. He turned his head back and smiled, showing the gap between his two front teeth.

"Hello, handsome," he said. "Where have you been?"

"At Ming's. Cass said she's seeing you after the play."

"Yeah, maybe. I'll see how I feel afterwards."

I dropped my bag by the sofa and moved into the narrow kitchen off the side of the living room. It was too small for two people to stand side by side. The appliances were off-white, stained with brown patches and rings, mixtures of dirt and rust and grease. It had been like this when we'd moved in. Rob had left a dish in the sink. I cleaned it up for him. There was a smear of something on a bowl on the drying rack, and so I washed that up, too.

I carried a half-full glass of water back into the living room and sat on the other end of the couch. The vase on the coffee table was full of yellow, orange and pink tulips.

"Do you like the flowers?" Rob asked.

"I do," I said. "Thanks for buying them."

A pang of affection strummed through my chest. We sat in silence for a few moments.

"I think I heard Cass throwing up in their bathroom last night," I said.

Rob's face lit with surprise. Mouth open, eyebrows high.

"Fuck, was she ill?" he asked.

"No. I mean, not like she drank too much. I think she was throwing up food."

"Fuck." He clenched his teeth. "I didn't realize it was that bad. That's bad, isn't it?"

"Yeah. Don't tell anyone I told you, though."

"'Course not."

Rob lifted the edges of his mouth into a wide but closed-mouthed smile. His eye curved shut like a sealed dumpling, his iris vanishing behind the condensed skin. My lips and eyes mirrored his. We laughed.

I pulled the blanket over myself and put my legs across Rob's. His hands moved towards my foot. He massaged the tender arch. His hands were strong, and the pressure of his broad thumbs soothed the knots that the morning's steps had tied. The ritual made me feel normal, in a way I didn't think I needed now that I was out and older, but which still felt good. When I was at school, nobody, including me, wanted to change next to the boy everyone thought was gay. And so I breathed in the suspicion that hung in the changing-room air, alongside the smell of chlorine and sweat and cans of Lynx Africa, and it clung to my insides like lead. Rob's touch drained the old abscesses. He was this way with his brothers. I'd seen it when I'd visited him at his parents' house in Manchester last summer. I was struck at how tender they could be. How they'd lie in each other's laps, or sit with their arms around one another. He was even gentler with me, no unprovoked slaps. Sometimes I wondered if he was comfortable doing this with me or if it was all pretend, but maybe the only way to close the gap between who you are and who you pretend to be is to keep pretending. After a few minutes he stopped, and I moved my foot off his lap, replacing it with the other one.

"Don't push your luck, all right?" He shook his head and laughed, and began to massage my second foot anyway. He knitted his eyebrows. "Sometimes there's a glint in someone's eye and you know they're just thinking, what is this or what are we? When I'm with Cass, I know she's thinking it, and it's like, fuck."

"Could it change?"

"I don't know. I really like being around her. She's so smart and interesting. She keeps giving me these books. Have you read *The Beauty Myth* by Naomi Wolf?"

I shook my head.

"It's really good," he said. "Kind of blew my mind, actually. But anyway, so with Cass, her being sad wouldn't make me feel good, and if she needed me for anything I'd be there. But I'm generally pretty happy, right? I don't really know what I need from someone. As in, I don't think I'd get anything out of it if we became more serious." Rob's fingers moved to massage my shins. "Maybe intimacy doesn't come naturally to me."

"Hm. Just be careful," I said. "She seems a little fragile, I guess."

"I don't know. You mean the food stuff?"

"Yeah, but maybe more generally."

Rob cocked his head in thought, like he was looking at a detective's corkboard, a web of senseless pictures and thumbtacks and string. Maybe I'm making connections that aren't there. Rob isn't responsible for Cass's shit.

"Ming's invited me to visit him in Malaysia," I said.

"Fuck." Rob looked at me, alert. "Are you going to say yes?"

"Yeah, for sure. It'd be cool. I've never been. To Asia, I mean."

"I bet Ming has a fuck-off house."

"It's pretty big, yeah," I said. "Wait, he sent me some pictures over Christmas break. I'll show you."

Rob and I shuffled closer and sat shoulder to shoulder as I scrolled past screenshots and photos of nights out, until I got to December. Rob took his time, zooming in on fixtures, then on Ming's dad. He zoomed in on Cindy, the woman the same age Ming's mother would've been, whose white teeth leaned out of her mouth. The woman who wore big Chanel sunglasses, straw hats and chunky gold jewelry. I'd once told Ming she looked like a teenager.

"For now," he'd said. "Give it ten years and she'll shrink a foot and get a perm."

As Rob and I spoke about Malaysia, I wondered what I needed from Ming, and if he needed anything from me. I remembered how displaced I felt after I broke up with Sarah, even though it meant being myself. Being with Ming had lifted my head out of the sand. I didn't know if I did or could do the same for someone as confident and comfortable as him.

★ ★ ★

Rob and I mooched around home for the rest of the day. We didn't have any lectures. I ripped open a few frozen pizzas for us for dinner and popped them into the oven.

After eating, I sat in bed and watched an interview I liked, then stopped halfway to watch a Boiler Room set instead. I wondered if this made me a bad socialist. No, of course not; most people haven't read *Capital in the Twenty-First Century* by Thomas Piketty. I fell asleep to it, and when I stirred awake, Sarah was at my bedroom door, in leather trousers and a leather jacket, holding a bottle of white wine by its neck.

"Were you napping to Rhythm Section, Tom?" she asked. Rob laughed from the couch behind her.

"I'll have you know," I yawned, "that I was watching a Mark Fisher interview before it."

"That's much worse." Sarah walked back into the living room. "It smells like a library in here."

I rolled myself out of bed and cracked open the living-room window. Sarah and Rob sat on the couch, and I on the chair with holes in the arms. A glass of wine each.

"How's Lisa doing?" I asked, rubbing my eyes.

"So worried," she said, exasperated. "She just thinks every-thing's going to go wrong, but she doesn't want solutions. This morning Lisa said that nobody was going to come, so I told her that if she was worried, she could do some last-minute social media stuff to promote it. Then that became a whole thing. All she wanted was me to tell her it was going to be fine." Sarah sat upright with an intense frown, an imitation of Lisa. "Wait, so, ah, fuck, do you actually think I should do that?"

Rob and I laughed.

"I guess you just have to be there for her," I said. "You can't really rationalize someone out of it, can you?"

"That's very astute of you, Tom," Sarah said. Her tone was suspicious, as if to suggest my wisdom was plagiarized, which it was. "You're right. But it's so frustrating, because if she just did what I said, she'd probably feel better."

"Do you know that, though?" Rob asked.

Sarah didn't respond, looking out of the window instead.

We each ordered pints at the drab, low-lit bar before moving into the L-shaped theater. Two groups of chairs were placed at either end of the L, the stage at the joint. We waved to Ming and Lisa, who sat at the back of the other set of chairs. Lisa had cut her fringe short, but its edges were crisp. Lego-man haircut. She looked on edge, like she'd just done a line.

The performance began. The woman who played Dorothy was a younger, own-brand Gillian Anderson. Ming watched the cast with his elbows on his knees and chin in his palms. His concentration transfixed me, the wash of relief across his face each time a joke landed. Rob and Sarah laughed the whole way through. Ming controlled the room. Pride swelled in my belly, and I realized I wasn't ever proud of anyone else like this, at least beyond the usual platitudes. What I felt for Ming's achievement was bigger.

The play ended when Dorothy, in her white veil and wedding dress, stormed past the audience and out of the exit. We all stood up and clapped.

Sarah, Rob and I waited in the crowded foyer with pints Rob had bought us. I could see Cass from the corner of my eye, standing by the bar on our right with some of her other friends.

"It had a lot of layers," Sarah said.

"Yeah, I suppose," Rob said, scrunching his eyebrows in thought as he looked up towards the ceiling. "When Ming and I talked about it, it just seemed like she didn't want to marry her gay friend. But fair play to her, right?"

"Well, yeah, but it was about the counterintuitive burden of comphet on women, Rob." Sarah took a breath. "She was going to have to give up a lot more if they were going to go through with having a family, and yet she still wanted to go through with it to escape herself. More than he did, until the end."

"I can see that," I said.

"What's comphet?" Rob asked.

Sarah shot Rob an insincere look of surprise.

"Compulsory heterosexuality," she said.

"Why would it be compulsory?" he asked.

Sarah rolled her eyes.

"I'll send you some reading."

Cass skulked near us before saying hello, hugging me and Sarah and then Rob. I opened a bit of space for her in our circle. The shaggy wool cuffs of her jacket were streaked with lime-green spray paint. She'd probably done it herself.

"What did you think of the play?" I asked.

"It was great," Cass said. "And you guys?"

"Good!"

"Really good!"

"So good!"

A heavy awkwardness crashed into the space between us. Rob wasn't doing a decent job of bringing her in. Cass looked uncomfortable. She fiddled with the straw of her clear, icy drink, taking a sip then stabbing the ice gently.

"Have you heard of comphet?" I asked.

"What?"

Before I could explain, Ming and Lisa came out from the theater doors. We clapped for them, and a small chorus of others who knew them joined in. Sarah and Lisa stood next to each other. I noticed how their appearances had begun to merge: Sarah's new eyebrow piercing, the black nails, the leather everything; but Lisa's mullet was a decided diversion from Sarah's bald head. Ming bought a round. He and Cass stood close, their arms and hands intertwining like vines as they drank. Ming whispered something in Cass's ear, and she seemed a little restored as she laughed into her glass. Sarah and Lisa held hands.

"Didn't I tell you it'd be fine?" Sarah asked her, lifting their conjoined fingers.

"Yeah, oh my god," Lisa said. "It's just, like, such a relief it's over. Everyone else did so well. They literally saved me."

Ming smiled. We stayed a while, then he yawned and told me he wanted to go home after his pint. Adrenaline comedown. We picked up our coats and got ready to leave.

"We're heading home, Cass," Ming said.

Cass looked towards Rob, her shoulders slightly hunched. He caught her eyes for a moment, and then addressed me and Ming as if he hadn't seen her.

"I'm feeling pretty tired," he said. "I think I'm going to head home alone."

I hugged Rob goodbye. He hugged Ming, everyone else, and then Cass. I couldn't help but watch.

"I'll text you," he said to her.

Ming pursed his lips, and then looked at me with a squint in his eye. The three of us left the theater and walked towards their house. Cass walked in between us, picking at the skin around her nails. When we got home, she whispered good-night before shutting the door behind her. Ming stood on the landing for a moment, then gave me an unsure look. I was already one foot into his room. I shrugged my shoulders. He glanced at her room again before walking towards me. We closed the door behind us.

We kissed naked on his bed, and then I twisted Ming's body so he lay facedown. Ming liked it when I put the weight of my body onto his. I placed my arms over his arms and his thighs under my thighs, my belly in the small of his back. My ribs tessellated with the gaps between his, and my hands hooked onto the webs between his fingers. After we finished, I lay down next to him and held his hand.

We spooned for a while, but then I felt his hand let go of mine. I knew it was to check his pulse. His breathing changed.

He was forcing himself to take long breaths. I pushed myself up and turned on the bedside lamp. I could see his face from above. Eyes shut and tears collecting at the sides, fingers pushing into his skin so hard it looked like they could slide through. I held his upper arm.

Sometimes people just have to be there. It was so easy to get wrapped up in comparing myself to him, feeling small next to him. If Ming is this, then what am I? What do I offer? Maybe it's enough for me to be here. I waited until his breathing went back to normal. He opened his eyes, wet and shiny. The room relaxed, filled with nothing but our quiet breaths. It seemed to grow hungry for words.

"I love you, Ming."

A small moment of silence.

"I love you, too, Tom."

Ming nestled into me, his breaths long and slow, growing steadier, more autonomous, as his body went slack. As I started to drift off, I heard the sound of doors opening and closing, and then Cass retching again. My body tensed, and I froze. Ming didn't stir. He was fast asleep. I still hadn't moved; I didn't want to wake him up. Does this have to do with Rob? The events of the day made it hard to separate the two, even if they were unrelated. It seemed confusing that she'd be at the mercy of him, but maybe it didn't take much. Look at me. Am I at the mercy of Ming? Maybe I'm not too far from Cass. After a few minutes the throaty heaves subsided, and I heard only the sound of a running tap. My body relaxed, and then I held Ming tight.

4
Swimming

"He's just texted me," Ming said as he scanned through rows of cars. "He said they're here."

We landed on a Wednesday morning. Ming had warned me about the heat. The airport had air-conditioning, but the humidity swallowed us when the doors opened to the pickup area. It was like we were standing in the wet heat of someone else's mouth.

I never knew how to dress for hot weather. It peeled back the layers of fabric and revealed shoulders that were bony and narrow, and the shoes and socks I wore looked childish against the shorts I'd had since school. I once confessed this to Ming, how sometimes I didn't know how to dress for the heat. Ming said that the white boys of Camberwell were like jellyfish, medusas in winter but polyps in summer. He'd bought me a pair of new shorts as a gift, which I'd worn on the plane.

"They're over there," Ming said.

He pointed to a champagne saloon car, which slowed to a

halt. It had tinted windows. As we approached, the boot lifted. Ming and I put our suitcases in and pulled open the doors to the back. We said hello in unison. A leathery man at the wheel turned to us with a white smile. I saw myself and Ming in his black aviators.

"I'm John." He released his hand from the wheel and shook mine. "Lovely to finally meet you, Tom."

Ming slipped his arm past the driver's seat to hug his dad.

"Thanks for driving to pick us up," Ming said.

"What's a morning off for my only son?"

Cindy, who sat in the passenger seat and was even smaller than in photos, smiled at me. There was an enormous and expensive-looking leather bag in her lap, one that I imagined she might hide in when people asked her what she did with her day.

"Pleasure to meet you, Tom. I'm Cindy." She turned to Ming and reached out to squeeze his hand. "He's so handsome!" she screeched. "What a waste!"

I smiled. She meant well. John stamped on the accelerator. The car shot onto the wide road out of the airport.

"How was your flight, boys?" John asked.

"Tom's never taken a plane ride that long before," Ming said.

"First trip to Malaysia?"

"First trip to Asia, actually."

John shared unsolicited observations, all of which reminded me that colonialism was alive and well. The thing about Asia is. What you have to understand about Malaysians is. Let me share a few words to summarize Kuala Lumpur: Hard Rain, Hard Sun, Traffic Jams, Oil, Kindness, Potholes. That's it.

"Aiyah." Cindy smacked John's arm.

Ming rolled his eyes. I laughed awkwardly and looked out of the window, staring at the rows of palm trees lining both sides of the tarmac, each tall and wide-hipped. I was grateful for John's opening gambit, not because it was funny but because it made me feel less conscious of my parents' slipups when they'd met

Ming. Gentrification is a real problem here, Ming. It all used to be much more colorful.

"Has Michael told you about the food?" John asked.

"He has, actually," I said. "I wanted to go to a Malaysian restaurant to get a feel for things before we came here, but Ming said I should wait for the real thing."

"Sounds like Michael to me."

John sped the whole journey. The needle of the speedometer launched upward after each tollbooth, wobbling at 160 kilometers per hour. Cars fell behind us. He drove with his legs as wide as possible, as if all before him had spawned from his crotch. I looked at the gravelly roads. The hydraulics dulled their texture.

Soon the palm trees fell away, and the roads became dense with traffic. A network of concrete overpasses and underpasses wove around us, surrounded by tall apartment buildings and shopping malls, separated by patches of green, pockets of insurgent nature resisting the built environment. The highways began to thin and bend into windier roads. A car in the right-hand lane cut John off as he took a left up a hill. He slammed the horn, rolled down the window and poked his head out as he tailed the tiny, shabby car.

"Fucking idiot," he shouted, pushing the horn again.

"Dad."

"These people don't know how to fucking drive." John rolled up his window and huffed through his nose. "It's about safety."

"Dad."

I squirmed. It might've been the first time I'd seen Ming embarrassed. I shivered at John's choice of words. He didn't seem to mean well. He seemed to mean to be a dick.

I kept my eyes focused out of the window. Speed bumps forced the car into a gentle cruise. Tall trees cast a flickering weave of shadow and daylight over us. John took a second left, and now among the trees were bigger, multi-story houses, some set far back from the road, disguised by deep driveways and rows of expensive cars. He took another left, and as we approached a dead end the gates of one house began to open. The car sailed in. Trees with gnarled spines hunched over the long driveway.

John drove on to an expanse of terracotta tile outside a mahogany front door, the same dusty red ceramic draped across the pitched roof of the large house. Ming had already told me that the house was upside down; the bedrooms were on the ground floor and the living space, for its light, was upstairs. It was as large and impressive as the pictures I'd seen, but up close the cream paint had weathered, some roof tiles had cracks, and there was just one dusty Toyota next to the car we climbed out of. We pulled our bags out of the back and rolled them into the house. A series of heavy shut doors choked the bright daylight out from the enclosed foyer.

"Please," Cindy said, gesturing towards a shoe rack.

I slipped mine off and tucked them into the bottom row, double-checking to make sure they were neat. The white tile was cool beneath my socks. I felt the sweat between my toes.

Ming opened one of the shut doors to our left. I put my bag at the foot of Ming's bed and walked the perimeter of the room. There were paintings of fruits, as he'd said, but there was also a painting of his mother above the dresser. Tall plants guarded the outside of the glass wall. The room wasn't as small as he'd described it. It was larger than mine. I wondered what he'd thought of my room when he had come to stay, walls covered in posters with crinkled edges, all stuff I'd discovered at school. Unknown Mortal Orchestra. Frank Ocean. Four Tet. Part of me had even felt a little proud. Look! I've had taste forever! Ming's room, which evoked the simple power of clean, modern design, made me feel juvenile.

Ming lay on his front on his mattress. I joined him and lay on my side.

"I'm really excited you're here," he murmured through shut eyes.

"You sound like it."

"I am."

His hand traversed the bedsheet to hold mine.

"Boys!" Cindy boomed. "Come upstairs when you're ready, ah."

Ming puffed air through his lips.

We climbed the single staircase to the upper floor of the house. It was open-plan, with a continuous row of enormous, square windows that ran across the walls of the room. The ceiling followed the shape of the roof. A pyramid of slats supported by wooden beams. A large ceiling fan dangled from the apex. Ming had told me the space was designed to encourage airflow, and that they didn't need to have the air-conditioning on, even though they often did anyway.

Cindy carried over a tray of dumpling-sized lumps in bright colors, setting it on a glass coffee table where we sat. John picked one wrapped in leaves and unfurled it to reveal a gelatinous green blob. He threw the whole thing into his mouth. Cindy chose a small wobbly block made of alternating white and pink layers.

"Try some, it's called kuih," Cindy said. I picked up one that was a similar shape to Cindy's, except with a green rectangle set above an equally thick layer of rice. "That's kuih seri muka."

The kuih was surprisingly oily in my hands. My front teeth glided through the top green layer and into the sweet, glutinous rice below. Aromatic wafts of coconut burst from the plump grains and across the roof of my mouth.

"Mmm," I moaned. "I don't think I've ever had anything like that."

"This one's my favorite," Ming said, picking up a pale-blue ball loosely pressed into a pyramid. He dug his thumbs into it and split it to expose its figgy innards. "It's desiccated coconut with sugar." He bit into one half and beamed, the kind of smile that came from his heart.

★ ★ ★

Friday morning was as hot as every other day of the week. Ming pressed a button on his key chain that opened the gates. He'd ordered a cab for us. Kuala Lumpur was too hilly to walk, even if something was round the corner, because that still meant a short drive with a highway and an overpass.

Over the prior few days I'd been a willing passenger in Ming's life. He dropped me in front of the things I ought to know; I took pictures and kept lists of places we went and of the things I ate so I wouldn't forget.

We leaned on his dad's car as we waited for the taxi.

"Did you ever learn how to drive?" I asked.

"Yeah. I don't drive anymore. Did I tell you about the time I crashed my dad's car?"

"No."

"I wrecked it coming out of the driveway."

Ming pointed to black scratches on the pillar by the gate.

"That doesn't look too bad," I said.

"I went into it really hard. It looked worse before."

"Was he mad?"

"He doesn't really get that mad."

I raised an eyebrow, cautious to believe that John's road rage was road love.

"When I crashed the car, he had this look. Like, so stern and fierce. I was crying and panicked and apologizing nonstop, like I was going to get spanked or something. But then it just kind of faded away. He asked me in a calm voice to explain what had happened, and when I told him he said that he was happy I was safe. He said we'd do a few more lessons together."

"Maybe he sensed your guilt."

"Maybe," he said. "But it's the same with everything, even when I'm being a real cunt. It's like something wipes the anger clean off and I can see what's underneath."

"What is it?"

"Fear, I think."

"Of what?"

"I don't know. Loss, maybe," he said, the tail end of his sentence adjoined by the sound of an approaching motor. "The taxi's here. I can go in the front. You can sit in the back with Alissa."

The small box of a car rolled into the driveway. We got in. The hairs on my arms rose from the air-conditioning. Ming turned to the taxi driver.

"Lorong Bukit Pantai five, please."

The taxi drove for a few minutes to the outside of a palatial house. Alissa emerged. She was tanned and leggy and had a loose smatter of freckles across her nose and cheeks. I would've pretended to fancy her a couple of years ago. Her beauty was obvious, the kind I'd long ago learned to spot in order to feel normal. When I was ten and boys started to put up posters of women in their rooms, I didn't quite get it, and so I put up a poster of Joanna Lumley. I swapped it for one of Megan Fox a few weeks later.

Alissa pulled the door open and stepped into the back seat with me.

"Hey," she squealed. "So nice to meet you!"

She hugged Ming from behind the seat. I leaned towards her for a hug, but the seat belt locked and sealed my hips to the seat. My back twisted to reach her. We began the idle chatter I'd had with most of Ming's friends I'd met on the trip. How did you meet Ming? So cute! Where in London are you from? I don't know it! I've been to London a few times. I went to some clubs. I think in Mayfair? You've never been to Asia? That is literally the saddest thing I've ever heard. Did Ming say anything about me? What did he say? No, seriously.

I scrambled my brain for facts, reciting them in vague terms: you're Korean, you and Ming went to school together, you were childhood friends, you go to university in California and you're in a sorority. She nodded, satisfied, smiling with synthetic warmth. I didn't tell her how easily I pictured her holding a megaphone, screaming at pledges to dive into the fucking Jell-O before she fucking drowns them in it.

The car rolled beyond the city. The houses lost structure and thickness, becoming shorter, narrower, rustier.

"What are we eating?" Alissa asked.

"Yong tau foo," Ming said.

"Classic Ming. So Asian!"

Ming hummed. The restaurant was a house off the side of a remote highway, surrounded by nothing but gravel and vegetation. The entrance was on the top floor, and as we walked in, a man in shorts and flip-flops jumped from his chair. He looked surprised to see us. He grabbed a red tablecloth from a podium by the door and spread it over a table.

"That's for you," Ming said. "The red tablecloths only come out for white people."

"Then it's for you, too, Ming." Alissa flashed me a look, as if she sensed that I was thinking it, too.

Ming received the joke with a flat smile. I realized, for the first time, that people in Malaysia might see him in a similar way to how they saw me. Ming ordered and food came on platters. Salty fish paste burst out of the pieces of eggplant and okra, the color of glue, splitting the seams of its vegetable host. We dipped the vegetables into a dark herbal broth. My hesitation dissipated as I bit into one, and although the texture was rubbery, the vegetables bore a rich savoriness. Ming insisted I eat the rectangles of bean curd with rounded corners, the fish paste sitting in the center like the dilated pupil of an eye.

"Really good, right?" Alissa said to me as she stuffed a bloated piece of okra into her mouth.

"I love them," I said.

It was true. I loved everything Ming ordered.

"He's not fussy," Ming said.

Alissa glowed with approval, the most sincere I'd seen her. I felt welcome. I wanted to squeeze Ming's knee, but remembered he'd told me not to. It wasn't okay, even if people knew we were foreigners. We'd moved through the city like friends. The most he did out of the house was shovel food onto my plate, affection buried in soup and grain.

The evening after yong tau foo we hopped between loud, narrow bars, mostly filled with white people. We huddled around tall tables neighboring a dance floor. Drinks came out in large, icy jugs. Ming was as drunk as I was, but he still kept watch for lapses in my memory; I tried to hold his hand and felt the jolt of his hardening neck and shoulders. I didn't like the change, how his body now spoke in words that pushed rather than pulled. It made me uneasy. It made me panic.

Alissa bought us shots. I didn't know why all the drinks had to be set on fire. She toasted us. It was sambuca. The whip of aniseed scorched my throat. We laughed, but as my arm dropped from Ming's shoulder to his hip, his body stiffened once more. I left his side to buy us more drinks. As I waited in the queue, the still heat of the bar hugged the crevices of my body. My forehead wept beads of sweat, coalescing into drips, drawing my hair into thick, wet strands. I brought the jug back to the group. His friends in tight dresses and T-shirts and cargo shorts and snapbacks thanked me as they poured themselves glasses of margarita. Ming checked the time. He brought his mouth to my ear.

"It's three a.m.," he said. "Can we go?"

As we walked out of the club I looked back at the money I'd wasted on the jug, but hoped they'd at least remember I'd bought it. Outside, Ming pointed to a light atop a local taxi, a boxy red car with a white roof and bonnet. We walked up to it and climbed into the back. He recited the address in the same way he always did, in the up-down cadence of Malay.

Our taxi driver wore a hat, the shape of a truncated cone, which the day before Ming had told me was called a songkok. Even in the darkness of the night I could see the birthmark on his hand, a small stain the shape of Italy on the pocket of flesh between his thumb and forefinger.

"It actually really fucked me off that she toasted us," Ming said.

"Alissa?"

"She's different now. I mean, they all are, but they were all dickheads about it when I was younger." He yawned, the top of his head against the window. "I know I say my school was liberal, but it was liberal for Malaysia, which actually doesn't say much, you know. Like, I didn't get beaten up or anything, but it just makes me angry."

"Then why are you still friends with them?"

"Because I put up with it at the time, and people change and people forget and they don't say sorry," he said, his eyes shut and arms folded. "And they're part of my life here."

"You don't really have to hold on to anything you don't want to," I said. "If it causes you pain, I mean. I'm here for you, anyway."

"Thank you," he said, yawning again.

I looked out onto the empty highway lit by orange lamps. Ming fell asleep, his head bobbing from the vibrations of the road until it landed on my shoulder. I thought about nudging him back to his side, but I liked it. The taxi driver looked back at us and laughed. I imagined he thought Ming would be embarrassed by the tenderness. In some ways, he'd be right. I laughed with him.

In the taxi I recognized the change I'd seen in Ming since we'd been in Malaysia. A flatness, a shrinking of self, as if we'd not only flown some distance away but also back in time, to a place before the Ming I knew had fully formed, to a hostility that dulled Ming into a quiet submission. And this Ming seemed not far from how I saw myself when I was with him back home. It made his brilliance feel more fragile, which didn't make me think of him as any less great, or of me as being any more spectacular. It just made me want to protect him.

I woke Ming once the taxi stopped outside the house. He lifted himself off my shoulder, wiping the corner of his mouth, and I followed him inside. We got into the shower together. The hot water restored us both. The cigarette smoke that clung to my skin swirled down the drain. Our wet bodies touched as we kissed. Ming began to laugh. I pushed the two chunks of his hair, soaked from the shower, to either side of his face.

"What is it?" I asked.

"It's just funny. I used to stand in this shower and think of boys."

The water sluiced onto our faces and into our open mouths, streams stuck in the vortex between our swirling tongues. We got out of the shower, and Ming made sure I'd rubbed my hair dry with the towel. His mother always said never to go to bed with wet hair.

As we lay in bed, I reached for Ming. He turned his back to me, wrapping my arm across his body and reversing into me. I held him closer and kissed his shoulder, and then his neck. He turned back around and kissed me. I bit his lip. I licked his ear the way he liked it. My tongue sank into the canal.

Ming's ears were sensitive. He once told me that his mother used to scoop the wax out of them. She used a thin metal stick, like the finger of a rake, long and straight with a small bend at the end. Doctors told her not to do it. Everyone knows you're not supposed to go inside the ear, even with a cotton bud, but she still did. Ming always said it was when he felt closest to her, and she liked to do it for him. They indulged in the lie that it kept his ears healthy and clean. A few days after he'd told me the story, I licked his ear on a whim, and he pushed me deeper into him.

★ ★ ★

The next morning Cindy brought roti canai home for breakfast while John was out playing golf. We sat around the kitchen
counter. I tugged at the crisp and buttery discs, which pulled
apart like raw dough. My fingers ran over the brittle speckles
of brown and black where the roti had burned. I dunked it into
the fish curry, which coated it in a vermillion wash. The sour
tang of tamarind softened the hot chilies. After my first bite, I
instinctively licked my thumb and forefinger, covered in a slick
film of curry. Cindy was elated.

"He loves it!" she shouted. "Typical ang mo."

Cindy left us for a long lunch with friends. The dough sat
heavy in my stomach, drawing the previous night's liquor from
my blood. Ming and I spent the day floating in the small lap
pool along the side of the house. We dipped in and out to re-
prieve ourselves from the heat. Ming monitored my skin. He
topped me up with SPF50 every couple of hours.

"You're literally a melanoma magnet," he said.

Ming sat in an inflatable doughnut; I swam beneath him and
pushed him out. He screamed, then pressed my shoulders into
the water and swam away from me, laughing. He hung on to
the edge of the pool with his elbows. I noticed the flecks of
black on his chin as I paddled closer. My torso touched the tile
next to him.

"You've got more stubble than normal," I said.

He rubbed at it as if it were a stain.

"I have to shave every day in Malaysia. It's something about
the heat."

I pulled my finger along the rough skin. He gently waved
my hand away.

"You hardly have any, though," I said. "You could just try
to grow it out."

"I don't want to," he said. "You know, I've actually been
thinking of getting it lasered."

"What if you want to grow a beard someday?" I asked. "Can't you just shave?"

He pushed off the side and lay flat on the surface of the water, spreading his arms and legs. He shut his eyes against the sun.

"It's the blue," he said. "Hair grows from beneath the skin, and if it's dark enough, then it colors it blue. The shadow's still there even if you shave. I don't like it. Could you even imagine me with a beard?"

"I think you look good with a little stubble. A bit rugged, I guess."

He didn't respond. His ears fell above and below the waterline.

"Can you hear me?" I asked.

"Yes."

"What did I say?"

"Nothing."

His voice had tightened.

"Is it because I said I'd like you rugged?"

"It's not because of anything."

"I just meant that the hair doesn't bother me, and that you don't have to go through with anything, or get anything done. I'm trying to say that you're fine the way that you are. If you said you wanted to lose weight or get more muscular, I'd say you didn't have to." I paused. "I'll go with you, if you want."

I swam towards him, but as I got near he descended into the water. The rejection hurt. He reemerged several meters away at the other end of the pool. I stood on the tiled floor on my tiptoes, still treading water with my arms.

"I don't even know if I'm getting it."

"Okay, well, then I won't go with you."

"Fine."

He pushed himself out of the water and wrapped himself in a towel. He lay down on a deck chair and picked up his book. I was annoyed at his cryptic stubbornness. I got out to dry myself with a towel and walked towards the house, feeling his eyes following me. I lay down on his bed, and soon after Ming was leaning against the doorframe.

"I was being irritable," he said.

Soft words melted me. I stretched out my arms to receive him. He collapsed on top of me and kissed my cheeks. The chlorine in the water had left our skin sticky. The whites of his eyes had reddened.

"Have you been feeling okay?" I asked.

He rolled over and lay on his back. I sat up on the bed.

"It's the same stuff," he said. "It's good. I'm distracted."

"I haven't seen you check your heart much."

He curled up facing me.

"You're right," he said. "It all helps."

"What does?"

"I don't know, being in Malaysia. Being here with you."

Being here with me. Me being here with Ming. He pushed himself up and kissed me. He strolled into the bathroom, standing in the yellow glow of its light. I could see his face in the mirror. He spread shaving cream over his skin. A razor blade mowed clean rows through the blue foam; he washed it and set it back down on the side of the sink. He looked at me through the mirror.

"Cindy has a karaoke machine," he said.

I smiled.

We put some clothes on and walked up the stairs and into the living room. I sat down on the sofa. Ming squatted in front of the machine and fiddled with the knobs until it and the TV turned on.

"How are we going to do this?" he asked.

"Why don't we request songs for each other?"

"What do I sing?"

"'Everytime' by Britney Spears."

"Okay. When I tell you to press play, press play."

Ming walked back towards the staircase, holding the microphone. He set it down at the top of the stairs before running
down again.

"Play!"

I pressed the button. The large television screen switched to
a field with long, billowing blades of grass and bright flowers. I
turned to look at him. He emerged from the stairwell wrapped
in the blanket from his bedroom. He crawled up the stairs, eyes
shut, looking down. He picked up the microphone and began
to sing without looking at the lyrics on the screen, walking in
slow, exaggerated steps towards the TV as he performed. At the
chorus, he belted the words in his Karaoke Voice. Loud, loose
with pitch, with an expression of unguardedness that was in-
trinsically guarded. Emphasis on volume over quality, because
quality is exposing, and trying too hard for it is embarrassing.

"Sing Seriously!" I shouted.

Ming burst out laughing, and the ball jumping over the text
for the refrain went from pink to yellow.

"My score!" he said.

"Sing Seriously!"

Sing Seriously was the game he and Cass sometimes played
when they were drinking. They'd each take turns singing as best
they could, which was still terribly, for minute-long stretches,
like they were auditioning in front of a blind panel. They'd let
me watch once. Cass sang "Call the Shots" by Girls Aloud to an
instrumental track they found online, a surprisingly back-catalog
suggestion they still knew all the lyrics to. Cass crumpled with
laughter on the first word. Ming hit pause. Sing Seriously, Cass!
Cass shut her eyes, and then began to give it her best. While Cass
sang, Ming was hunched over, his back wobbling. I could see
tears budding out of the corner of his eyes. There was something
amazing about it. Not her voice—she sang like a squeaky door—
but because it was so painfully earnest. That was the point, each

of them serving their pride on a dish, the other shaking with vicarious embarrassment. Being honest was hard.

Ming focused on the television with intent. Sing Seriously stripped him of confidence, no longer the boy who'd perform in drag. There was nothing to hide behind. He stood still and looked shy, rotating his hips in the thick blanket. A grin stretched across my face.

"Stop smiling," he said.

The image on the television changed to a couple in white linen shirts, holding hands as they walked past a rolling stream. He jumped back into the song at the bridge. His voice was soft, more careful to hit the notes, the raspy but thin timbre of his voice emerging.

His voice cracked at the chorus, and I started to laugh. He picked up a cork coaster from the coffee table and threw it at me, continuing on with the chorus with his eyes shut. I held the coaster flat against my stomach as I tried to bury my laughter. When he finished the song, we both had tears in our eyes, him from trying to force the honesty and me from trying to hide it.

He threw the blanket over me, knocking over a sealed glass swing-top water bottle. I pushed the edge of the blanket beneath my chin and looked at him as he held the remote, searching for a song for me to Sing Seriously. He picked "I Gotta Feeling" by the Black Eyed Peas. An act of cruelty. He held out the microphone.

I raised my shoulders and tilted my head in the direction of the open balcony doors. Ming rolled his eyes and shut them. I started to sing half-heartedly, somewhere in between speech and song. Sing Seriously! I started to sing more melodically, but with affectatious inflections in the words. Ming wasn't satisfied. Sing Seriously! I sighed, and he laughed, and then I shut my eyes and tried to sing seriously, like I was a wanker in a fedora by a campfire, fingering an acoustic guitar. Ming roared, and I couldn't help but join him.

★ ★ ★

On my last evening, we sat down to eat with three bottles of wine, serving ourselves from a big bowl of Hokkien mee. The warmth of my tongue melted the pork fat, and in turn dissolved the small hat of crackling, releasing the salt into my mouth. John and Cindy asked questions about what I would do for the rest of the summer. We talked about my flight the next day. John explained to me why I should never go to Singapore.

"It's sterile. And materialistic." He set his fork down, and wrapped one fist in his other hand, gearing up for a punch line. "But maybe I'd be as uptight as them if I had to stuff chewing gum up my ass at customs."

Ming's face flushed with dismay. I offered a polite laugh, which John received as a big laugh. A week at Ming's house and my first impressions of John hadn't changed, nice to me as he was. Still, I couldn't help but settle quickly into the comforts of his life. Did I want what John had? Part of me thought yes, even if I was embarrassed to admit it.

I drank three glasses of wine. Ming and I washed up after dinner. We retreated to our room, brushed our teeth and went to bed. I couldn't sleep. My mind wouldn't settle; it ran through the events of the last week—the bars we'd visited, the meals we'd eaten, Ming's friends—but I couldn't follow them in detail, like watching race cars through binoculars. The time disappeared from me and left regret in its place; I wished I'd come for longer—I'd thought of suggesting two weeks before I'd booked my flights, but I hadn't wanted to impose. My thoughts sped in winding circles.

I lifted my arm from Ming's body. He remained fast asleep. I put on a T-shirt and gym shorts and walked upstairs to get some water from the filter tap. My head began to split. The half-bottle of wine drew away like an ebbing wave. I saw Cindy smoking one of her thin Marlboro Lights on the balcony. She was alone. I slid open the glass door.

"Trouble sleeping?" she asked.

"Yeah. I think I'm a bit overtired."

"Come. Lepak." She tapped the rattan chair next to her. "Those boys are always sleeping."

I sat down and she offered me a cigarette. I lit it myself. The yellow light hanging above us sharpened her cheekbones into a cliff edge. Cindy looked much older than she did during the day. She sucked in her cheeks as she inhaled and extended her thin legs from the chair, hooking her ankles onto the balcony railing. She'd drunk more than me at dinner and was half my size.

"You have a very handsome face, Tom," she said. "Just like Ming."

I nodded, unsure of how to receive the compliment.

"Kamu cinta dia? Or, in English, do you love him? Hah." She inhaled once more and coughed.

"I do."

"Good. That boy"—she put a finger to her head—"is always thinking too much, you know. He drives himself to sadness, but he looks happy when he's with you."

I held the glass of water in my hands, rubbing my right thumb across its base. Sad felt heavy and permanent. I'd never thought of Ming as sad. Anxious, yes, but he'd hardly checked his pulse this holiday. Sometimes understanding Ming felt like treading water, and sometimes I was ashamed for not knowing its depth. I smiled uncertainly at Cindy.

"Kamu cinta dia?" I asked.

"Aiyah." She whacked my arm. A wild laugh pulsed out of her. It faded into a hum. "You know, when I started dating John, I was so scared, man. Ming's mother died two years before, and here was this teenage boy, just like his father. I was like, alamak"—she tapped her palm against her head—"Cindy, you have it coming. One day this boy is going to explode at you, say you are some hiao po trying to replace his mother."

"I don't think he's ever hated you."

"Maybe, lah. But I waited and waited and waited, and it never came. John sold their old house and Ming understood. I moved in here and Ming said nothing. We got married and Ming said nothing. I mean, John asked him to speak at the wedding—you know, a few words here and there or something—and Ming said no, but he stood in the pictures and he smiled, and for our present he painted something for me and John. A painting of jackfruit in a bowl, like the Western ones with the apples and oranges, but with pieces of jackfruit. A new friend comes over and they say, wow! Jilei ho sui! And I say my stepson painted it for me. He is the closest thing I have to a child, not that I'm a parent, lah, but you know what I mean." She paused and dragged her finger along the top of her wineglass, and if she had pulled it any faster, it would have sung. "Sometimes I worry. I love him like a son, even though I don't know what that's like, but his mind is always tutup. You know, shut away from me. After I moved in, I heard him crying in his room, and I was so scared I just stood outside the door. Aiyah, it's like that woman, you know, with the snakes on her head."

"Medusa?"

"Ya, it's like I looked at Medusa and froze." She jolted and stuck her arms out as if she'd been petrified. "I worried it was because of me, and because of me and John, and because of his mother. And then I realized, he might not say anything, but..." She held up her hand like a claw towards the sky as if summoning a word, but then gave up and released it. "Ming, he sometimes holds on to and swallows pain, I can tell. Just like John. But sometimes you need to be a bit kiasu when you're young— selfish and spoiled, to get it out, lah. And so I worry, and sometimes I wish and pray he would scream at me, or scream at someone, because when I look at him sometimes I can see."

"See what?"

"That it's stuck." She clenched her right hand into a fist and knocked it lightly against her sternum. "The sadness, lah. But what can I say, I am not his mother, and I'm still scared."

"Of what?"

"That he'll tell me it's not my place."

I nodded. We both took deep, loud breaths.

Tutup. Ming's mind was shut off to Cindy, and sometimes I felt the same way. I could never be sure if or how much he liked or loved me, even if he said it, and when he recoiled from my touch in the club it became harder to take his word for it. Then I had to rely on other things. He said his heart is much better when he's around me. He needs me. And then I wondered why I wanted so much reassurance, anyway, why I'd let myself arrive at a place where I was so uneasy, why I couldn't just be happy that he transmuted me into a more tolerable version of myself.

And then I thought again about all the things I didn't know. Three months to learn about his OCD. Four months to learn his name. Eight months to think of him as sad. Things that forced me to acknowledge there was a gap in the completeness I wanted between Ming and me. Maybe we stood at either end of a rift, two bluffs separated by the things I didn't know. Experts know how little they know. That's what Dad liked to say. Still, not knowing could be painful.

Swirling thoughts filled the long silence between Cindy and me, and I remembered how much lighter my relationship with Ming felt when I was asleep next to him. Cindy set her wineglass down and stretched her arms above her. She yawned, and I yawned shortly after.

5
Sweat

I shouldn't use the word crazy, but I feel like I can. In the same way I can call myself a faggot. Sometimes the shoe fits if you put it on yourself.

I hold my phone in my hand as I pace around my room. My finger hovers over the call button. Tom has his last exam tomorrow, but I'm in a real fucking state. The last year was good. My OCD waned. The heart stuff left. In the ten months since he visited Malaysia, Tom and I have ticked over in ways peaceful and lovely. Ten months! A world away. He moved into a house with Rob and Sarah, taking the shitty attic room because he's just that kind of guy. He watched my plays. I watched Tom and Rob's monthly set, played to a loose but committed audience, at the only club in town that didn't blast "Mr. Brightside" on repeat. I spent nights in their new house, sometimes staying a bit longer in the mornings, after Tom and Sarah had gone to the library, to eat breakfast with Rob in the kitchen. Tom and I held hands in the supermarket. I even nodded along to a video essay setting out a socialist defense of Hegel. I'm still not sure why he needed defending, but I watched it, and without reminding Tom that his family are middle-class Camberwell gentrifiers who worship at the church of Ottolenghi and knitted alpaca cardigans. Something in me felt increasingly present. Maybe it was the laser, which I know sounds stupid, but each time I ran my fingers along my hairless face, I was calmer for it.

But then the pressure of *Death's a Drag* started to get to me. Lisa and I dressed up as our dead parents to pontificate on whether they'd be disappointed in their gay kids. Um, so, Ming, I just think there's a really good opportunity to explore, and maybe, like, usurp the expectations society places on non-white parents and their queer children. I thought the idea was brilliant. Lisa was brilliant, even if she struggled to see it. We each wrote scraps of soliloquys that we edited into dialogue. The whole thing brought Lisa peace, and even though I loved it, could do it over and over, for some reason I started to crack. And then it was exams and dissertations, which I'd done fuck all for. My OCD waxed. At first it was manageable, but then it wasn't.

I sit at the end of my bed and lock my phone. A GP put me on a small dose of citalopram a few weeks ago, but it makes me feel jittery and for the first week I shat my guts out. It'll take another few weeks to help, if it does anything at all, and so for now I'm stuck here. I shut my eyes and hug my legs. I feel a twitch in my calf. And then in my eye. I panic. I'm dying! It's amyotrophic lateral sclerosis, more commonly known as ALS. Do I have ALS? Oh my god, I have fucking ALS, don't I. I give in and open my laptop at my desk and head to the forums. Is twenty-one too young to have ALS? Yes, it is very unlikely. A bit of relief. Is the twitching in my leg ALS? It is a very rare disease; it is very unlikely. More relief. Does lasering facial hair increase likelihood of ALS? No results. Okay! Youngest person ever to have ALS? Eight. Fuck! The cycle starts again, and

I am researching and researching through a hamster wheel of improbability and death. This is what I do instead of studying. I spend my days on support forums and checking my muscles in the mirror for atrophy, which sucks because I fucking hate looking at my naked body in the mirror. When Tom and I go to the library, I slip into the bathroom to look stuff up in private. He's cottoned on that something's up, because nobody needs to piss four times an hour.

I could go to Cass or Lisa instead, but Cass has her own problems and I don't know what Lisa would do. She'd understand, but it'd also send her into a flap. Um. Ah! Okay. So, Ming, first of all I'm, like, so sorry. Ah, this is just awful. I'm so worried about you, Ming! I think that'd send me over the edge. None of this is Tom's fault, obviously, even if he suggested watching the fucking Stephen Hawking biopic that started it all.

The panic swirls in my stomach and stretches its arms towards my jaw. It all feels too much. I bite my lip and roll it over my bottom row of teeth. If Tom fucks up his exams, he won't get his job. I don't think that'd be the worst thing in the world, but I know that it would be to him, and that's what matters.

People I once thought were cool applied for jobs at places like Goldman Wank and PricewaterhouseShitheads. It's disappointing that Tom and Rob did the same. As Tom told me about one of his interviews, I stared at the copy of *Capitalist Realism* on his bookshelf behind him. The cognitive dissonance amazed me, and when I said this he reminded me that Engels was a textile magnate. I didn't care enough to remind him that he wasn't Engels. Besides, it was what he wanted to do, and who was I even to judge. What office would have me? What skills do I have? All I want to do is write. To dress up as my mother and perform *Death's a Drag* at any cost.

I shut my laptop and stare out of my window. A lone streetlamp glows. I pick up the phone and call Tom. There's a tremor in my throat, and I know my voice will wobble like small ripples in a pothole puddle.

"I'm scared, Tom," I say.

"I can come over." He pauses. "I'll bring my revision notes."

"Are you sure? Your last exam's tomorrow."

Silence on the line.

"I'll see you in a bit," he says.

"I love you."

"I love you, too."

I leave my phone on the bed and lie down next to it. I rub my hands over my face. It's smooth, but I can feel a few follicles burgeoning, some resistance, like running over sparse hooks of Velcro. This sends another pang of unease through me. I start to cry. The world feels too much. Booking another session feels like too much, even if it makes me happy.

Laser's expensive, and to pay for it, I had to dip into the special pot of money my mother gave me on the final Chinese New Year before she died. She handed me an ang pow stuffed to the brim with British currency. It was absurd, as thick as *War and Peace*. We all knew she was going to die at that point. She was so weak from the chemo, bound to a wheelchair, oxygen tank in tow. I received the packet with two hands and said thank you, just like any other year. She said it was for the future, and so Dad took it from me to put into a UK bank account, which I could only access when I moved over.

Sometimes I try to think of what she was doing, what feeling or assurance this informal inheritance gave her, even though she knew Dad would still be there, and that if something happened to him, there'd be much more for me than what was in the envelope. Spending the money feels like I'm exhuming and deleting her memory, but there was no other way both to pay for the laser and feel like the decision was my own.

Maybe I need food. I run downstairs. The lights are off. Cass is in her room. I open the white kitchen cabinets and throw six digestive biscuits and a stick of chorizo into a bowl. I pour cashew milk into a glass. There's no almond milk in the house because it kills bees and I don't want blood on my hands. I sit on the countertop with the cabinets poking into the back of my neck and dip five of the digestives into the milk one by one. I eat the chorizo and down the final biscuit and the rest of the milk. I wash my mouth out with some water, ditch the bowl and glass in the sink, and sit down at the kitchen table. For a second I feel calm, but then my leg twitches again. What if I have ALS? I look directly up at the ceiling light and beg my mind to stop.

The doorbell rings. It's Tom. I walk to the door. He hugs me tight. I rest my cheek atop his collarbone. I love him so much. His hair's a little damp. He smells so clean. Like passionfruit. I wonder if I smell of chorizo.

"You're here," I say.

"How are you feeling?"

"Better since we got off the phone. I ate some food."

We walk upstairs together towards my room. I look at my messy, unaccommodating desk. Tom hates how my belongings splat over any surface like jam.

"Do you want me to move some stuff?" I ask.

"I'll just sit on your bed."

He slips his shoes off his feet. He takes a book and pencil out of his satchel and lies stomach-down on my black sheets. When I'm certain he's comfortable, I sit back at my desk and open my laptop. I shut the forum tabs. My leg twitches. The what-ifs come, but I don't open the tabs back up. Feeling his eyes on me helps. I know it's not a permanent cure, but sometimes when he's around me the mania melts, and I feel like I can swallow the fear. The panic spikes a few more times, but I don't open the browsers, I don't go to the mirror.

I make notes in the margins of a book to the sound of high-lighters screeching across his papers. I wonder what I look like from behind. Do my shoulders look broad? I sit cross-legged on the chair and play with the toes on my bare feet. I imagine Tom's face. The nub of his tongue pokes out from the side of his mouth when he works. There's always a furrow above his nose.

I read until my mind eases, and a dry fatigue begins to creep over my eyes. The curves and the lines of the letters on the page fatten. Tom yawns. I dog-ear the corner of the page and swing around.

"Do you want to go to bed soon?" I ask.

Tom looks up from his book and smiles at me.

"Sure."

He stretches his arms above him and the bones in his back crack. His body is long. He flicks through the flash cards like he's shuffling a deck of cards, then puts them atop the book and looks at the corner of the room.

"I see the fan's arrived," he says.

Thank fuck. The citalopram gives me night sweats. It's fucking gross, my body crying into the sheets like that. Sex sweat is hot and salty, but cortisol sweat smells like ass. I stand up and we take our clothes off. Tom folds his over the end of the bed while I hang mine on the standing rail next to my desk. I leave my T-shirt on. Tom is naked. He crawls into bed and pushes his legs beneath the duvet. I turn the fan on and position it towards him. He gives me a thumbs-down. I move it to the right a little. He gives me a thumbs-up. I crawl in next to him and he turns off the bedside light. We cuddle and fall asleep.

I look at my clock when Tom wakes up. It's three in the morning. We're drenched in sweat. Cortisol sweat. I feel the moisture everywhere. In the rim of my ear and on the hairs on the back of my neck. I've soaked into him. All of this came from my body, and it's because of the fucking citalopram that I have to take because I'm crazy. I start crying. I can't help myself. Shit!

"I'm so sorry, Tom, it's the fucking citalopram," I say. "I really thought the fan would help, you know. It's so disgusting. I'm so sorry."

I feel beastly, like one of those white PE teachers from my school sweating under the equatorial sun. It all horrifies me. Tom leans in to hug me, squeezing more sweat from the pores of my wet T-shirt.

"It's fine," he says. "It's fine. Go and rinse off. I'll change the bedsheet."

I turn on the bedside light and stand up. I watch as he flips the duvet off the bed. He pulls the bedsheet off, gets a new one from the cupboard and stretches the corners over the mattress. His movements are precise and methodical. It's disturbing. It suggests a response to a pattern of behavior. Three times is enough to evidence a pattern. The T-shirt I wore to sleep in is cold and heavy on my body. I need to take it off, but I can't move.

"Go and rinse off," he repeats.

This gives me the push I need. I cross my arms along the hem and pull the T-shirt off in one clean motion. I go into the bathroom on the landing. I squint. The bright halogen lights are like fingers in my eyes. I stand in the white bath, rubbing my belly with a bar of soap. I barely pull the shower curtain because I'm scared of being too enclosed. Water from the showerhead drips onto my tummy and runs down my legs. Some splashes onto the bathroom floor. Tom comes in a few moments after and pisses into the toilet bowl. He forgets to pull the seat up. It's unlike him, and this underscores to me that he must be tired. I remember he has an exam tomorrow, and I feel so guilty that I want to cry again. He unspools the toilet paper and wipes the drops of urine that bounced onto the seat. He throws it into the bowl, shuts the lid and sits on it. My eyes twitch again. What if it's ALS? I press my palms into my face and groan.

"What is it?" he asks.

"My eyes are twitching," I say. "I'm worried it's ALS."

He keeps silent. He doesn't say it's nothing to worry about.

Part of me hates him for it, even though it's good for me. I know he's read the blogs. I once looked something up on his laptop, and on a whim I typed OCD and saw what came up. Endless visits to forums on how to support your partner. Support your partner in other ways. Support your partner in ways that don't provide them with reassurance. Being a good partner is counter-intuitive. Being a good partner will sometimes feel like being a bad partner. Everyone prefers the feeling of handing out sweets over broccoli. But sometimes I want candy.

I turn the shower off and step out of the bath. He grabs the towel off the rail, but when I reach to take it he ignores me and dries me off himself, then hugs me through the fabric. My leg twitches. What if it's ALS? What if I'm dying? He seems to sense this and holds me longer, and when the panic fades I shift out from him and hold on to the towel.

He steps into the shower and pulls the curtain all the way. I wait for him, and when he finishes he takes the towel from me and dries himself off. I check the clock. Half an hour gone. An hour if he can't get to sleep right away.

When we go back into the room, Tom sits cross-legged on the bed. The corner of his pillow touches the small of his back. He curves his spine and yawns. He looks worn, his body crumpled like wet petals. He taps the space in front of him and tells me to sit down.

"Let's do that Meisner stuff," he says. "Do you remember?"

I'm confused for a moment, but then sit down in front of him without a word. We look into each other's eyes.

"You look worried," he says.

"I look worried," I say. "You're knitting your eyebrows."

"I'm knitting my eyebrows," he says. "You're lifting your shoulders."

"I'm lifting my shoulders," I say, trying to relax them back down. "You look sleepy."

"I look sleepy. You moved your hand."

"I moved my hand," I say. "You're pursing your lips."

"I'm pursing my lips. You're taking a deep breath."

"I'm taking a deep breath," I say. "You're smiling a little."

"I'm smiling a little."

We carry on with the Meisner technique for a long time. I try not to think about how it's Tom's last exam tomorrow. For the first time this evening I am out of my own head. I wonder how what to do comes so easily to Tom. I've never been able to imagine myself with another person like this. A month ago, when Tom told me that his parents had said we could move into their house after graduation for a while, I was unsure. Not just because moving into his childhood bedroom is fucking weird, but because I never thought I would be the kind of person who someone could date and love enough to live with. At least by choice. But as we narrate and repeat each other's movements and expressions, I almost believe it.

6
Voids

I'm sitting in the gastropub toilet. I need a break from my dad harassing me over the dinner table. Why would you lie to us about your marks, Michael? Are you planning to get an actual job? Do you intend to live with Tom's parents forever? What would your mother think? The last one hit like a dump truck. Cindy looked aghast. Aiyah, John! We never whack out the M-word. He might as well have shat on the table. Dad, you wouldn't know what she'd fucking think, and by the way, undoing that many buttons on a white linen shirt makes you look like a sex tourist.

My trousers are at my ankles but nothing's coming out of either hole. I tense my pelvic floor and a few drops of urine fall into the bowl. I fold a single square of toilet paper to dab the excess wetness. Two brown brogues walk along the bottom of the stall, and when they go into the cubicle next to me, I stand up and fasten my trousers. I tuck the billowy shirt into the waist that comes up higher than my belly button. I stand with my hand on the stall lock and wait for a moment.

Term is done. We finished our exams. It's a time to celebrate, but it doesn't feel like it. Tom fucked up his last one, and while his job didn't end up caring, he still didn't get the grade he wanted. Neither did I, but I didn't deserve to, and even calling it a want for me was a stretch. He says it wasn't my fault, but we both know that's not true. The worst part is that when I finished my exams, I booked a doctor's appointment to talk about the twitching, but as soon as I did, the worries about ALS simmered down to nothing. It can be like that sometimes; an obsession cannonballs through the living-room window, only to shoot right out the other side a couple of months later. It's obvious to me now that I didn't have ALS, which makes all the pain I put Tom through feel futile.

When I stopped worrying about my heart, I started worrying about ALS. Now that I've stopped worrying about the ALS stuff, I'm worrying about something else. I can't tell Tom. I can hardly tell myself.

I flip the lock and walk back into the pub, bouncing down the short staircases cascading to the seating area that overlooks the river. My dad and Cindy are sitting next to each other in silence and on their phones. I take the spot across from Cindy. Cindy acknowledges my return. Dad ignores me. I look out of the window.

Tom and his parents are standing on the bridge next to the restaurant, pausing to look at the view. A gentle channel of wind rustles Janice's chocolate mane and exposes Morris's high widow's peak. I don't think they can see us. Janice and Morris have their elbows on the parapet and Janice is gesticulating, her angular, expressive face caught in an explanation. Morris nods along, a smile rounding his dimpled cheeks. Tom paces in circles. He looks restless, and I know it's because his parents are mindfully slow and they're a few minutes late. They eventually push off the bridge and head into the restaurant.

When they join us, everyone stands up to introduce themselves. I make eye contact with Tom then look askance at my dad, who tells them that he's ordered a bottle from the wine list. This is the kind of chest-puffing people like Janice and Morris don't care for. Tom sits next to me, and his parents sit across from each other at the end of the table.

"That's a beautiful necklace," Janice says to Cindy, nodding at the thick gold choker around Cindy's neck.

"Thank you!" Cindy beams. "It's Dior! Half off!"

"Ooh," Janice says.

A young waiter brings a bottle of wine to our table. The apron and shirt sit loose on his gangly frame. He looks like he's playing dress-up. My dad inspects the label. I wonder if he takes anything in when he does this, or if he's playing dress-up, too. He sips it and nods. The waiter fills his glass, and then Cindy's and Janice's, then Morris's, then mine, and Tom's last. His hand wobbles as he tips the wine into Tom's glass, and some splashes onto the tablecloth. His voice cracks when he apologizes, his cheeks steaming red. We all pretend nothing's happened.

There are bad vibes in the room. My dad and I still don't make eye contact.

"Ming's told me about your job, Tom. Congratulations." My dad turns to Tom's parents. "You must be very proud."

Morris looks surprised at my dad's enthusiasm. Janice and Morris pretend to hate banks as much as any white, middle-class *Guardian* reader. He raises his eyebrows before relaxing them into an agreeing smile.

"Tom seems excited to start," Morris says.

"Thank you," Tom says, fiddling with his silk shirtsleeve.

Tom's parents were as confused as I was by his job. They've spent years nodding along to Tom's Fisher-Price socialism, but stop short whenever Tom mentions a wealth tax. Yes, tax the

millionaires. No, not our kind of millionaire. Not the acci-
dental property millionaire! They'll be the first to bury their
cordless Dyson in the back garden when the class war erupts
and the purges begin.

"A pretty packet for your first job, too," my dad says. "Doesn't
sound too bad, does it, Michael?"

I glare at him.

"Aiyah, John." Cindy places her hand on my dad's shoulder.
"Leave Ming alone."

"He'll have to get a job eventually. You can't trouble Janice
and Morris forever."

"Don't worry about that." Janice holds her hands up, palms
open in protest. This clears the awkwardness collecting around
the table like plaque. "We're excited to have them both at home
soon, more than Tom would let us admit."

I smile at Janice. I fucking love this woman, even if she once
introduced me as Tom's Malaysian boyfriend. She gets the shit
I write. She's actually seen my plays, whereas Dad's a philis-
tine. He's the kind of man who looks at a Pollock and says he
could've done it. His favorite actor is Nicolas Cage. I decide to
be diplomatic and repeat what I said to him earlier, minus the
ad hominems.

"I'm going to find a job, Dad," I say. "It's not banker or bust,
you know. There's this door-to-door flower-selling thing that
I've looked into doing. Lisa's going to do it, too. It's becoming
really popular in London. You can earn a surprising amount
of money."

"Oh, brilliant!" my dad says, the venom in his tone bright.
"Fantastic use of your degree. Wonderful return on investment."

"I couldn't get a job like Tom's, anyway. With my grades,
you know."

"Oh yes," he says. "The grades. That's another conversation
altogether."

"Dad," I say. "Stop it."

My mother would combust at the state of him, airing shit out in public like this. She always said we had to save face. Don't shout—you're not some ang mo brat. Just smile if Auntie Melinda says you look fat. No need to tell Auntie Jasmine that you failed your flute exam.

My dad grips his cutlery. His eyes swing between me and Janice. He looks on the cusp of saying something, but takes a sip of his wine instead. He's doing that thing where he takes stock of himself mid-tantrum, but it's obvious he's still upset. It's a bit pathetic.

"The wine's lovely," he says.

"Very lovely," Morris says.

I stare out of the window. Some of the thoughts crowd back. These what-ifs are painful. I tap a silent finger on the tablecloth. Tom is looking at me. I wonder what he sees, how deeply he sees, if he knows that I'm hiding something. Does he know? Maybe he knows. Would that be so bad? Yes. We exchange small smiles.

"Ming's a brilliant playwright," Janice says to my dad and Cindy. The compliment pulls me back into the room.

"So good at it," she continues. "As I'm sure you know. Morris and I came up to see *Death's a Drag* at the start of the year. It was such a beautiful premise, him and that girl Lisa dressing up in clothes—"

"In drag," Tom says.

"In drag. It was phenomenal, really. The makeup, the acting. I shed a few tears."

I look at my dad. He's pretending to be distracted by something out of the window. He never liked the idea of *Death's a Drag*. I first told him at dinner back home in Malaysia one night, over curries and pickles surrounding a dome of rice like moons, all served on a banana leaf. I expected him to be touched, but he just sat there in silence, and so I began to explain. It's a way for me to feel close to her. Lisa feels the same way about her dad. We've already written it. Sometimes it still really hurts, and writing always makes it hurt less. I think she would've found it quite funny! He didn't say anything for a few moments. He picked up the stem of a crisp chili, preserved and dried in salt, its skin black and flaked gold where it caught the halogen light of the restaurant. He nibbled at the end and set it down again before he turned his eyes to me.

"The dead can't say no, Michael."

He picked up his fork and spoon and heaped rice into his mouth. His tone was grave. He was never one for aphorisms, only cheap slogans, and so this wasn't something I could brush off as typical Dad shit. My mother couldn't say no, but I was the one who had to live without her. I stayed silent, and when I flew back to England for the start of term we put the play on anyway. When I told my dad about it on the phone, he just hummed and wished me good luck. And now he's sitting here with his eyes fixed out of the window, pretending as if it never happened.

"I saw pictures," Cindy says. "I wish I could have seen it in person. He looked just like his—" Cindy stops herself. Her using the M-word has always felt sacrilegious, but this time I'm almost sad she doesn't say it. "He looked very pretty, right? Much prettier than me! Cantiknya. And that girl, Leslie. Wow! So manly! Ming showed me pictures of her father. Died in a car accident. So sad! Spitting image when she dressed up for the show, I'm telling you."

Our food arrives. Seabass for the women. Steaks for the men. Fish and chips for me and Tom. My dad begins to look less sour. I ask for more ketchup.

"Have you spent much time around the town?" Morris asks.

"Cindy likes to shop," I say.

"Only a little." Cindy clicks her tongue and rolls her eyes with a smile. She turns to Janice. "I'm telling you, the imported clothes in Malaysia are very expensive, you know. When you buy them here you can get at least ten per cent off." She grows more animated. "And then another twenty per cent when you go through customs because of the VAT. Haiya, it's cheap! How can you not buy?"

"Any excuse to shop," my dad says. "Cindy even bought something from Royal Selangor today."

I burst out laughing. This is the first I've heard of it. She hangs her head in playful shame. Janice laughs along, too, though I don't think she's ever heard of Royal Selangor.

"What's that?" Morris asks.

"They sell pewter ornaments," my dad says. "It's a Malaysian shop. Cindy bought pewter imported into England from Malaysia and is now going to smuggle it back into Malaysia at twice the price."

"It's not twice the price! And it's different designs for the shops here, lah," Cindy says, turning to Janice. "You understand."

I am certain that Janice doesn't understand.

"It can't be twice the price, Dad," I say. "Not with the VAT refunds."

Everyone laughs. The joke's not even funny, but there is a collective yearning to shift the mood. The shakes in our ribs are enough to connect the empty spaces between the chairs and across the table. The conversation turns light. Janice and Morris share their observations about the graduation ceremony. Tom's was yesterday. Mine's the day after tomorrow. Cindy's palms meet in tight, rapid claps, growing quicker the more antediluvian the detail. We finish our food. Waiters clear our plates and the adults fight over the bill. My dad wins because he has to. The six of us trifurcate outside the restaurant, where it's still light.

Tom and I walk in silence until we reach the path towards my house.

"I can't wait for this all to be over," I say.

"What?"

"This." I gesture towards the Gothic buildings in front and to the side of us. "I just really want to leave."

This seems to wound Tom. His hands are in his pockets. I feel bad. Places move into people just as much as people move into places, but that's not what I mean. I just really want to leave. He looks down at his shoes.

"Only a couple of days," he says.

"Are you spending tomorrow with Rob and Sarah?"

"Yeah," he says. "Last night in the house, I guess."

We turn onto my road and step into my house. Cass and Lisa sit at the kitchen table drinking. Cass is in a mesh bodysuit and Lisa is wearing a booby crisscross top. They greet us loudly. Lisa's the only person I've seen who manages to look healthy under the sobering kitchen floodlight. Cass is hunched over. Her clavicles are steep. She's not doing any better, but she's still the most beautiful woman I know, and the smartest; she got first-class honors in her degree and a fancy job at a big think tank.

"You both look so lovely!" Lisa says. "So how was dinner? Did they, like, get along?"

"It was good. Everyone got along." Tom turns to me. "Right?"

"Yeah, for sure." I walk over to the kitchen cabinets and take out two glasses. "More than I expected. Are you guys still going to Rosie's?"

"Cass was telling me about the prize thing," Lisa says quickly.

"What's that?" Tom asks.

I notice Lisa's ignored my question, probably because she doesn't want to say that she isn't coming. I remind Tom that Rosie once won a two-thousand-pound prize for her exam results, only to spend it all on ketamine and resell it at profit. She was my and Cass's dealer for a small chunk of second year.

"What's she doing after graduation?" Lisa asks.

"Venture capital," Cass says.

Lisa laughs.

"Are you guys coming?" Cass asks.

"Of course. Tom and Rob are playing," I say. Cass looks at her cup. I feel bad. I pour drinks for me and Tom, then look towards Lisa.

"You're coming, right?" I ask.

"I was," she says. "I really want to, to be honest, but Sarah's just texted to say she wants to stay in. She's going to meet me at mine."

I want to say that Sarah could stay in alone, but in some relationships one person stands and the other bends. It'd be nice if Sarah stood for fun. I turn to Tom.

"Let's drop some stuff off upstairs."

I walk out of the kitchen and Tom follows me to my room. I sit on my bed. He changes into some loose pin-striped trousers and an oversized T-shirt he's left in a drawer. He lies down on the bed, his back on the duvet.

"I think I have a pill somewhere," I say. "We could split it."

"Sure."

I get up and rifle through my drawers until I find a small bag with a red pill that looks like a battery. I throw it underarm at Tom. It lands on his chest but he doesn't move. He holds his glass atop his navel, looking up at the ceiling.

"Is everything okay?" he asks. "There was a moment at dinner where I thought you might be thinking about something. You were staring out of the window, kind of glazed, I guess. The way you get when you're panicking."

I look at Tom, but he doesn't reciprocate eye contact. I don't know how to respond.

"Was I?" I ask. "I haven't thought about the ALS stuff recently. Not in a way that scares me."

"Was it something else?"

I move some things around in the open drawer.

"It wasn't," I say. "I was just thinking."

He furrows his eyebrows and opens his mouth, but then bites his bottom lip. His face relaxes. He sits up and takes the baggie off his chest.

"Will one pill be enough between us?" he asks.

I'm dancing with Cass next to the decks and speakers set up for the party. None of us have seen Rosie. Apparently she's already passed out upstairs. Tom and Rob are playing. Rob's wearing a noisy button-down with no discernible pattern, just random technicolored streaks and lines. A high Cass uses an app to find the names of the tracks with mixed success. I take my share of the pill halfway through. Rob finishes off their set with a remixed version of "My Neck, My Back." The crowd cheers. I'm coming up too hard to assess the politics of that choice. Someone who looks just like Tom and Rob replaces them at the decks. Tom joins us. Rob disappears. I give Tom his half of the pill.

I feel a warm rush in my chest. My tongue curls and fishes out the metallic-tasting crumbs between my teeth. My hands writhe in their joints, and my fingers bend into claws. We're in a corner of the long living room. Cass and Tom are locked in conversation. She's being gushy.

"You know that I love you. And it's not just because you're Ming's boyfriend. He's so special, but you are, too." She puts Tom's hand on her chest, pushing his palm against it. "I hold you guys so close to here."

I wonder if she knows I can hear her. She lets go of Tom's hands and hugs him tight, then brings me in, too. We all waddle in tandem, and when we release, Tom smiles at me. It's not that Tom doesn't like Cass; he does, I just think he doesn't totally get her. He thinks she sometimes looks at people in a condescending way because she tilts her chin downward, but I know it's just shyness, not judgment. Maybe the stuff with Rob doesn't help. Tom goes off somewhere, and so I'm dancing with

Cass again. I know we're fucked because we're quoting Tiffany Pollard from *Flavor of Love* as we dance. You're the only bitch in the house I ever respected! Beyoncé? Beyoncé? You fucking look like Luther Vandross!

I need to take a poo. I peel away from everyone and climb up the stairs. I shut my eyes as I walk up. My fingers run along the wooden banister. The nicks in the wood feel much bigger and the dimples much deeper. There's no queue for the loo. Miraculous! The lights don't work and the floor is wet. Tea towels, heavy with water from a leak, run along the bottom of the wall behind the toilet. I step on one beneath the sink accidentally. It squelches and bleeds onto my trainers. It's disgusting, and if I'm saying that, then it must be pretty fucking gross. I sit down and do my business. I wipe, flush and I look at my faded face in the mirror, its contours hidden in the dark. I wash and dry my hands and then feel my jaw. There are a couple of bristles. Anxiety flutters in my chest. I'm due another session.

I need to lie down for a second. Sometimes when I get overwhelmed, I just want to lock myself away. It's not always the case. Sometimes I want Tom, but for the moment I want somewhere dark and empty. I stumble into a tiny bedroom by the landing. It's the only one that I don't hear voices coming out of. Part of me expects to find a comatose Rosie, but instead I see Rob lying on the bed.

"Rob. Why are you in here?"

"I needed a moment to myself. I started to come up when we were playing. Bad idea, right?"

"Can I join you?"

He gives me two thumbs up. I lie down next to him on the single bed. Rob's wearing his cologne. The smell reminds me of the droplets that spritz onto my hands when I peel a mandarin orange, anchored by notes of sandalwood. I stare at our shoes. I think of the water from the bathroom and feel bad for whoever's room this is.

"You guys did really good," I say.

Rob looks at me.

"Yeah?"

"Yeah," I say. "Why'd you drop during your set?"

He laughs.

"I don't know. I thought it'd be fun." He pauses. "And I got a bit nervous about fucking up the set and letting people down because it's graduation and expectations are high, so I took some of the pill to take the edge off. It's so dumb, because it's just a house party, right? It's stupid, isn't it?"

"Rob!" I say, hugging him. "It's not stupid. It's really human. None of us want to let people down."

"And I get that feeling with my parents a lot," he continues, and I'm briefly taken aback by the sharp turn. "They're so proud of me that sometimes it hurts. So proud of me for being here. Rob's going to do this! Rob's going to do that! It's a bit overwhelming, right?"

"Yeah," I say. "I can relate."

I'm not sure I can relate. My dad's pride has always felt more subdued, more knowing, as if the small successes are a given. It wasn't ever as warm, and these days it's stone-cold.

"It's why I think it's nice to live for yourself sometimes, right?" Rob says. "Not for other people."

We fall into a brief silence. Rob rests his head on mine.

"Your family left this morning, didn't they?" I ask.

"Yeah. A bit of a squish having everyone," he says. "It was nice that Tom and Sarah didn't mind. Not that their families would've wanted to stay in the house, anyway. But it was good. They all loved the ceremony, even my brothers."

We talk more about dinner, and about Tom's parents. Rob slips his phone out of his pocket, and we take a photo of ourselves. Our eyes are droopy.

"Cass is here tonight, right?" he asks.

"Yeah."

I wonder if I should say something. Tom fucking won't. It's probably the only thing he wouldn't do for me. I know Rob worries about disappointing people, but it's never an excuse to hurt someone. Cass would be mortified, but I'm high and it seems urgent for him to know how much he hurt her. Rob can be a doofus about this stuff. It's a straight-man thing. Not that I'd know. He dangled her on a string for over a year. Each time he slept with her, he pulled away, swooping back in right after she started to feel okay. Facts are facts, even if Cass plays them down. He's not the reason she has an eating disorder, but he doesn't help, and I know it'd be a tonic if he admitted some wrong.

"I think it would mean a lot if you apologized to her."

Rob turns his body so that he's lying on his side, facing me. He looks worried.

"For what?" he asks.

"She really liked you, you know." My tongue feels dizzy in my mouth. "You strung her along for too long. I get that you might not have wanted a relationship with her, and that she might've said she was chill, but it's not always that simple. Especially when someone's ill."

I know it was stupid of me, and I know I shouldn't have done it. What if he tells Cass I said something? Who am I to call her ill? I'm not even sure that's how she sees herself. I wouldn't want her to think that's how I see her. I pray that Cass never finds out. Rob exhales, and then lies down on his back again. His palms are flat over his tummy. He rests his elbow on the inside of mine.

"Okay," he says. "It'd be the right thing to do, right?"

"Yeah."

There's a knock at the door. It opens. It's Tom.

He lies down on top of us. His weight is comforting. We don't talk about Cass, but instead we retrace the dinner. Tom mentions that Morris texted him to say that Cindy was engaging and hilarious. Rob rolls off the bed and pulls me and Tom up by our arms.

"All right, you two," he says. "Time to have fun, okay?"

Tom and I groan.

"Classic only children," he says. "So stubborn."

We walk back downstairs into the crowded living room. We squeeze to the front of the decks. The three of us dance together. Maybe I'm just high, but it really does feel like it's the three of us, me and Tom and Rob, like when Rob hugs us like brothers, or when we watch movies with my head on Tom's lap and my legs across Rob's.

Cass joins us, and we dance in the throng of people until Rob and Cass peel off. I see them in the corner of the room. He stands over her. They hug for a long time. I think about how being ill really sucks. Cass may think Rob's affection could somehow fix her, and maybe the apology will help, but part of me also knows the effect will underwhelm against the expectation. Sometimes a person, an achievement or a place— whatever is missing—seems the perfect shape to fill a void, so much so that its absence seems to be the cause of the problem and its presence the solution. But up close, the voids are always much larger. Tom and I dance close. I don't let go of his hand.

7

Litter

I was packing up my attic room. The sun shone through the windows. Rob and Sarah didn't like the slanted ceilings. I didn't either, but Sarah had got first pick because she wouldn't move in with us otherwise. I got second pick because I'd found it, but Rob needed a room with more light than mine. He said he'd be fine with the attic, but he was masking his disappointment. I'm sure I could get a few more lamps, right? I could always just work in the living room, couldn't I? But I'd known Rob meant none of this, so I'd pretended to grow enthusiastic about it. Look at how much more I can see from up here! I've got windows on both ends!

I crashed down onto my bed, stretching and rolling the tiredness out of me. It was afternoon, but I still hadn't gone downstairs. I got back up and stared at myself in the mirror. I looked sallow and gaunt. More so recently. I scratched the itchy scalp beneath my mop of messy hair.

I got changed and descended the forest-green carpet that

ran past Sarah's and Rob's shut doors. It was a terrible color. It made the house feel crowded and clammy, and its dark, rough tendrils entombed red-wine stains and dirt.

The living-room door on the ground floor was shut, too. I heard murmurs, and through the bottom sliver I saw the flickering light of the television. I ducked my head inside. The whiteness of the screen was harsh against the otherwise unlit room, its curtains drawn. Rob was curled up in the fetal position on the couch to my left, his arms folded and head on Sarah's lap. Sarah was on her phone. Rob twisted his head and smiled at me. His face was mushed up from this angle, like a happy baby in a Renaissance painting.

"What are you guys watching?" I asked.

"Rob's never seen *Thelma & Louise*." Sarah put her phone down behind Rob's back, turning her head towards me. "Shall we open the bottle?"

I retrieved it from the fridge at the other end of the room, the bottle we'd split between us and saved for the last night in the house. It had been Rob's idea. We all moved into the garden, onto the furniture we'd found in a skip at the start of the year. Rain had colored the iron beneath the chipped paint with moss and rust.

Sarah popped the bottle open. The cork flew over the far edge of the garden and into our neighbor's. Rob hid tired eyes behind sunglasses. I poured the bottle into a mason jar, our single flute, and a heavy red-wine glass that dinged like plastic when I flicked it. We clinked them together.

"How are you feeling after Rosie's?" Sarah asked me.

"Really dead."

"I'm not surprised." Sarah sat up in her chair. "Have you seen Rosie on a night out? It's like watching Ms. Pac-Man. She just guzzles what's in front of her."

"She was passed out at her own party," I said. "Like, just after midnight."

Sarah laughed, then slouched with her legs stretched out towards the ground.

"Kind of feels like we're going backwards, doesn't it?" I said. "Moving back home."

"It's only for a bit," Sarah said, holding her hand above her eyes like a visor, blocking them from the last of the evening's sun. "For me and Rob, at least. If they make me permanent at the charity, then I can afford to move out."

"When I'm with my parents it's like I walk through the front door and I'm twelve again," Rob said.

"Your voice cracks?" I said.

"Do your pubes drop off, Rob?" Sarah said.

"Yeah, fuck, basically. Pubeless and squeaky." Rob laughed. "But it's the other stuff, isn't it? Sharing space with my brothers. All the stupid fights you have with siblings, right? You know everyone's pressure points."

"What are yours?" Sarah asked.

Rob folded his arms.

"When they make fun of my accent," he said. "They say it's gone posh."

"You still sound Northern to me, Rob," she said.

"That's the problem, isn't it? Caught in between."

"There's a spoken-word poem in there," she said.

We laughed, then sighed into a collective lull. I knew that the coming change would be different for others than it was for me, how each step backward or forward could be longer or steeper or harder. Going to university had felt like one thing falling into another, the next domino in a row.

Sarah leaned forward and brought her shoulder blades together. They cracked, and she exhaled as she relaxed back into her chair.

"I regress into this really cunty teenager when I'm with my parents," she said. "There's just so much yelling."

"I can't really remember the last time me and my parents raised our voices at one another," I said.

"Of course you don't, Tom."

I shrugged my shoulders. Sarah tucked her knees towards her on the chair and tilted her glass to her mouth. She often compared our families, rolling her eyes at the simplicity of a white, middle-class home. Does your mum call you fat and say your ass is flat like a pancake in the same breath, Tom? Did your mum pretend to faint when you told her you were gay? Did she open her eyes to tell you to call an ambulance before pretending to faint again? I couldn't always separate her judgment from humor.

"I still don't want to move back," I said.

"Ming's moving in," she offered, voice light but mocking. "That'll be different."

I shifted my bum in the seat. The curves of the hard iron pressed into my back.

"It's not forever, obviously. It just makes sense for now. To not stress about too much at once, I guess. Until after he and Lisa submit the play to festivals in London."

"Lisa said it could take a while."

I hummed. I didn't want a while. I didn't want it at all. I wanted our own place. A reset to normal. But a suggestion by my parents had become something much more, and while Ming was tentative, he was also enthusiastic, and so I'd relented.

"To be honest," Rob said, "I'm finding the idea of moving to London more stressful than moving home."

"It's not like London's the only place to live, Rob," Sarah said.

"Yeah, yeah, I'm aware of that." There was a rare flicker of irritation in Rob's voice. "But nobody wants to be left behind, right? So I have to move, and I wouldn't be able to do it without the sign-on bonus from my job. It's different for you guys because you grew up in London."

"St Albans isn't quite London." Sarah's voice was sharp. "And it's not like I'm getting a sign-on bonus, Rob."

"You know what I mean, though," he said. "Not all of us can do three-month internships at LGBT charities while we figure things out."

She knew what he meant. We all did. There were times I tried to talk about it, how the difference might feel frustrating, but he always brushed it off with a laugh. I shifted in my seat a bit more. Sarah's posture softened.

"Do you really feel like you'll be left behind, Rob?" Sarah asked.

"A bit, yeah," he said. "You have Lisa and Tom has Ming, most of you grew up in similar places. And I'm fine and everything, but all of it just makes me worry a bit."

Sarah stood up, walked behind Rob and hugged him. I reached out and squeezed his arm.

"You don't have to worry," she said.

We relaxed back into our chairs and stared out from the patio as if we'd planted something to be proud of, even though the grass was long and uneven and flowerless. I looked at the wooden shed at the end of the garden. We hadn't dared open it in case anything inside became our responsibility. Rob took off his sunglasses and turned to me. He pursed his lips, then fixed his gaze on the stem of his glass.

"Ming spoke to me about Cass last night," Rob said. "When we were on the bed. He said it'd mean a lot to her if I apologized for everything. I hadn't even thought about apologizing, to be honest."

"Are you glad you did it?" I asked.

"I am, actually," he said with a lift of his shoulders. "Like a weight off that I didn't realize was there. It's funny, isn't it?" He paused, drawing a finger to his bottom lip, mouth open. "When I stopped sleeping with her last year, I kind of just thought that was it. And when we hooked up again a few months ago, and the other times, I didn't really think anything of it. But people can think of you and you not think of them, right? It's not like

I forgot about her, but I also kind of did. I don't know. I feel bad, but I'm glad I said sorry. I didn't want to fuck her around. Maybe I was naive. I probably knew how she felt, didn't I?"

"Did you?" Sarah asked.

"I don't know," he said. "I mean, did you guys know?"

Sarah looked at me, but I avoided her gaze. I knew that Cass loved Rob, or thought she loved Rob, because Ming had told me. He didn't need to. It was obvious to any onlooker. I could've told Rob not to sleep with her again. Ming wanted me to. I told him they were adults, that it wasn't our place. Maybe all I was doing was protecting Rob, stopping him from feeling bad about himself.

"I thought we all did," I said. "But that it was sort of unspoken."

Rob hummed.

"Yeah, maybe," he said. "Is Ming doing any better?"

My heart sank a little. I took a deep breath. He was, I supposed, but saying so felt conjectural.

"Yeah. Better, I think. For now. He said the OCD's gone away."

Sarah let out the beginning of a word, but then leaned back into her seat. I wondered what she was thinking. Probably that I couldn't be sure. Of anything. Of whether citalopram was a long-term measure, of whether the OCD could really just go away, of whether he'd stick with the CBT he said he'd do anyway, of whether I was actually helping him. How can you be sure, Tom?

I thought about what I'd seen at the dinner table the night before, and how Ming had denied anything was going on. I knew his habits; I knew his faces. It was a lie. But what does a person do in front of a lie? It was never as simple as saying something. I had questions. What did him not telling the truth mean for us? Why didn't he want to tell me? But to put these questions to him seemed selfish and unreasonable, and so I'd let the lie slide. I wanted to direct the conversation elsewhere.

"Lisa's moving in a couple of weeks, isn't she?" I asked Sarah.

"Yeah," she said. "To her mum's flat. She'll have it all to herself."

Rob let out a short, sharp, closed-mouthed laugh. Sarah ignored it.

"How's she feeling?" I asked.

"I think London will ground her," she said. "She's lacking in confidence a bit. Like, even in how we interact with each other. We don't always have to do what I say. She just goes with what I want. I know I can be domineering—"

"No!" Rob gasped.

We laughed, then fell into silence again. Bubbles leaped off the sides of the wide glasses, rising to their deaths where the champagne met the air. Sarah topped me up, then Rob, then tended to her own depleted glass.

I got up from my chair and walked onto the grass. I stared back at the house. You could see clearly through the windows. The staircase leading up to my attic, and Sarah's room. I wondered if people across the way watched us moving around like small figurines in a doll's house, and whether they would notice we were gone. It was dwarfing that a place could feel so littered with my memories of it and yet have no visible trace of me. Flakes of skin, hair, fabric would all have fallen into the cracks of the wood and deep within the carpet, down into places where the sweeping bristles of a broom or the wheezing mouth of a vacuum cleaner couldn't reach. But even then, when the time came, that dark-green carpet would be ripped out and the floors replaced, and eventually our hair and skin would decompose, replaced by the hair and skin of whoever came after us.

8
Home

The job was as bad as everyone said it would be. Late nights. And taxis home. And a manager called Judith who controlled my life and who, in Ming's words, looked like a sexy Miss Trunchbull.

I got on the Northern line. It was seven a.m., still not early enough to get a seat. I stood sandwiched between clammy commuter bodies, lobotomized from a night of spreadsheets and another chicken–Caesar–and–bacon sandwich from Pret. The monotony was excruciating. I could hear Ming laugh at the melodrama. But it was. A constant shuttle between home and office. One was the place where Ming and my parents cooked and laughed without me, the other was the place where angry people threw holepunches at entry-level analysts. I pushed out of the train and the turnstiles and marched to the gym.

People, although particularly my parents, had strong opinions about the job. Why did you even apply? Rob helped me with the applications, and then it sort of made sense. Is Rob making decisions for you now? No, Dad. The hours will be very long, Tom, and I've never really thought of you as a banker, and didn't you once say that banks were evil? They are, but I need a job, Mum, and it's a really good one. The thing about money is that it often dooms the havers to misery. And you and Dad have just the right amount of it, I guess?

Jason stood outside the gym, his girthy hand holding his leather duffel. He wore a gray wool coat that went down to his shins. He always waited for me, even as threads of winter had begun to ice the November air. He looked up from his phone, smiled, and reached to open the doors.

"Good morning," he said.

He let me walk in first, and as I did he put his hand on the small of my back in greeting. Mornings with Jason had become something to look forward to. We walked up to the brightly lit changing rooms and stripped off next to one another. As we changed, we swapped stories of the weekend. I caught glimpses of Jason's body while he spoke. His back bulged with muscle. I noticed again how hairy his legs were, swarms of hair that appeared again on his chest, a thick line moving up from the bottom of his abdomen, erupting at his pecs like a volcanic plume. I both wanted and didn't want a body like his; I wondered how it'd feel to inhabit the kind of power and size that Jason did.

We moved into the dark room filled with stationary bikes. The spin class was divided into three sections by fluorescent lines along the floor. Jason and I climbed onto adjacent stations.

Our instructor patrolled the front of the class as if we were flight risks.

"Are you ready to give it a hundred and ten per cent? Are you going to give it a hundred and sixty per cent?" She jumped onto her bike in a clean swoop and cycled fast. "Listen to me, guys. It's Tuesday morning, but you're here. You're ready to do this. Half the journey is sitting on the bike. From now, it's just us and the road. Let's go!" She lifted her butt off the bike seat;

we all followed suit. "It takes courage to add resistance. But you know what? You know what? You lot are my Tuesday-morning heroes. The bravest people I know. Now, turn up that fucking resistance."

I pushed my feet against the pedals and felt my hamstrings scrunch. The sweat on my forehead rained onto the control panel and magnified the numbers. Towards the end of the hour, the instructor led us through a cooldown. We cycled slowly. We stretched our legs using the bike pedals.

After the class, Jason and I stripped off in the changing rooms and went into different shower cubicles. I finished before him. When he walked out of the shower, he tied the towel low. Two ridges curved downward from his hip bones to the top of his pubes. We changed side by side by the lockers, and my eyes drifted towards the fat veins that his muscles pushed to the surface of his skin. I put my underwear on without taking my towel off my hips, burying the beginnings of an erection beneath two layers of cotton.

The first time I'd told Ming about Jason, he'd asked a lot of questions. Is he hot? Yes, but in a stereotypical kind of way. He doesn't really sound like your type, though? I think he's everyone's type. I didn't think that was yours!

I'd stopped mentioning Jason after that, because I knew Ming wore a new prickliness over his appearance, which he'd strongarmed into a kind of anti-pubescence. Are you sure you're fine with me not having facial hair? Yes. Are you fine with me shaving my legs? Sure. Are you fine with the longer hair? Of course. It was always are you fine with, and not do you prefer, and I was grateful because it meant that I didn't have to lie. Small preferences didn't matter. Attraction ebbed and flowed. Preferences adjusted. Why would we be having as much sex in my parents' house, anyway?

Jason waited at the edge of the lockers for me. We left the gym and headed towards the office in pleasant silence. Chilly wisps settled in my wet hair. I caught a glimpse of myself in the tinted glass of an office building, my navy cigarette legs bending at the knee. Ming made fun of the suit. It's the contrast! It's just so different, you know. I laughed along, but the weak chuckles betrayed my resignation. He hadn't made fun of the first suit, which I'd found secondhand. The jacket hung loose on my shoulders and the trousers were slack on my legs, but a week into the job I saw that others looked vacuum-packed into theirs and I looked shrunken in mine, like a teenager borrowing his dad's suit for prom. And so the second suit conformed, and the next time I got a haircut I asked for something neater and slicker, still spilling out of the center parting but shorter and pushed further back. These things were supposed to be superficial, but the change felt greater than the sum of its parts. How flimsy is the self if cut away by steel scissors? It concerned me that I might've always been closer to the boys at university who wanted to become bankers and consultants, who wore Patagonia gilets and salmon shorts and had PR girlfriends in floral dresses called Emily or Sophie. Am I just another posh cunt?

All of this seemed easier for Jason. He was one of those gay men intent on queering corporate London, which made as much sense to me as queering drone warfare. He was already organizing events for Prism, the LGBT committee at work. Nobody seemed to clock how close it sounded to prison. Jason was unmoved when I suggested that capitalism and the liberation of queer people were incompatible. Yeah, Tom, I'm sure Prism would love to hear that.

Jason and I turned onto the street with our office building. I looked up at its windows, which punctured the sand-colored lattice like holes in a grater.

"I booked my flights to Mykonos," Jason said.

"Didn't you just go?"

"Never too much Mykonos for a Clapham gay," he said. "Gotta spend it somehow."

I wouldn't have been friends with Jason but for sexuality and circumstance. His online presence informed me that he was the only gay friend of many straight blondes from the Home Counties. Jason represented the kind of gayness I'd always felt alienated from, one that felt distinctly uncool.

I didn't think Jason understood this. If anything, he thought the same of me. This provoked an existential anguish in me, one that I knew was completely ridiculous, yet I could ignore it all at work and at the gym. And I worked in finance, too, and so any leg I'd once had to stand on had been ripped from its socket. Maybe it was better to pin rainbows to the walls if you planned to submit to the man regardless.

We stepped through the automatic doors of the staff entrance and swiped our access passes against the sensor, which opened smaller gates into the eight-story atrium. It was lined with columns of glass, elevators and offices that looked inward, down on us and onto each other. A capitalist panopticon. We veered right into the staff canteen and got breakfast from the self-service counter.

Jason and I sat down across from one another. There was a pile of scrambled eggs on his plate and a couple of chicken sausages. He stabbed the head of one of his sausages with his fork. His knife sliced through it in one pull. The oil from the meat made the steel glisten.

"How's Judy?" he asked.

"She's Judy."

The points of Jason's fork pierced the taut skin of another sausage. He lifted it to his mouth. My hands moved to imitate him, but combining some beans with a bit of soaked hash brown instead.

"I hate blindly following orders," I said. "It's the deadlines she sets. They're all arbitrary. I sent in that presentation because she told me it was due. I don't think she touched it for three days."

"I swear she's always in the office. Does she have anyone?"

"She's married, so I guess," I said. "But they're fighting a lot."

Jason laughed. His teeth were too white. I wondered how much they'd set him back.

"How do you know that?" he asked.

"She told me. She started telling me things after I told her that I'm gay. Do you know she's only a few years older than us?"

"Seriously? Christ, what's wrong with the air in this place?" Jason took his phone out of his pocket. "Do you like this photo?"

It was a topless picture of himself, standing over a pool, his chest wet from the water, holding a cocktail. I wondered what I'd have to be threatened with in order for me to post a photo like that. A Prince Albert piercing. Lactose intolerance. My eyes drifted to his abs.

"You look hot," I said.

His thumb hovered over and tapped the button to post. We finished our food and put our trays in the collection area, then rode the elevators to our different floors. I set up at the desk by the same window I tried to sit at each morning. It looked over the street with the gym, now littered with people, ants scuttling to their offices. I felt Judith's eyes on me from across the room. I looked up as she walked towards me in her fitted teal dress, one from her lean wardrobe that I'd learned started at dark blue and ended at green. She talked at me in bursts for most of the morning. Can you take notes for this meeting? Can you send me some slides? Have you even finished the slides? Look at Fatima. Be sure you make time to date, Tom, or you'll end up like her. She's not even that good at her job. And she's single. Don't end up like her. Judith was afflicted with the kind of self-loathing that made her shit on everyone else as much as possible.

I moved between slides and spreadsheets and emails. At lunch I ate a boxed tuna Nicoise salad and some bread at my desk. Each bite rolled in my mouth and down my throat like tumbleweed. I copied graphs from spreadsheets into slides and proofread them.

All afternoon I tapped away at my screen, and without notic-

ing the falling sun transform the gray sky black. The blue light
from my computer needled further into my eyes. I finished at
eight, an early night, and went back home.

I could hear my parents' and Ming's voices from the front
door. They shouted my name from the table. I put my satchel
down by the stairs and walked over to the dining room. Ming
had worked that day. He'd texted to let me know he'd cooked
a green curry. There were slices of cake in a box on the kitchen
counter, something Ming would bring home from the bakery
down the road when he'd had a good day of selling flower subscriptions. Middle-class families across London were showing
renewed interest in farm-to-vase subscriptions sold by charming young people, and Ming was riding the wave. We all said
hello. I kissed Ming on the head. I sat down at the place laid for
me. All their plates were empty. The bottle of wine was near
empty. Mum was chewing her last bite and moaned in a way
that made my skin crawl. Absolutely gorgeous. Truly stunning.
The flavors! She always did this with Asian food. I knew Ming
had just used up the store-bought paste in the fridge.

"You got out early today," Dad said.

"Not early enough," I said.

"How was work?" Ming asked, reaching over and massaging my shoulder.

"It was good."

I spooned out some curry from the blue pot at the center of
the table. Chunks of chicken, peas, carrots and baby corn swam
in the ladle of bright-green sauce. I served myself from the large
bowl of white rice.

"I was just about to give your parents the flower pitch,"
Ming said.

"Go on, then," I said.

I took a bite as Ming cleared his throat. The warmth left

on the forkful was teasing, and vanished soon after hitting my tongue. Ming rolled back his shoulders and sat up.

"Hi! How are you?" Ming said, his voice effusive. I almost mouthed the words along as he said them. I'd helped him rehearse it. "My friend Bella—"

"Have you ever met Bella?" Dad asked.

"Never—my friend Bella has started a new business called Bella's Bunches." Dad couldn't contain his laughter. "We deliver flowers to houses in your area every week, although it doesn't have to be that often, as our flowers last a lot longer. Twice as long as the ones you'd get in the supermarket. You can cancel the subscription at any time. We have one at home and we love it, to be honest!"

"That's clever," Mum said.

"You know, there's absolutely no pressure to sign up, but if you do want to sign up now, I've actually got a discount code on me that gives you the first bouquet for free."

My parents guffawed.

"Hook, line and sinker," Dad said.

"Absolutely terrifying," Mum said.

I laughed through my nose with my mouth shut. Mum's glance passed over me for a moment. The three of them talked about going on a day trip to Margate the following weekend to visit the Turner Contemporary, something I couldn't commit to outright in case I had to work. Dad explained to Ming the narrow windows in which various berries were actually in season. My jaw slowly volleyed bits of chicken between the sides of my mouth. As they spoke about nothing and everything, I began to feel left out.

My shoulders hunched over my plate. This wasn't an annoyance I could bring up, because if I did, then it would come back to the job. They said the same things over and over. If you're unhappy, then you could find a job that lets you off a bit earlier. I've been there four months, Dad. People have many other jobs, and your first career often isn't the one that you end up with, and so all that I'm saying, Tom, is that you may find a period of exploration will be enormously helpful. I don't want to quit, Mum. Ming did the same, too, but within the confines of our bedroom. Maybe they have a point? I always kept quiet, even if it enraged me. What job would cover most of the rent if we move in together? What job makes sense if he wants to write plays? And I knew thinking like this was silly. I knew what he'd say. What the fuck, Tom, why are you thinking so far ahead? We're literally in our early twenties?

I took the last bit of chicken and lapped up the thin layer of sauce that clung to the bottom of my plate. I placed my fork and spoon touching and parallel, and this drew their chatter to a close.

"That was really nice, thank you," I said.

We collected our plates together and I brought them to the kitchen sink. Ming followed me with the pots. We washed and dried the dishes side by side. Some of the vegetables had caramelized and stuck to the base of the pot. I scrubbed it with a brush until I could see the enamel underneath.

"Lisa and I submitted to that festival today," he said. "Vault. The one in Waterloo."

I waited for a fraction of a moment with an imperceptible raise of an eyebrow, expecting something to follow. An offer to look for somewhere else to live, or an admission that he'd already been looking and that he had a flat to show me. Look at this one! It's next to that Thai place in Peckham that Asian people never go into. Ming sealed the gap between his lips and no words followed.

"That's amazing," I said, handing him the pot. He set it on the stove while he dried it with a tea towel, then opened the cabinet below the counter to put it away.

"I'm a bit nervous," he said, drying handfuls of cutlery at

once. I noticed some water at the end of a knife as he put it in the drawer. "That nowhere's going to accept it, I mean."

"They will." I turned the tap off and leaned back on the kitchen counter. "And you'll get a whole load of reviews just as good as the ones before."

"A hilarious and hopeful meditation on loss and queerness?"

"Exactly."

Ming stopped drying for a moment and tapped his finger on the edge of the counter, his eyes on the kitchen tiles. I'd noticed him doing this again for months, ever since our graduation dinner with our parents. Eyes vacant as they stared into the dark garden over dinner, frequent toilet breaks with his phone in his hand. There were lies deflected by a calm smile and a nothing. I'd broached it all with him before. What are you looking up? Nothing. What are you thinking about? Nothing. Is everything okay? It's nothing. Is it the play? No. Well, if it is something, you know you can tell me, right? I know.

We finished washing up and went upstairs. On the journey between ground and first floor, and in the change from work clothes to a hoodie and gym shorts, those things Ming didn't say rattled me. Submitting the play was supposed to be a milestone beyond the submission, one unspoken but shared. One I'd waited for. And then there were the secrets. I lay on my bed and took deep breaths. Six seconds in, six seconds out, like my mum always said to do. It was worse than his worries about his heart and ALS. Those things had form, a name. This was an unidentified body in the room. One I tiptoed around.

Six in, six out, until I felt calm.

"Everything okay?" Ming asked.

I opened my eyes and saw him standing by the door.

"Yeah."

He changed into his bathrobe and left the room. I could hear the running taps. When the splashing stopped, I knocked on the door, announced myself and walked in. Ming sat on the edge of the bath, applying piles of shaving cream to his leg. The other foot was planted in the clear bathwater. His legs were stubbly and patchy from the last time he'd shaved.

"Can I watch?" I asked.

He nodded. I pulled the toilet seat down and sat fully clothed with my legs wide, watching him spread the foam over his calves. He'd got into the habit of shaving over the summer. A full month of it, doing it once every couple of days. Now he did it less frequently, but he said he preferred the feel of a clean leg, of bare skin against the bedsheet.

He rounded his spine and tucked his leg towards him. He drew the razor up his leg, over the shaving cream, clearing it to reveal clean patches of tanned skin. Every couple of lines he would shake the razor in the water, expelling the foam from the blade. Small black leg hairs floated in the cloudy bathwater, like bodies after a shipwreck, or strings of untethered dead cells.

"Do you think we should find somewhere else to live now that you've sent the play off?"

Ming looked up at me. The razor halted. A drop of water glided from the edge of the blade down his leg, cutting a path through the white foam. The sight of it annoyed me. Ming did whatever he wanted. The irritation I thought I'd muffled inside began to boil. I was ready to defend my right to leave.

"Okay," Ming said. "Let's move out."

He guided the razor back up his leg and reset it at the adjacent column of shaving foam next to his ankle, face still.

"What's wrong?" I asked. "Aren't you excited?"

"Nothing's wrong." He didn't stop the razor this time. "Should something be wrong?"

"I just thought you might be a bit more enthusiastic, like I wasn't asking a favor and you were capitulating."

"I don't really know how you want me to react."

"With enthusiasm," I repeated. "I thought you'd be excited to move out, to not squat in my parents' house."

I winced inside at my choice of words, although my face remained impassive. The razor stopped again and he looked at me. His expression was one of deep hurt, of betrayal. He put the razor down on the side of the tub and set his leg into the contaminated bathwater. He straightened his knees and allowed himself to slide under the waterline, until all but his head was submerged. He'd pushed his hair back with a headband. The ends dipped into the water.

"Do you think I'm squatting?" Ming asked, his voice calm. He pulled the bath plug chain with his toes.

"I just really want to not live in my parents' house with my boyfriend, Ming."

"You're not exactly making me want to move out with you."

"What does that mean?"

"You're being a dick."

"How?" I grew defiant, even though I knew exactly what he meant; my voice was aggressive, I'd interrupted a peaceful bath. He didn't respond. He didn't move. The water level climbed down his body, debris of hair and foam collecting along his chest. "Everyone thinks it's weird."

"I don't think Sarah counts as everyone, Tom." His voice thickened, becoming caustic. "If you want to move out, that's fine. I said it's okay. I do not know—and I mean this—what in the fuck you want from me." He flicked his arms up; droplets hit my face. "I said okay, but you're being really crazy. Like, I don't get why we have to have this conversation right now?"

His palms returned to the sides of the bath. There were things I wanted to say but couldn't. I'm nervous and angry because something's off. We're barely fucking, and it's not just because I come home late. You're hiding something, Ming. You're the nervous one. It's been like this for months. Is this really fine for you? What's going on in your head?

But how could I demand entry? He was going to therapy again. He was sorting it out. And maybe it was a good thing that he didn't feel he needed me in that way. I knew about his heart and the ALS stuff, but not whatever this was. I knew the house was making it worse, and if we just lived in our own place it would get better. But I didn't know how to intimate this to him, because as I tried to sew together the scraps of thought into words, they felt pallid and ridiculous. Maybe I'm just paranoid. Maybe I'm not trusting him. Surely that's my hurdle to clear.

All the bathwater had swirled down into the pipes, and a snail trail of small hairs lined up in the center of the bath, leading into the drain.

"Look, I'm sorry. We can obviously wait a bit," I said. "I just wanted to float the idea again."

"No floating required," Ming said. "We're on the same page. I'm going to rinse off."

I didn't move as he pulled the shower curtain and turned the water on. The steam danced around and settled on my legs. Regret rushed through me. When Ming turned the shower off and opened the curtain, he looked surprised and irritated to see me there. It was rehearsed. He knew I hadn't left. I got him a towel and wrapped him in it. His face softened.

"I'm sorry," I said again. "You're not squatting. I think I'm just getting cabin fever. I was being unreasonable."

"Whatever," Ming said. "Let's just start looking."

I cuddled him through the towel. He walked out of the bathroom and across the landing into my room. I followed him and shut the door behind me. When Ming had moved in, Mum had made sure I left enough space for his clothes, and made me change things in my room to make it look less like a teenager's. We cleared out textbooks, old notes from school, so that Ming would have somewhere to leave his stuff. She made me paint over scuff marks and scratches from mounting putty that had hardened over the paint.

He dropped his towel as I sat down on the bed, then opened a drawer and pulled out a T-shirt and underwear. I looked at his feet. I'd always liked his ankles, defined more by negative space than skin and tendon, the curves on either side of his Achilles tendon like empty eye sockets. Ming put the clothes on the bed and picked the towel up from the floor. He scrubbed it over his head with vigor, then dropped it to the floor again.

"I've actually looked at a few places," I said. "Not gone to them, just on apps, I mean."

"What are they like?" he asked as he pulled the T-shirt on.

"They're nice. One-beds. Still in South, not too far from where Rob lives."

"Are we sure we want a one-bed?"

"Where else would we live?"

"I don't know. I thought we would get a room in a house. But a one-bed sounds nice."

Ming put his underwear on. He picked the towel off the floor and patted it over his head again before hanging it up behind the door.

"I could pay for most of it," I said.

Ming turned around, looking confused.

"Why on earth would you do that?"

"Because you earn no money."

Ming's jaw slackened. He narrowed his eyes.

"Is it going to become, like, a thing where you get dicked on at work and then swing your dick around at home?"

"Oh, come on, Ming."

I wanted to smack my palms against my forehead. It was coming across all wrong. I got up from the bed and walked to the window. Maybe Ming's right. Maybe I'm just trying to strengthen my hold. He doesn't need this. A deep breath. Six in. Six out.

"Sorry," I said.

He was silent. I stared out into the dark. I'd always liked that I could see the backs and gardens of the other terraced houses, borders set up in the form of thin wooden panels. The houses in the square looked contained in their own world. I couldn't see anything else. I didn't know lots of my neighbors, and yet our houses shared brick; there were probably roots that went from our garden into theirs.

The bed squeaked as Ming tucked his legs under the covers. I leaned against the windowsill.

"I have my last CBT session next week," he said, his tone matter-of-fact.

"I know. How does it feel?"

"Good. But I haven't really needed it recently. I feel good."

The things I'd seen said otherwise, and maybe he knew that I knew it. We stared at each other for a moment too long. I met his tentative smile with my own, and within each smile was a lie. His, but also mine, the one that said I believed him.

I pushed off from the white wood. I took off my clothes and hung them behind the door, then turned off the main light and slipped under the covers. Ming sat up against the headboard with the book from his bedside table, reading beneath the light of the yellow lamp.

I curled up away from him, still in the shadow of his body.

"I can stop reading," he said. "If you'd like the light off."

"No," I said. "I don't mind."

I turned back around, resting my arm across his body. He smiled gently. I nestled into his side and listened to the rustle of turning pages.

9
Ash

Ming wanted to go to the party, but junior analysts didn't get plus-ones. I stood in front of my bedroom mirror, weaving the tie around my neck. The noose was taut, each end of it folding in half at the tight knot. The body of the tie was off-center, and I knew that at some point it would flip to show the stitching and label.

I'd come home early to get changed, even though the dress code wasn't far from what we already wore to the office. Judith said everyone did it for this one day every year. Ming and I were home alone. My parents were away for the week.

Ming lay on the bed with his laptop on his chest.

"You look nice," he said. "Can you take me next year?"

"Of course," I said, bending down to relace my shoe. "Did you sign the lease?"

"I did."

Two weeks until we'd move. We'd waited another month to start viewing flats, right after the festival accepted *Death's a*

Drag. And then Ming was fussy. Is there enough light? Imagine how hot it'll get during summer. It's a bit cramped in here, you know. This is, like, really expensive. After some push-and-pull, Ming had agreed to put in the offer on a basement flat with a small garden in Peckham.

I put the things I needed into my pockets. Phone, cards, keys. I turned towards the bed. Ming straightened his legs against the duvet, fanning them in and out, as if he was making the lower half of a snow angel. My heart jumped when I looked at them. They were inflamed, covered in uniform pox across their length.

"Ming. What's wrong with your legs?"

He shut his laptop and sat up.

"I got them lasered a few hours ago," he said.

"Is that something you're doing?"

"Yeah."

"Is it expensive?" I asked.

"Yes."

"Is your dad paying for it?"

"No," he said. "My mother is. That money she left me when she died."

I puffed air out of my mouth. I knew what that money meant to him, how guilty he'd felt when he used it to blast the hair off his face. Ming wasn't quick to forget his mistakes, which meant that this mattered to him. It mattered a lot. I rested my forearms on the black iron at the foot of the bed.

"Why wouldn't you tell me?"

"It's my body, Tom," Ming said. His legs stiffened. He took the flat computer off his lap. "I don't have to tell you anything."

My lips wobbled in dismay, and my stomach folded. He didn't have to tell me anything, but people didn't have to tell anyone anything, and this was important. I brought my shoulders over my forearms. Deep breath. Six in. Six out.

"I get that," I said, turning my head back up to him. "But it seems like something you'd share."

"It's just laser, Tom." He leaned forward, but his voice was passionless. "If you don't like it, then I don't have to do any more sessions. This one will hardly make a dent, okay? I already shave my legs, you know."

I stood back up with my hands on my hips.

"It's not about that, Ming."

He sighed, massaging his forehead with his thumb and index finger.

"What is it about, then?"

"If I spent hundreds of pounds on a tattoo sleeve, I'd probably discuss it with you first."

"You shouldn't have to."

Nobody should have to. But they do. I lifted my arms from my sides and brought them above my head. Deep breaths. Six in. Six out. I shut my eyes and paced in circles.

"Don't you think this is, like, a bit of an overreaction?"

Maybe it was, but this felt bigger than legs, and I couldn't say why because I knew he wouldn't give. Nothing. It's Nothing. It's Nothing, Tom. I stood in front of him again, my arms and spine slack, my palms towards him. His posture was unforgiving.

"I want a boyfriend," I said, unable to peel myself away from the cruelty. "Not a naked mole rat."

"Oh, fuck you, Tom." He looked as angry as he did wounded.

"Why are you pretending this isn't weird?"

"What's the analogy? Getting a fucking eighth of a tattoo?" he snarled. "It'll all grow back if you hate it. It's my body. Do I have to ask your permission every time I take a shit?"

I looked away from him. This was childish, the going to lengths to sound like an adult, and I knew that he knew it because of the sardonic lift to his voice. I checked the time. I took my thick coat from the wardrobe and punched each suited fist through the sleeves. I rummaged through my pockets again. Phone. Wallet. Keys.

"I'm going to be late," I said.

He got up from the bed as I walked out of my room. I sensed his body at the top of the stairs as I ran down them and out of the house. I stood at the bus stop and wrote a text to Ming.

We're moving in together. Keeping secrets like this doesn't feel like a good place to start.

He responded right away.

We already live together. We're not going to see eye to eye on this. Just drop it.

I got onto the number 12 bus and sat on the top deck.

You're a dick, I wrote.

Yeah and you're a real fucking gentleman.

I put my phone on airplane mode. Fucking Ming. The rest of the bus journey was long. There was traffic. Why the fuck did I take the bus? I checked my watch. If the traffic didn't clear, then I would be late. Agitation thrummed. The sway of the bus made a nauseous lump press onto my throat. I shut my eyes and put my head against the window until I heard the bus stop for Oxford Circus. I took my phone off airplane. He hadn't messaged. Fucking Ming. I texted Jason to let him know I'd be a few more minutes.

As I got off the bus, the queasiness clung to my neck and began to expand into my head. I took a deep breath of cool air, which did little to temper the heat in my cheeks. I marched in the direction of the hotel.

I knew I needed to calm down, so I lit a cigarette outside the entrance, putting it out after a couple of drags. I walked through the lobby and into the top level of the ballroom, where I handed in my coat. There was a mezzanine that wrapped around a pit filled with round tables. The women wore long, flowing dresses and intricate updos, towering over portly men who looked just like they did at work. Jason said he was at the bar, which was at the far end of the balcony. I found him waiting in the corner.

His suit creased from the bulge of his body. He wasn't wearing his glasses.

"Are you okay? You look stressed," he said, hand firm on my shoulder. His thumb massaged the base of my neck. "You're tense."

I wiped the sweat from my forehead and tousled my hair. Deep breath.

"I was worried I'd be late. I've just had a tough day," I said, taking another breath. "I didn't expect it to be so nice."

Jason took two glasses of champagne from a waiter and gave one to me.

"Here," he said. "Relax. We're in for a good night. I'll make sure of it."

We clinked the glasses against one another.

A bell rang to invite us to the tables down below. Hunger banged against the walls of my stomach. We walked towards the sound, over the art deco carpet that swallowed the room. Jason put his arm on my shoulder again as we approached the curved staircase. It slid down to my waist, along the back of my ribs, before falling off. The static of his touch set my nerves ablaze. My groin pulsed. Fuck. As we glided to our table, he gossiped about the other analysts in our intake. Poppy and Rupert were fucking. Felix had thrown up at a BAME networking event. He cupped the side of my hip for a moment to guide me towards our seats. My spine straightened. I tipped my drink down my throat and took another from a woman holding a tray.

The starter arrived during the first speech of the night. It was bland soup. A senior partner anesthetized the crowd with anecdotes from his forty-year career. We've come a long way. We're proud to be here today. A tall, thin woman was next to me, the wife of a partner, looked like Olive Oyl. Her husband's face melted into a wide double chin, unable to resist the aging force of the hours he worked. He'd once told me it was a scary time to be a straight white man in the workplace. She laughed at every weak punch line, smiling at her husband, who didn't speak to her, and then at me and Jason.

"That was lovely," she said. "Such a funny man."

Jason and I nodded.

"We've known him for years," she said. "I actually used to work at the firm. I don't anymore, but I'm sure you know my husband."

We nodded again. He didn't turn to look at us, his attention redirected to the other partner seated next to him.

"Which one of you works at the firm?" she asked.

"We both do," I said.

"Oh, I assumed you were together. Pardon me."

"You wouldn't be wrong," Jason said, leaning forward in his chair. My face swung towards his. He put his left hand on my knee and winked at me, resting some of his weight onto it. I felt my cheeks blush, and beneath it a whisper of guilt.

"Oh. Wonderful! Everything's come a long way, hasn't it."

Jason and I laughed in agreement, but then his hand lingered. He didn't remove it until the waiters served us our mains. I made polite conversation with Olive Oyl over bleeding beef tenderloin and limp roast vegetables. She had two daughters. They're eleven, so very busy. You know how it is! She told me how it wasn't really a done thing in the past for women to wear trousers, like it is now. She filled me in on her reformer Pilates regimen. She'd rather be waterboarded than slip out of ketosis, sliding the silky oblong of mashed potato to the edge of her plate. Jason was busy charming the couple next to him.

I could hear them laughing over Olive Oyl's babble. Maybe if she'd thought I was straight, then she would've spared me all this. If Gwyneth Paltrow told her to lick the bottom of a dirty flip-flop, she'd lick the bottom of ten. Olive Oyl carried on. What school did you go to? Oh, I don't know that one. And university? Oh, very good.

After they took our mains away, Jason's hand returned to my knee, and he kept it there over dessert. He ate the chocolate torte with one hand. Every so often he'd look at me and smile, eye contact that felt assuring, but which also lasted a moment too long. I drank the wine on the table.

As they took our plates, I turned to Jason. My fingers touched his thigh, and I felt the power of his hard leg. What does cool get anyone, anyway? What does cool even mean? I thought again about what he looked like with his trousers off, the curve of his thigh when he faced the locker and took the towel off his waist at the gym. I thought of the wild hair beneath them. Thick hairs bursting from strong follicles, evading the lasers and blades that had obliterated Ming's. I let my hand rest on them.

After dinner, most of the senior staff vacated the tables and ascended to the mezzanine. A band started playing on the stage, and the rest of the guests migrated to the dance floor at the center of the basin.

"Come with me," Jason said.

He led me to one of the tables at the back, making a bee-line for a bottle of white poking out from a wine cooler. He held it up.

"Ta-da!"

We sat at the back, laughing at some of the partners who'd stayed downstairs to dance clumsily with their spouses. Jason imitated their gawky arms as we drank the rest of the bottle. He leaned in a bit closer to me, his voice a smooth whisper, even though nobody was around us.

"I brought a bag," he said. "If you want some."

"Is that the vibe?" I asked.

"It could be."

Maybe so. Maybe it'd be fun. I followed him up the stairs towards an accessible toilet at the end of a quiet corridor off the hotel lobby. We went in together. I sat on the ledge beneath the mirror that joined the sink to the toilet.

"Feeling better?" he asked, taking some keys from his pocket.

"What?"

"You weren't yourself earlier," he said. "When you arrived."

"Yeah," I said. "I feel better. Thanks."

"Good."

He keyed some coke onto the back of his hand and snorted it in one. He gave me the baggie. I snorted a bump from my house keys. When I looked up to give the coke back to him, he started laughing.

"What is it?" I said.

"You've still got some on your nose."

"Fuck," I said. "Jason."

I spun around to check my nostril in the mirror. My heart started to beat faster, a rush in my chest and shoulders.

"Hold on," he said. "Relax. Sit back down."

I turned and sat back down on the ledge. Jason approached me. He stood with his large thigh between my knees and his body inches away. He reached for the tap and wet his finger, using it to clean my nostril. I looked towards the ceiling. There was a tenting pressure against my suit trousers. I prayed that Jason wouldn't look down. When he was done, his eyes met mine.

"Perfect," he said. "How am I?"

A couple of nose hairs dipped below the line of his nostril, but there was no trace of white powder.

"All good," I said.

He didn't move, and neither did his eyes. He kept his body close. Is he hard, too? I was scared, because in that moment

I could say for certain that I wasn't just fascinated by Jason's strength, his presence, but desired it.

I leaned in to kiss him. He didn't wait to kiss me back. He brought his body closer, and I could feel his hard-on against my knee. He was a forceful kisser, and each motion brought a powerful wetness, a slimy flood. His tongue overpowered my own, forcing it to cower behind my teeth as he lunged into my mouth. It didn't feel real. It was a sequence of events that moments before hadn't seemed possible, whether I wanted it or not. My eyes were shut, but my vision was speckled beneath the black of my lids.

He pulled away from me, undid my belt and trousers, and flipped my hard dick out of my underwear. I opened my eyes, but looked behind him at the marble tile. He pulled the skin back and forth with a strong grip. Desire and guilt boxed one another in a roped ring. I let him take me into his mouth. The suction lifted my hips, splayed my fingers, straightened my knees. I looked down at him. The space around us grew crisp. The outline of his face sharpened. I could see the dry skin around his knuckles, the lines in his forehead as he looked up at me, the stray hairs between his eyebrows, white spots on his nails. These details overwhelmed me. They weren't things that existed in fantasy.

"No," I said. "Jason."

He released me and looked at me for a moment. I shuddered out of him and rattled my belt and trousers back up. He stood, still sandwiching me between himself and the sink.

"What's wrong?" he said.

"This is," I said. "I have a boyfriend. You know that I have a boyfriend."

His face took on a quiet maliciousness, painted in the grooves of his gentle smile.

"It's just playing," he said, leaning forward and kissing me.

I didn't pull away, but didn't kiss him back, either. He stroked my leg. "It's not a big deal."

"You're fucked up."

"What the fuck are you talking about? You kissed me?" Jason laughed, but venom washed over him. He straightened his back. "When you're fucking cheating?"

I fastened my belt and pushed past him. I opened the bathroom door and left, storming down the corridor and towards the cloakroom to get my things. On my way out, I saw Judith standing in the lobby on her work phone. She looked up, and while the sight of me made her smile, it soon dissolved into an unfamiliar look of concern, something aside from the worry she'd feign over projects. I turned away from her and walked through the sliding doors onto the street.

Home was my only option. I could've bided my time at Rob's, but I wanted to be at home, because that's where Ming was. I couldn't bear the thought of sitting still on a bus or train. Time would crawl if I couldn't focus on the rhythm of my legs and feet, and so I walked. My heart was rushing from the coke and adrenaline. People's heads turned as I walked through the street. The sweat on my forehead absorbed and intensified the cold.

As I crossed Westminster Bridge, a gust billowed across the Thames. It shook me sober, the anxious high supplanted by a terrifying low. I couldn't tell anyone before I told Ming, and so I imagined what they'd say. You obviously have to tell Ming, Tom. Okay, Sarah. You haven't done anything that wrong, and Ming might not even mind! It was just a kiss and a quick blow, right? But I'm scared, Rob. What might seem like random acts have an underlying pattern, and I think you may want to disentangle what led you here, for both you and Ming. Not the time, Mum. What your mum's suggested sounds sensible. Thanks, Dad.

My legs ached by the time I reached Camberwell. I was back

home in ninety minutes, but loitered on the front steps of my house for another ten. The walk had sobered me, the drunkenness shrinking away, but leaving the sharp sting of stupidity. I sat on the doorstep and banged my fists against my head.

Ming can make things right. Ming can tell me what to do. Ming can solve things. It goes beyond confession and absolution; he knows things I don't. Maybe he's a little selfish, but I'm worse. I stood up and turned the key. I shut the front door behind me. I heard him call my name from the bedroom, and I climbed up the old stairs towards him. He was on the bed, in the same clothes and position as when I'd left hours ago. The bedside light was on. The swelling on his legs had died down. He held a book in his lap, but looked up towards me.

"I'm sorry about earlier. I should've told you," he said. "I just wanted to get it, and I think I was scared of what you'd say."

He turned to face me fully as I stood in the doorway.

"How was it?" he asked. "You're back early."

I didn't say anything. He froze.

"Tom?"

I stayed silent, but used my wrist to lean against the doorframe, pressing my hand against my face for a moment. When I finally looked at him, his expression turned amnesic, as if I were a stranger.

"Tom."

His voice was resolute, like he was talking down a threat. I didn't move.

"Tom," he said again, not a question, but an order. To stand up straight. To speak. My body wriggled, but I couldn't take the weight of it off the door.

"I have to tell you something, Ming," I said, my fists clenched.

"What is it?"

"I fucked up."

"Fucked up how?"

I began to cry. Ming's body turned to stone, and through my wet eyes I could see his face tighten with consternation.

"What is it?" he asked. "Tom?"

"I hooked up with Jason."

"What?"

"I don't know what it was, but I kissed him, and then he sucked me off for a second. We got drunk. And, I don't know, it was wrong. I don't know what to do. I'm so sorry, Ming. I'm so sorry."

He sat at the edge of the bed with his back towards me. Ming sighed. It was slow, a steady release of air from his mouth, not short, not sharp, not with frustration or exasperation. He cocked his head down. We stayed like this, in stalemate, unmoving, for a while. And then he buried his head in his hands and began to cry. He didn't call me names, he didn't scream at me, he just whimpered, and then kept saying shit and fuck. I was helpless. I wanted to touch him, but his body seemed flammable.

I thought we might cry together, but against his tears my own felt awkward, glib, unwelcome, like I was speaking over him. I stopped sniffling, watching him from the door.

His cries became guttural, wet heaves, the kind of tears I'd only ever seen in films. They suffocated the room, thickening the ether between us. My chest seized, and I couldn't move past the door, but when his wails dulled I trod towards him and cautiously sat on the bed. I felt like a child, watching emotion that felt too big to wield or to help control.

"Ming?" I asked.

He said nothing, his body still hunched over.

"Ming?"

I extended a tentative hand to touch him, but he raised his right hand to halt me. It was slow, like a sloth's paw. He returned it to his lap, and stared at his book. He fiddled with the corners, passing the paper between his thumb and index finger. Then he sighed again. A deep breath. Six in. Six out.

"Ming?"

"How did it even happen?" he asked.

I opened my mouth to respond.

"Actually, no," he said, "I don't think I want to know. Not now. Why'd you do it?"

"I don't know. It was stupid. Because I was drunk, and it just was so stupid. I don't know. What do you want me to do?" I asked, my voice weak, pleading. "Should I leave?"

Ming finally looked at me. His head fell a few degrees towards me with a slight scrunch of his eyebrows.

"Your own house?"

We sat in silence. Ming's sobs retreated. His eyes were red with hurt, but his eyebrows relaxed, and his lips parted.

"Tom?" he said, fiddling with his thumbs. "There's something I have to tell you."

My heart began to pound. Thick beats against my chest. I shifted on the bed and straightened my back. I seemed to know that he was going to weave the months of nothings into something, to close that distance between us. I was coming into knowledge, the tips of my toes on the edge of a plane. Did I want to know? Both states of knowing and unknowing could be torture. But I did want to know, because with Ming all I'd ever done was want to know.

"What is it?" I asked.

Ming looked back at his lap and gripped the book. He began to shrink, growing smaller, like a child. He took a wobbly but deep breath, and then looked in the vicinity of my face but not at me. He opened his mouth. A tear rolled out from beneath his eye and onto his cheek.

"I don't think I want to be a boy," he said. "I mean that I think I can't be a man."

An anxious dread radiated from my stomach. It climbed my bones up to my jaw. It sat in the bays of my teeth.

"What does that mean?" I asked.

"I think I've realized that now. I've been thinking about it for a long time. Since before we went to see my dad and Cindy in Kuala Lumpur. Much more since we graduated. I know you thought my OCD had got better. Or at least that's what I said. I know you've been asking questions. It has got better. That wasn't a lie, but in a lot of ways it just turned inwards," he said, growing more lucid as the words piled on. It was alarming. He moved his body back and sat against the headboard. "The thought came to me: what if you're trans? And then it stuck. It came in and out, but then I was obsessed with my heart and ALS and it all took a back seat. It was so scary, you know, because it's a big thing, and it means losing so much." He cleared his throat. "I've thought about nothing else since, to be honest. Like, I've been analyzing memories and imagining myself this way or that way and seeing how I feel. It takes me to different answers. When the answers tell me I'm trans, I panic and I do it again until I can convince myself I'm not. But it sticks, Tom. And I think it's real. It's different from the heart and ALS stuff. It was easier when I thought I was dying. Sometimes this feels bigger than death, you know."

My mouth was open, my jaw slack, my hands on my lap. I didn't know what any of this meant, the suggestion that he was in his head but also not in his head.

"So is it your OCD?" I asked.

"I'm trying to say that it was and it wasn't. Everyone questions things, but I question things in an unhealthy way. When I finished the CBT, the obsessive part stopped but the rest of it stuck. And then I realized that I don't think I want to be a man. That I like the changes I've been making a little too much. And I'm scared, Tom."

I realized how milky my brain was, curds of gray matter floating in alcohol. The legs. The face. The hair. The drag. The things before this conversation came in like a flood from a burst dam. Things I had willed to have no greater meaning, which now meant everything. He held his knees towards him. I didn't move from the other side of the bed. I knew what I wanted to ask. Do you want to stay together? But that felt too soon.

"Do you want to be a woman?" I asked.

"I don't even know sometimes. I think so. But then I ask myself what does living as a man or woman even mean?" He shook his head. "And I tell myself it's all sexism, but at the same time it's a sexist world, and those things still mean something, you know."

"Right."

I moved to sit with my back on the headboard next to him. I peeled one of his hands away from his knees and held it. It was as cold as ever. I still didn't know what to do, but I no longer felt like my touch was corrosive. I waited for him to speak.

"I feel like I've been drawing an outline of myself using negative space," he said, rubbing my knuckle with his thumb. "Like, maybe I can be a boy if I don't have thick facial hair, or as much leg hair, or if I dress a certain way, but the list keeps growing. It's an endless list of conditions." He paused. "It feels ridiculous and unsustainable, like J. Lo's backstage rider or something."

Ming flashed me a weak smile. I puffed a stream of air through my nose, my body too in shock to laugh. He squeezed my hand. "I think I've realized that even if I did everything on the list, life would only be tolerable."

Ming looked out of the bedroom window. Tolerable ripped me in two. It delivered the truth of my shortcomings, the limits of what I could do to close any gap I thought was between us. He continued.

"But if I imagine it all having been born a woman, then the conditions vanish. Like, if I put all the scary stuff aside, I can think in terms of can rather than can't. I don't know where that leaves us, or where me being this way has left us. Maybe if I'd been on the outside to all of this, I'd have hooked up with Jason, too."

Do you want to stay together? The question sat in my mouth.

"Are you going to transition?" I asked.

Ming looked in front of him. A small gap opened between his lips.

"That word kinda winds me," he said. His thumbs poked one another again. "I think so. I booked a consultation with this private clinic. It's in a couple of weeks. I got all these blood tests and stuff done for it."

More secrets, but drips in the flood. He looked at me, crest-fallen. My heart had always been supple against his face. I brought his head to my chest and stroked his hair. My fingers sailed across the black strands; the reminder of its length pained me.

"Does anyone else know?" I asked.

"No," he said. "Just the clinics."

I felt a little better. A little more on the inside.

"Do you want to stay together?" I asked.

He gave me a look, one that said that the world and fate were cruel, and that maybe I'd always been too naive to know it.

"I don't have all the answers, Tom. I don't know how it's all going to work."

Ming let go of my hand and lay on his back, his neck on the pillow. His eyes were dry. He tilted his chin down, his eyes fixed on the wardrobe across the room.

"I feel stupid for saying this, but all I ever wanted was a boy to fix me," Ming said. "That's all I thought about growing up. That somehow I'd meet someone and then I'd feel okay, you know. And I met you and I fell in love and life was better. But something's still wrong with me, and I've been too scared to say it until now."

I sat with his words. Is this the end? Where do we go? I didn't know. To know my role was palliative rather than enriching made me and Ming seem bleak. And at the same time, I felt closer to Ming. It was devastating, and yet I felt relieved. The thing he'd hidden had nothing to do with me, but he'd hidden it because he was scared to lose me, just as I'd always been scared to lose him. And therefore maybe that distance, these changes to his physicality, his secrecy, didn't matter.

We slept in the same bed that night. The next morning, I couldn't recall how or when I'd changed out of my clothes, or when the lights turned off, or how he ended up in my arms beneath the covers.

Mum and I sat across from one another at the kitchen table. Dad was in the garden.

"Will it be that different?" she asked.

I didn't answer. She held a mug of tea in her hands. Steam pirouetted out of it, leaping into the air.

"I mean, in a lot of ways Ming already looks very feminine," she said, linking her fingers. "I can't imagine he'll need to do much. Will it even be that big a change?"

"I don't know. Maybe not, but it's the small things. I look at pictures from a couple of years ago and he already looks different."

"I suppose. Those things feel surface-level, though, if you really love someone. His body wouldn't change that much for now, would it? Does he want to go the whole way?"

I got up from the chair and opened the sliding door to the garden to freshen the air. I stood by the gap.

"I don't know. I mean, I don't think so, but hormones make you grow boobs and stuff. It's not just genitals that you're attracted to in someone else." I shivered as the air danced on my neck and on my chin. "That's not to say it's not important, but there's a whole bunch of stuff."

"That's true, attraction is more holistic. I can see that."

The sun intensified. I looked back at her. She blew over the surface of her mug. The brown liquid rippled from the force of her breath. I looked back out towards the garden. Dad was kneeling at the border of a flower bed, plucking matter from the soil.

"Would you stay with Dad?" I asked.

"You know, Tom, I've thought about this before. A while ago, actually. When all that stuff with what's-her-name—the American ex-decathlete—Carmen Kardashian, came out."

"Caitlyn Jenner."

"Yes, Catherine Jenner. My friend and I—you know Tia— were discussing it, and she asked me that same question." She sipped her coffee; her lips rasped from the suction that drew the tea into her mouth. "I said that part of me thinks no, because if I were going to be with a woman, I'd prefer someone prettier than your father." I broke out of my solemnity and laughed. "But in all seriousness, I also said to her that I would stay." She sipped and exhaled, releasing the heat of her drink back into the air of the room. "I think I would still be attracted to him, too, even though that's become less important." She shrugged her shoulders. "But I don't know, we're older, and our bodies are probably less pliable. He probably wouldn't look that different. In many ways I don't know what the alternative is for me, because I know I'll never meet someone else I love as much as him. There aren't enough years left of life to share as much with someone else."

I returned to my seat and the table. Mum stared out into the garden.

"You know, Tom, I don't know if I've told you this, but before I gave birth to you I was so paranoid." She scratched her chin with her index finger. "It'd been so hard to conceive, and the thing that panicked me the most was that you'd somehow be swapped at the hospital. Isn't that interesting?" She shook her head and laughed at herself. "I was worried you'd be taken away and I'd be given another boy that wasn't mine. I don't know why that worry went away, but as soon as we took you home I realized that, yes, it could be a tragic story if you'd been swapped and left with a bad family, but I had a child all the same, who I'd love and care for anyway."

Her stare was fixed out of the window, eyes vacant, as if lost in the worry she'd felt twenty-two years before. I stacked my forearms on the table and hunched over them.

"Who's the baby in this analogy?" I asked.

"I don't know." She shook her head again and turned back to me before taking another sip from her mug. "I don't really know what I'm saying, exactly, but if I'd got a changeling of you as a baby, then I could maybe have coped. If someone were to swap you now and give me another twenty-two-year-old and tell me he's my son, I don't think it'd work at all, would it?" She bit her bottom lip. "I think that all I'm saying is that you're still young, and I know you might not know much more than Ming, but it'll be fine." The doorbell rang. Mum stood up. "I'll get it. Don't move."

She disappeared through the kitchen door. I supposed that both Ming and I were the babies, that Mum was saying there we were, still at a stage where we were both replaceable, that there would be other people. But I didn't know if that was true, or if that was a view stripped of sentimentality and duty. Mum came back holding a brochure, placing it on the table as she sat back down.

"Green Party," she said.

"Would you stay with Dad to support him?" I asked.

She smiled, taking the mug between her two hands once more.

"Yes. I think that'd be a big part of it. The support. I love him, and I imagine he would've been in a lot of pain, even if keeping that secret seemed in one way or another to be a betrayal." She released one hand from the mug and rubbed her temple with two fingers. "I don't know if I would trust him to manage alone."

"Right."

She reached out to touch my knuckles. Her fingers carried the warmth of the mug. I let my hand rock onto its side so that she could hold it. Wrinkles and surfacing veins covered her fists. I ducked in and out of making eye contact with her, but she maintained a steady gaze.

"Trust me, I know I put my foot in it sometimes when it comes to certain things. I'm not an idiot. I don't always say the right thing, and this stuff with Ming, the transitioning, is fairly new to me. I mean, one of my clients has a daughter who's trans, but still." Her touch grew a degree firmer. "I'm here, Tom."

"I know, Mum."

She exhaled and leaned back in her chair, her hands returning to her mug, the liquid's surface no longer whispering steam into the room.

"I wish I could figure this out for you."

"Do you say that to your clients?"

She laughed.

"Not in those terms, no, but I often want to."

10
Hole

Half the view from the bedroom window in my and Tom's flat is brick wall, and the other is street and railing and strolling feet. Black metal bars hug the outside of the window. Shoes vanish behind them and reappear. Vanish. Reappear. We're coming to the end of our lease. Tom thinks we should stay on for another year. I'm not going to call it prison—I'm reading one of Tom's books about abolitionism and it seems in poor taste—but sometimes our home feels like a cage. One that costs most of what I earn.

Tom hasn't left for work yet. I'm naked, pottering around the room. I can hear things clunking and knocking in the kitchen. I put on the pink robe on the back of the door. Tom's sitting by the kitchen island, eating out of a bowl of cereal. He's hunched over it, slurping the milk like a suited barbarian. I sit across from him. He smiles.

"I didn't hear you come in last night," I say.

"You were asleep."

"What time did you go to bed?"

His head descends back towards his bowl.

"Late," he says. "I was watching this documentary. It's about detransitioners. Have you seen it?"

He tilts his head back up towards me.

"No, Tom. Why would you suggest that?"

"I just thought you might find it interesting."

This is cruel. And yet there's no way that I can express that it is cruel without also being cruel. Tom's a master at this, being the good guy without actually being the good guy. It's the way he phrases things. He can't mask his discomfort. Are you sure you're comfortable? I just want to make sure you're comfortable with your doctors. It's nothing to do with trans stuff, I just think you look better in those overalls than in that dress. It's just a personal preference, I guess. You don't have to dress feminine to be beautiful! That's what happens when you keep mum about what you want. He's an overfilled Tupperware. Liquid seeps out. I don't want to let this go. I take a deep breath.

"Why would I find it interesting?" I ask.

"I don't know. Detransitioning's under the trans umbrella, right?"

"Why were you even watching it?"

"It just came up when I was looking for something to watch." He pauses. "Have you ever thought about it?"

The question hurts for all the reasons he knew it would. He lifts his bowl, empty but for the milk, off-white from the yellow sweetness leached from the cereal flakes. He decants it directly into his mouth, then hiccups and wipes the white rim around his lips with his shirtsleeve.

"It's been a year. I'm pretty deep in, Tom."

"I know, but so are the people who do it."

I don't know if I should be honest. I know what it'll give him if I say I've thought about it, that everyone thinks about it, that everyone worries they're not doing the right thing. Every-

one has to accept that they might not be. I'm taking each day
as it comes, but as far as I know, this is what I want. It's what I
want. I don't need to carry the burden of other people's doubt.

"Everyone thinks about it, you know. It's normal."

There's a look in his eye; he's away somewhere in his head.
Imagining something, unable to restrain the corners of his lips
from turning upward. He picks up the bowl and brings it to the
sink. He rinses it under the tap and puts it on the drying rack.

"It wouldn't be so bad, would it?" he says with his back to
me. "If it's what you wanted, I guess. It must be nice to know
you have the option."

Nice for fucking whom? I wonder how a therapist raised
someone with so little self-awareness. This sucks. The dynamic
in which I owe him, the dynamic in which I shut up about what
I want. And then I wonder if I'm going to become an overfilled
Tupperware. Am I an overfilled Tupperware? Maybe everyone
shuts up about what they want. Maybe that's normal. Maybe
everyone in the world is a fucking overfilled Tupperware.

"Yeah," I say.

He turns around and picks his keys off the table. He kisses
my head and leaves for work. I go to the bathroom in the hallway between the living space and our bedroom and sit down
while I pee. When I'm back in the bedroom, I take one of my
progesterone pills and place it under my tongue. I already apply
estrogen gels, but this is supposed to make my boobs grow. Results pending. If I pierce it with a needle and put it up my asshole it'll work better, but absolutely fucking not.

The hormones make me really sleepy. At first it was the lack
of testosterone, but then I adjusted. Now it's this pill. It makes
me drowsy, and so my endocrine nurse told me to take it before I go to bed. All I heard was to take it when I want to sleep.

There's no work today. I don't sell flowers anymore. Sometimes I miss it, but the new cinema job feels more trans-friendly,
and the shifts are still flexible. On mornings like this, when I

have fuck all to do, I slip some progesterone under my tongue and crawl back into bed. I let the plastic-tasting liquid swim into the vascular flesh of my tongue and sail into forced slumber. Sometimes I'm surprised at how much I sleep. I set an alarm for one in the afternoon.

Later, I get changed into a bodysuit, skirt and some tights. I splash water on my face, apply some makeup, put on my jumper and jacket and start the hour-long walk to Elina's house. I play lyric-less music on the lowest volume setting and try to think about nothing. Walking in public with headphones on makes me nervous. They're the large kind, and I think the way that they press down on my ears and hair makes my chin and jaw look stronger. Each time someone approaches me on the pavement, I feel anxious and cross the road. It adds five minutes to the journey, and so I quicken my pace towards Elina's leafy Dulwich street.

I go through the garden door at the side of Elina's semi-detached Georgian house. She's my therapist. I've never been through the main door. When Tom and I decided to stay together, I also decided to go to therapy. Not CBT, but proper talk therapy. It's not for my OCD. After I got my first prescription for hormones, all of that started to fall away. Sometimes I still think my heart is stopping, but it's getting rarer and rarer. The therapy is for all the stuff I can't blame on an anxiety disorder. Despite his occasional shittiness, deep down I know Tom lets me get away with murder, he always has, and him staying with me through my transition feels like I'm taking the piss. Ten months into HRT and he's still reminding me of shit admin I'd never think to do. He sits with me at doctor's appointments. He tells me when my tuck looks off in jeans. The least I could do was see a therapist.

Each time I walk towards the converted shed at the back of the garden, I try to spot things that tell me about Elina's life.

There's a new trampoline in the garden. I can't imagine Elina, in her heeled booties and leopard-print shift dress, jumping up and down on the black polypropylene, but I can't imagine Elina doing much of anything.

It's a nice shed. The windows overlook the garden. As I approach, she opens the door. Her timing is precise. I imagine her counting down the seconds each time I ring the buzzer. Knowing the beat of my feet would be very Elina.

She's wearing the same black heeled boots, a leather jacket, leggings beneath a skirt and layered tops. When people think I'm working, I'm often watching reruns of *What Not to Wear*, mostly because I still can't believe that Trinny Woodall was allowed to be so mean on television. Elina dresses like she got made over in 2005 and just stuck with it. That's not mean. She still looks smoking, but there's a datedness there that highlights that we are one and a half generations apart. Her hair looks nice: ringlets of auburn that come to her shoulders, framing big blue eyes and a pair of strong Anastasia Beverly Hills eyebrows. Elina waves me in and I walk to the other end of the low-ceilinged studio, over the Persian rug. I sit down on the mustard couch, across from the chaise longue just a few tones lighter. I take my arms out of my coat and let it rest behind me. She sits in the mahogany armchair, relaxes her elbows on its curved and uneven arms, and smiles at me.

"How are you, Ming?"

"Hm."

I look at the bookshelf to my left. Some are popular-psychology books, some are textbooks, and sometimes Elina goes to the shelf and picks one up for me. I've read the ones she's lent to me, like *The Body Keeps the Score*, which told me that my body is probably as fucked up as my head is, and that I should probably do some yoga. I've also read *Feel the Fear and Do It Anyway*, which told me to do shit I'm scared of. Last week she gave me one called *Attached*. Aren't we all? I glance over the books at the start of each session. Not for long, though, because I'm not like those white people on TV who go to therapy and sit in silence. My bank balance bears an inverse relationship to the clock behind her, and every forty seconds a pound coin pops out of my ass and rolls towards Elina.

"I'm feeling a lot of, like, trans panic," I say.

She raises her eyebrows. Her face relaxes.

"Describe trans panic."

"It's like a paranoia. Even on my way here. Like, I assume everyone's looking at me, even if they're not. I'm always on edge, you know."

"Why does that make you panic?"

Elina asks questions she knows the answers to.

"Because people knowing I'm trans leads to danger."

"Does it? I know you're trans—is that dangerous?"

I sigh. I look at the clock. She's warming up. She always takes a few minutes to recalibrate from whatever dipshit sits in this chair right before me. I imagine he, she or they haven't read *Feel the Fear and Do It Anyway.*

"It's not dangerous," I say. "But trans people get tranny-bashed, and when you hear about it, you think you're next. We need to be responsive to danger. It's not a bad thing. But when your fight-or-flight is engaged, then you're hyperaware, and everything becomes a threat. It's irrational." I take a breath. "And I know the only way I can subvert that kind of faulty data-gathering is to push through it. And then eventually I'll be able to see a real threat from a fake threat and give people the benefit of the doubt. It's an exercise in distinguishing between types of thinking, you know."

She smiles. We circle around the things that my paranoia disrupts. Going to the shops. Getting the night bus. She allows some, but points to the disorder in others. It's okay to skip the night bus, but I should probably try to buy some groceries, even if I'm alone. And then I complain again because it's hard. Although we agree on what's wrong about the world and me, she doesn't offer an immediate fix other than to keep going. I want answers, but good therapists don't like to give them.

Elina uncrosses her legs and recrosses them. I imitate this motion. My eyes drift to her knees and when I look up she's still staring at me.

"Do you ask for support?" she asks.

"In what sense?"

"Do you ask other people to help you? To come with you."

We have a back-and-forth about what we can and cannot ask people to do. We conclude that if they love you, they'll do these things for you, but you'll never know if you don't ask.

"There is an urge to deny yourself support," she says.

Check. I know where this is going, and so I decide to cut the shit.

"Maybe I don't think I'm deserving of support."

She sits with this for only a moment.

"If we think about you after your mother died, crying in the closet. There is a shame there. A shame in being seen, in being helped. Being helped can mean being seen."

I nod. We return to this image a lot. My memory blacked out after my mother died. I vanished and hid in a closet and fell asleep like a five-year-old, except I was fourteen. My dad only found me after he'd called the police. I was loath to tell Elina at first. The symbolism was so rich and ridiculous that I knew any therapist would have an aneurysm. I put out at week five. She brings it up often, as I expected, but in ways I didn't expect. You have to connect to the Ming curled up like that. You have to speak to the Ming crouching in the dark. You have to think about what that Ming needs. See her as your friend!

"The response to needing others is to withdraw. It's restrictive. It starves you of nutrition," she says. "Why don't you want to rely on Tom?"

"I do rely on Tom," I say. "He comes to my doctor's appointments with me."

I am certain that, for a moment, there's a minuscule smile in the corner of her mouth.

"Do you ask him to?"

"No."

"Are you scared of your medical appointments?"

I sigh.

"No."

Tom is something I want to avoid, but I allow her to probe the reasons why I don't rely on Tom for the things I'm actually scared of. She is gentle at first, but then punches her fist in. I unfurl. I tell her that I'm a burden. I tell her that in his eyes I'm on a warpath to destroy my own body, that I'm a freak, a hormonal griffin. Elina doesn't move her face, but she can't hide the sympathy and sadness in her eyes. I know she wants to tell me to hug Ming in the closet, but she's used up her coupon for this session. She asks if he's said any of this to me.

"No," I say. "But he's gay."

"His sexuality and those statements about yourself seem to be different things."

We both know what this means. I look down at my arms. Shame floods through me, like I'm seeing new bruises for the first time. I feel like a dipshit. She smiles again. I remember that Elina's still often three steps ahead of me, and that's why I like her. I may have a better handle on the stars, but she draws the constellations; the bull's horns, the crab's pincers.

"The solutions are often simple," she says.

"A Brazilian butt lift?"

The edges of Elina's lips curve into another soft smile.

"Connection," she says. "Relying on connections."

She asks if I am making an effort with the trans support group I go to. I tell her this week's session was rescheduled for

tonight. Double therapy. We talk about how that's going. The
session ends. I thank her and leave the office-shed.

I'm waiting for the Overground to Lisa's. The two of us are
brainstorming our next play. All my ideas are shit. I've been
straying away from transness. My last idea was a man leaving his
partner after he catches him being breastfed by his mum. Lisa
said it was too similar to *Friend of Dorothy*, which was a polite
rejection because the idea was deranged.

I'm glad I didn't tell Elina I've booked my nose job or about
the detransition thing. I'll save that for support group. They get
all the light stuff because I like to front-load emotional trauma
for therapy. For that reason, I also won't tell support group how
I'm paying for it, how I've used up what was left of my mother.
These small bits of information-control help me twist my feet
in the sand. They make me feel safe with Elina. I'm aware this
is a problem.

When the train arrives, I climb on and sit opposite a girl who
smiles at me. She's wearing loose trousers and a stripy top with
a cardigan. She has her hair in a bun on top of her head. She
looks like an ally. The kind that doesn't know any queer people but makes her boyfriend watch *Drag Race*. I wonder what's
going on in her head when she looks at me. Probably nonsense.
Slay coochie mama queen yes god tongue pop!

I get off the train and get on another two until I reach Angel.
I beep through the gate. Lisa's flat is only a few minutes away
from Angel station. She makes such a big deal about being a
state-educated woman of color, but I learned a year into knowing her that she's actually rich-rich. There are two bedrooms
but her mum lets her live alone. Sarah lives between there and
her hovel in Catford. I ring the buzzer for the flat. The lock
buzzes back and I walk through to the hallway and up the stairs.
Sarah opens the door just as my fist's about to knock against it.
She's in a gray sweatshirt and matching trackies, but her pixie

cut looks freshly trimmed. She hugs me and gives me that smile English people give each other when they pass one another in a hallway. Come on, Sarah! We're Chinese!

"Sarah," I say. "You're in."

"I'm working from here today. From the spare bedroom, though," she says. "Lisa's just in the loo."

I take my shoes off at the base of the stairs and walk up the seagrass carpet, following Sarah to the living room with its rubber floor. The ceilings are so high. I think I'd die if dropped from them. At least if headfirst. The windows are tall and thin and open up to a Juliet balcony. I put my bag on the sofa facing them and sit on the arm.

"How's Tom?" she asks, as if she doesn't speak to him all the time.

"He's good."

She hums and then pours two glasses of water from the tap behind me. She hands one to me and I say thank you. I don't know if Sarah and I would be friends if it weren't for Lisa and Tom. I don't know if we're really friends now. She sits on the sofa, and because the length of the arm is along my crack, I have to twist uncomfortably to talk to her.

"How's work going?" I ask.

"Yeah, it's fine. The charity's doing a fundraising push at the moment. We have this big comedy thing coming up."

"The lesbian one?"

"Yeah, the lesbian one."

"What's the lineup?"

She lists a bunch of comedians. I know none of them, but she tells me there's a surprise guest who's had a special on a major streaming platform, and I manage to guess that one. There's a lull in the conversation. Sarah's so hard. She's been cold to me ever since Tom told her I was going to transition. Or rather, the coldness I'd long felt from her intensified. Blaming trans-exclusionary politics would be convenient, and would help me shift responsibility, but there's next to no evidence of that. She works for an LGBT charity. I think it's caution on her end. Or suspicion. There was a shift around a year after Tom and I started dating, when things stopped being all fun and got a bit difficult because I went fucking crazy. She knows more about me than she'd admit. She fights for Tom, and I know that in part means fighting against me. I'm the difficult one. Rob's different to Sarah. Rob accepted the oxymoron of my transness and Tom and I staying together without much question. Tom told him it was the right thing to do and Rob seemed to support it. Sarah didn't, and it reads in her body language as she sits on the couch. Her tightly crossed legs. Her placid smile. The tension in her forehead.

Lisa enters the room. She's wearing a sage-green sweatshirt and complementing bottoms. Sarah and Lisa are like those matching couples in Kuala Lumpur shopping malls, except I don't think they ever plan it.

"Sorry!" she says. "I was doing a poo."

Sarah gets up from the sofa.

"I'll leave you guys to it," Sarah says. "Good luck."

She waves me goodbye and retreats out of the living room.

"You look so nice," Lisa says. "How are you doing?"

"I'm okay," I say. "Just had therapy."

"Maria Therapova?"

I nod. I get up from the sofa and follow Lisa to the wooden dining table, which has built-in seating on one long and one short end. I sit on one of the white wooden chairs.

"How's Bella's Bunches?" I ask.

"I'm going to quit," she says. "For good."

"What happened?"

I'm genuinely surprised. Lisa wasn't any good at first, but when she stopped apologizing to people for knocking on their doors, she started doing much better. She outlasted me. I thought she'd outlast all of us.

"It's run its course," she says. "I'm going to take a leap and push for more theater work."

"Good for you," I smile. "Seriously."

We begin to talk through some ideas we've had. It's been three weeks since our most recent run of *Death's a Drag* at the Battersea Arts Centre. We've milked the idea dry. It's a dusty udder, and we've decided it's done. It's time to work on something new together. She opens up her notebook to a page on which she's written the word brainstorming in capital letters, surrounded by a border of radiating lines. I can see that beneath it she's only written four words. Honesty. Ming's journey. Transness. I release an inaudible sigh. In moments like this I wonder if I'm the brains of the operation.

"So I've had a few ideas," she says.

I put my finger on the notebook.

"An honest play about Ming's honest journey through transness?"

She stares open-mouthed at the ruled page.

"No. Well, I mean. Like, have you thought about what's good about the old stuff?"

This is the same roundabout way she always speaks, peppering her sentences with filler words and vague references.

"The old stuff?"

"Look, I mean, like, um…" Her pen lies flat on her thumb, and she uses her index finger to tap the page on either side of her hand. "I've been thinking about why *Death's a Drag* did so well, and I think it's because it was vulnerable and honest. And I'm just thinking, what's—I don't know—new and honest for either of us."

She turns her dark eyes towards me, peeking out of her overgrown mullet.

"So we should write something about my transition?" I ask.

"We don't need to write it together. I could take a slightly different role. But maybe we could work some stuff out. You're so amazing, Ming, and you're going on this incredible journey—"

"What aspect of transness?"

She suggests surgery. I say that it is probably not worth writing a play about my nose job. It's just not a big enough deal. I also haven't had it yet. Also, lots of trans people can't afford them. It's tone-deaf! She suggests something to do with Malaysia, and I tell her I'm not the right voice because I'll never live in Malaysia again. She suggests something about trans medicine, and I tell her I jumped the queue because I could pay to go private. Again, tone-deaf.

"How about something based on you and Tom?"

"What do you mean?"

"I don't know. I mean, like, surely it's, like, an interesting lens?"

"On what?"

"Relationships. You guys have been through a lot."

There is nothing stage-worthy at the intersection between my transness and my relationship with Tom. What is there for anyone to learn? There's no Ming's Journey in our relationship. Tom has strapped himself onto a plane with a faulty engine, and it's not interesting because the plane has yet to crash.

"We don't know where all of that is going yet, Lisa," I say.

I read something in Lisa's face—the raise of the eyebrows, lips open but curving downward. It's like something's dawned on her. Even though she can doubt herself to the world's end, she's clinically optimistic about other people and, I imagine, by extension, other couples. I wonder if she and Sarah have ever argued about me and Tom. If Lisa has defended the relationship. No, but, like, I think they're quite good, I mean, they seem to be doing okay, right? That's not true, Lisa.

"Okay," she says. "Surely, like, the nose job idea isn't that bad, then?"

For the next hour we brainstorm a play about a nose job. We

think of titles. *Nobody Nose. Nosthrills. Transplasty.* She suggests *Saving Face*, but I let her know it's already a movie. It's all pretend. We both know we're never going to write a play about a fucking nose job.

"Do you want to stay for dinner?" she asks.

"No, it's fine. I'm not hungry. Support group starts early today." I pause. "Are you going to be at Cass's later?"

"Me and Sarah haven't decided yet," she says.

You haven't or Sarah hasn't? I want to ask, but I shouldn't interrogate anyone on any relationship, least of all one that, aside from an entrenched power imbalance, still seems to function okay. I hug Lisa goodbye and shout the same to Sarah. She ignores me. I leave the flat and head back to the Tube, riding it a few stops until I'm at Elephant & Castle, and then walk towards support group. My stomach rumbles. I'm really hungry. I stop by a Pret and pick up a chicken salad with brown rice. I tell them I'm taking it away and then walk downstairs to eat it in the basement. I sit on one of the tall stools and tuck in.

When I was younger, watching any adult eat alone made me want to cry. I see myself in the reflective black walls of the restaurant and wonder if the two teenage girls in the other corner feel sad for me. I take out my phone and send Tom a pointless text to prove that I'm eating alone by choice. I have loads of friends, actually! And a boyfriend. And a therapist! Leftover grains of rice cling on to the sides of the box. I use my plastic fork to pick them up one by one, sucking them off the tines.

I finish my meal and look up how many calories are in a beet and in an ear of corn. Women have an hourglass figure if there's at least a ten-inch difference between hip and waist. I'm three inches off. No more rice after this.

I empty my tray into the bin, walk back upstairs and head towards support group. Everyone pushed me to join because I didn't have any trans friends, but I'm certain as fuck I won't make any here. Noah is the exception. I enter the community

center, a brutalist hellscape in SE1, and walk to the repurposed
sports hall. Despite having time to kill, I am the last one to arrive. I sit in the empty chair and smile at Noah. He's wearing
a yellow beanie, which speaks for itself, really.

Twelve of us sit in a circle. There are eleven white people and
one me. Flynn leads the meetings. He's a counselor in his forties,
a rotund trans man with glasses and a bushy beard. He's wearing a multicolored striped shirt and a small enamel pin of the
trans flag. I've seen thousands of him in movies and on television, or at least the cis version of him; the Seth Rogens and Zach
Galifianakises of the world. The type of guy who gets with hot
women in a way that doesn't make sense but also kind of does.

I usually hate a lot of what's said during the weekly hour of
tranologues. I normally categorize the irritation I feel by playing a game called Do I Hate It Or Do I Hate Myself, but today
I'm too tired. I switch off for the first forty minutes, looking
through everyone else but maintaining an appropriate level of
eye contact with Flynn. I think about what Lisa said about a
trans play, and then I really think about it for the first time. I
can see the set. I can see our bedroom onstage. I can picture
the mechanics and the lighting and shit. And yet I'm imagining a play to tell a history of something that has yet to happen, and that feels fucked up. But I allow myself to go there
for most of the session, clapping only when I hear other people
clap. Would it be weird if I played myself? What could Lisa do?
Would there be sex?

I decide to tune in for the last twenty minutes of the session.
Only Abby, Sophie and I have yet to speak this week. Flynn
turns to Sophie. Her lips look freshly plumped. If she could get
paid in Juvéderm, then I know she'd take five syringes at the
end of the month.

"Sophie," Flynn says. "How was your week?"

"It was okay," she says, her eyes examining her nails, then
flattening her PVC skirt with her hands. "On my way here

some boys pointed at me. They were like, is that a woman? I got up from my seat and went to the other end of the carriage. They all laughed at me, though. I told them to fuck off, which made them laugh more."

Faces in the circle melt with pity.

"I'm sorry that happened to you," Flynn says.

"It's fine." Sophie rolls her eyes. "Day in the life."

Everyone shuffles in their chairs. I notice how Sophie's clothes and makeup age her. I wonder if she knows that all the drag makes her more clockable. A thought beginning with, well, maybe if she didn't...cracks into my mind like lightning. This is a firm I Hate Myself.

"How are you doing this week, Ming?" Flynn asks.

"I'm doing good. I set the date for my nose job. It's in a couple of months. A bit less than that, actually."

Abby claps with gusto from across the circle, the kind of blind and affectionate enthusiasm afflicting parents over fifty. Some of the others clap with her. Sophie forces a smile.

"That's a big deal," Flynn says. "Does it feel like a big deal?"

"It does and it doesn't, you know. It's something I've always wanted, even before I knew I was trans. I don't think I'll even look that different. It's just the angle of the tip."

"But it must feel like a step forward."

"Yeah, I suppose so."

"How does your boyfriend feel?" Sophie asks.

I catch the Schadenfreude in her emphasis on boyfriend. Flynn shoots her a look, but I speak up before he can say anything.

"I don't know. I probably would've got one anyway. Even if I wasn't trans, I mean, but something's still changed between us." I fiddle with my thumbs. "It's always changing, but I talked about detransition with him; like, how it's natural to sometimes have thoughts about going back, you know."

"I don't have those," Sophie says.

"No interrupting, please," Flynn says.

"Well," I say, turning my eyes to Sophie, "then, sometimes I have thoughts about going back. I don't think there's anything wrong with that. I mean, you can't be a hundred per cent sure about doing anything." I hear these words in Elina's voice. "But anyway, Tom can't really hide how he's feeling. And I don't think he knows how much he shows on his face."

"What did his face say?" Flynn asks, his palms open on his lap.

I think of Tom in the kitchen, his back straightening, asking leading questions while holding in that fucking smile. He was trying to be coy, but he's easier to read than a neon sign.

"I saw hope," I say.

"How did that make you feel?"

"Like shit. I feel scared of being honest with him. The support feels conditional, or strained, maybe. I don't know. It brought home that we want different things, you know. But anyway, that's where I'm at."

"Thank you for sharing."

Flynn turns to Abby.

"How are things with you, Abby?"

"My wife, like, still doesn't want to speak to me," Abby says. "My kids are being brats about the whole thing. But it's their mother. She tells them things like, Daddy's going to chop his willy off. I heard that from my ten-year-old."

The room is silent, but everyone winces. Abby looks down at her shift dress. I stare at her new boobs. She got them done six weeks ago.

"Sorry," Abby says. "It's just been really, really hard. I've had some luck with positive affirmations, though. I just say to myself in the mirror: Abby, you're a woman. You were born a woman. You will always be a woman. And I feel a bit braver for the day."

The room claps for her. I bring my hands together, and they collide and release without making a sound. I wonder if a clap is a clap if nobody hears it. What bothers me most about Abby, I think, is how she speaks. She feels like a relic, but also so fresh, like she was thawed from a shitty cryogenic sleep that froze her mind but not her body. She talks a lot about feeling like a woman and about destiny. I imagine she takes notes watching episodes of *POSE*. I know this is an I Hate Myself, and I also know it's because I hate my proximity to Abby, and that all that separates us is time. I think about the things Abby's ex-wife says about her, and it pains me to imagine Tom ever saying the same.

"All right, then, that's all for this week," Flynn says.

We all clap once more, stand up, fold our chairs and take them to the wall. I survey the room from the side, and note once more how most of the people at support group have fallen into the Great Regression, the involuntary rewind of speech and behavior when a person transitions, the deep psychological urge to relive youth that prejudice and self-loathing stole from them. They're trans in the psychosomatic sense, but also trans in that they're teenagers stuck in the bodies of adults. I'm grateful to have mostly escaped it.

Noah comes up to me.

"Hey, beautiful," he says.

His voice is teasing but sincere, and with the nasal affect of a gay teenager. He hugs me. My arms wrap around the top of his back, across his oversized sweatshirt and jacket. I'm impressed by the illusion of breadth along his shoulders. I feel the beginnings of his beard on my cheek. He'll soon have more facial hair than Tom could ever grow.

"Sorry about Tom," he says. "You look really fit tonight."

I smile. His labored flirting is his own version of the Great Regression, but my brain and neck still tingle. I suppose this is what's left of mine.

"Are you going to the pub?" I ask.

"Yeah, why not," he says. "Let's go for a couple."

We trail behind the group on the way to the lofty pub around the corner. I'm not sure I'd date Noah, but I think it's funny that we'd be a straight couple no matter where you stand on the ontological question. I order a vodka soda for myself and a pint for Noah. Our group takes three low mahogany tables in one corner. Noah and I sit next to each other on the edge. By the time we finish our drinks, some of the others are doing shots. I check the time. It's eight.

Noah tilts his head towards conjoined mops of brown and pink-and-blue hair. It's Amber and Anarchy, who suck each other's faces so hard that I ponder the possibility of oral prolapse.

I try not to look at them. I see an elderly couple watching Amber and Anarchy in shock. They turn their stares to me and Noah, which makes me uncomfortable. Noah goes to buy us another round and I start to make conversation with Abby. She tells me about some clothes she's bought, but I can't focus on anything but her wig. It's an expensive lace-front with bangs, but she hasn't glued it down properly. I fight the urge to tug the parting so that it rests at a sensible place on her scalp. Noah returns with a vodka soda and gives it to me. He says he's just got a call from his parents and that he's got to run. I hug him goodbye.

I let Abby tell me about being misgendered at work while I take slow, continuous sips of my drink.

"They slap wrists but, like, nothing happens," she says, shrugging her shoulders. "That's construction for you."

"That sounds fucking horrible."

"It's fine," she says. "Like they say, it gets better."

Does it? I hope it does. For Abby, at least. I find it a little devastating that people can become this inured to cruelty. I look at my watch and tell her I'd best be off. Abby hugs me. There's an unexpected softness to her embrace, and the safety I feel in it disarms me. The gesture means more than I'd like to admit. I try to repay her warmth.

"You don't have to take everyone's shit, Abby."

"I know," she says. "I know."

She squeezes a little tighter then lets me go. I look back as I walk out of the pub and see Abby checking her phone. She always stays until the end. I don't think she has many other friends. The loneliness I see in her makes me ache.

I check my messages when I'm out on the street. Tom has texted me to tell me that he's going to work late, but he'll see me at Cass's house party. I hop on the bus and climb to the top deck. There's a man with a scar on his chin who looks at me, and a woman in her twenties sitting at the back, staring out of the window. The man has his arms folded, and he's slouching in his chair with his legs spread past the width of the bench. He's holding a can of Strongbow Dark Fruit. His eyes stay on me too long. He smirks. I sit down closer to the front window. I turn up my headphones. The air behind me shifts. The nerves in my cheeks bloom, and I begin to feel nauseous. I look back and he's now sitting two seats behind me. His brow-ridge shadows his eyes, and the corners of his lips curl into a wicked snarl. I pick up my things and trot down the stairs. I hear him say something to me, but my headphones submerge the noise. I jump onto the pavement and feel the cold wind twirl around my shins.

The next bus arrives, and I climb on. I sit near the driver. I open up my phone and look at the 3D mock-ups of my nose job. I put it through a feminizing face app that makes my hair even longer and my cheeks much fuller. I've done it before, but I don't save the picture because I think seeing the before and after makes me feel better. It makes things feel possible. The photo comes up. I look just like my mother, and that makes me feel better about using all the money, like I've just exchanged one representation for another.

I know better than to show my dad these photos, even though he's the only one who'd understand how freaky it is. I think about my dad and when I flew back to Malaysia. It was just after I'd paid to get onto hormones. To pay for the flight, I used all the flower money, some cinema money, and the money left over after the second run of *Death's a Drag*, which I only had because Tom's parents didn't charge me rent.

On my first night back, my dad and I sat on the balcony when Cindy was out, and I told him everything over a beer. The words were rehearsed, and he took them in without a stir. He stared out to the sky and sipped his beer slowly. He asked if it meant that I wanted to be a woman, and then he interrogated where my body was and where it would go, as if drawing the chalk outline around an old shape to understand the new. He was calm, but rose from his chair and walked inside. I heard the fridge open and the clink of bottles, and the hiss from dislodged bottle caps. The air was still, and the humid heat rose into the backs of my knees and armpits. A thin layer of sweat appeared beneath the hair that covered the corners of my forehead. When he returned, he sat back down on the chair.

"I support you, that goes without saying." His voice was low and impassive. He brought his large hand to my shoulder. "But life is going to be difficult, Michael."

"I'm better off than most trans people," I said.

"Being lucky isn't always enough," he said, and he took a long sip from the bottle. The meniscus wobbled and descended the glass. "I have to ask, really. Do you think it has anything to do with your mother?"

"No, Dad. It doesn't work like that."

"Okay. I just had to ask."

He took another sip.

"I think," he said, "I think you've always been more like her. You've always looked like her. More Ming than Michael."

More Ming than Michael. I return to those words all the time.

The bus arrives at my stop, and I step off so that I can walk home. I feel dehydrated. When I reach our building, I hop down the stairs to the lower ground floor. The tall Georgian windows of the flats above us glow yellow. Inside our room, the bed is made, but my clothes are on the floor. Tom will get mad if I don't pick them up. I top up my makeup, but in the living-room mirror where the light is better. I can hear our upstairs neighbors in their section of the garden. I pull out the creams and serums from my makeup bag. All of it's natural-look stuff, to make me look like I bleed hyaluronic acid and shit dew.

There's a cavity opening in my stomach. The old anxiety, which I tell people has gone, rushes to fill it. There's a bottle of vodka in the cabinet, and so I pour a vodka soda into a yellow mug and take some leftover chicken and a lime wedge out of the fridge. I lie on the sofa that Tom's parents gave us because they had it in storage. It's beat-up, but it's a low mid-century piece. And it's leather. I drink, but the cold liquid pools at the top of my chest and I cough. My mother always told me not to drink or eat things lying down. It gives you poor digestion. Everything came back to digestion for her. Eat your fruits first or they'll rot in your stomach and you'll get diarrhea! No cold water after hot food—the oil will coagulate and you'll have a tummy ache! Don't eat goreng pisang from that stall. My friend said they melt plastic into the oil to keep it crispy—you'll get stomach cancer! I sit up.

I take another bite of chicken and wash it down with a gulp of my drink. More Ming than Michael. Michael is something more than the name my father called me. I spoke about it with Elina last week. Michael is the gay me, the me who isn't men-tally ill, the me who could live as a boy. The boy who likes to fuck like one. Michael would want a job like Tom's. Michael wouldn't fuck up an expensive education because he was wor-ried he was dying. Michael could be what Tom needs. After I came out, I began to see that maybe Tom loved Michael in-stead, and the question for us was not where Ming would go, but how much of Michael would stay.

I lick the bones clean and throw them into the compost bin, then place the plate and empty mug into the sink and wash my hands.

Cass's is twenty minutes away. I'm feeling brave enough to walk. I carry the bottles of vodka and soda water in a tote bag and head in the direction of the house in Brixton. The backstreets help to avoid attention. Lisa opens the door when I arrive. Her boots reach all the way above her knees. She's slathered in chunky silver jewelry.

"Hey, beautiful!" she says.

"You came!"

I hug her. I feel more relaxed. The party is split between the kitchen and living room. People spill out into the garden. I pour myself a drink in the kitchen and find Cass in her room upstairs. She's wearing a mesh top with no bra underneath. I should wear more mesh. The smell of incense sticks weighs down the air. She's talking to a girl called Tabitha, whose shoulders are narrow, her makeup pristine and her hair gently coiled into long and loose curls. I've not seen Tabitha in nearly a year, almost as long as I've been on hormones. I hug both of them, and we all sit together on the floral quilt covering the bedspread. I lie across it while Tabitha and Cass settle cross-legged near the pillows.

"Cass was just telling me about her promotion," Tabitha says.

"It's not a big deal," Cass says.

"It is, Cass!" I say.

"I went from research assistant to policy researcher," Cass says. "I'm doing the exact same job."

"It sounds completely different," Tabitha says.

"Also money, Cass."

"Look what I bought to celebrate." Cass jumps off her bed and pulls a white silk corset from her top drawer, the cups in the shape of seashells, Selfridges tags hanging off. I should wear more corsets.

"Are you going to wear that to work?" I ask.

We all laugh. Cass sits back down. Tabitha bats her annoyingly wide eyes at me.

"Congratulations on everything," she says. "You look beautiful."

"Thanks," I say. "How's everything with you?"

"Oh, I'm still interning at that gallery. I saw that play you did with Lisa is showing at Battersea Theatre."

"The Battersea Arts Centre, yeah. It finished a few weeks ago."

"So amazing," Tabitha says. "Are you still selling flowers?"

"No. Not for a bit. I'm doing shifts at a cinema until I find something else."

"Why'd you stop?" she asks.

I laugh.

"I'm trans."

Tabitha's eyebrows pinch together. Her head cocks sideways and her lips extend into a flat smile.

"You can't be trans and sell flowers door-to-door," I say.

"Why not?" Tabitha asks.

"Here we go," Cass says.

"Trans people are scary in the way that gay people used to be. When you're trans and don't pass, you're no longer charming. They'd think I was selling them a—"

"Bouquet of poppers," Cass finishes the sentence with me. We laugh.

"It's ridiculous," Cass says. "Ming's the most charming person I know. That doesn't just go away."

I look at the wall of photographs behind Cass's bed. I notice she's taken down the pre-transition photos since I last came over, which is all the photos of me. There are no pictures of her from university, when she was at her thinnest. She goes to therapy now. She looks healthy. Her reconstruction of history is compassionate to me, but it's hard to know if that compassion extends to herself. I still worry.

"I'm sure things will change," Tabitha offers. "You still pass, anyway."

"Not really," I say. Neither of them protests. My fingers rub the lacy border of one of Cass's pillows. "Does anyone want another drink?"

They nod and head down with me. Tabitha walks in front of us. Cass holds my hand and whispers in my ear.

"You look really pretty tonight," she says.

I squeeze her hand. It means more from Cass than almost anyone else, even if I'm sure she feels she has to. At the bottom of the stairs I see Tom by the bookshelf in the front room, talking to a boy I recognize. I tell Cass and Tabitha I'll meet them in the kitchen. I swirl through the loose crowd. The boy is wearing chinos and a jumper and tortoiseshell glasses. I can't remember his name. Both of them lean against the bookshelf. They cross their legs. Tom's still in his work clothes. White shirt, blue trousers. I quickly go up to hug and kiss him. Then I hug the boy, who kisses me on my cheek.

"Hey," Tom says. "You look nice."

"Ming," the boy says. "You're looking great."

His short, moussed curls bounce. I squirm at the compliment and say thank you. I meet Tom's eyes. His lips purse into a soft smile.

"Did you come straight from the office?" I ask.

"Yeah," he says.

"So late on a Friday," the boy says. "Fuck me."

"Yeah, it's mad," I add, then ask the boy, "What have you been up to?"

"Oh, you know, working at Goldman's."

"Like, Goldman Sachs?"

"Yeah," he says. "But, you know, work hard, play hard."

"Is this what playing hard looks like?"

He doesn't laugh. Tom smiles. The boy pushes his glasses up his nose and Tom takes his satchel off his shoulder. I notice how my body disrupts their symmetry, a third ruining a game of seesaw. I excuse myself to get a drink, and I offer to pour Tom and the boy one, too. I push through the crowd to get into the kitchen, hugging Sarah on the way in. Nice to see you again! She's friendlier at parties. When I get back, they're sitting down, and I join them on the hard arm of the couch. My bony bum pushes through the upholstery and into the skeleton of the sofa. I wonder if it hurts women with big bums to sit like this. I motor through my drink and make conversation with the two girls standing in front of me. Tom's back now faces me, and so I return to the bookshelf and inspect the spines. Cass comes up behind me and puts her hands on my waist.

"Do you want a line, Mingy?"

"I've brought some ket," I say.

"Fun!"

We head upstairs to a random bedroom with one of Cass's handsome flatmates. Cass gets out a tablet and tips out fat lines of coke and ket. She mixes them together with two cards. Her gestures are grand, like she's mixing ice cream with scrapers. I take a fiver out of my wallet and hand it to Cass, who snorts a line. The flatmate goes next. I'm last, and as my head rises from the black screen, Tom is at the door. I pick the rim of my left nostril with my thumbnail.

"Do you want some?" I ask.

Tom sits down next to me, and he does a line off the tablet on my lap. I wipe some more residue from his nostrils, and he holds my hand for the first time that evening. I notice how warm it is, and know that means my skin must feel icy on his. Cass comes to the other side of me with her laptop and we play music from the speakers. Tom introduces himself to the flatmate. We dance in the meter-wide moat of carpet around the bed.

"Is Ming your girlfriend?" I overhear the flatmate say.

"Yeah, she is," Tom says.

Girlfriend. My ears focus on the music, and Tom and the flat-mate talk while Cass and I dance. My legs start to feel lighter. The ketamine starts to hit. I really like ketamine. I've always liked ketamine. There was a UK-wide shortage of ketamine during my first year of university. It was impossible to get it anywhere. I excuse myself to go to the bathroom and stare at my reflection in the mirror.

"Ketamine drought two-K-fifteen," I slur to myself.

I take another key. I don't rush on drugs as much as I used to, and that makes going to parties hard. There's a tipping point that comes on nights like these. Where I go from feeling hot to seeing stubble that isn't there, and to inspecting the hair on women's upper lips to see if the amount I have left is natural. I see the angle of my cheeks and size of my jaw. I see the width of my shoulders. The hormones could dissolve the muscles around them, but they'll never shave bone. I wonder if they're really that wide, and whether drugs distort or purify. I wonder what I actually look like and who the fuck can tell me. It feels like when I used to look in the mirror when I was younger, when I would push and prod at my face and question whether I was real.

I look at my man-face in the mirror. I ask if the hormones will really change anything, and if I'm going to be taking this shit until I die. And then I think about the hormones, and the health risks, the number of times I've googled an older famous trans woman to learn that if she didn't die of AIDS then she died from a heart attack or organ failure. And I wonder to my-self, is it the estrogen? All I wear are A-line miniskirts. What the fuck is up with that?

And the only way to get over these thoughts is to leave the monster in the mirror, and so I head back downstairs to the crowd in the living room. Tom's talking to Sarah. I do a bump. Fat keys until I'm somewhere other than here. And then the cor-ners of the room feel far away, but the room also feels so small, and my friends' heads look bigger and out of proportion to their bodies, like I'm dancing with Bratz dolls in a fish-eye lens.

Rob was once so high he thought people were trying to snort him. I try to tell this to the girl next to me, but she just nods and hugs me. She didn't hear what I said. And then I'm dancing with my eyes closed, and someone asks me if I'm okay, and then Tom comes out of nowhere and holds my hand and we dance together, and we sway, and I feel safe again, and I realize I'd take any medication forever just to have someone hold me like this, and then I remember that I'm doing the opposite. He takes me to the couch and I lie in his lap. He talks to other people until I come out of the hole and I'm social again.

"I'm alive!" I say.

Tom laughs. So does that boy from earlier.

"We didn't think you'd come out of it!" says one of them.

Well, I did, and I can dance again. And then I can do a line of coke and I'm feeling better, I'm alert, but then the sinkhole reopens, and I see the size of my hands. I see the ridges and my long fingers and the squidgy blue veins that you can press down. And I look at Tabitha's hands and they're plump and round and not knobbly like mine. My mother had hands like mine. It's nothing to do with being a woman, really. Anyone can have any hands. Absolutely anyone. But I'd also really like to have small hands.

I ask someone where Lisa is, and they tell me that she and Sarah went home early. I drink another vodka soda, squeezing in a lime because I still have self-respect. I want to tell everyone in the room that I'm going to look different. And so I tell some people that I'm getting a nose job.

Did you know? Oh, you think I look different already? Thank you, that's so kind. It's all pretty crazy, really. I tell them about how Tom and I are still together. And I can probably do a tiny bit of ket again. I fumble with the keys in my pocket and shovel it into my nose. Do you want any? He's been amazing. He has, really. No, I know I don't need a nose job, but it's something I've always wanted. It doesn't even really have to do with being trans. It's just the angle of the tip! I believe in doing as little as possible. I think that's the best philosophy, personally, otherwise you don't know what you'd regret. The good stuff has to come from within, and I'm doing much better. The hormones are amazing.

Tom hugs me from behind. He says we should go home because it's five in the morning. I say that's fine, and I ask him if we have any paracetamol. He tells me it's bad for my kidneys. We get into the cab. I fall asleep on him. When we get home I take my clothes off and lie in bed, and when I wake up at eight I forget that I've slept at all. It's not like I lost the memory of whatever dream I had, but there were no dreams at all, like for a while I didn't exist, like I'd been unplugged. I crawl back into bed, and Tom reaches over to spoon me. His mum once told me how touch can lower cortisol. Hugging and cuddling reduces stress. It makes people feel safer. My head is groggy. Opening my eyes feels like lifting weights and so I don't. I love it when he holds me. I wonder if I'm lowering his cortisol. I can't wait for my nose job, but I know it's the nail in the coffin. It's not worth it. Tom deserves someone he wants to fuck. He deserves someone who lowers his cortisol. His mum told me I'm pretty. She's so nice. Maybe I will be pretty. I'll look like my mother. My beautiful mother. I miss her. My dad says she would be proud of me. She was so open-minded, he says. She taught him so much.

Poor fucking Tom. Stupid fucking Tom. It'd all be a good play, wouldn't it.

11

Thin Frames

I sat in my chair. A scintilla of light pierced past the clouds and onto my desk. I straightened the papers in front of me and placed them small stack by small stack into a large ring binder. The deal was done, securing finance for a Finnish energy company to build four onshore wind farms. It was one of the few things that crossed my desk that didn't make me feel terrible—it wasn't oil like last time—but the hours had been tormenting. For the final few weeks we'd had early starts of eight thirty and late finishes of four in the morning. I'd worked on it for five months. Judith had put me on it two days after Ming broke up with me. The project was a distraction, and the odd hours meant fewer awkward run-ins with Jason in the elevators. People on the team were sleep-deprived but at least more relaxed.

It was three in the afternoon. I yawned a wide yawn.

Judith came up to my desk. She was uncharacteristically friendly, struck by a tired delirium. She touched the new Cartier watch on her wrist as she spoke, as if reminding herself it was there. Oh my god, Tom! You've worked hard. Isn't Fatima's new haircut horrible? Don't worry about doing much today. David took me aside and told me the partners have been talking. It's all on track for me. Director by next year. God, clarity is so good, isn't it. I said that you've been really helpful recently. What are you eating? Have you heard of the five-two diet? It's two five-hundred calorie days and you can eat whatever you want on the other days. I just ate an entire roll of Hobnobs! I wonder what they've said to Fatima. She doesn't deserve a promotion.

I really didn't care about what anyone had said to Fatima. I was exhausted, but it was a wired kind of fatigue, where a body shuts down but the circuits are still sparking, still trapped somewhere between no and all systems go. When Judith left me alone, I messaged Marco to ask if he was free later that evening. I'd met him on an app. He was one of a few people I'd slept with since Ming and I broke up, but the only one I'd enjoyed. He was a fashion photographer, a transplant from Australia, one who wore black T-shirts and silver jewelry and saw himself as an authority on all things aesthetic. He'd go on tirades about IKEA. He'd spend hundreds of pounds on dog shit as long as it was mid-century. It wasn't clear to me if it was just sex, but the sex was good. He was built and manly in the ways Ming never was, and he had hairy legs and a beard. I'd let him top me. It was the first time I'd ever done it. I almost never thought of Ming when he fucked me.

I sat idle at my computer, waiting until the clock reached four. Marco hadn't read my text yet. I'd felt so confident when sending the message, but grew increasingly worried that I'd done something wrong. Was saying that it would be nice to see him with an exclamation mark passive-aggressive? Or was it too keen? These questions always led me to the same anguished place. I wanted to make plans, to do something fun. Rob was busy that evening. Sarah was out of London.

I searched things on the internet to distract myself. My fingers flicked through social media apps, my tired eyes steeping in the flashing images and bright colors. The flicking stopped, and then my index finger pressed onto the search button. I typed in Ming's name.

I hadn't looked her up for a couple of months, but exhaustion had worn down my defenses. There was an enormous pinch in my chest as I looked at her page, as if gripped by Alsatian-sized pliers. I saw a post advertising *Thin Frames*. The play. The poster was an image of two topless bodies, shot close-up, sitting back-to-back. Their faces weren't in it, but they must've been Ming and me. That's what *Thin Frames* was about: Ming and me, which meant that it was about me, because for the last year or so it was hard to know where I ended and she began.

I'd been upset when I'd found out about *Thin Frames* a few months ago. Everyone else had been, too. Rob and Ming had stopped speaking after a blowup at Lisa's flat. Rob had said it was bad. It's just fucking crazy, right? Who the fuck does she think she is? What a cunt. I know, Rob, but let's not talk about it. Sarah had said it was really bad. She'd been upset with Ming and Lisa. It's so narcissistic, Tom. Can we please just stop talking about it, Sarah. I hadn't asked either of them for details. I hadn't wanted them.

Lisa had broken up with Sarah soon after. It'd surprised everyone, not least because Sarah had always been the one to complain: about Lisa's anxieties, that Lisa wasn't her own person, that she didn't respect Sarah's space. But Lisa had fallen out of love. Sarah had scrunched her face up when I'd apologized for all the stress Ming and I had caused them.

"Are you serious?" she'd laughed. "Not everything's about you, Tom."

I'd appreciated the reassurance, but still, *Thin Frames* can't have helped. Sarah hated that they'd made the play, that Lisa was riding shotgun.

I clicked onto the ticket website. It was showing that week. In just a few months the production had come together, which made me certain that the groundwork had been there much earlier. Marco still hadn't read my message. My mouse hovered over the drop-down list. I reached for my wallet and pulled out my bank card. Watching *Thin Frames* hadn't been something I'd allowed myself to consider. I'd buried Ming as much as I could. I didn't talk about her. I still don't want to talk about it. I'm fine. I'm moving on. I don't even care that she got to stay in the flat for a month longer, or that I had to move home for a bit. Look at this guy I fucked. It's so good to be free!

Wanting to go felt illogical, but I punched in my card details and bought a ticket for that night at seven, back of the theater, near the exits. The confirmation pinged into my inbox, along with a fresh spike of anxiety. I left my desk and went to the bathroom by the lifts. I didn't have to go, but I needed somewhere to be alone and sleep it off, and I couldn't put my head on my desk even if I wasn't doing anything. I went into a stall and sat on a toilet with its lid closed. The tiled wall was hard on the corner of my head, but I folded my arms and shut my eyes.

Ming and I had scarcely spoken since we'd broken up. She'd sent texts. Thinking of you, Tom. Hope you're doing good! I heard your and Rob's new place is lovely. For a while I'd replied with scant answers. You too. Yeah, it is! And then she'd asked if she could call me because she had something important to talk to me about. It was a month or so after we'd broken up. The call was about the play. Can I do it, Tom? It'd be really good, you know. I think it'd help other couples who are, like, going through what we went through. Or explain it. Does that make sense? Would you be okay with it? You'll totally have the right to veto anything you don't like!

I didn't understand why it was necessary, or what it would provide the world. What was there to glean from any of the years of me and Ming? Don't trust narcissists! Even if they're trans! But I wanted a clean break from Ming, and so fighting about the play felt stupid. I said yes. Not: yes, but I'd like to see the script. Not: yes, but I'd like to decide who plays me. Just yes. A yes with a flat smile. I could sense that she was disappointed, but that she knew I wouldn't give her anything more. Folding felt obvious. Folding felt sensible, but then I stopped speaking to Ming altogether, scaling down from scant words to none, and that was that.

I timed my walk so that I'd get there just as the curtains opened. I didn't want to bump into people or hang out in the foyer or bar or hallway. I didn't want anyone to see me. When I walked through the doors at the back of the theater, I could see the stage. A heavy dread wrapped its arms around my esophagus.

I danced past the knees of two women to get to my seat. The one right next to me had pale-pink hair, and small black polka dots covered her long white dress. Nobody was more than two meters away from that dress that summer. There was a bed in the middle of the stage, lit under a wide spotlight. Its back feet were raised, and I realized it was so that the audience, who sat level with the bed, could see the two bodies lying in it; cigarettes at either end of an empty pack, parallel lines tucked in white cotton. It was me and Ming, or the people who played me and Ming, a white man and an Asian trans woman. He looked nothing like me. Blonde hair and face like a fucking pug.

"It's me, Li," the man in the bed said.

I was startled. It was our bedroom in the flat we'd shared. Not just because it was a play about the end of us, but also because of what the blonde actor who looked nothing like me said. It's me, Li.

It's me. The scene before the curtain opening replayed in my mind. It was a few weeks after her nose job. It had healed, but the tip was still swollen, such that the fluid forced the very end to upturn a little. At that point I didn't know if it'd ever go down, where her face would settle. Right before that opening scene I was slumped over Ming, thrusting into her. I'd stared at the budding lumps on her chest, the chemical rosiness of her cheeks, the synthetic length and points of her mascaraed lashes, the nostrils that I could now see more of; some lines in sand and some lines in concrete. At the time, all I could think about was the first time we'd had sex, the night when I'd worn Sarah's dress, how life had felt easy, how it had felt like riding a bike downhill, fingers off the brakes, and how that meet-cute tentativeness, that simplicity I'd discovered years before, had since dissolved into a cold numbness, a soft collapse in my loins that made me slow and fall onto her and say sorry. It's me, Ming.

The actor got out of bed and walked in circles. He was short and solid. He put his hands on his hips as he did this, barefoot, wearing only boxers.

"It's me, Li," he said again.

The actor playing Ming sat up in bed. She'd been looking to her side, away from her partner, away from me. She turned her head towards the blonde actor.

"I don't think it's you, George. We both know it isn't you."

"It's my dick."

That's what I told her. In some senses, it was me; it was my soft dick that used to be a hard dick. It wasn't explained away by anything I'd done, but it was my body and its response to her body. It was an exposition of my limits, and this seemed but another way in which I was confronted by the things I couldn't be. A person attracted to a woman who used to be a man who used to be my boyfriend who became my girlfriend.

Li put her head in her hands. I couldn't remember if Ming had done the same, but Li doing so made me think she had, and this made me doubt what memories were mine or Ming's and what was just the play. From my memory, Ming had begun to cry, but maybe that wasn't how plays worked, how creating art worked. I remembered the aphorisms Ming used to repeat about writing. There's no release without tension, you know. There needed to be buildup, and there wouldn't have been any buildup if Li had started crying on her first line.

"It's the nose, isn't it? I knew this would happen, you know. It's all fucked. I've fucked it."

Li stood up. She wore lingerie. George looked at her from across the bed, his hands still on his hips. The heat of his eyes seemed to crease her stomach, and she crumpled towards the floor, squatting with her arms around her knees. George sat back down on the bed, his back towards her. Their nakedness filled me with discomfort.

"It's just a nose job, Li," he said. "You don't even look that different. Not in a bad way, but you're the one who keeps saying it was a spiritual rhinoplasty."

Li sat on the floor with her back to the side of the bed, playing with her fingers.

"It can be like this when I drink," George said.

"You're not drunk, George."

"I guess we're just getting older."

"How old do you think we are?"

George's bum slid down the side of the bed, symmetrical to Li's. I remembered that at that time our bed had felt like two halves. He sat with his legs wide, forearms on his bent knees. They spoke to one another for a while.

It had been in that moment with Ming, some months before, that all the small stuff had weighed up to something insurmountably large. Larger than it had felt when she'd told me she was trans, because the threads of transness had danced into something that was no longer a hypothetical scary, but a big and present and undeniable thing. It was there in front of me, on her naked body and on her painted and scalpeled face. And then I couldn't keep it up, and so my dick seemed to measure the distance between the new Ming and the old Ming. And still, I didn't leave.

Li got up from the floor and faced the audience.

"I'm on hormones via a private gender clinic. I knew I'd have to wait four years if I went through the NHS, and I wasn't going to spend my twenties looking like Noel Fielding."

"You've never looked like Noel Fielding," George said, his head hanging between his legs, all while Li kept her eyes on the audience. "Tell them about when you first called them."

"So the woman on the phone sounded like Jennifer Coolidge, but if Jennifer Coolidge was from Sunderland—"

"I said when."

"Oh. I booked the appointment over a year ago."

"Tell them about when you told me."

"I only told George after I'd had all my bloods done, and only after I'd booked it," Li said. "I know it's bad, but it's what made sense. You didn't mind, did you?"

This went on for a while, Li speaking and George directing, splicing and recombining old anecdotes, things I remembered and things I didn't remember, things I thought had happened weeks after, closer to when we broke up, and then things I thought might have happened before.

George moved to the front of the stage, while Li moved onto the bed, reclining sideways, her arm resting in the fold between her hip and ribs. She stared at George as he spoke.

"Li has this thing she calls her corner shop voice. She speaks in a higher register when she's in a corner shop because she's scared of being misgendered. But it's not like you only hear it in the corner shop. She does it everywhere. Restaurants. Cinemas. More and more when we're with friends."

"Tell them about the ice cream," Li said.

"We were standing in a queue with two tubs of Ben & Jerry's. The shopkeeper had done a two-pound markup on each tub. Li says"—George cleared his throat—"Can I pay with card, please?" He imitated the corner shop voice. High, but weak and strained. "But when she looks at the till and sees the price, she goes"—

George lowered his voice an octave or two—"What the fuck?!"
The audience laughed. "Everyone started laughing. The cashier.
The people behind us."

"I call it doing a Paris Hilton," Li said.

"She laughed with the rest of the shop."

"And when I got home I cried."

I remembered the ice cream. I remembered how before she
started crying she'd taken off the skirt she was wearing and
thrown it across the room, and how as I held her I couldn't
help but acknowledge that part of me that hoped she'd never
put it back on. That she'd take some trousers from my side of
the wardrobe, bin the hormones and just go back to before.

At one point, George and Li went to bed. Each of them woke
up at different times, one of them asleep while the other spoke
more privately with the audience. The audience laughed with
Li. The reactions of the woman next to me were crude and primal. She swung her arms like the end of a metronome's baton.
My memories and life had become offerings for hungry cis-het
women. Her laughter made me sick. I cycled through versions
of the same thought. Fuck Ming. Fuck Her. Fuck You.

George got up and explained to the audience the intricacies
of rhino-tip surgery, the small differences between a male and
a female nose. I paid even closer attention to him. Again, to his
physicality, this stale bap of a man. He was apart from the reality of Tom, of me. I knew that it would've been intentional,
but I couldn't decide if this was a gift or an insult from Ming,
or if it was both. Maybe George wasn't me because he didn't
have to be. It made me wonder if it could have been anyone, if
I could have been anyone. There was no exposition of his dif-
ficulty, his grief. What about the things worth showing? The
things I went through. The things that made George me. Fuck
Ming. All that ever mattered to her was that she had something
to write about.

I began to feel angry, so angry that I clenched my fists and dug my nails deep into my palms, and I wanted to bring my hands to my face and slap it all out of myself. I was angry at the sunk costs, the care I'd given to a relationship that had erupted into this play, the life that had become cannon fodder for lines in a script. And here I was, paying her for it, letting her make an idiot of me in life and art.

George and Li woke up from their sleep, the climax of the play, and the dim stage light turned to a brighter yellow for the shift from night to day. They had the conversation that Ming and I had had weeks after that night. The one in which she broke up with me, the thing I would never have done to her. They lay in bed just as they had at the start of the play.

"There's more out there for you, George."

"What do you mean?"

"More out there than me. You won't say it, but this isn't what you want."

George took a deep breath.

"That's not true," he said.

Li got out of bed, her back to George and her hands just below her waist, thumbs along the rise of her jagged hips.

"I don't want to be with you anymore," she said. "I need to feel wanted, George. I need to stop feeling like my transition is a burden."

Hapless George got on his knees on the bed, sitting on his feet with his arms slack between his thighs.

"That's why I go to all of that stuff with you, Li." George's voice was wobbly. "The appointments, the admin. So that it's not a burden."

Li pursed her lips and looked out towards the stage lights, facing the audience, her arms folded.

"I'm not saying it's a burden to me, George. It's one to you, and it's one I'm carrying. It makes all these happy things blue. I know that you know, even if you don't want to say it."

George begged. He cried in Li's arms when she knelt in front of him on the bed. Please! I'm not ready to be alone! It'll be fine! Please! I can't, Tom.

The play ended. The curtains shut. I shuffled through the jubilant, clapping audience, my head down, hoping that nobody would see me, that Ming wouldn't emerge from backstage to bow and recognize me in the audience. It was painful; I felt old pain bursting out of fresh pain, identical but distinct, amplificatory. It made me wish the last few years had never happened. A world in which I'd never met Ming, or at least in which Ming wasn't trans.

I walked to the bus stop and sat on the bench. Deep breaths. Six in. Six out. It didn't work. Waves of anger spread from my stomach to my chest and towards my neck. Six in. Six out. I took the keys out of my jacket and squeezed them tight. The points of the blunt teeth felt good, but not enough. I wanted them to cut through skin, or for the keys to snap in half, for something to break, but they were just a set of stupid keys. I put them back in the pocket, wrapped my jacket up into a ball and looked around. Nobody was walking towards me. I dropped my head to my knees and screamed as loud as I could into the bundle of fabric. As I came up, a middle-aged woman appeared from behind the Nicole Scherzinger supplement ad covering the side of the bus stop. A blind spot. I looked away. A few people further down the road had turned back to look. I was too angry to feel embarrassed.

The bus arrived after a couple of minutes. I climbed on and sat at the back of the bottom deck. What was the point of it all? Ming and I had stood over the empty grave of our relationship for more than a year, and it had felt at once like forever and also like much less, like dividing a number by zero. Maybe I'd known that some end was inevitable, but when a person loves another, they don't leave, and when a person is sick, the other doesn't leave, and when Ming stopped being sick and wanted to change in ways that were painful and alien, I stayed because she needed it. And I wasn't ready to be alone, and so the breakup was a betrayal, and *Thin Frames* was a spit in the face of the years I'd spent holding her shaking hand. It was a looting of privacy, pulling me inside out and shaking me for coins.

By the time the bus had crossed Waterloo Bridge, I'd started to cry. As I wept, I thought of how inseparable all those years were from Ming. The lines and borders used to define myself had faded, ink spilling onto the stage. My stories were her stories, but that didn't mean she could use them like that. Everyone on the bus looked away, except an old woman standing by the doors with a shopping trolley, who set sympathetic eyes on me. She got off the bus, and I got off at the stop after. Maybe it wasn't the right thing to feel, but I hated Ming. I really, really hated her.

12
Blonde

It was Sunday, just after lunch. I nodded at the stoic bouncer, a large man who looked, and maybe had always looked, somewhere between thirty-five and sixty. He checked my ID and waved me through the black gazebo outside the walled-up underpass.

I joined a small cluster of fully clothed men waiting to get inside. The queue stood single file. I was glad. It made me look less lonely. When I'd told Mum I was gay, she'd told me that she didn't care. My only worry, Tom, is that you might never meet someone and make a family, but maybe that's a stereotype that I've never been able to shake. I mean, look at my and Dad's gay friends—they all have partners and are perfectly happy; it's funny how those things stick, isn't it? She never mentioned it again, maybe because I'd met Ming, but after Ming and I broke up I started wondering if I was lonely, or if others thought that about me.

The boy in front of me was tall. Bleach had drained the pigment from his short hair, leaving it lifeless and coarse. He turned back to me with a curious stare, his beady eyes deep-set against his high but narrow nose. They lingered for a moment, and so mine escaped downward. He wore big leather boots and a long black coat, the tails of which swiveled back around as I glanced up again to smile at him.

Ming had the same slim and slopy shoulders as him. I wondered what Ming was doing; probably cooking something complicated, squatting in front of the oven, watching a soufflé rise in a ramekin, her spindly fingers twirling and tugging at her fine black hair. *Thin Frames* had opened something in me, a cavity from which anger met obsession. I thought about it a lot, which meant I thought about Ming a lot. And maybe that was the final cruelty upon cruelty, to intensify the not wanting to think about her and thinking about her in tandem. Nobody knew that I'd watched *Thin Frames*. I didn't want to tell anyone. It'd been six months since the breakup. Too much time had passed for me still to be talking about her, and the more I talked, the less I could show that I'd moved on. But I was still in pain. Sometimes it was spread like fire across my chest, but sometimes it was a dull and persistent ache, haunting my body.

I'd muted her on every app, but not before I'd seen she was moving to New York for a master's she'd never mentioned. I hadn't even known she'd applied, and this seemed like another secret between us, even though we hadn't spoken properly since she'd called me about the play. It still made me angry.

There was a gap between the gazebo and the club, with barriers along the edges, protecting us from outside view. Two bears in leather vests guarded the front doors. Men in purple robes smoked on either side of them. I checked my phone. No text from Marco, but one from Rob with a link to a Kode9 set and a timestamp.

Have a listen!

When I got to the front of the line, one of the bears gave

me a garbage bag. The other frisked me. He winked at me, and his rough hands softened as he patted my shoulder into the club foyer.

"That's eighteen pounds please," the doorman said. He was older, but looked like he was fighting it, desperately clinging on to twinkdom, with his bony frame and crop top and paralyzed face. He grinned at me as I tapped my card against the reader, unable to move anything but his mouth.

"Thanks, hun!" He stamped my hand. "Drinks token or herbal Viagra?"

"Herbal Viagra, please."

The week before, Marco had told me that you always got to pick, but that everyone chose the herbal Viagra. The doorman pressed a gelatin capsule into the cup of my hand. He pointed me towards an interlocking room. I pulled the heavy velvet curtain and saw the blonde boy. He peeled his clothes off and stuffed them into his bag. He left his shoes and socks on. I copied him, but slipped my pill and bank card into my shoe, and the condom from my jacket into my sock. The corner of the packet scratched my foot. Before I put my phone in the bag, I checked it again to see if Marco had messaged. He had.

Not going to make it today. Really sorry, should've let you know sooner. You should still go, though. You might like it.

My heart sank a little. Sometimes I wondered if, over the last couple of months, Marco and I had fallen into a pattern. If when Marco said Marco, I said Polo, and if when I said Marco, he said nothing. I told myself this was normal, that it was still early on.

I considered turning back, but I'd come too far; I was already naked. I gave my bag of stuff to the man behind the counter at the opposite end of the foyer. He wrote a number on the top of my hand. The marker's gasoline scent was sharp against my brain.

I moved into the club. Techno blared through the speakers. Purple beams of light swung over the hive of dancing men.

The bodies in the crowd were half hard, fleshy but not veiny. I knelt down to fish the pill out of my shoe. It'd fallen beneath the tall arch of my foot, escaping the force of my weight. I dry-swallowed it, but it clung for life on to the walls of my throat. I swallowed once more, but the pill lodged itself in the dent of my neck. Bleugh! I went to the bar to get a drink.

After moving into an empty space near the front, I noticed that I was next to the blonde boy. He turned towards me and smiled.

"Do you want a drink?" I asked.

"Sure."

His voice was low and hoarse. We waited for the barman's attention. The blonde boy's arm hair courted mine, and soon after his skin pressed hard against my own. He wanted a vodka soda. I ordered two. We shuffled out from the bar and leaned on the arched wall of the tunnel together. I knew that, without a shadow of a doubt, Marco was fucking other people, and that I should probably do the same.

"What do you do?" he asked.

My eardrum rattled from the closeness of his mouth.

"I work in finance. What about you?"

"I'm a model." He gave a shy chuckle and reached out towards me. He pulled the skin of my dick back and forth. I reached back to touch him. He was bigger than me. "You're fit. I'm un-detectable, by the way."

"Do you still use condoms?"

"I'm undetectable."

"I'd prefer to use one, if that's okay."

"Find someone else, then." He let go of me and walked away. I stood by the wall, petrified and sullied with guilt. His bob-bing head disappeared into the mass of bare shoulders.

I was on PrEP, but I'd only ever had unprotected sex with Ming. I'd trusted Ming more than wind in winter. I used con-doms with Marco. He didn't like it, either. He was also on

PrEP but I still wouldn't go without. Sometimes I felt silly, and I wanted to let go, but whenever Marco asked, my whole body hardened. It was the kind of fear sown young, the roots of which stretched too far to know life without it. Marco still slept with me, though. I tried to believe this meant he liked me.

I studied the dance floor. There were rolling men, sober men, fat men, scrawny men, beefy men, sagging men, young men, men like me. Most bounced to the music, but those clustered at the sides chatted with their heads close. It reminded me of the gym saunas from when I was a teenager. Dad had been trying to lose weight and had bought a membership to an expensive gym. He'd got enough guest passes to bring me along once or twice a month. We'd play a short game of squash followed by a trip to the steam room. Dad and I would wear towels, but some of the older men would be naked, unbothered by the carousel of eyes in and out of the room.

I held my dick against my stomach at the dance floor's edge. I began to move in. My shoulders grazed sweaty arms and backs. Hands reached for my bum. One played a short riff on the curve of my cheeks. The surrounding crowd of fat and muscle grew denser. My heart bashed against my ribs. I went back the way I'd come, out from the dance floor and towards the entrance.

The bouncer handed me a purple robe at the door. I slipped it on and went into the smoking area. The blonde boy from the queue stood alone, smoking a cigarette against the brick wall. He lifted his head towards the roof of the gazebo, releasing a trail of smoke into the air. I walked towards him.

"Hey, I'm sorry about that earlier," I said. He turned around, leaning on the corner of his right shoulder. He was staring at me without a word. "It's honestly got nothing to do with you being undetectable. I just don't really do that. With anyone, I mean."

He slumped back onto the wall. His spine collapsed against the brick. He looked away from me.

"It's fine."

"Is it?"

His eyes met mine.

"It's just a bit boring after a while, to be honest. Like, having to explain the same shit again. It's like going back in time." He held out a pack of cigarettes towards me, the sides scrunched and corners beaten. "Do you want one?"

I slid one out of the open pack. We touched tips, and the force of his breath spread the orange glow from his cigarette to mine.

"Thank you," I said.

He observed the group standing next to us. Three swarthy and muscular men with balloon biceps. Their toothpick legs poked out from beneath their robes.

"Is it your first time here?" the blonde boy asked. He puffed smoke out of the corner of his mouth. The wind brought the loose cloud towards my face anyway.

"Yeah, it is. You?"

"I've been coming on and off for a while. I live nearby. It's just kinda here, you know. I don't even hook up with people half the time."

"Really?"

"Yeah. Sometimes I'll just have a drink or two then leave."

"Oh."

He pinched a small bit of robe by my hip, as if examining the quality of the blend. My heart jumped. I couldn't contain my smile.

"I'd be down today, though," he said. "Do you want to go back inside?"

I nodded. He stamped out his cigarette with his shoe. I did the same; I'd barely had two drags. We gave our robes to the bouncer and he led me hand in hand back through the club. We glided through the dance floor. He parted the crowd. I let my dick hang loose, and I noticed only the feeling of his palm squashed against mine.

At the other side of the club there was a long corridor submerged in blue and green light. He walked me to the end of it and drew me into a room. It was pitch-black, an abyss that swallowed everything but the slaps and grunts of grown men fucking. The angle of his hand changed and he pulled me down gently. My hand mapped out a wooden bench, and on it his reclined body.

"You can use a condom," he said, his breath hot on my ear. "There's some in the corner of the room in a basket. There's lube, too."

He pointed to the basket by moving my hand with his. I walked there slowly, bumping shoulders with another man. I pressed on to the film packets and found a sachet of lube, soft like a tiny waterbed. When I got back to the blonde boy, I dug out the condom I'd stuffed into my sock. I realized we hadn't kissed yet. I leaned in, and our lips touched. His tongue plunged into my mouth, wide and slimy. Its size and its warmth and the mixing of saliva comforted me. A hand, neither mine nor his, squeezed my shoulder. I swatted the stranger away and lubed myself up. I began to push into him.

Is this okay? Yes. How does that feel? Good, stop asking, you're good. The blonde boy's hand squeezed my chest with approving undulations. He had cold hands, just like Ming, who'd always had poor circulation. He could probably feel my heart. Hard thumps against his palm, betraying the nerves I tried to hide.

Our moans grew louder and drowned the room's chorus. I came in the condom. I took him into my mouth and stroked him until he finished. I threw the condom onto the floor. He held my hand and I took him out of the room. We kissed again in the corridor and walked into the adjacent bathroom, where I gave my dick and hands a quick rinse and returned to the empty doorway. I watched the blonde boy wash his bum, lit by halogen light.

I just think there's more out there for you, Tom. Maybe this is what Ming meant. There's more out there.

The blonde boy came back out to me, each hand scratching the opposite tricep.

"All clean," he said. "That was fun."

I leaned back against a wall.

"Do you want to leave for a bit?" I asked.

"What do you want to do?"

"We could sit in the park?"

He smiled.

It was warm at Vauxhall Park, but the air still carried a chill from the first breaths of autumn, and cold crept over when the sun hid behind the clouds. We walked along the park's diagonal. The branches of tall trees mingled above us. I heard the pop of prosecco. Children played on slides and swings while their parents watched from the sides. A small terrier off its lead leaped from group to group.

We found a spot untouched by the long shadows of the tree trunks. He sat cross-legged and I lay down next to him. He yanked blades of grass from the ground and placed them in a small pile on my belly. I closed my eyes.

"Do you like modeling?" I asked.

"Yeah, I do. I've been doing it for a while, but work's dried up."

"Why?"

"I don't know. It's hard to say, really. Maybe I don't look as good as I used to."

"Do you want to do anything else?"

"I don't know. I fell into it, and kept doing it because I thought it was exciting, but I think the people who do well from it are the ones who have something else to them, and I don't think there's something else to me, you know? Not in a bad way, but I can't act or sing or design or anything, and I'm not that smart."

He dropped a handful of grass onto my shirt. I opened my eyes, blocking the sun with my hand, squinting at the blonde boy.

"Sometimes I feel like I fell into my job, too," I said. "I was good enough at school, and I wanted to make money. It was the path of least resistance, I guess."

"Ha. It's not the same though, is it. Brains start out wrinkly. Skin doesn't."

"I suppose you're right."

My stomach rumbled. I hadn't eaten lunch.

"You know, you could model," he said.

I blushed and laughed.

"No, I couldn't," I said. "Anyway, you'll find something else. I could always look at your CV, if you'd like."

Fuck. Why did I offer to do that? He raised his eyebrows and then pushed them together, drawing the corner of his mouth into a smirk.

"I'll let you know," he said, sprinkling another handful of grass onto me.

We sat in silence for a few minutes. I watched the pile of grass on my belly grow and grow from the bottom of my eyes. I wondered how long it would take for me to be buried in it. Maybe a day or so.

I told him I was hungry and he said he knew a Vietnamese place round the corner. We got up and I swept the blades of grass off my T-shirt. He did one final sweep as a courtesy, then leaned in to kiss me. We held hands as we walked out of the park.

The restaurant was near empty, with only a few other bums squished against the pink plastic seats inside. We stared at the big laminated menus for only a minute before the waiter asked us what we wanted. We both ordered the rare-beef pho. Our eyes fixed on one another as the waiter took our menus away.

"Are you lonely?" I asked.

"What?" He smiled with his mouth ajar.

"Sorry, weird question. I guess a lot of the time I'm not, but going to that club made me feel quite lonely."

He paused in thought. His eyes moved to the tiles on the wall next to us, and he lifted his fingernail to trace the stems of the flowers printed on them.

"Well, what are you looking for?" he asked, meeting my gaze.

I laughed.

"I've only ever been asked that on apps."

His eyes remained fixed on me. It was clear he wanted an answer. A real one. My jaw was low, as if to speak, but I wasn't sure what to say. It seemed like a question I could get wrong, an opportunity for mismatch between us, grounds for dismissal.

"I'm pretty open-minded," I said.

He shook his head, almost imperceptibly.

"I think that's what everyone who wants a relationship says."

I flushed with scarlet unease. Do I want a relationship? Why is that so hard to admit?

"But can you really have a relationship if you can't say it's what you want?" he continued. "People act like saying what they want is a bad thing. You see it everywhere, right? Like in movies or TV shows, where the woman's like, I wanted flowers for my birthday! And the man's like, you didn't ask for them. And she's like, I shouldn't have to ask! But why shouldn't you have to ask? Why can't we just tell people what we want? Why is everyone in the market for a mind reader?"

"What about the club?" I asked. "It seemed pretty clear what everyone wanted."

"Are you a mind reader now?"

I hung my head towards my forearms, placed neatly on the

table, and laughed. He was right; I had been there, after all. Maybe it was wrong to make assumptions.

"What do you want, then?" I asked.

He thought about it for a moment, turning his head back to the flowered tiles.

"I think I'd like having a boyfriend, to be fair," he said. "But I also see how sex can be safer and simpler. Relationships can feel a bit scary."

A cocktail of nerves and longing poured through me. I leaned back in my chair. "You shouldn't say you're not smart, by the way," I said. "You have a really nice way of putting things."

"You sound a bit patronizing, by the way," he mocked the cadence of my voice. "Even when you're saying nice things."

The blonde boy grinned and grazed the top of my hand with his thumb. My mouth stretched into a flat smile.

Our food arrived. We dived into the noodles and slurped them out of the bowls. The broth was rich and salty and full, and it reminded me of the holidays I'd taken with Ming. I'd always let her order for us when we shared food because, unless left with no other option, my prosaic palate yearned only for the familiar. She'd once made me try boiled snails she had found in the frozen aisle at an Asian supermarket near our flat. Fifty snails. She'd arranged them in a spiral on a large plastic plate, a snail shell made of snail shells. I didn't share this memory with the blonde boy.

"My parents have this book in their house about this artist I love," I said. "He's called Gordon Matta-Clark."

"I know him," he said.

"So you know how he split houses in two," I said, the blonde boy nodding, elbows on the table, leaning forward. "When I was younger, I'd look at the pictures and think that people had just built two halves of a house. But that's kind of how relationships work, right? You're just building, most of the time blindfolded, just trusting that your neighbor's building too. But

I guess there's always that worry you'll take your blindfold off and see an empty plot of land in front of you."

"Hm," he said, resting back into his chair. "That's the most pretentious shit I've ever heard."

He laughed, and I laughed. It was fucking pretentious.

There were things I wanted to ask him, all of them as weird as asking if he was lonely. Have you ever been in love? I'm sure you have. Who was the last person who broke your heart? Bet he was a dick. And then it occurred to me that I only wanted to ask these questions because I wanted him to ask the same of me. It didn't seem an unusual thing to dress vanity up as curiosity, but was it even vanity if it all came back to Ming? I still couldn't square wanting never to speak about Ming again with wanting others to pry it all out of me. I was supposed to be okay. It'd been six months. It would never have worked.

The blonde boy and I took no more than ten minutes to eat our pho, more or less in silence. He must've been starving, too. We got the bill when our bowls were clean. I offered to pay and he let me. After leaving the restaurant, we realized we were heading in opposite directions. I asked to exchange numbers and he picked my phone out of my hand to type it in himself. His name was Ben.

We hugged goodbye and, with an elegant twist of his ankles, he strode away from me and I from him. We both turned back and waved, I with my hand and Ben with his whole arm.

I put my keys in the bowl when I got home. I thought of Ben as I watched a movie. I imagined us doing fun things like going on holiday. Let's get out of London for the winter! Barbados? Okay! And boring things, like picking up a block of feta on the way home. Does it have to be organic? Obviously! After ninety minutes, I sent him a text.

Hey. It was really nice meeting you. Let's do it again, maybe somewhere more private?

He hadn't messaged me an hour later, but Marco had. He wanted to hang out. I ignored it. Ben hadn't responded by the time I went to bed.

I resolved not to check in the morning as I got ready for work, nor on the way in. I waited until I went for lunch. When twelve thirty came, I got my things and walked into the downward elevator. I pulled out my phone as the glass box sank towards the ground. He'd replied at ten thirty in the morning.

Hey. It was nice meeting you too. I'm sorry, but I don't think it's gonna work. I'm sure I'll see you around.

13
Tarpaulin

"Did you fuck anyone?" Marco asked, lying across my chest on my crumpled bedsheet, tracing the nail of his finger over my stomach, his head facing away from me.

"I did, actually. His name was Ben."

Saying his name stung, but I was still glad to relay it all to Marco. His nail stopped. He lifted his head and twisted his neck towards me before setting it back down.

"Which room?"

"The first one. The vanilla one."

"Look at you," he said. "Calling things vanilla."

"You're hilarious."

"No, no, sorry." He pushed his forehead into my side for a moment. "I like it. It's not a bad thing. You have a stable vibe."

Here lies Tom. He had a stable vibe. He might as well have said I was nice. I rolled my eyes.

"Okay," he laughed. "Let me turn this around. You're fun,

but you're not completely unpredictable. I mean, you're younger than I am but have this grown-up job—"

"We're basically the same age."

"A couple of years younger," he said, his nail continuing in smaller loops around my belly button. "But anyway, I admire it. It's nice to be around. Better than photographers."

"What's wrong with photographers?"

"Don't you already know?"

We laughed. A little self-awareness from Marco helped soothe the sting of his fickleness.

"I'm sorry again for bailing, by the way. It would've been fun to see you there." He pushed himself off my stomach and looked me in the eye, his thick brown hair tucked away from his face. "It's nice to see you now, though."

He offered me a half-smile. Marco could be so tender, but the way he moved in and out of my weeks and weekends resowed old fears of withdrawal, so much so that I was cautious even to say nice things back, and would certainly never initiate them.

"It's nice to see you, too," I said.

He pursed his lips for a moment and then got up from the bed. Small muscles radiated from his spine like veins from a petiole. His back was hairless, which always surprised me because of the dark patches that sprouted from most of his chest, a rich and tangling bed of keratin. It was like two sides of a carpet. He pinched his clothes from the floor between his toes and dropped them onto the bed in a loose pile, then turned with his back towards me as he got dressed.

Marco lived in a warehouse to save money but also wore Le Labo. I breathed in through my nose and caught a whiff of him floating up from my bedding. It wasn't until I'd started bringing people home that I'd realized how little time it took for someone's smell to hang around. It always lay dormant until it erupted from a fluffed pillow or agitated fabric. Each waft vanished as quickly as it had come. The smell of a one-night stand would linger for a couple of days, longer than anyone would want it to.

My bed had smelled of Ming when we were together, and before that of Sarah, but there had been a permanence to them that made it make sense, to the point where I had stopped noticing what they smelled like. I shifted further up the pillow and another cloud of Marco floated towards my nostrils. I thought of him bent over me a moment ago, biting my back where it curved into my armpit, pushing himself into me.

"I'm going to cook some food," I said. "Do you want some?"

He smiled at me as he emerged from his T-shirt.

"What are you making?" he asked.

"It's called char kuey teow. It's a Malaysian dish. It's fried flat noodles with prawns and a few sauces, and other shit like bean sprouts and cockles, which are those tiny shellfish, the size of a marble, maybe."

"I know what char kuey teow is," he said, rolling his eyes. "And cockles. We have Malaysian food in Sydney."

For all his wonders, Marco had a funny way of making me feel uninteresting. I stood up and grabbed a bathrobe from the back of my door, then smoothed the duvet hunched over the edge of the bed like a seasick passenger. My room smelled stale. I crawled over my bed towards the window and pulled on the roller blind, then lifted up the creaking sash window. Fresh, cool air flooded in. After a few seconds my room smelled like leaves, laced with the aroma of sizzling chicken from a barbecue in my neighbor's garden two houses over.

"Where'd you learn to make it?" he asked.

"From my ex."

"The trans one?"

"Ming. Yeah."

Ming's name stung. More than Ben's. Bone-deep venom. I backed away from the window. Marco followed me into the open-plan living room and kitchen, and threw himself onto the sofa in the alcove of the bay window. Light shone through the glass and onto his face. He shut his eyes and smiled, and I felt a rush of affection as I watched him. I put some Brian Eno on the speakers, quiet enough so we could still talk, and filled the kettle with water.

"Your flatmate's never here," he said.

"He's a strategy consultant," I said. "His hours are terrible at the moment. They've made him go in today."

"What does that job actually mean, though?"

"Do you really care?" I asked. Marco gestured for me to go on. "So he's on a project where their client wants to buy another company that makes valves for pipelines. He's been working on a model to predict future earnings. I think something went wrong with the figures, so he's gone in to fix them."

"Wow," Marco said. "Valves for pipelines. Very sexy."

"We can't all be photographers, Marco."

"Anyone can take a photo."

I moved towards the white kitchen cabinets and started to take ingredients out of the cupboards.

"What's he like?" Marco asked.

I explained what made Rob special. The way he asked people questions about themselves. The way affection was always so simple for him. His newfound passion for DIY. How he'd send me songs and sets at all hours of the day, with little notes about why I'd like them. I stood looking inside the fridge. There was some water spinach I'd bought from a Chinese supermarket. I found some dried shrimp paste in the cupboard.

"Do you need any help?"

"Nah." I smirked at him. "You just lie there."

"You're so giving," he said.

I felt warm. With my fingers and a cleaver, I peeled and chopped the garlic and ginger. I softened the rice noodles in a bowl of boiling water, rinsed the bean sprouts from the pack and cut off the ends of the water spinach. I reached for the wok above the kitchen cabinet and set it on the gas cooker. Ming had said that the most important ingredient was high heat. The noodles wouldn't come out right until I'd bought the wok, which let me get enough heat at the base to char the noodles properly. I tipped a couple of tablespoons of vegetable oil into the wok.

"How was it for you?" he asked me. "Your boyfriend transitioning."

I was startled. It seemed to come from nowhere, even if I'd mentioned that I'd learned how to make the dish from Ming.

"We tried until it didn't work," I said, not turning away from the hob.

"It must've been weird, though?"

I fought the urge to divulge too much. Hey, Marco, imagine if somebody's vision of happiness was moving away from the version of themself you loved! Pretty weird, yeah. Pretty fucking weird. Also pretty weird to profit from someone's pain and humiliation. So weird. I raised my shoulders towards my neck. The bones clicked, and then dropped back to rest.

"We don't speak anymore," I said. "We're not a part of each other's lives."

The hot oil glistened and raced around the curved sides of the wok as I swirled it. I threw the prawns into the pan. They sizzled, and the wok spat drops of oil onto my arm. I tried my best not to flinch. I gently poked the prawns as the blue proteins in their translucent flesh bloomed pink. I took them out of the pan and threw the eggs in to make a quick omelet. When the scramble solidified, I folded in the bean sprouts and cockles together with the soy sauce.

"Where does she live?" Marco asked.

"New York," I said, nudging the noodles around the pan, careful not to break them. I didn't want to talk about her, but it was a war between reason and impulse, a craving for tailspin. I bit my lip then lifted my teeth. "She writes plays. There was one about our breakup."

"Shit. Sounds messy. Did you see it?"

"No."

The lie made things simpler. Once the noodles were charred, I put some onto two ceramic plates from the drying rack, transferring the remains to a container, just in case Rob was hungry when he got home. I carried them to the table by my bedroom door. The steam from the plates aroused Marco's spine upright. He walked over and we sat down together. I opened the chopsticks like wide jaws and pinched some of the char kuey teow together, then brought it to my mouth. The salty char of the blackened noodles, stained brown from the dark soy sauce, sat on my tongue. I chewed the rough, scorched sections into their glutinous tails.

"This is really good," Marco said. He looked up from his plate, a broken noodle stuck to the corner of his mouth.

I smiled, poking a few strands that had fused into a ball. I chomped on them. Water gushed from the bean sprouts and bounced off the rubbery flesh of the cockles. I looked at Marco, who grinned up at me. The top end of his chopsticks pointed towards his face. He had his elbows on the table.

"What was the play called?" he asked.

"*Thin Frames.*"

"Cool."

Marco finished before me.

"I'll wash up," he said.

He insisted when I said I'd do it. I crossed my legs and leaned back on the chair, my head against the wall, and watched him wash the plates. He went to the bathroom when he was done. I got up from my chair and dried everything, storing the dishes on the floating shelves that Rob had installed.

When Marco came back, he sat down in the groove his body had left on the couch. I fell onto his lap, my neck supported by the curve of his thigh. He drew a finger along my eyebrow, pulling the skin at the top of the arch. I shut my eyes.

"I looked the play up when I was in there," Marco said. "Have you read the reviews?"

My stomach dropped. I stayed silent.

"You were two-dimensional. Apparently you put them to sleep."

"That's not funny."

He continued to caress my eyebrow, but his touch became rougher, his finger imprinting its ridges and canyons onto my forehead.

"This one says you were desperate and weren't believable."

"Fuck off."

He laughed. A tempest stirred beneath my sternum. I waved his hand off my eyebrow like it was a fly. He laughed again. This was the side of Marco that could be mean. I shoved my foot on the brakes.

"Can we please not talk about it?"

"All right, sorry," he said. "I was trying to be funny. I'm sorry."

He stroked my hair again. I breathed in through my nose, and again until my body relaxed. Six in, six out. Marco's thigh felt stiffer. I opened my eyes. He stared at his phone. The white light lit his face, like he was telling a ghost story around a campfire.

He tilted his head down towards me.

"You know, I'd like to take your photograph," he said. "At my studio."

"Really?"

"Yeah, I would," he said. "I've thought about it for a while. You've never modeled before, have you?"

"No."

"You have the face for it."

"Do I?"

I thought of Ben again and felt a little sad.

"You know you do," Marco said. "Let's do it tomorrow."

Nerves pinged in my chest. He tapped my forehead twice

and began to lift his thigh. I pulled my body up as he collected
his things from around the room.

"What do I wear?" I asked.

"It doesn't matter," he smiled.

Marco's warehouse in Seven Sisters had poured-concrete
flooring and high ceilings. Some of the other tenants were
photographers, and so they used one of the rooms as a studio.
There was a beige sheet of tarpaulin held up as a backdrop. It
rolled down onto the floor and faced the large window to the
walled-up outside. I'd never had my photo taken. Not like
this, not by a professional. I thought I might feel uncomfortable, being focused on like that, but I still wanted to do it, to
challenge myself a little, to allow some of Marco's flattery in.

"You'd look good against the beige. Can you get naked?"
he asked, all business.

I clenched my teeth. His eyes took in my unsure posture.

"Trust me." He let out a gentle sigh and softened. "The photographs will look a bit more delicate this way. No direct shots.
I promise."

I took a deep breath, nodded and took off my sweatshirt and
the T-shirt beneath.

"It always starts with a tasteful nude, Marco."

He laughed. I slipped my shoes off and unzipped my trousers, pushing them down with my underwear. It felt like I was
undressing a mannequin, pulling clothes from a plastic shell.

"Cold outside?" he asked.

"Fuck off."

He fiddled with his camera, loading it with film, then twisted
it and clicked without warning me. The light flashed.

"Test shot," he said. "Sit on the sheet."

I sat cross-legged, holding my hands loose in front of my
dick. He snapped a picture and looked back at the knobs on
his camera. Orders flew out of his mouth. Cross your legs but

have your knees high. No, that doesn't look good. Yeah, just
like that. Relax both your arms but have your palms upward. I
said relax, you look stiff. Shake it out of your shoulders. Relax.
Nice. Maybe link your hands under your knees. Cool. Okay,
now look at me. Don't do that with your eyes. Relax a bit. Soft
expression. That doesn't look soft; stop doing that with your
eyebrows. Now can you open your mouth just a tiny bit? Cool.
The orders were strict and almost cold, but it felt good to have
so much of Marco's attention on me, undivided, certain. He
put the film camera down and picked up the DSLR by his foot.

"Do you prefer using film?" I asked.

"Sometimes, but I've noticed a lot of photographers in London like doing this boring, airy, Taylor Swift kinda shit. Flash
is good. It's more intrusive. There's less pretense."

I'd never thought of Marco as aiming for less pretense. I
moved with each order he gave me. My eyes followed the clicking lens. I tried shifting slightly from one picture to the next,
a little twist of the chin or a repositioning of the arm, like I'd
seen models do on television. Please stop moving. I said stop
moving. Cool. Marco looked tall and Herculean in his oversized black T-shirt and slouchy white cords.

"Lie on your front," he said. I lay down on my back. "Is that
your front?"

I rolled over, setting one arm by my side and placing the
other above my head.

"Open your mouth slightly. Slightly. Hold yourself there."

I lay still and stared into the glass at my curved reflection
in the lens, my face transparent, consumed by the envelop-
ing emptiness behind it. Marco pressed the shutter once every
ten seconds or so, and each time my face disappeared into the
clicking black hole. Spit pooled in the cup of my cheek. A drop
rolled into my mouth's corner, hurling itself over the edge. I
focused on the humming of the studio fan and thought about
Ming. I thought about us laughing at a story she told about a

woman she had sold flowers to. I thought of the blonde boy at the restaurant table, slurping his noodles from his bowl. And Marco. All of them conjoined on a paper people chain, then crumpling into each other, grinding into a rolling tumbleweed of skin and bone. It seemed that whatever I did with this body, wherever I took it, my mind carried the past and all its wrongs with it, even as I lay naked on the tarpaulin. It seemed that the harder I tried to ignore Ming, the more she invaded the present, the more I felt her inside me, swimming around in my belly. I wanted her out.

"Beautiful," Marco said. "That's exactly what I wanted. I think we're done."

I sat up, unable to contain a smile. I wiped the side of my mouth. A drop of saliva had stained the tarpaulin.

"I want to get another picture of you. Just plain digitals. Is that all right?"

"What for?"

"They're nice to have. I like holding on to some of models. Put your jeans on but leave your shirt off."

I stood next to a white wall while he took pictures of me on the DSLR. He made me turn to show my profile.

"Do you want to have a look at some of them?" he asked. "I can't show you the ones on film, obviously, but I can show you the other ones."

I stood over his shoulder while he scrolled through the photos. He went through them quickly, but zoomed in on my drooling face when we got to the photos on the tarpaulin.

"You look really striking here," he said.

My cheeks blushed with a loving feeling, but I felt some distance from the face in the photo the longer I stared at it. In the small glass confines of the preview screen, my eyes were vacant, pleading, but aware. A cadaver brought back to life, taking its second first breath, or something living taking its last.

14

Beckett

It's eight a.m., and Alissa is already out of the house for her job at Blackstone. I don't think I could've lived with anyone else. Not because I didn't want to, but because Alissa wouldn't have let me. Oh my fucking god! We're going to New York, baby! NYC! Can you even imagine? Our thirteen-year-old selves would literally die. We're gonna have that Empire State of Mind. I nearly canceled my flights there and then, but now that it's come to it, I quite like living with Alissa. She's my oldest friend. I've always thought the more dense the city, the more atomized it becomes, as if people are so sick of people that they unwillingly cart themselves towards loneliness, and so Alissa feels like an emergency brake. Familiarity is comforting. We are very different people, but there still are moments when it's just like when we were at school together in Malaysia, lying in bed and gagging at a pirated MP4 of *The Human Centipede*.

I stroll into the kitchen-living room and take my jade rollers out of the freezer. I walk to the bathroom and begin rolling under my eyes, across my forehead, over the smile lines I hate, and then along my jawline. The cold massage stimulates blood flow. I stare at myself. My skin is red, but also fetal. I look back at the freezer. Alissa gets mad that I leave the door open. She blames me for the ice that's building inside. The walls are covered in frost, thick and delicate like white fur, but I still don't really see how two minutes can make such a big difference, and so I haven't stopped doing it. I tie my hair up with the scrunchie that I sleep with around my wrist. It's silk. I'm not an animal! I wash my face with some water and put on a bit of moisturizer.

The jade rollers go back in the freezer. I return to my bedroom. There's a small gap between the end of my bed and the wardrobe, so that when the wardrobe doors are open, they graze the edge of the duvet hanging over the mattress. I put on some fishnet tights, a kilt, a Singapore Dragon Boat Festival T-shirt that I cut into a crop, and a lime-green jumper with a knit so tattered and loose that it is functionally useless. Over it I wear a long jacket I bought in Brighton, and some knock-off tabi Mary Janes that still cost two hundred dollars. I look amazing. I stare out of my window, which looks directly into another building and nothing else. Maybe it's Stockholm syndrome, but I can't imagine wanting to be anywhere else.

It's a schlep to get to class on the Upper West Side, but I can't complain because it's still a shorter commute for me than most of my coursemates. I wanted to live in Brooklyn, but Alissa was willing to fork out the extra cash and so now we live in Chinatown. I sit on my bed and go over some of what I wrote last night. Some days I think I'm trans Beckett, and other days I feel like I've come no further than when I was sixteen, writing things centered on words I don't understand. Totalitarianism! Machiavellianism! Verisimilitude!

It's literally miraculous that I got into Columbia, especially with the grades I applied with. People at Columbia have years-long professional repertoires of the boring stuff everyone loves, laden with existential pain but plotless as a queef. Sometimes I think I got in because I'm trans. A trans woman of color. A triple jackpot in the hierarchy of oppression. The all-cis admissions board probably couldn't have cared less that I don't face most of it. I'm privileged to shit.

I pack my bag, lock up and walk down eight flights of stairs and onto the loud street. A fishy pong hits me. The store at the bottom of our building sells dried fish. Large ivory husks hang from a wire, and crisp silver fish are layered in plastic trays. I take a deep sniff of it. It reminds me of the dried cuttlefish snacks I used to eat at home; thin, burnt-orange squares of cuttlefish seasoned with chili and salt and MSG, like tough sheets of nori in negative. I love it. Alissa loves it. Neither of us can ever be bothered to explain why to white people. I head off towards the subway station. The weather is crisp. As I descend the stairs, a man trotting down bumps into me.

"Sorry, dude," he says.

He doesn't look back. I feel a sting in my chest. I walk down the steps, swipe my subway card and walk towards the platform. I look at my feet on the grimy gray tiles, shifting my weight between them. My train arrives. There are no seats. I put my headphones over my ears. I can't stop thinking about it. Was his intention to say something gender-neutral? It's a no, and so I run through all the things Elina told me to do when something like this happens. Don't assume his state of mind. He didn't even see my face. I'm dressed in this loose jumper. I'm already tall and I'm wearing heels. The same could happen to a cis woman, after all. It's not you, it's him. You can look trans and look beautiful. You might pass to some and not to others, and that's okay! The train moves up through Midtown and towards the Upper West Side. Bodies file in and out. I want to take my shoes off, or at least sit down. I want to wear what I want, but I also feel so tall, like my head's above a molehill and someone might play Whack-a-Tranny. The train stops and lots of people get off. I manage to get a seat. I turn up my music to distract myself, and when I arrive at 116th Street I stand up and alight from the train.

It's a short walk to the lecture theater. I'm a couple of minutes late. I sit at the back. Our lecturer is an Asian woman named Linda, who also facilitates a lot of our workshops. It's awful, but whenever I see or meet a creative Asian I always wonder what their parents think. At least she's an academic, even if it's theater. It's a full house. I make notes. I nod enthusiastically. I look off into the distance when Linda says something thought-provoking.

At the end of the lecture I walk back out through the doors to wait for Bunting and Malcolm. Bunting's the only other British person in our playwriting concentration, although her mother's side of the family is American. Her real name is Alice, but she kept the nickname Bunting from boarding school. Nobody else in our course understands how ridiculous this is. She emerges from the door. Her blonde hair grazes the top of her black turtleneck. If my coursemates aren't wearing black turtlenecks, then they're dressed like British evacuees. The vibe of an academic thesp is cross-continental. Malcolm is behind Bunting. He's also wearing a black turtleneck, stark against his red hair, as well as round tortoiseshell glasses with thick frames.

"Me and Malcolm are gonna get some breakfast," Bunting says. "Do you want to join?"

I nod. We walk slowly to somewhere off campus. Sun floods the pavement. The streets here are nice. Nothing smells like fish. I think of how lucky I am to attend a university like this, and then I get a pang of guilt. It's the guilt that hits when I think about it all too deeply. I think of the fees, the remortgaging my dad did, how he probably won't retire until he's wearing nappies again, how I begged for it all like a child, how I built the case that I'd be destitute without it. This is my chance! I know I fucked up the first time, but this is my redemption arc!

It's all a little deranged. I smoke a cigarette as we walk. This is
not doctor-recommended. I'm not supposed to smoke on hormones because of clots or heart attacks or whatever, but I sneak
one in every now and then. It's funny how scared I used to be
about my heart stopping, and how careless I've become once
presented with an actual risk of it.

We find a café with a white front and sit inside by the window. Malcolm and Bunting order breakfast, but I think about
money and order their cheapest green juice with zero fruit.
The cigarette has cut through my hunger. The light hits my
face, and I remember that I'm not wearing SPF. UV rays still
get through glass. I'm aging by the minute.

We talk about the lecture. No, but I don't actually think that's
what she meant by that. Ah! Interesting! This is grown-up chat.
It's learned chat, and sometimes I'm wowed at the thoughts I
have and the way that I participate, and the way that I feel good
after I say something, even if other people think it's dumb. It
makes being in New York feel special.

"Well, with my theater company," Malcolm says, "we often
had to consider this. It boils down to praxis."

Bunting and I nod. Malcolm's from Minnesota. He went to
college in state, in Minneapolis. He doesn't look his age, and so
when he told me he ran his own theater company for five years,
I nearly shat myself. Malcolm's gay, and I think he's drawn to
me and Bunting because we're young and British. My relative
freshness to American theater and Bunting's kindness mean
we're probably the only people in New York who care about
his theater company back home.

A young woman in an apron brings my juice, Bunting's
smoothie and Malcolm's black Americano. We sip and laugh.
The food arrives.

"Are you sure you're not eating?" Bunting asks as she cuts
into her pancakes.

"No, I'm fine. I ate, like, seven hundred bananas for break-fast."

A lie.

"Do you want to try some of mine?" Malcolm asks.

"I'm not hungry. I promise."

I want to be honest and say that I'm trying to save money, but something stops me. I miss my old friends. I miss Cass. We speak as much as we can, but it's hard to overcome long distance. I miss Lisa, too, more than I expected. Rob going nuclear at that dinner made me grow avoidant. Towards the play. Towards Lisa, who oiled its engines. So, when *Thin Frames* was over, I peeled away. I said I was too busy with shifts at the cinema. Then I was too busy getting ready for New York. Then I was in New York. But I miss everyone.

Still, Bunting and Malcolm will have to do. Bunting and Malcolm are shiny and new. I wouldn't have much patience for ultra-posh girls like Bunting in London, but she works for New York, even if I suspect she's only drawn to me for the cultural capital of having a trans friend. We're not too far apart, anyway. Her writing is intimate. Like me, she self-cannibalizes.

"I've been so anxious about our workshop next week," Bunting says. "I haven't been sleeping."

"You'll be fine," I offer. "You've been working so hard."

"That's easy for you to say, Ming."

It's true. People have been kind to me. I could probably wheel out trans retellings until graduation. Trans *Medea. The Trial*, but trans.

"I think I'm just a bit traumatized from last time," she adds.

Bunting wrote a campus play about a woman who agrees to provide good-character evidence for her boyfriend, who's been accused of sexual assault, but over the course of preparing she becomes awake to the untoward behavior he displays in their relationship. I thought it was good. Other people were mean. One person said that it was written to be comfortable and marketable, an insult by the standards of our course, and yet was still boring. I later learned, while consoling a crying Bunting in the bathroom, that she'd been assaulted by a man, and that the play was a means to empathize with the women who supported him.

"It's really, really good," I say. "I honestly think that last time people were just a bit jealous."

Bunting smiles at me, swallows a big mouthful of pancake and turns to Malcolm.

"Can you come to my party this evening, Malcolm?" she asks. "Ming's coming."

"I'm supposed to be having dinner with a friend."

Bunting raises her eyebrows.

"He's straight," he says.

"Bring him," she says.

I take another sip of my green juice. It's suspiciously sweet. They must've added in an apple and some lemon. Maybe two apples. For a second I worry about my blood sugar. Bunting looks at me.

"You are coming, right?" she asks.

"Yeah, of course." I set my glass down. My fingers are wet from the condensation. I wipe them on a napkin. "What can I bring?"

"Some wine. Although you don't even need to, to be honest. I've got a few boxes I'm trying to get rid of." She turns to Malcolm. "And bring your friend."

Back at my apartment, I open my files with my plays-in-progress. I take my computer to my room. I like my room. I'm often more functional in confined spaces. Less space. More control. I crawl back into bed and turn to my plays.

Sometimes New York feels like creative freedom. I can write about whatever I want here, and nobody back home really has to know about it. I've started writing a comedy about two overly therapized friends who speak to one another in clichés, but in doing so reinforce each other's bad behaviors. I don't know if it's inspired by me and Cass, but the distance makes it less of a question. Art comes with responsibility. I know that, I'm not an idiot. But I think that responsibility might go away under the conditions of intimate workshops, where a lot of what we write won't go to production, and if it does, then only to limited audiences. Nobody here knows who I am or my history; conversely, the people I may or may not be writing about don't know that I'm doing it. It's not like Bunting and Malcolm know that Cass exists. She's planning to visit closer to the summer, but even if they met her they wouldn't put two and two together, and who knows if I'm writing about Cass at all. As far as anyone knows, what I produce is born from my mind and my mind only. For the first time in a long time, I am writing without guilt.

After an hour I get bored and switch windows to the second play I'm writing. I'm not going to submit it until much later on. I've been thinking how it's going to be when I'm old and demented. Sometimes I have dreams where I'm still a boy. It makes me wonder if one day I'll forget I've transitioned, look down at my body and scream. It's a scary thought, especially given the state of things. A crumbling NHS. The fact that some Americans wear dog tags telling people not to call an ambulance if they have a seizure because they're so expensive. I write for a little while longer. What if I lose my mind? It's weird to think that one day someone will have to explain to me that I used to be a boy, but that I've become an old lady. I wonder if there'll be anyone there to explain at all.

Bunting lives in a penthouse apartment in an older building on the Upper West Side. The walls are lined with bookshelves of old paperbacks. The living room has glass sliding doors that go onto a balcony. I can see so much of the city. I can see campus. I can see lights and bars and cars. People drink box wine out of expensive-looking wineglasses. Lots of students from our course are here. Some of us are sitting around a table on the balcony. Some people comment on Bunting's apartment. This is insane! She tries to repent for her privilege. It's a co-op that cost pennies when they bought it in the fifties, and her family aren't allowed to rent it out, anyway. She tells us that her grandma's circulation means she can't fly back from the Cotswolds, and that her mum's brother got meningitis when he was eight and died, and because of that she has no cousins. She's also an only child. It would literally be empty if it weren't for her. I wonder when it became so fucking hard just to say thank you.

I stand up and lean on the edge of the balcony. For a moment I imagine myself falling off. An intrusive thought. I still get these. Behaviorally speaking, the OCD's pretty much still gone, but recently, now that things are going my way, I've been thinking about death more. Worrying about death used to mean thinking about the decline and suffering that comes with degenerative disease, or the scary suddenness of a heart attack. I never really thought about the cost dying would entail, the loss of the years I could've lived. The worries were primal. The bog standard I Don't Want To Die coded into my amygdala. But now when I think about death, I think about the things I wouldn't get to do, the things I want to do, the people I want to kiss and fuck but whose faces I've yet to see, the things I've yet to write. It's not so much dying that scares me, but dying young, because in a lot of ways life has only just begun to feel like it's worth living. I'm catching up. I'm only just learning what it means to want to live. Nobody should die young. My mind doesn't go in circles like before, but sometimes I can't help but be careful. I take extra care when I'm crossing the road. I walk slowly down the stairs if I'm in heels. I'm aware that none of this squares with the smoking, but some risks feel less real.

I go back inside. People dance to a playlist comprised of the

Hot 100 and American EDM, played on a Bluetooth speaker that's too quiet. There are two rolled-up rugs against the wall of the living room, one of the few spaces not colonized by books. I'm trying to embrace it. Sometimes I wish the New York I inhabited was a bit cooler, or a bit more queer, but parties like this feel like a second chance. It's still early days, and so I'll dance anyway, because this world is open and possible. And it's a party without the burden of personal history, without people who knew me as a boy and, I suspect, deep down, still see me as one. I laugh. I hold hands with Deandra, another friend from my course. She's a few years older than me. Her long black hair is in two French plaits. I sing along. Some wine spills onto the parquet floors. Carte blanche! Vita nova! Dua Lipa!

There's a bearded man who's shorter than me and is staring as I dance. Each time I look at him, he looks away. I think he's a friend of a friend of a friend. I ignore him. This is cautious eye-fucking if ever I've seen it, but maybe I'm delusional, and so there's not much else for me to do. I won't go up to him to talk. I don't want to embarrass him. I don't want to be embarrassed.

The doorbell rings again. Bunting leaps in from the balcony and opens the door. It's Malcolm and his friend. They take off their jackets. Malcolm's in the same black turtleneck. His friend is tall, with messy dark-brown hair, wearing a plaid shirt over a T-shirt. I'm still surprised Malcolm has straight friends. Malcolm begins to introduce the tall man to people in the crowd. I walk a bit closer. He's excited to see me.

"Ming!" He waves to me, then looks to the tall man. "This is the girl I was telling you about."

Malcolm and I hug, and then I hug his friend.

"I'm Roland."

He's a few inches taller than me, even in my fake tabis. I ask them how dinner was. Where did you go? Oh, I've been there, I literally saw a rat in the bathroom. As we talk, I unzip my thrift-store Hello Kitty bag and reach for my cigarettes and lighter, holding them in separate hands. I zip up the bag.

"Do either of you want one?" I ask.

Malcolm holds up a gentle palm and shakes it, but Roland nods. We make our way to the balcony. I open the pack and give him one, lighting his cigarette before my own. We lean on the balustrade. He's a friend of Malcolm's from college. He tells me that he grew up in the city. Well, Hoboken. He wanted to try something new, and so he went to college in Minneapolis. I tell him that I know Malcolm through our course, although he already knows. I tap the cigarette with my index finger. The ash falls down towards the city.

"I've written a screenplay," he says, elbows on the stone barrier.

"What's it about?"

He laughs.

"The CIA wrongly suspect that a woman is a Russian disinformation psy-op, but she's actually just really poorly informed," he says. "She's like an influencer. So, like, they start following her, but over the course of the script they can't decide if she's really smart or really stupid."

I open my mouth and nod. I'm speechless. It sounds fucking terrible.

"I feel like that could star Melissa McCarthy," I say.

Melissa McCarthy doesn't deserve this. He's flattered by it. He gives me a look. It's three-quarters on with a smirk. It's a look that says, I like you, and then he laughs in the direction of his hands. There's an edge of humility to his unjustified confidence, and I find all of this extremely charming. I don't know why. Patriarchy, I guess! He asks me about my plays and I tell him about *Thin Frames*. When we speak, we lean in close. He asks me if any of them are based on real life and I say no. I'm not sure if he believes me. I realize I've taken him outside before he's had a chance to get a drink.

"Do you need a drink?" I ask.

"Yeah," he says. "That'd be great."

We go inside and head right towards the kitchen, but as we're about to enter, he asks me where the bathroom is. I point in the opposite direction, down the corridor. He leaves me. I move into the kitchen alone. There are black-and-white mosaic tiles all over the floor, and older light-brown cabinets with Italian ceramic knobs. The fridge is new. The ice-maker has five different options. I take the bottle of white that I brought from the fridge. I wonder if I should pour Roland a glass. It's a no. I don't want to be more than friendly. I don't want to embarrass him. I don't want to be embarrassed.

When I get back to the room, he's talking to Deandra. They seem friendly, and so I don't interrupt. I walk back to the balcony and sit on one of the chairs around the low table. I join in on the conversation between Bunting and her friends. Oh my god, no! You didn't! She did! No! Yes! Every once in a while I look back in. They're still talking.

The night rolls on, and I put men out of my mind and enjoy the company. We smoke cigarettes. My throat feels sandpapery. I wet it with box wine even though the alcohol dries it out again. I lean into the feedback loop as time drips on. We're talking plays again, and I'm drunk enough to talk about my own to the crowd. I even tell them about my play about trans people with dementia. Everyone is floored.

"That sounds groundbreaking," Bunting says.

Maybe it is groundbreaking. Maybe I'm groundbreaking. I'm trans Beckett. I'm a literal genius. I look around again. Roland's not there. Maybe he's left without saying goodbye; maybe he's not a hugger. Deandra still is, and at this I feel some relief. Bunting stands up. Let's all go inside! She puts on some reggaeton. Everyone dances. There are about twenty of us here.

Bunting's arm is hooked around the neck of the short man with a beard. He's laughing and nodding. They hug once again.

I wonder if they fancy one another. I'll ask her on Monday. I walk back to the kitchen and open the fridge. I stare at the cold bottle, but this genius feels tired. I close the fridge door and order a cab instead. After hugging everybody goodbye, I stand in the elevator alone. In the taxi I yawn and think about how much it'll cost to get home, but I feel happy and safe. I take out my phone and open the hookup app. I close it immediately. At least if I've opened it, I'll come up on people's home pages for an hour, which means that the messages will pour in.

I get home and take a deep sniff. It doesn't smell as fishy when all the shop fronts are shut. A man at the end of the street shouts at me. Hey, lady! I fumble with my keys and shut the door behind me. I climb up the stairs and open the door. Alissa's out. She's on a date with another banker tonight. She has three types: banker, lawyer, consultant. No accountants.

I go into the bathroom and use a cold cream to dissolve the makeup on my face. The sharp black lines around my eyes rub into smoky clouds, and then into pale streaks. I cleanse and moisturize and end it all with some tretinoin I bought via a pharmacy in India. They didn't take online card payment, and so I had to bank transfer them before they sent the shipment to me. I get under the covers and check the notifications from the apps. There are many. I go through them. Dick pics. Some cash offers. Some saying I'm pretty. One message catches my eye.

You looked beautiful tonight.

I check his profile. It's faceless, but according to his stats he's twenty-nine, toned and tall.

What the fuck?

Sorry. We were at the same party earlier.

Maybe I'm not as delusional as I thought.

You should've said hi.

I did.

It's fucking Roland.

Who are you?

Can't say. Anyway, you're gorgeous. Have a good night.

As my fingers move to interrogate him, his profile disappears. He's blocked me. Some of his shame seeps through the phone. I feel sad for him, and I wonder what my world would look like if men didn't cower from their desires. Maybe not that different, because male desire has rarely done much good for anyone. I scroll through the rest of the notifications. The picket fence of dick pics is at once both offensive and vile, but I feel a thread of gratification that I am loath to admit, even though it shouldn't be a crime to say that it feels good to be desired, especially behind the safety of the internet. I hug my phone, a portal to a sea of dicks.

The front door opens. I listen out for talking, but I don't hear any. It's just Alissa. No boy. I get out of bed and stand by my doorframe. She's fussing around the kitchen in a black cocktail dress.

"How was your date?" I ask.

"I should've been suspicious when he said he was in the financial sector. Too vague. Financial marketing. What the fuck? Worse than an accountant." She opens the fridge and looks back at me. "I'm going to make some tteok-bokki. Do you want some?"

I nod and approach the kitchen counter, sitting on a stool. She takes out some kelp-and-anchovy stock she made last week. She could work twenty-four hours in a day and still find time to buy groceries. She pours it into the pot with gochujang, fish balls, spring onions and rice cakes. I watch it boil, and the hot, spicy scent floats into my nostrils. I feel much more sober, and I want to stay awake for a while longer. The sauce thickens as Alissa stirs, and then she pours it all into two bowls. She gets some mozzarella out of the fridge because she knows I like it. She sprinkles it over my bowl and nudges it towards me.

"Wanna watch a movie?" I ask.

She nods. We sit on our couch. I bring my laptop and place it on the coffee table with the warm bowl in my lap. We watch *Spy*. A movie Melissa McCarthy deserves.

15
Exhibition

Sophia commanded me to take my shirt off. I walked the length of the studio, in front of framed prints of magazine covers, while she filmed me with a camera she held at her chest. Her blonde bob was tucked behind her ears. She looked like she'd play herself in *Zoolander*.

"And again. And again." Her German accent vacillated, sitting in the peak and trough of each swing. I walked over the same five meters, towards the kitchen, and then back towards the window. "Faster. Hunch over, like you are late for the bus, ja?" I picked up my pace. "No, not so quickly. Keep your cool."

I slowed down. I did another length and arrived at the window. I didn't make eye contact with Rob because I knew he'd be trying not to laugh. He was sitting behind Sophia at a wooden table, next to a brunette with a fringe. He initially hadn't come in with me, but when I'd told her I had a friend waiting outside, Sophia had buzzed him up to the agency. I could see her melt a little when a red-cheeked Rob burst through the door, beaming.

"Now stare out the front. Look a little bit more relaxed, like you are being massaged."

I softened my face.

"Look a little bit less relaxed. You are worried you left the oven on."

I tensed my eyebrows.

"Good. Stay there."

The agency was on the second floor. Marco had sent Sophia the pictures he'd taken of me. He'd asked if he could, and I'd said yes. As strange as the whole experience in Marco's studio had felt, part of me thought the prospect of something else, something exciting, overrode it. Part of me also noticed a change in how Marco saw me. I didn't want to lose that.

Sophia owned the agency and, after seeing the photos, she'd emailed to invite me to Cologne. Marco said it was so she could decide whether they wanted to sign me, and if she did, then she would start putting me up for jobs. He'd reassured me that it was reputable, that they only really supplied models to high-end brands and magazines.

I could see a park from the window. Sun drenched the grass and lake in light. A couple in camel coats pushed two small babies in a pram, a complicated assembly of plastic bends and ergonomic levers.

Sophia watched the screen of the camera. Her tense eyebrows formed a canyon right above her sharp nose. I imagined her running, the sweat plunging down like it was on a luge, and flying off the tip to its demise.

"Now look towards me! Can you walk into the center of the room, please?"

She took slow, wide crab steps around me. The camera hovered at an even level. We talked a little more. Tell me about your job! You don't like it? How sad!

I caught Rob's eyes. He rested his chin on his palm. He didn't laugh at me, but his lips were parted with wonder. He nodded and I looked back at Sophia.

"Beautiful," she said. "That's all we need. You can put back on your shirt. Okay, so, the plan is this. I own the agency, but sometimes I work as a casting director. I would like to recommend you to our client for their show. We can see if they like you, and if they do, then I think we can sign you with my agency. Elisa, can you please get the paper?"

The brunette jumped from her seat towards the printer. She picked up a white sheet and handed it to me. It listed the details of a spring show for the autumn/winter collection of a huge brand, the clothes of which nobody I knew could afford. As Sophia spoke about it, I looked over to Rob again, who mouthed the word wow.

"Hopefully the client is interested," Sophia said. "Book the days off work. I have a good feeling!"

Sophia hugged me tight and waved me and Rob out of the door. We carried our bags down the dark staircase, into the old brick courtyard that enclosed the agency, and out onto the street. We'd come straight from the airport. Traffic and trams separated us from the other side of the road; above the steel roofs I could see a glass-fronted office the size of a large town house, next to a block of seventies flats, next to a long period building.

"That's a big designer," Rob said as we stomped along the pavement. "I didn't realize the agency wanted you for something specific."

"It is. And me neither. But I haven't got it yet."

"It was worth the early morning to see."

"What?"

"The pictures. And you. I don't know." He shrugged his shoulders. "It seems exciting, doesn't it? Being flown out to a different country for something like this."

The thuds of my heart warmed my chest against the cold air. We walked towards the city center until we reached the apartment we'd booked. Our host was a man called Viktor. The listing had pitched Cologne and the flat but hedged Viktor against any liabilities. Conveniently located to all of Cologne's hottest restaurants. No noise after ten p.m. Amazing bars nearby. No drinking in flat. Walking distance from hottest clubs. No parties. No party people. Do not water the plants.

We carried our bags to the top floor of an old block. There were period accents. A fresh lick of white paint covered the inside and outside. As Viktor had instructed, the keys were in a locked box outside the front door. Rob led us in. It was a bright studio with a Murphy bed. I walked around it. Everything was plastic. It looked cheaper in person. Plastic furniture. Plastic fruit. Plastic plants. I understood why he didn't want us to water them.

Rob pulled down the bed frame and lay on it facedown. He said something, but the fluffy pillow swallowed his words.

"What did you say?" I asked.

He turned his head to me.

"Would you quit your job? If this got big, I mean."

"Would you quit your job?"

Rob rolled onto his back and stared at the ceiling. I moved towards the small kitchen island by the door and sat on a stool.

"I don't know," Rob said. "I think the point is that not everyone has options like that. Most of us give up on this kind of stuff when we're kids. People have to get real, right?"

I played with a fake lemon in the wooden fruit bowl.

"I think I want a break from work," I said. "It'd be fun to try something different."

"A couple of years and you've done your stint in the City?"

"Sure." I threw a plastic satsuma at Rob. He caught it and put it on the floor next to him. "Change would be good."

"You're due some." Rob let out a sonorous yawn. "This could be your New York, right?"

"I guess."

Is this my New York? Maybe this is moving on and letting go. I cringed. I was embarrassed at my transparency, but protesting would only make it worse.

Rob shut his eyes. His hands linked on his sternum. Ming used to say that Rob looked like an adult baby, because his head looked large on his body and he often had his mouth open. She thought it was adorable. I picked up my phone and played some Susumu Yokota on the apartment's speakers. The airy, reverbed notes filled the room.

"I like this," Rob said.

"Me too," I said. "Are you still feeling unsure about the shroom girl?"

"El? She's doing a PhD on fungal pathogens, Tom. Have some respect." Rob laughed, then sighed. "I was going to see her this weekend, but I canceled to come here." He let out a long breath. "I don't know. She's nice, and hot, and so smart. But I thought we were just having fun, and the way she's speaking to me and stuff has sort of changed. Like, getting annoyed when I don't respond quickly enough. I think we want different things. Maybe I could've been clearer from the start. That would've been better, right?"

"What do you think you want?"

"I don't know." He rubbed his eyes and dragged his hands down the sides of his nose. "You can always tell if someone really, really likes you. Fuck. It's like history just repeats itself, doesn't it? I could always sense it with Cass. And I'm sure if you feel the same it's the best feeling in the world, but when you don't, it's like, shit, what have I done." Rob got up from the bed and squatted in front of his suitcase. My elbows stayed planted as he unzipped it and started unpacking. "Do you remember Lily Dowding? She was that really hot, super-religious girl from our course. She wore those clips in her hair."

"Pious Nigella?"

"Yeah, her." He laughed. "She got married last year, and

she posted an announcement that she's pregnant. It's a picture of her and her husband holding the corner of an ultrasound." Rob shot up, popped his hip and held his passport in front of him between his thumb and index finger as if it were a sonogram picture. "The caption was something like, oops! We did a thing! And I just thought, fuck, that's deranged."

"Not everyone wants kids."

"I think it's everything, though." He took his top off. His body was a few years ahead of mine, doughy in the right places. "When I think about that stuff, I just panic. All the other stuff, too. Like talking about what to eat for dinner or what to watch on telly."

"That's just life. It makes sense to do it with someone else, I guess. Do you think it's because you grew up in a big family?"

"Maybe, but why does the why of it matter?" He looked at a spot on the wall, a fresh T-shirt in his hands, then shook his head. "I know things change for people, but I don't want any of it. I don't think I will." He twisted his body towards me. "And sometimes it makes me worry a bit, because I think there's something wrong with me. But when I look into the future, I see fun. Fuck-off holidays, buying a fuck-off house for my parents—"

"When you're a crypto billionaire?"

"Exactly," he smiled. "But if everyone's moving on and settling down, I also think, what does that mean for me? I'm going to be left behind, aren't I? Just, like, this adult playing kid. I get a bit scared when I think about it all. But I like my friends." He brought up his hands and twisted his long arms around his body. "I like hanging with you. I like sex, too, but I'll always pick weekends like this over dating." He paused. "Maybe after Ming you'll start to feel a bit more like me, right?"

After Ming. Rob pulled the white T-shirt over his head. The clothes he wore had become plainer, still loose but more tailored. I smiled the nonplussed expression off my face by the time his head emerged from the top. He put on an oversized corduroy shirt, leaving it unbuttoned.

I stayed quiet, tracing circles the size of grapes with my finger on the kitchen counter. Did I want all the small, sedate stuff with Ming? Do I want that with Marco? The obvious answer was yes, but it was a question I never asked, maybe because somewhere along the line I'd decided everything would be fine as long as I had the small stuff. Rob sat down at the end of the bed and placed his forearms on his thighs, his palms open in the space between his knees.

"What time is it?" he asked.

"Half past one."

"Should we go to that museum Sophia recommended?"

We got there by foot. The museum's walls were white. Steel railings clipped to panels of glass, fixed to a bed of red terracotta tiles, similar to those at Ming's house in Malaysia. We sat on a bench and stared at a Rothko. One rust rectangle against a royal-green one, both on an indigo-blue background. The room was mostly empty.

"My art teacher in Year Seven used to make a big song and dance about Rothko," Rob said. "He said people burst into tears looking at his paintings. Then the next week he took us to a museum with a big blue one and everyone had these crazy reactions to it, really hamming it up. One girl collapsed in front of it."

My laugh echoed through the gallery chamber, so I attempted to keep my voice low.

"What the fuck?"

"Weird, right? It was fucking mad, and nobody ever talked about it after. I think everyone felt ashamed." Rob smiled. "I do remember feeling super sad, though. It all felt real at the time, like those dancing plagues."

"What does this one make you feel?"

"Fuck all."

The old woman nearby scowled at us. I tapped Rob's leg and we walked towards the entrance to the room. Rob pulled us into a corridor of sculptures to the left. One was by an artist called Hans Arp. It looked like the Henry Moore sculptures I'd seen back home, except it was shiny and gold. It was a long blob, the shape of wax in a lava lamp. I could see my body stretched in the curved reflection of the sculpture. The text said a lot of Arp's work was biomorphic, inspired by the form of the living, the shape of a human body. I squinted my eyes. I could see it.

"I get that," Rob said. "Most skyscrapers in London could be dicks."

"They're also filled with them."

"Including you."

"And you."

We walked towards the museum café on the ground floor. Rob held the door open for me, and we sat down at a table along an exposed built-in cabinet filled with red-wine bottles. A young waitress came over and Rob ordered us beers. They exchanged flirtatious looks. The waitress came back with the opened bottles within a minute. The beer was metallic on my tongue.

"I think I would quit my job," I said. "I'd have to know it was really going to work out, though. I couldn't just take a leap."

"Interesting."

"I'm not being funny, but I don't really know what I like or care about anymore. Do you remember Jason?"

"Are you joking?" he asked, coughing with laughter as he brought his bottle back down to the table.

"Fuck off," I said. "Anyway, Jason really bought into the big picture, right? But I just can't really do it. I feel like a fucking lug nut."

"Lug nut. Sounds like *The Matrix*."

"Yeah," I said. "I guess, but a lug nut in something bad. Like that oil exploration job I was on. It's fucked. Sometimes I just wonder if you can work for bad companies and still be a good person. I don't get how you could."

Rob smiled at me, and it seemed like he buried a small laugh beneath it.

"I think lots of people don't care about the big picture. But some people don't have a choice, right?" he smiled. "Not everyone's as lucky as you, Tom."

I felt embarrassed, and wondered if the me from two years ago would balk at me now, or if I'd always said shit like this and people just let it slide. I had a narrow field of vision. That's how Ming would've described it. Maybe that'd always been my problem, thinking too small.

"And good or bad doesn't boil down to one thing a person does," he added. "You might do some good on some days and some bad on other days. Nobody's asking you to dismantle capitalism with a Bloomberg Terminal."

"Do you care about your job?" I asked. "I know you like it, but I mean, do you really care about it?"

"Yeah, a bit, to be honest. I like it and getting a salary and enjoying life. I don't really need much more." He savored another sip of beer. "Plug me in, baby."

"Do you ever worry about being beholden to an institution?"

"Beholden to an institution? Classic Tom." He laughed at me again and leaned against the wooden frame next to him. His face wandered towards the sun. "But yeah, I guess. You know how my granddad worked for that car manufacturer, right? He gave fifty years of his life to them and they ended up forcing him out because he was too old."

"Yikes," I said.

I looked at my fingernails, imagining an old man rotting away behind factory walls, his lungs blackened and heavy from exhaust fumes, his bones crumbling to soot. It seemed far and away from the world I knew. I wasn't trapped. The world was open. That was why we were here.

"Yeah," he said. "But it's like a story you've heard a thousand times before, right?" He stretched his arms behind him and yawned. "People say they've given their lives to something. They're always fucked over in the end. Part of getting people to work hard is helping them to forget that a company can't love you back. I like the work, but I still see the job for what it is. It's not heroic stuff, but it's not like I'm an arms dealer. And so it's chill."

"I get you."

"But if you don't feel good, like, if something's not right in here"—he tapped his chest—"and you have options, then it's a different story, isn't it?"

I stared out towards the courtyard. There was still some sun. Rob clicked the head of his bottle on the neck of mine. I looked back at him and picked my bottle up.

"I think I hate it," I said. "I always have."

"Then something's got to give."

We sat in silence, staring back out of the windows, until our bottles were empty. Rob asked for the bill and paid for us. We left the museum and walked out near the end of a bridge across the river Rhine. We leaned on the pale-green railings. The sun sat low in the sky.

"What did you mean when you said that thing about Ming earlier?" I asked.

"Which thing?"

"When we were talking about not wanting relationships and family and stuff. You said you thought I might feel the same after Ming."

"Oh." He paused and looked over the bridge, across the river. "Looking back, I guess you were in a relationship that wouldn't have worked, right? And then that fucking play. Sometimes I still think you feel shit about it all, don't you? Even if you don't say anything. It's true, right?" He shifted the weight between his elbows. "I thought you'd eventually come to me. I don't know, maybe I'm just projecting. But you've been a bit sad, haven't you?"

Rob faced me; his back was towards the river. I looked away, shifting my eyes to the gray-and-terracotta exterior of the museum.

"And listen," he said, "I think Ming was fucking shit for that play, you know I think that, but I also don't think you're moving forward, or taking enough away from it, stuff that you could've done differently, too. You could've said no, right?"

I didn't respond.

"Now that you're seeing Marco, it's worth meditating on Ming a bit, I think."

"I don't want to fucking meditate on it, Rob." I pursed my lips, unsure of what I should or could confess. "Sometimes it's all I think about, even when I don't want to. She just makes me so angry."

"She makes me angry, too, but I know that I'm going to have to let it go at some point. We might not go back to how it was before, but it's also not going to be bad forever, yeah?"

He released an agitated breath. It seemed semi-performative. Rob twisted his body, the railing pushing against his ribs. I set my feet further back, deepening the angle of my lean. It felt like Rob wasn't on my side. I knew he wasn't on Ming's, but there seemed to be a shift in blame, some for Ming that was now trickling onto me. Rob put his arm across my back.

I felt his eyes examining my face, and so I focused on the faded balustrade, dusty and dirty and chipped.

"You know, I got chatting to Marco a few nights ago. He came out into the living room while you were asleep. I could tell that he really likes you."

A smile crept across my lips as I imagined Rob and Marco whispering about me in the dim light of the living room. We pushed away from the railings and walked off the bridge in the direction of our flat. The sun had nearly set, but the clouds broke once again, and the last of it bled onto the concrete pavilion at the end of the bridge.

"I don't think I've ever asked you this," I said, "but what would you have done?"

"Broken up." He paused. "And probably supported her through it if she needed it."

"Easier said than done."

We both stopped at a traffic light, waiting to cross. He looked at me.

"You'd already been with Sarah," he said. "You knew you didn't fancy girls, and even if Ming—I don't know, physically—sat somewhere in between, it would've been further from what you wanted."

"Why didn't you say anything, if that's how you felt?"

The pedestrian signal went green. We began to walk.

"You said it was the right thing to do," he said. "I also don't think I understood it as much as I do now. That's just time, right?"

"Yeah, but I knew I loved Ming. I guess I wanted to test the limits."

"They'd already been crossed, hadn't they? Isn't that why you nearly fucked Jason?"

My jaw dropped. He kept his gaze on me as we paced on, and I realized he wanted an answer. Any words I had fell out of the wound he'd opened. I wondered how much he'd thought about this, how much else he'd chosen to hold back.

"I think there were a lot of reasons for that," I said.

Rob hummed, raising his eyebrows. The sun had retreated by the time we reached the flat. We walked up the stairs in silence.

"I feel like you're blaming me for it all," I said, feeling pathetic as my voice echoed up the stairwell. I took a deep breath. "You're being hard on me. It's not really like you."

"I'm sorry." He turned back to me at the landing, a few steps ahead of me, looking down. "But it's not about blame, is it? You can make decisions and not be to blame."

I caught up to him. He put his arm around me and kissed my head. I thought about how Mum liked to say something similar. It's important to remember, Tom, that accepting responsibility doesn't mean accepting blame, and that you can take charge of your own life without it being an admission of guilt or fault. My decisions were my own. There was nobody else to claim them. I'd chosen to stay together with Ming. It was my choice not to break up. I'd said yes to *Thin Frames*. All the cursing and bitching and the hate inside my head came easiest, but it was all just pirouettes on the same big toe, moving fast but going nowhere. Maybe I have to stop hating Ming if I want to stop thinking about her, and maybe part of that means taking blame out of the picture altogether. It was so basic, so fucking obvious, and yet so impossibly hard.

Back inside, Rob took a shower, and I lay down on the Murphy bed and fell asleep right away. My dream was a version of the day we'd just had. I was back in the agency. Sophia told me I'd got the job. I called Judith on the spot. What the fuck do you want? To quit! And then I woke up with Rob next to me on his phone, his hair damp, smelling of oranges. He put the back of his hand on my forehead, as if I'd gone for a fever nap, and said we should go for dinner. There was a text from Viktor.

Saw you got in okay. Enjoy your evening, boys.

Creep. I went to the bathroom and washed my face. The floor was wet and soaked into my socks. I peeled them off, removed my other clothes and showered, inspecting the showerhead for a hidden camera just in case. I used Rob's deodorant and cologne and started to brush my teeth, staring at myself in the mirror as white built up at the corners of my mouth. Beau-

tiful. I thought of the word, flying from Sophia's lips towards
me. It was something I'd say to Sarah, and to Ming. I'd never
thought of myself as being beautiful. I felt gawky and uncomfortable. Sometimes I felt handsome, but handsome was different. And when I thought of Rob's face as he sat behind Sophia,
I thought that maybe he saw it, too. I spat, wiped my mouth and
walked back into the room in a towel. Rob sat on the kitchen
stool facing the bed.

"Do you ever match with trans women on apps?" I asked,
unzipping my bag to take some clothes out.

"Yeah, I have actually," he said, a bit taken aback by the question. "There's been a couple on this new app I'm on. I haven't
met up with any, though."

"Why not?" I asked.

He cocked his head towards the far corner of the room,
mouth open.

"I don't really know what I can ask. I mean, about surgeries
and stuff. It feels private, and like I can't address it, but what's
down there also feels relevant, right? I'm not sure how I'd feel—
I don't know—I'd have to live it."

I put on a gray sweatshirt and some fitted jeans, then hung
up the towel.

"Do you think we have to wait and see, or actually test
things out?"

"Hard to say. We're all in a rush and short on time, right?
Nobody wants to invest in something that might be doomed
from the outset." He shrugged his shoulders. "And I think the
fear of not knowing what you are draws the lines thicker for
some people, right?"

"Or it blurs them when you're scared of losing someone."

"Yeah, fuck," he said. "But you can't tell someone their lines
are drawn too thick, can you? People have to come to it themselves."

I tried to close my bag, struggling to get the zip over a bump in the teeth.

"Yeah," I said. "You're probably right."

As I stood up, I noticed Rob was watching me. I let my hands rest at my hips.

"I'm sorry again for earlier," he said. "Being hard on you, I mean."

"I probably could've used it sooner, to be honest."

"Hindsight, right?"

Rob gave me a sympathetic smile. I sat down on the bed, my forearms over my knees.

"I watched *Thin Frames*, you know. One night after work."

Rob looked surprised. I could see worry lines deepening across his forehead.

"I'm sorry," I said.

He shook his head.

"You don't have anything to apologize for," he said. "Why didn't you tell me?"

I looked towards my suitcase.

"It opened all of this stuff up, but the emotions felt delayed, like I'd missed the window or something. I just wanted to move on and get over it."

"Fuck, there's no window for this shit. I don't think that's how it all works, is it?" The stool squeaked as he got up and moved next to me. I shifted my bum further along the bed to make room for him. He put an arm around my back. "You can talk about this stuff with me. You know that."

I squeezed my eyes shut. My back began to shake. Rob tightened his grip on me.

"Was it really shit?" he asked.

"It was really, really shit," I said. "I looked like a fucking mug."

He placed his other arm on my lap, his hand holding the inside of my elbow. I rested my head on his shoulder.

★ ★ ★

Later, we ate dinner at a Lebanese restaurant near the flat, then went on to a bar. Rob knew someone who had a number for pills, so we picked up and dropped at a club that played discordant, droning techno. We danced and smoked with strangers and danced some more.

Rob and I stayed close. He was gushy when he was high. He said it was because he always rushed like it was his first time. He told me how much he loved me. I said the same to him. We walked home at five. We swallowed some Valium and plunged into sleep.

I woke up at ten, groggy. My chest felt hollow, the same way it did whenever I was coming down, but dulled by the lead glow of the diazepam. I got up to get some water, and took two paracetamol that I'd kept in my bag, glugging them down with a second glass. I sat by the kitchen counter and rubbed my eyes, and then I watched Rob sleep on his back. His rib cage rose and fell. His body jerked for a moment, then he sighed, and then let out a half-laugh. His breathing returned to pace. I'd taken most of the blanket in my sleep, and now it only covered one of his shins. One of his hands pinched its edge.

Our Cologne apartment was chilly, and I turned the central heating up by a degree. I walked over to Rob and covered him with the blanket before crawling into my side of the bed. He turned onto his side with his back to me. I stared at the short hairs on his neck as my heavy eyelids shut.

16

Sifu

Cindy should be coming out of the JFK arrivals gate any minute now. I'm trying to look excited, but I'm very anxious, and so I'm smiling like I've learned how to from a manual. Cindy and I are not a unit. Hanging out as a pair isn't a thing that we do. Dad is a surprisingly useful buffer. I feel some form of kinship with her: she's devout with sunscreen, her death row meal would be Spam, a fried egg and white rice, and she frequently sends me blurry pictures of clothes she thinks I'd like. I appreciate all these things, but the prospect of an entire weekend with her is still daunting to shit.

She rang me one evening. The call fell out of her basic taxonomy: butt-dials, asking me where something in the house is despite my not having been home for two years, and urgent warnings. Tornado in Florida. Be careful! Young man punched old lady over TV at Black Friday sale. Don't go shopping!

"Sharon has a fistula and needs me to take care of her after her operation," she said. "I'll stop by New York on the way home. Only for a weekend."

Sharon is Cindy's sister who lives in California. Her husband is a geologist for Big Oil. I've only met her once, at the wedding. She spent most of it screaming at her sons. You want me to send you to live with Ah Ma, is it? She told me that my nostril shape meant I'd be prone to losing money, and that I needed to be careful. She wasn't wrong.

"You could stay at mine?" I asked.

"No need, lah, I can stay in a hotel."

It was a trap if ever I saw one. Cindy is my family. She, but mostly my dad, would never forgive me if I let her waste money on a hotel. There was no other option.

"No," I said. "Please stay with me. Alissa and I would love to have you."

"Okay!" she said. "I'll bring curry paste for you."

I'm still smiling weirdly by the time Cindy emerges from arrivals. She looks like she's in witness protection. Big sunglasses. Hair in tight bun. Enormous black coat. She wheels her suitcase, waving maniacally, jogging so slowly towards me that she moves no faster than walking, but at least gives the impression of enthusiasm. She hugs me.

"How's the fistula?" I ask.

"Aiyah," she says. "I brought her red dates. Bird's nest also, to make soup. Can you believe they confiscated my bird's nest at customs? They said it can bring in disease. These mat sallehs so bodoh. What disease? Luckily I hid the red dates in the secret compartment in my suitcase."

"Can't you buy all that stuff here?"

I take the suitcase from her. She looks grateful.

"Too expensive," she says. "Also, Americans add so many chemicals to food. I don't trust them." She leans in. "And they dare call us third world!"

We take a cab from the airport to my apartment in Manhattan, even though it'll be slower than the train. Cindy's paying. We learn that our taxi driver is Vietnamese. Duy is a boyish-looking man with thick black hair and tanned skin. He speaks in a hybrid accent, part Vietnamese and part American. Cindy asks him personal and invasive questions, each of which makes me flush with embarrassment. Your family's been here for how many generations? Do taxi drivers make good money? Do you have children? What do they do? Is your wife a good cook? I keep looking at her with wide eyes, trying to signal her to stop. She ignores me.

"You're being so kaypoh," I whisper.

"What?" She clicks her tongue against the roof of her mouth. "It's just conversation."

I look out of the window. Duy doesn't seem to mind any of it, anyway. When Cindy asks how old he is, and he says he's fifty, she gasps. Good genes!

Cindy leans back in her seat.

"Can you believe?" she asks. "Not one of my nephews came back to visit their mother. Haiya, that's the problem with ABCs—they forget their values." She turns her attention to Duy. "This younger generation don't give us the same respect we gave to our elders."

Duy nods. I wonder what exposure to American Born Chinese Cindy has outside of her nephews, other than the children on *Fresh Off the Boat.*

Duy nods with a polite smile, but stamps his foot on the accelerator.

When we arrive, Cindy shrieks at the cold. This week has been chilly, even for New York. A little bit of snow, but crisp and sunny. Clear skies. I find weeks like this more manageable than in the UK, where the wind and wet and gray vacuum up any shred of hope and joy.

I haul Cindy's wheelie suitcase up to my floor. In the apartment, Cindy calls out Alissa's name while she takes off her shoes.

I love the way she says it. Ah-Lee-Sah! Alissa comes out of her room in expensive jeans and a white cashmere roll-neck.

"Auntie Cindy!" she shouts.

They run up and hug each other.

"How is your sister?" Alissa asks, rubbing Cindy's back. "And your nephews."

Alissa's always been good with parents.

"Recovering! Otherwise same old." They pull apart. Cindy gasps.

"Your face is so thin. You're working too hard."

Alissa smiles. Cindy didn't mean it as a compliment.

Alissa has agreed to accept me into her bed for the next two nights. Sharing a bed with Cindy would feel a little weird. We have an airbed, but I got a stiff neck the last time I slept on one. I hardly wrote for a couple of days. The world doesn't deserve that! Cindy also snores. It's hard to believe that noise comes out of such a small woman.

I wheel Cindy's suitcase towards my room.

"How was your flight?" Alissa asks.

"I woke up at three a.m. for the plane."

"Are you tired?"

"Nope!" she says proudly. "I slept the whole way."

Cindy starts looking around the apartment with an expressionless face. She strolls around our kitchen and living room. Alissa and I follow her.

"No washing machine?" she asks.

"No," I say.

"Hm."

"But nobody in New York has one," I add. "Even famous people. I once saw Chloë Sevigny in our laundromat."

"She lives in Tribeca, Ming," Alissa says.

"It was definitely her."

Cindy ignores us and walks into my room.

"Your wardrobe looks nice," she says.

"Thanks," I say. "We found it on the sidewalk."

Alissa elbows me. Cindy looks at me like I stole it from an orphanage.

Cindy moves through the rest of the apartment, releasing an occasional short hum or nod. I can tell she's disturbed by the reality of our home. The nice things that we, but mainly Alissa, bought for the apartment haven't plastered the cracks, like the standing clothes rails that Alissa uses in lieu of an actual wardrobe, or our bathroom, which can fit a maximum of two people if one person's on the toilet and the other's in the bathtub. I know that Cindy is concealing terror. The apartment's activated her fight-or-flight. She will report to my dad that Alissa and I are living in cramped squalor. I try to think of things I can say to make it better. We're two weeks cockroach-free. Our radiators no longer leak. The neighborhood could definitely be more dangerous! All of it would make it worse.

We allow Cindy some time to unpack in my bedroom. I cleared some of the wardrobe for her, stuffing the drawers beneath to their brim with satin and mesh.

Cindy surprised me last week when she said she'd bought us tickets to an off-Broadway production of *Little Shop of Horrors*. I've had no contact with the musical since I was twelve and played one of Audrey II's tentacles in my school's production. Cindy wasn't there—it was before my mother died—but there's a picture of me painted green on one of the living-room sideboards back home. Our showing's at eight p.m., and I've made a reservation at a Korean barbecue restaurant twenty minutes from the theater for an early dinner. Cindy emerges from my bedroom at five wearing a full face of makeup. Red lips. False eyelashes. Hair curled at the ends. Her heels are metallic. This is High Drag.

"Time to makan!" she says.

Alissa, Cindy and I get the N line, sitting in a row of three across from a homeless man sleeping along the opposite row.

"So sad," Cindy says in a half-whisper.

I feel a prickle at the back of my neck. I want to tell her to stop staring.

"You shouldn't—"

"Nobody wants to smell like that," she continues. "Nobody should have to smell like that. You don't see this kind of thing in Malaysia. In Malaysia it's easier to be poor. In America, how to survive?"

Alissa nods. I feel like a dick. Sometimes I'm just a bit on edge.

At the restaurant, the hostess leads us to a small wooden booth. Alissa and Cindy sit across from me. Cindy places her hand on Alissa's arm.

"You choose everything, okay?" Cindy says.

Alissa leans into Cindy. The tops of their heads touch. I struggle to be like this with Cindy, so casual and warm. The reasons are clear to me; the same things I blame for just about everything. My mother. And being trans, because since transitioning I've become overly worried about other women thinking I'm a perv. But it'd be nice to share in those small gestures of intimacy, to feel a little closer to Cindy. When the waitress comes, Alissa orders beef, tongue, brisket and pork ribs. Cindy asks Alissa to add mandu, spicy octopus and kimchijeon, which Alissa probably would've ordered anyway. Alissa mans the grill, and we dip meat in oil and salt and wrap it into ssam parcels. Cindy piles the sides onto our plates. Eat, lah! Finish. Don't waste.

"Alissa," Cindy says, "are you dating?"

"I'm trying to, but it's hard to date here," she says. "It feels very transactional. I'm also just busy, with work and everything."

"You should make time. You're looking so pretty." Cindy shovels more octopus onto Alissa's plate. "You too, Ming. You make time to date, okay?"

"I'm not interested in dating at the moment," I say, and by this, I mean I invest only in transactional encounters with minimal returns. I'm part of the problem Alissa has described. "And I'm enjoying writing and things. I'm putting my energy towards that."

Cindy smiles.

"Okay, that is fine, too. Study hard." She turns to Alissa. "I keep telling people my stepdaughter is acting in the Ivy Leagues."

I make eye contact with Alissa. There's a wide grin on her face, disguising her urge to laugh as shared enthusiasm.

"I'm not actually acting," I say. "It's all playwriting."

"Oh, I know it's writing. I just thought you're looking more and more like an actress." Cindy pauses. I smile. "Any new plays?"

"I've finished a play about a trans woman in a care home with dementia," I say. "She's forgotten she's transitioned, and when she looks down at her clothes, she doesn't know why she's wearing them, and why all her parts are different. We're going to take it to production, which is exciting."

"Ah," Cindy says.

"People in her class love it." Alissa nudges Cindy. "Brain disease. Trans people. Literally, what more could you want?"

I smirk at Alissa.

"So she doesn't want to be trans anymore?" Cindy asks.

"She does," I say. "But imagine you have all these private desires, and suddenly they appear in the real world without you saying anything. Wouldn't that be terrifying?"

"Hah," she says. "It sounds like a dream until it happens."

"A dream?"

"Wanting things and getting them, lah. Without having to say anything."

I take another bite. I'm unsure if Cindy has missed the point, or understands it beyond my comprehension.

We clean our plates. I feel up to my eyes in mandu, and regret wearing the jeans with the tight waist. The button feels close to popping. It could kill an innocent bystander. We ask for the bill and Alissa refuses to let Cindy pay, until Cindy enforces a mock sternness that allows Alissa to back down. I feel a little small, not really having my own money, not even thinking to offer. Cindy pays in cash.

We say goodbye to Alissa and walk to Westside Theatre, a tall, church-like building with a brick facade. The wind is gentle, and even Cindy isn't complaining about the cold. At the theater bar, I order us two large glasses of red wine. I limply hold out my card, but she insists on paying. We settle into our seats near the front. She tells me that she's been listening to the soundtrack on repeat since buying the tickets in Malaysia.

From the moment the curtains open, Cindy has an incredible time. When "Skid Row" plays, she sings along every time the ensemble sings the word downtown. A blonde woman in the seat in front of us keeps looking back at Cindy with disdain. Cindy seems or pretends not to notice, but I keep scowling back at the woman until she turns around. Maybe it's the wine, but I'm feeling more tender towards Cindy. I don't like people being rude to her. Cindy buys us another two glasses during the intermission, and by the second act I'm a little buzzed. During the reprise of "Somewhere That's Green," Cindy holds her hand over her heart, swaying in her seat. She's mouthing the lyrics, and even though she's silent I can tell she's doing it with questionable accuracy. It's remarkably sweet, and I'm moved by the thought of her being so excited to see the musical, to see me. Cindy has tears in her eyes. I cry a little, too. At this play. At Cindy's tears. It's so nice to feel something. It's refreshing not to have to think, just to watch something onstage and enjoy it for what it is. Not everything has to make you think. I recognize suddenly how much I needed an evening like this, and then a small wave of homesickness creeps across my chest. For Malaysia. For London.

★ ★ ★

Cindy and I spend Sunday walking around Manhattan. I sense that Cindy and Brooklyn can remain unacquainted. She leaves tomorrow, which I feel surprisingly sad about. A weekend's not long enough.

We walk into a pizza place with good reviews. It still serves big slices on paper plates. Cindy and I share a slice. She didn't like the idea of pizza for breakfast, but I wasn't sure how else to fit it into our day. She dabs the surface of the slice with a napkin, for which I am grateful.

"So much oil," she says. "Can die."

After breakfast we walk a little more, stopping by shops. I watch her try on clothes. She picks out dresses for me to try. I keep saying no. We find a consignment store, and I give in when she pulls out a vintage Alexander McQueen gown. It's a pale-pink taffeta with a sweetheart neckline. I would literally never wear this. Where would I wear this? Cindy zips me into it. I look at my reflection. I look absurd, but also very pretty. Cindy claps. The shop assistant beams with rehearsed awe.

"See," Cindy says, holding up her phone to take a picture. "Like an actress."

I don't let her buy me the dress. It's too expensive, even if it's a good price. She sends the picture to my dad. She shows me his response.

Beautiful.

I try to think if he's ever called me beautiful. It feels like the first time. I know that beauty isn't supposed to mean all that much, but sometimes it means a lot.

We eat a dim sum lunch in a shabby restaurant. It's filled with Chinese people, which means that we trust it. Steaming plates and baskets collect on our small table. Slippery, glistening sheets of char siu-stuffed cheong fun, in a shallow bath of soy sauce. Square pucks of lo bak go, the shredded turnip caramelized on its surface. A few har gow, because it feels obligatory. A leaf-bound parcel of lo mai gai, which Cindy teases apart with her chopsticks. Some kai lan with thick wedges of garlic. For digestion!

Cindy insists that she wants to see some museums, so we walk lunch off on our way to MoMA. She doesn't trust the coat check, and so she wears her puffy, fur-collared black jacket, cinched at the waist, across the entire museum. She yelps and gags when she sees a Louise Bourgeois spider sculpture. Its great steel legs stretch across all four corners of the room, and Cindy hides behind me as if it'd move to attack her. I take her to the Whitney afterwards, which she prefers because of the expansive views from the glass-fronted terraces on the upper floors. She speeds through all the rooms, reading none of the explanatory plaques.

Racking my brains for other touristy shit to do, I suggest getting dessert at Levain. I've never been. Before I moved to New York, people always brought up the food. You're going to eat so much! Tons. So lucky! Maybe it's my neuroses, but I kept sensing they were hoping I'd gain weight. Levain is a place I've avoided for that reason. There are nearly six hundred calories in each cookie. Ten veggie sausages. Eleven Oreos! But Cindy's here, and she'd like them. I can let go. We walk over. There's a small queue outside the shop.

"The cookies here are supposed to be really good," I say.

"Let's just share one," she says. "I'll only have a tiny bit of yours."

Although I'd planned to share, I'm weakened by the saccharine scent of the bakery. Also, Cindy never stops at a mouthful.

"I'll buy two," I say.

"No need."

I decide to pretend.

"I'm hungry," I say. "I want two for myself."

At the front of the line I order two cookies and pay for them.

We get them in small white bags. I take a bite of one outside, and hold it out for Cindy so she can have a nibble.

"Too sweet," she says, chewing. She leans in towards the bag. "One more bite."

I hand her the bag with the cookie and start eating the other one.

"How long to walk back home?" she asks.

"It's a twenty-minute walk," I say.

"Aiyah."

I realize then that being on our feet all day, exacerbated by poor navigation and transportation planning, has left Cindy exhausted. She isn't used to walking this much.

"I'm sorry for all the walking," I say. "We can get a cab."

"No," she says, lifting her knees up high for a few steps. "It's good for circulation."

At home she takes a long nap in my bedroom. When I check on her, she's lying down with her arms flat at her sides, sunglasses on. I stay at the doorframe, watching her for a little while. There is something about her sleeping position that is aspirational and glamorous. Anna Wintour probably sleeps like this.

We sit in the famous, modern East Village ramen bar that I had to reserve weeks in advance, and even that was a stroke of luck. The owner's muscled his way onto every inch of culinary TV for the last five years. I contemplated a non-Asian meal, but Asian food in New York is excellent, and Cindy feels faint if she goes too long without noodles or white rice.

Cindy leaves tomorrow morning. I wish I could go with her. It's been two years since I've been home, which feels like a very long time, but I don't feel safe. I didn't expect Cindy's visit to kindle this much homesickness. Telling her this will make her sad, and so I don't.

She bites into one of the pork belly bao we ordered. Her

chomps are big and rhythmic. I pick up a piece of smashed cucumber with my chopsticks.

"Who plans to visit next?" she asks.

"Cass is coming," I say. "A bit later in the year. She would've come earlier, but she has a new job assisting this Labour MP who's high up in the Shadow Cabinet. She writes a lot of her speeches."

"Wow!" she says, raising her eyebrows, a little bit of bun in her cheek. "Could you do speechwriting?"

There was a time I'd get defensive about questions like this. I'd probably still get defensive if my dad asked the same. Dad! Believe in my art.

"Yeah," I say. "Maybe."

"What about your other friends?" she asks, taking another bite. "Lesley?"

"Lisa," I say. Lisa and I haven't spoken in a while. Just a couple of superficial messages since I left London. It's hard to explain the growing chasm between my New York life and London life to Cindy. "I think I'm just enjoying a fresh start and meeting new people, you know. I have good friends here. Like Bunting."

"Okay," she says, dabbing her face with her napkin. "It's good you have Bunny, but you can only fresh start so many times. Good to remember."

I swallow another piece of cucumber. It seems obvious that I can't keep swapping out old people for new ones. There aren't enough visas in the world. As I pick up the pork belly bao, Cindy's words sink in, reminding me that I may not be in New York forever, that in the quest to find my people I may be abandoning some of them. No. These all feel like issues for another time. I'm enjoying new opportunities. I'm taking the space I need. I really need the space.

Our noodles arrive. We dive in. Cindy moans, taking her first slurp of the thick broth and perfectly tough noodles.

"So good," she says.

We eat in silence for a couple of minutes.

"Do you speak to Tom?" she asks.

"No," I say, slowly. "Why would I?"

"I don't know. Just asking, lah," she says. "I don't speak to any of my ex-boyfriends. One messaged me the other day to ask how I am."

"What did you say?"

"Sorry, baby!" She picks up her phone on the table, showing me her screensaver, a tightly cropped photo of her and my dad. He's looking old, but happy. "Too late!"

I laugh, then slurp a little more.

"You can do what you want," she says, setting her chopsticks down for a moment. "You are very blessed. Enjoy it."

"I know," I say, drawing up a row of yellowed noodles into my mouth, chewing, then speaking with my mouth a quarter full. "I mean, I do. All of this feels so lucky." I pause for a moment, hesitating. But maybe if I opened up a bit, then I wouldn't feel so bad. I might not ache for home so much. "There are times when I feel like I've signed a Faustian pact or something, like a deal with the devil."

"Aiyah," she says. "What devil? Such nonsense."

"I mean it," I say. "I just worry there's a price to pay for all of this, like something's going to come back to bite me."

Cindy waves her hand.

"Trust me," she says. "I never worry about you."

"Why?" I ask, dabbing my mouth with my napkin.

"Because of the sifu."

"What sifu?"

"The sifu at the Temple of the Goddess of Mercy," she says. "Sort of like a nun or master, lah. We gave her your personal information."

"You gave my personal information to a nun?" I ask.

I am beyond confused. It's like she's been body-snatched by a random-word generator.

"Are you sure I never told you?" she asks.

"I think I'd remember, Cindy."

She picks up her chopsticks and takes another mouthful, and then bites into the soy-soaked boiled egg and its jammy yolk. She clears her throat to prepare to speak. Her voice is clear, like she's reading out the nun's last will and testament.

"A while ago, my sister—"

"Which sister?" I ask.

"Cynthia."

"Ah."

Cynthia is Cindy's other sister, who lives in Malaysia. I've met her several times, though not since transitioning. She's an even louder version of Cindy with red hair and cat-eye glasses.

"Cynthia went to pay respects to the Goddess of Mercy at the temple in Ipoh on the way to Penang. Anyway, they know the sifu, so my sister asked me for your time and date of birth."

"Why would she do that?"

"To give to the sifu, lah," she says, exasperated, like all of this is extremely obvious. "I told my sister you were stressed. I didn't tell her the reason, but it was about that time you said you wanted to transit."

"It's transition—"

"How is your meal?" A waiter has appeared out of thin air, wearing a forced, tight smile. Cindy turns to him and beams.

"Very good, thank you!" She turns back to me. "So she asked for it, so I asked your dad for the time of birth and gave it to her. Anyway, she went to the temple and gave it to the sifu, who can tell fortunes."

"And?" I ask, leaning forward.

Cindy clears her throat again. I'm taken by how drawn in I am. This stuff is usually bullshit to me. I always put my hands over my ears whenever Cass tried to read me my horoscope. Stop ignoring me—it's so Taurean. Maybe that's your rising sign? I feel differently about Cindy's story. It feels important, like something I need. She continues.

"The sifu consulted her book of life—"

"What's the book of life?"

"Aiyah." She waves her hand in front of her again. "I don't know if it's called that. But it has lots of charts, and she uses it to determine your path of life, okay? Anyway, the sifu said: Why are you worried about this person? This person is a girl, and when she figures out who she is, she will be very success-ful. She is very lucky. Don't spend your time worrying about her. Worry about yourselves!" Cindy smiles, and her posture relaxes. "Since then I don't worry about you."

"Your sister told her that I'm trans?" I ask.

"No," she says. "My sister didn't know about you being trans at the time, but the sifu told her that you are a girl. Not even that you are trans, just that you are a girl, but my sister took it to mean that you are trans. Afterwards, she sat me down and began to lecture me. Cindy! Ming is a girl! You must accept her. Only then can she be successful!"

My jaw is slack. I'm not quite sure what I'm hearing.

"What did you say?" I ask.

"I was laughing, lah! It was after you told me and your dad. I said to Cynthia, duh! Ming told me already; I thought you would be the ones to not accept her!" Cindy and I start laugh-ing. "See! People can surprise you."

I can't help but smile. Cindy reaches for my hand across the table and squeezes. I hesitate, but then squeeze back. We keep them there, just for a moment, before she lets go and returns to her noodles.

"Never tell anyone your time of birth, by the way," she says, her face turning grave. "People can use it against you. Dark magic."

"I have no idea what my time of birth is."

"Six-oh-nine p.m.," she says loudly.

I nod.

"Did you tell my dad about all of this?" I ask.

"Of course," she says. "You know your father, lah, he's not so into this kind of thing. Just like you. But even then, he was smiling big and laughing. But I know it made him happy. I could see him worry much less. Amazing, eh?"

"Yeah," I say. "Pretty amazing. Thank you."

Cindy glances at the soju slushies that have arrived at the next table. She leans over to get a good look. She's about to speak to the adjacent diners. I stop myself from saying anything. I should let her be Cindy.

17

Underwater

I hadn't heard back from Sophia. From what Marco had said, they probably wouldn't dignify me with a rejection and would only get in touch if I'd got the job. It'd been weeks. The fashion show was a couple of months away. The excitement had dissipated a few days after landing in London, realizing that it was just one show and that my old job was waiting for me. It all seemed ridiculous. Anyone I told would probably have thought I was lying. I'd have sounded like a twelve-year-old insisting they had a boyfriend at another school who modeled for Abercrombie. As the high of possibility eked away from me, an anxiousness around Marco grew. I'd been telling myself to chill out, but realized that I was not, and maybe never would be, a chilled person. My self-esteem had plopped itself into one basket. I didn't know where else to put it. I was never going to get it from my job. Amateur pottery always looked shit, fermentation was just a lot of waiting around, and marathons were for people who had something to run away from.

My friends. I knew my friends were another basket, but when something's always there, it's easy to take it for granted. But that's what friends were for, subject to calendar clashes and Tube travel. I got out of bed and opened the door to the living room. A soft sizzle filled the room. Rob stood at the stove in a bathrobe. He turned to me and smiled.

"Good morning," he said. "Do you want any eggs?"

"Yeah, sure, please. If you're making some."

He rolled scrambled eggs out of a pan and onto a plate, then took the final three eggs and cracked them into a bowl one by one. I walked over to the bread box and started cutting slices from a half-eaten sourdough boule. I toasted as Rob stirred. When we were done, I reached for the colder plate. We sat down at the round dining table and tucked in. Rob always ate his eggs with ketchup. I thought it was fine. Sarah thought it was barbaric.

"Do you want to go and see a film today?" I asked.

Rob shook his head with a mouth full of bread, toast in hand, crumbs on lips.

"I'm still going to that daytime party at that club in Canning Town. I reckon you can still get a ticket, if you want to join? I'm heading in a couple of hours."

"Oh shit, yeah. I forgot about that."

I'd said no because I'd wanted to keep the day free for Marco. I looked down at my plate. I wanted to tell Rob about how Marco hadn't responded to my text, but I was embarrassed, and I didn't know if Rob's analysis of our situation would help. Rob swallowed some food and then looked at me.

"Wait," he said. "Aren't you seeing Marco today?"

Heat bloomed in my cheeks.

"He hasn't got back to me."

"Oh," he said. "That's shit of him, isn't it? Maybe there's a good reason."

"No, it's fine." I shrugged my shoulders. "And you're right, there's probably a good reason."

"You should come today."

Spending a winter Saturday clubbing in an old industrial estate would hollow me out even more. An irrational part of me imagined myself bumping into Marco there, which would've hurt. Another part of me didn't want to commit in case he got back to me. Whether this was also irrational, I didn't know.

"I don't think I'm in the mood for it," I said.

"I get that."

After breakfast we washed up together, and I went back to my room and lay on my bed. I reached for my phone again. No response from Marco. I messaged Sarah, who I knew would definitively not be going to the club in Canning Town.

What are you doing today?

She started typing back instantly. Reliable, responsible Sarah.

Taking nephew to aquarium. Do you want to come? I'll be there at 1.

London Aquarium was a bit shit. It had a bad rap, but Marco definitely wouldn't be there, and I could put him out of my mind.

I'd love to.

I got there before Sarah and Chlo, and so I bought three tickets and waved at them as they came in. Sarah was growing her hair out. It was a few inches long. Chlo grinned at me. He was taller than the last time I'd seen him, at his third birthday party. He'd dressed up as Elsa from Frozen. Ming and I had gone together with Rob.

Chlo wore a black puffer jacket that matched Sarah's and tripled his width. He looked more like his father than Sarah's sister. God, Tom, it's so fucking sad that Chlo looks so white. You can only tell he's Chinese because you know he is. Blonde wisps of hair wove through the brown, glowing in the blue light of the aquarium.

"Hi, Chlo!" I said.

He folded his arms and wore an exaggerated, cross expression.

"My name is Claudius."

"I'm sorry, Claudius."

"Don't call him that, Tom."

"It's my name."

Sarah rolled her eyes. Chlo plunged his fists into his pockets but also smiled at me.

We checked in our coats and walked into the ticketed section. Chlo screamed when he saw the sharks in the tank beneath the glass floor. I locked eyes with an octopus, its mantle a purple scrotum, billowing in the synthetic current of the tank. We took Chlo to the glass and I lifted him up. The octopus crawled away from us. Its skin darkened from gray to maroon, and it buried its tentacles beneath its body before it relaxed back into the color of stone.

"I think we made it angry," I said.

Chlo laughed. I dragged him along the window like a library ladder, and put him down where the granite was low enough for him to see over it.

"What's that?" Chlo pointed into the tank.

"Eels, they're kind of like snakes."

Chlo shrieked. We walked into the glass tunnel that ran through the bottom of a tank. Schools of fish swam around us, twirling between fronds and coral. Sarah and I kept a couple of feet behind Chlo.

"Weren't you going to that thing with Rob?" she asked.

"No," I said, slipping my hands into my pockets. "I thought I was hanging out with Marco."

"Did he cancel?"

"Not really, we just never followed up."

"That's worse! Why didn't you follow up?"

"I did. This morning. He hasn't replied."

Her face turned anxious and sympathetic, like she'd just stepped on my big toe.

"That's really shit, Tom."

I hummed. Maybe it was shit, but I still wanted to see him. I couldn't imagine that he was still asleep. I wasn't sure what else he'd be doing. Maybe someone he knows was in an accident. Maybe there's been a cancer scare in the family. Maybe he just doesn't want to see me. I wanted to change the subject, to shift attention elsewhere.

"How was work this week?" I asked.

"So shit, Tom," she said. "The layoffs feel relentless. Everyone is burned out, even in the fundraising team, and our jobs aren't even on the chopping block."

"Do you think it might calm down?" I asked, looking at the metal grating under my feet.

"No," she said. "Too much negative coverage about the charity. Too much negative press about trans people."

"That's fucked up."

"Mhm."

She looked towards the side of the tank. An aquatic constellation of yellow fish swam past us.

"I saw Lisa this week, actually," she said. "As in, we met up."

I turned to her, surprised. Lisa had been avoiding Sarah since the breakup. Bump-ins at parties were amicable but light.

"Yeah? Did you get that postmortem?"

"No," she said. "I don't think I want it anymore, to be honest." She clicked her tongue against the roof of her mouth before breathing out. "There's not much more talking to do, Tom. I kind of got the gist of it on my own."

Sarah stopped walking when Chlo stood stationary to look up at the fish. We leaned against the railing.

"Gist of what?" I asked.

"As in, I know why we broke up, beyond the reasons she gave me. What more do I need?" she said. "I was always in control, which I resented. There was part of me, I think, that saw her as being a little weak. I criticized her a lot. I mean, I know I do it with everyone. You and Rob. I find things to nip at. For the longest time, I thought I was just getting her to stand up for herself, but then when she finally started to do it, I couldn't really handle it."

"What do you mean?"

Sarah pursed her lips and bobbed her head from side to side, a forced display of grasping for the right words.

"So, *Thin Frames*, right. She literally didn't give a fuck, Tom. And it set me off. I've told you all of this, but I've spent a lot of time going over it, and it was obvious that I wanted her to stand up for herself, but only on my terms. What does that say about me? Firstly, that I'm a control freak—"

"You?" I said. "Never."

"Yeah, yeah," she laughed. "But also that it was less about helping her be better, and more about being as hard on others as I am on myself. Does that make sense?"

I nodded. It was clear, even if unfair.

"I do think you make people better, though," I said. "You're all about helping others. And your friends. You challenge people in the right ways."

Sarah locked her arm into mine.

"You don't have to say any of that," she said. "But thank you."

I looked up. Fish swam in loops above me. I could see the surface of the water just above the glass curve of the tunnel. I remembered coming to the aquarium with my parents and

refusing to look up, or even at the sides, because of how panicked I felt at seeing the ripples above me. My body must have
thought it was drowning. Chlo and the other children looked at
ease, their minds plastic to the engineering that let them walk
along the tank floor. Chlo carried on, and so Sarah and I followed him, still linking arms.

"You never told me that *Thin Frames* became such a big issue,"
I said. "Even when I asked."

"To be honest, Tom…" She paused. "I wasn't sure if you
were in a position to understand how little it had to do with
you. You seem better, though."

Chlo ran back to us. He held my and Sarah's hands and we
swung him between us. Better. I meditated on better for a moment.

"I do feel a bit better," I said. "I sort of feel like I have my
own stuff going on. I don't really mean that stuff in Cologne,
although that helped for a bit. I guess I'm focusing more on
Marco, too. And I've stopped feeling like all that time with
Ming was wasted."

She opened her mouth as if to say something, and then shut
it, changing tack.

"Do you feel good about Marco?"

His name conjured whispers of so many different emotions.
Pride. Dread. Anxiety. Joy. Often all at once.

"I do," I said.

"Even if he's ignoring you?"

"He's not ignoring me."

Sarah squinted. I'd responded too quickly. Defensively. But I
wasn't lying. I felt good about Marco; it was just sometimes that
I didn't. It was the hot and cold. He'd told me that he thought
about me a lot, but I still hadn't met his friends. Once, when we
were at a pub, Marco said the woman working the bar had asked
if we were together. How funny is that? Anyway, I was think-

ing we could go to Lisbon to escape the bad weather. It was a
flip-flopping opacity that I'd grown regrettably accustomed to.

An old woman smiled at me, Sarah and Chlo from a bench
at the end of the tunnel. She wore a sensible gilet and necklace
of Malteser-sized pearls. She must have been eighty. She had
canyons around her eyes and mouth, but her long gray hair was
youthful bar its color. We sat on the adjacent bench while Chlo
ran up to the shark tank.

"How old is he?" the woman asked.

"Four," Sarah said. "He'd remind me to say he's four and a
half, though."

"What's his name?"

"Claudius," she said. "Or Chlo."

"He's lovely, a perfect blend of the two of you."

"He is, isn't he," I said.

Sarah looked at me and laughed. I flashed my eyes at her and
lowered my voice.

"She would've thought you and Lisa were just good friends."

"Oh yeah." She framed her mouth with two fingers. "Gal
pals."

We watched Chlo stare into the tank. The blue light drowned
the details of his back, and he dissolved into a dark silhouette. I
used to picture moments like this long before I came out, going
to things like aquariums and theme parks and parties with a
faceless wife and child. These imaginings had seemed to repre-
sent everything I'd no longer have if I told everyone I was gay.
Being at the aquarium with Sarah and Chlo made wanting all
of that feel so facile and silly, especially at the expense of my
own happiness. And as we sat there, staring at Chlo's outline, I
thought about how life repackages and regifts and counterfeits.

"Sometimes I want to talk to Ming about Marco," I said. "As
much as I'm still angry with her, I know part of me still misses
her. Or needs her."

Sarah looked at me. It was true. I did want to talk to Ming.

Not to brag, not even to complain, but just to talk; see what jokes she'd make, what she'd say about Marco to make me laugh. Wow. Secretive and emotionally unavailable? Sounds like your type! There was a thread between Marco and Ming, its texture and shape oblique. Sarah didn't say anything, and so I let the admission float off into the abyss.

Chlo tapped his nail against the enormous pane of glass. The tip of his finger tracked the path of a shark like the barrel of a sniper.

"I'm still trying to figure out what place Lisa can have in my life, if any," Sarah said, looking ahead. "But I'm learning you can take your time."

"How'd you get so wise about Lisa, anyway?" I asked.

"New therapist," she said. "She's bleeding me dry."

"Do you guys ever talk about me?"

"Yeah," she said. "Only for the first forty minutes. We save the last ten for me."

I laughed. Two young children returned to the old woman. As she got up from the bench, both kids held their hands behind her legs, steering her towards the next room. She turned to us and rolled her eyes with a smile. I returned it as if I'd seen the same in Chlo. They walked out of the room together. Sarah looked back at Chlo, who stood hypnotized by the sharks. Eventually, he ran back to us.

"Do you wanna go and see the seahorses?" Sarah asked.

Chlo nodded. We got up and walked, Chlo in front of us again. Sarah held my hand. Chlo turned back to us and giggled. Sarah's hands were always soft. Each ridge of bone cushioned in smooth skin. She used hand cream every day, even when we were nineteen. It was the first thing she did in the morning. When we woke up, she'd go to her dressing table and put a dollop in her hand before getting back into bed. Her hand would still be oily from the excess, and I could smell the lemons from beneath the covers.

We stood right behind Chlo at the main seahorse tank. A long seahorse, yellow in color, flapped its wings to no avail, too weak to ascend, but holding its position. Chlo ran up to one of the smaller tanks, which stood in front of the main tank like rows of museum plinths. He stared at the miniatures dancing in the water. Sarah let go of my hand as we walked after him.

"Do you remember the ceiling in your room in first year?" Sarah asked.

"No. I can't imagine it was nice, though. Do you?"

She didn't look up.

"It's one of the only ceilings I can perfectly picture," she said. "I used to look at it when we had sex."

"Oh."

Something heavy within my abdomen woke up; the tension in my body kneaded it like dough, braiding it into knots. I didn't know why she was bringing this up. Sarah and I, after all these years, never spoke to each other about us having sex. I hardly spoke about it to anyone. Ming had asked questions, but otherwise it was something Sarah and I avoided, to the point where it had stopped feeling real. To have spoken about it was to have undone the toil of burying it.

"There were these water stains," she said, drawing a shape on the top of the tank with her finger. "I remember there being a big one and a bunch of smaller ones. I would stare at the ridges and pretend they were the edges of a cloud. But I think my brain wandered because I had to disengage." She walked around one of the other tanks. I followed her. "I think part of me really wanted to believe that sex was a certain way for men and a certain way for women. It couldn't go on for long, could it, Tom?" Her voice wore a feigned humor, and so I smiled in return. "But anyway, for the longest time I couldn't get that image of the ceiling out of my head. I'd just think about it, and the fact that I could remember it, and I just felt gross. Sometimes

I still feel so embarrassed about it. Isn't that ridiculous? And I guess it's shame, right? Some kind of trauma."

We stood in silence on either side of one of the tanks. Sex with Sarah had been painful and fruitless, yet at the time it had been so important, to uphold an image of myself that I could no longer even recognize. It hurt to think about it again. It was fresher than expected.

"I'm sorry," I said.

"Don't be silly, Tom. We both did it to ourselves."

I took a deep breath and looked around us. The seahorse room was empty besides me, Chlo and Sarah. Chlo darted around from tank to tank, a small pinball, sometimes from one straight back to one he'd just looked at. Sarah and I kept walking around the room, drawing figure eights with our bodies, keeping our distance from Chlo.

"I'd sort of feel good after we did it," I said, lowering my voice to escape the echo of the empty room. "I felt like I'd ticked some kind of box."

"Yeah, me too. But I don't think I felt the cost until after we broke up. It's like the event plants a seed, but you don't really know how it'll grow. It was shit."

"Shit," Chlo muttered to himself from across the room, and Sarah's neck snapped towards him.

"Don't say that, Chlo," she said.

I walked around one of the smaller tanks and stared at the placard, which explained the difficulties with seahorse husbandry. The babies usually died because the plankton feed was too big for them to eat. A small number of aquariums, including this one, had solved it by feeding them smaller plankton. It didn't say why it had taken them so fucking long.

Chlo appeared next to me and started to read the placard. He put his finger over the metal square and ran it along the lines, much faster than it would have been possible for him to

read. When he reached the end, he turned to us and asked to
see the penguins.

Sarah and I led Chlo to the penguin room. We sat on another
bench. Children put their heads up against the glass, leaving
greasy impressions.

"Why'd you try so hard to stay friends if you had all the bad
memories?" I asked.

"I don't think I was fully aware." She looked down at her
folded arms. "But maybe staying friends with you felt like I'd
commanded it in some way. I'm glad I did. Aren't you?" She
unfolded her arms and leaned back, hands slack on her thighs.
"I guess I felt bitter. And there was some of that for you and
some for myself, and in some ways neither of those were different. It wasn't easy. Sometimes it'd feel like there was this huge
gap between the person who'd sleep with a boy to prove that
she was straight and the person I thought I'd become. But I'd
have moments where I'd think about the ceiling, and then I'd
feel it in my stomach." She brought her hands to her belly, as if
something inside had kicked. "And then I realized that the gap
wasn't always there. Like I'd wandered around a maze to end
up right where I'd started. But it was worth it."

"Was it?"

She huffed. It might've been a pathetic, fishing question, but
I ached for emotional symmetry, to be reassured of my worth,
that there was good attached to me and to time spent on me.
Ming felt so out of reach, the us of it all becoming victim to
time and neglect. But Sarah was here. I leaned over, my elbows
resting on my knees. My insides were knotted. I felt a guilt that
was both fresh and old, a new sprout from a dormant seed.

"You're a good person, Tom. I really love you. We've shared
a lot, and even though it was a long time ago, you still know
me in ways other friends won't."

I started to tear up. I felt so tender. She paused for a moment,

and then she pulled my outside shoulder towards her chest. I
sniffed on her as she stroked my hair.

"Stop it, Tom. This is my sob story."

I laughed, and when I pulled away I saw that her eyes were
wet. We looked back at Chlo and watched him giggle as a penguin dived from air to water.

"Thanks for telling me that," I said.

"It's all good, Tom," she said. "I'm speaking the shame away.
I'm showing you my belly."

"What?"

"It's this analogy we're using in therapy," she said. "There's
a lot of fear in showing it, for some animals. Because you're at
risk of being mauled."

I nodded slowly.

"Our insides aren't worth much to other people, I guess."

"Some people," she said. "It sounds like hippie bullshit, but
I think the risk is worth it. It's how you learn who cares, and
it stops you from punishing yourself so much for being you."

I supposed that I hadn't always been much of a risk-taker.
Had I shown my belly to Marco?

"Chlo," she shouted. "I think it's time to go."

Chlo ran back to us and told us that penguins got married.

"Sick," Sarah said.

We got our coats from the cloakroom. We walked out of the
aquarium with Chlo between us, holding hands once again.
The sun, although low in the sky, blasted the entrance of the
aquarium, its swan song before the winter afternoon pulled it
beneath the skyline.

I stretched my arms above me. The stiff dark of the aquarium
had rusted my joints. I shut my eyes, but the sun painted the
inside of my eyelids orange. I let out a roaring yawn.

I thought of Ming stretching in the morning, standing in the
fresh light of a new day, and how I would wince at the arpeggios
that erupted from her cracking spine. Her laugh would fill the

room. I'd spent years feeling happy to be nourished by Ming's light, so much so that I'd never asked what I could be for myself, only what I could be for her. I'd long suspected that Ming shone brighter than me, the same way I'd suspected Sarah did, too.

As my arms returned to my sides, I filled my lungs. The petroleum notes of the city settled on my sinuses, but it was sweeter than the stale air inside. Chlo reached for me again. We walked down the steps away from the entrance.

I checked my phone with my free hand. Marco still hadn't texted, but there were a few messages and an email from Sophia. The designer had booked me. Sophia wanted my details to reserve my train ticket to Paris.

I stabbed holes into the plastic cover of a frozen lasagna and stuck it in the microwave, then went back to the sofa and watched the black container spin in the silver box. The slowness of its rotation, the dull yellow light of the microwave, would've normally filled me with a dreadful unimportance, but tonight I felt the opposite. I read Sophia's email over and over. And Marco called me. Been shit with my phone today! Can you come up to Dalston? I'll probably eat at home, but I've told a friend she can join us. You'll like her. I hope you don't mind? I didn't tell Marco that I'd got the job. I wanted to save it for when we saw one another in person. I wanted to see him smile.

I ate the lasagna straight out of its container, washed my mouth out and left the flat. The Overground train went straight there. I walked along Kingsland Road. We were meeting at a Japanese restaurant-slash-jazz-bar. I had a peek inside to look for them. White globe pendant lights hung from the ceiling. Oak chairs and tables sprawled across the oak floors. People drank and ate sushi and spoke over jazz. They didn't seem like jazz bar regulars, but they looked like they were pretending to be. There were black turtlenecks and buzz cuts and wide-legged trousers and lots of people on their phones. I couldn't see Marco, and so I sat on an empty bike stand outside.

Ten minutes later, Marco approached from up the road. He was in a long leather jacket, silver jewelry and relaxed jeans. He'd trimmed his beard. He walked with a woman around our age in an identical coat, her platinum-blonde hair tied back in a bun. She had heavy eye makeup, and wore a champagne corset and flared trousers the color of rust. She looked like she was appropriating something, but I couldn't figure out what. We said hello. Her name was Thea. Marco ducked away from my kiss, directing my lips to his cheek instead.

"Why didn't you go in?" Marco asked.

"I only got here a couple of seconds ago."

We walked into the bar, towards the far end of the room, and sat at a table.

"I actually really hate jazz," Thea said.

Marco scoffed, but the admission warmed me to her. I didn't hate jazz—I didn't really know much about it—but I knew that dunking on it wasn't a done thing. People looked at you like you'd said you hated culture.

Thea glanced around the bar, and then at the DJ booth. A minimalist poster advertised an open decks night. She gestured towards it.

"Maybe we came on the wrong night," Thea said.

"I used to DJ," I blurted out, attempting an ironic smile.

"I forgot about that!" Marco said.

Thea laughed. I worried the joke was lost on them. She looked on the verge of asking follow-up questions, and so I changed the subject. I learned that she was a photographer, too. That's how she knew Marco.

"How do you guys know each other?" she asked.

Thea's question was a fist in the gut. It was humiliating, and it revealed how Marco spoke about me, or how little he did. I'm just meeting someone for drinks, Thea; you should come.

When I told people about Marco, I volunteered details. We're dating. We're seeing one another. We are, in some senses of the word, together.

"We met on an app," Marco said.

Thea puckered her lips and nodded her head. I accepted this in-between, which at least acknowledged some connection. I asked Thea about her photography.

"Fashion. Or I'm trying to do fashion, at least. I've done a couple of editorials recently."

I knew from Marco that this meant fighting other young photographers for an unpaid two-page spread in an indie magazine called *Probation* or *Wet Wipe*.

"I've been getting a bit more commercial work recently, which means fewer sex parties in Mayfair."

"Sex parties?"

"I take photos of the before, when everyone's still in black tie. They always invite me to stay. The women are beautiful. The men are disgusting."

Marco's phone screen lit up on the table. I saw a notification from the app on which we'd met. Another whomping pang of anxiety. He flipped his phone around. I'd deleted my apps weeks ago, partly because the only reason I'd go on them was to check if Marco was online, which he often was. We weren't exclusive, but it still made me uneasy. Maybe he's just online because he's checking if I'm on there, too!

"Tom?" Thea said.

"Sorry?"

"I asked you what you do," she laughed.

"He works in finance," Marco said. "He's really clever."

"Oh, wow!" Thea said. "What specifically?"

"It's boring."

"No, tell me!" Thea said.

"I'm an analyst in the Mergers and Acquisitions team at a

boutique investment bank. I mostly do energy and infrastructure work at the moment."

"I have no idea what any of that means," Thea laughed.

"No one does," Marco added.

I smiled and put my finger over the tip of my straw, drawing circles with it, jostling the ice at the bottom of my glass. Is that it? Is that what I'm about? When I talked about the books I liked, those video essays, the DJing, they all felt less like things I liked to do and more like things I used to do, shrunken and shriveled in the corner of a room. I cringed again at telling Thea I used to DJ. There was something pathetic about it, trying to reclaim some sense of personhood.

"I sent some pictures of Tom to this agency abroad. They liked him. The owner's one of the casting directors for a show and they flew him over for the go-see."

"That's a good sign," Thea said.

"I actually heard back from them earlier today. They've booked me."

Marco looked shocked for a moment, but this melted into a knowing smile, as if it couldn't have gone any other way because he'd put it together. Thea clapped and we clinked our glasses. I felt a cozy pride. As we withdrew our hands, Marco put an arm around my hip and squeezed. It was the first time that evening he'd shown me real affection, and I could almost forget that Thea hadn't known who I was until that night. We ordered another round of drinks, and a few more. A new friend joined us. He was a boxy man with a lime-green mullet, in a white vest and yellow-lensed glasses. When he asked me how I knew Marco, I told him we were dating. Marco looked at me with a smile.

They cleared the tables in front of the bar at eleven. More drinks, and an hour later we had a dance by the decks. Marco's body felt like distance. Its size, its power—not quite Jason's, but leaps and bounds from Ming's—felt like growth. I ordered a cab for us back to his warehouse. On the way back he told me why he thought Andreas Gursky was overrated, even though Thea and his ex-boyfriend loved him. I listened and asked questions until the cab pulled up to the warehouse. We walked through the dark common area and kitchen, and then into his bedroom.

After climbing up to the top of his mezzanine bed, he took off my clothes. I told him he was beautiful. He buried his face in my ass. I held him close to me as we fucked. We lay next to each other, his tummy down and mine up, breathing short, labored breaths. I held his hand.

"Do you want to come to Paris with me?" I asked.

Marco flipped onto his back.

"I might be busy with work. I'll have to think about it." He paused. "But yeah, that would be really nice." He kissed me on the cheek. "Hang on, I need to piss."

He rolled away and climbed down the ladder from the bed. His phone was plugged into the charger by the pillow. I reached for it to check the time, but saw once more an unread stack of notifications from the app. My insides scrunched a little. I flipped the phone over, putting it back where it was. When Marco came back, I shut my eyes, pretending to be asleep.

18
Walk

Trance music flooded the room, the sort of thing you'd hear at a festival in Bulgaria filled with white people with dreadlocks. I could feel my feet in my shoes. They were a size too big. The woman in front of me wore a dress with the widest shoulder pads I'd ever seen. She looked like a shower curtain. Backstage was claustrophobic, a little darker than the runway beyond, which was lit by white light. The audience was barely visible. I yawned. We'd had an early start, and I'd hardly slept the night before.

I tried to recall Sophia's words when she'd met me outside the auditorium. It wasn't clear to me why she was there, but she seemed to know the other models. She'd probably cast all of them. She'd squeezed the arm of a woman with prosthetically enhanced cheekbones, then walked over to me. Her blonde hair was slicked back. She held my shoulders and stared at me, her eyes piercing from the shadows of her deep-set eyes. She didn't lift her chin.

"Remember to walk," she'd said. "Purposeful posture, not like you are holding a grape in your butt. Maybe like you are holding a watermelon in your hands. No, you don't understand, just like there is weight there. Put your hands back at your sides."

I said those words to myself again, as I'd done when the stylists dressed me in the oversized suit, buttoning my trousers and putting my feet into the shoes. No grape. Watermelon. I'd said them again when the makeup artists drew dark circles around my eyes that made me look ill.

The woman in front of me walked onto the onyx runway, which was depressed an inch and filled with water. I watched her feet make gentle splashes as she stomped, her body rippled in the reflection beneath her. My mind snapped back with the touch of a man's hand on my spine. Go! Go! Go!

I walked behind her, the rows of people on either side of me cloaked in darkness. I stopped breathing. My neck tensed. I kept my head straight. All I had to do was finish the long, rectangular loop. My feet pushed in and out of the water. Some droplets hit my ankles, running down into the shoes. Don't stop at the corners! Turn. Walk more. Turn! Watermelon. On the final stretch I noticed my heart in my chest, beating wildly, my head pulsing with it. And then my walk was over. I started to laugh, and someone I didn't know patted my back and told me that I'd done a good job. What the fuck was that? The waiting and anticipation distilled into less than a minute, a small vial that I could swallow in one, and I laughed again because time felt stupid, because at one end of the curtain I was an imposter and at the other end I felt special, and I didn't know if that change was powerful or wondrous or fragile or all of those things combined.

It wasn't how I'd imagined. We didn't all walk out in a procession at the end, like in the shows I'd looked up. We just stood in silence as the rest of the models finished walking, collecting behind the curtain like drops in a puddle. After the audience clapped, they unrobed us, undoing the hours and hours of work. People fluttered around me like fairy-tale mice and birds, their hands deconstructing the ensemble, returning me to myself. Someone eventually came with makeup wipes and swiped the dark circles and the rest of the makeup away.

I walked over to my clothes, arranged in a small stack at the side of the room. I redressed myself into the ordinary. There were thank-yous and we're-dones flying across the room from everyone involved, and then the crowd dispersed out of the film studio complex. I saw Sophia near the makeup tables and waited for her to finish a conversation with another model. She turned to me, her face brighter than before.

"Well done," she said. "You were great, just enough weight at the front. Perfect watermelon. I will send you an email. Not right now, but soon! Maybe this evening. Or later! Just check your phone, okay?"

I thanked her and walked out into the main hallway. Marco had said the complex was a renovated power plant. The windows stretched the length of the thirty-meter walls, and a skylight ran along the center. With each step I grew more aware of the building's size and my body shrank. I walked with my face towards the sky. I smiled. A warmth pulsed through me, and I tried to ignore the uncertainty that tailed it, two circling koi fish in my chest. Marco stood outside the main doors. They'd paid for my hotel. All Marco had had to do was buy a train ticket.

He jogged towards me, and as he hugged me I felt big again.

"How was it?" Marco asked. "Did Sophia say she'd sign you?"

"I think it all hinged on this job. So yeah, I guess."

Marco hugged me again, and then his strong hand squeezed my bum.

"You're gonna be something."

As he held my face, the uncertain fish swallowed the warm fish, and I could feel the coldness of Marco's arms against my neck. My arms sank to his waist. He pecked my mouth twice.

He flagged a taxi and told the driver the address of our hotel in French.

"How did it feel?" he asked.

I thought of walking the runway, and what I'd experienced. It'd been hard not to be blown away by it all, but something had also felt off. It hadn't been fear of what I was doing, but an internal sense of distance, as if I'd woken up from sleep to find that I was floating in space. It was the same feeling I'd had when I lay on the tarpaulin in Marco's studio, like I was a little out of my body. I wondered if the idea of it all was more enticing than the act.

"It was exciting," I said. "I don't know how to describe it, though. I felt like I wasn't myself."

"You weren't yourself, stupid. That's the whole point, isn't it? You become who they want you to be."

"Yeah."

I tried my best to smile back at him.

The taxi drove into the city and stopped outside our hotel. We walked through the doors together holding hands. Two women a few years older than us sat with their suitcases in the lobby. They wore UGG boots and berets. They looked at us, smiled, and then smiled at each other.

In our hotel room, I leaned against the ornate wallpaper along the outside wall of our bathroom. It had vines with pastel flowers painted onto it. Marco knelt by the mini fridge. He opened the silver door and took out a bottle of Veuve Clicquot.

"They won't cover that," I said.

"I bought it earlier."

"Sneaky."

"You deserve it."

He unwound the wire and pulled off the top. At the call of the pop, a small white stream leaped from the bottle's mouth. The foam landed on Marco's arm, dissolving into clear stickiness. He licked and sucked at the dripping fluid and reached for two glasses. The champagne glugged too fast and bubbles rose up the glass, fighting to the surface for breath. He waited for the line to fall and filled them up again, then gave one to me.

I walked over to our Juliet balcony and sipped at the champagne, hoping that it'd quell the uneasiness I felt about the chat I'd been rehearsing in my head, the one I knew I needed to have with Marco. He stood beside me and we looked out at the view, at the setting sun, the delicate cream-colored building across from us, a mosaic of yellow light and blacked-out windows; taller buildings poked out from behind.

We stood in silence as I drank, and he hugged my waist as soon as my glass was empty. His hand squeezed tight. We swayed to the silence of the room, to the dull white noise of the air-conditioning, the rattle of a luggage trolley outside. He kissed my neck, and then my ear.

"I'm going to fuck you so hard," he said.

The words ran down my neck and shoulder blades, the muscles twitching against the bone. I kissed Marco. We walked to the bed, and I sat on top of his hips. I set my lips onto his neck. His stubble scratched my cheek. I unbuttoned his shirt and belt buckle and took him into my mouth. He held the back of my head and rotated his hips.

I pulled my T-shirt over my head and unbuttoned my trousers. I straddled Marco's body, shuffling my knees up to bring my hips towards his face. He went down on me, then, with his hands at my sides, motioned me to roll onto my back. He slipped a condom on and began to push in, and soon the strokes of his body were vigorous. The muscles and veins on the sides of his neck tensed and released to the rhythm of his hips. With his hands he turned me over, his body on my body and his hot breath on my ear. He came, then flipped me over again and nibbled on my neck until I did, too. He tied the condom and threw it into the bin. A clean shot. After disappearing into the bathroom and returning with a towel, he wiped my cum off my chest and threw the towel onto the floor.

I stayed in bed a moment longer before moving again towards the balcony, hiding my dick behind a column of the balustrade. The chill skirted over my chest. Marco moved behind me, resuming our position from before, as if nothing had happened but the vanishing of our clothes. He kissed my neck again.

My phone rang. I moved away from Marco and the balcony and found it in my trousers on the floor. It was Rob. I went into the bathroom and closed the pocket door. My thighs spread across the cold wood of the toilet seat. I cleared my throat, and the sound echoed off the marble fixtures.

"Hey," I said.

"How did it go?"

"Good, I'm back at the hotel with Marco now. The whole thing was crazy."

"Send me pictures, okay? I'm fucking proud of you."

I blushed.

"Are you still coming home tonight?" he asked.

"Yeah, we get in quite late."

"I'm heading out, but I'll see you when I get back, or tomorrow morning. Have you spoken to Marco yet?"

"No. Not yet."

"Are you planning to?"

"I think so."

"You should, okay? Good luck. Well done, again. Love you."

"Love you."

I hung up. Balance reentered my body. I looked into the mirror, buoyed by Rob's voice. The face staring back at me had done something great, something interesting, a world apart from my job in London. Maybe it didn't matter that I'd felt a little outside of myself. Maybe that was a good thing. I flicked through my phone and texted my parents to let them know that everything had gone well.

I washed quickly, thinking about Marco, and again about the conversation I'd told Rob that I'd have with him. Six in, six out. These are conversations that people have with people they're dating. It's normal for a person to express their needs. I thought of the worst he could say. You're fucking delusional. You? And me? Hah! My hands slid the pocket door back into its socket and I walked out into the room. Marco had put on some underwear, and so I put some on, too. I leaned against the small mahogany desk in the corner, next to the empty glass I'd set down. Marco lay on the bed, looking at his phone, the small of his back on the slant of the down pillows, his knees bent and the weight of his thighs on the sheets, his body catching the last of the day's light.

"Marco."

He cocked his head towards me.

"I've been wanting to talk," I said. "About us. I thought this weekend would be a good opportunity. I don't know, I thought I could wait until the train or after, but I guess it makes sense to chat while we're in private."

He shifted on the bed. The sheets rustled as he pushed himself upright.

"I want us to be more than whatever we're currently doing," I said.

"You want us to be boyfriends?"

He wore a blank expression, nothing but a silent command for honesty.

"I do," I said. "I want a relationship."

The outline of Marco's body seemed to soften, relaxing back into curves. He patted the space next to him on the bed and I sat down, facing the wall across the room. Our legs overlapped at the knee, his on top of mine, and I avoided his eyes, comparing the meatiness of his thighs to my own slender frame.

"I quite like you," he said. "I think you're cool, Tom. I like spending time with you, but I don't want to be with just you."

"I didn't say I wanted a monogamous relationship." The words crumbled out of my mouth. He took a pause, placed his hand on my knee and squeezed.

"I mean, I don't know if monogamy works for me," I said. "I cheated on Ming."

"Like, cheated-cheated?"

"Kind of. It was this guy from work. It was a one-off."

Marco laughed. I felt childish. I imagined myself in his eyes. Small and naive, as if people and relationships were too big for me to understand, like that night when Ming told me she was trans, or when she broke up with me.

"I'm not diminishing it," Marco said. "But I'm going to take a guess and say things ran a bit deeper there than wanting non-monogamy."

I got up from the bed and stood by the balcony. A grayness hung in the darkening sky between the city lights and the emerging moon.

"I think we have fun," Marco said. "But can we just stay as we are? I'm not in a place for a relationship, and if we commit to anything, it'll add strain. I don't think it's worth it. Let's not change things."

"Okay."

It was worth it to me. To know it wasn't to Marco wounded me. I had shown myself to him, and with a blind flick of his hand he'd ripped me open. I moved away from the balcony and picked up my clothes from the floor around the bed, like I was gathering my insides. I went into the bathroom to collect my toiletries. We were leaving that night, and not in the morning, because Marco had plans in London the next day. The bottles of moisturizer and serum clacked in my travel bag; things I'd been told to use but didn't care about. Marco had already packed all his things.

I was shocked at how quickly I'd capitulated, denying myself what I needed to accept what he wanted. And I knew it was because part of me believed that I was lucky to get what I was given, that there would never be anybody else. This all felt too much like one tile in a matching set, and I knew I fell short of myself. I zipped up the bag and walked into the room. Marco had changed back into his clothes. He stood fastening his belt on his trousers. I set the bag of toiletries and clothes on the dressing table.

"I don't think I want something casual," I said.

Marco looked at me. I reached for my T-shirt and put it on, hiding from his eyes behind the black fabric, and when I emerged from the top, he'd released me from his gaze.

"I don't want a relationship," Marco said.

"I don't know where that leaves us."

I paused. Something inside me collapsed again, and I fiddled with my trousers in the hope that I could distract myself from the tears collecting around my eyes, ready to launch like projectiles from artillery. I stepped into my trousers and fastened the belt, then sat on the corner of the bed.

"I still want to see you," he said.

"I don't want that."

"Why not?"

"Because I'll get hurt," I sniffed. "And even though that feels like the easy thing to do, that's not how it should be. I don't think it's what I want or need. I know that much." Tears slid along my cheeks. I wiped them off with the back of my hand and stood up. I walked towards my shoes in the corner of the room, turning back to Marco once I'd cleared the wetness from my face. "I think there's more out there for me."

Marco's lips curved into a grimace.

"More out there for you?"

"I don't mean more out there than you, but more than what you want to give. You said it yourself. You don't want a relationship, but all of this." I waved my arms around me. "Coming here with me. It's like you want me to deliver myself to you without giving anything in return."

"I got you this job, Tom."

"You sent the photos to Sophia," I said, my words firm but calm. "I'm grateful for that, but you can't claim all of that, either. There's some of me there, too. And I'm not talking about those kinds of things, anyway. You know what I mean. I kind of just want to know that someone's there."

"Sounds like a hang-up from your ex, if I'm being honest," Marco said.

"Yeah, maybe, but is that wrong?"

The question seemed to deflate Marco, and he sat on the bed while he fiddled with his shoes.

"I think you need some time to figure out what you want," I said. "I don't actually think you know, either. You wouldn't be pressed now if you did. It's as confusing to me as it is to you, but I don't think it's all on me."

His hands moved towards the laces of his trainers. He tightened the white strings and drew them into loops, dancing them around one another until they formed a double-knot.

Marco said nothing.

"We should probably get going," I said.

He nodded, sitting still for a moment before getting up.

Marco and I waited in the terminal for our train back to London in silence, stranger's distance apart. When we got to the waiting room, I bought him a sandwich from a shop, and he took it from me without eye contact or a word of thanks. None of this was as sad as I'd thought it'd be; there were still some dormant tears, but I was okay, and I knew somehow that I would be okay in a way I hadn't before. Maybe it was the high of the show, but also the knowledge that I'd done what I could, left nothing unsaid. Our train came up on the departures screen.

"Should we go to the platform?" I asked.

He nodded. He pushed himself off the seat and we walked to our carriage, he a step behind me. We got onto the train and sat on our seats across from one another. The train was empty. I took out my phone to let Rob know what had happened.

Fuck! Sorry to hear! Let's talk about it in person, okay?

Marco let out a stubborn humph and folded his arms, his body language cartoonish. A furrowed brow, eyes out of the window.

"Is everything okay?" I asked.

"Everything's fine."

"I feel like you're mad."

"I'm not mad."

"Okay."

I took my book from my backpack and started to read. My eyes ran over the lines but couldn't take them in. I kept reading them until they started to mean something. The train pulled out of the station, and when I looked up from the top of my book, Marco's arms were still woven beneath his elbows. His face was still sour. I smiled at him, but he didn't look at me. I moved through the pages until I grew less conscious of time, until Marco finally spoke.

"I think you're right."

I looked up at him. He'd unfolded his arms. The tension in his face had melted. I folded the corner of the book and placed it square in front of me.

"It makes sense," he said. "I think it just felt like rejection. I reacted badly to that."

"I feel a bit rejected, too, but I think that probably means neither of us is rejecting the other. It's just hard, isn't it," I said. I took a deep breath through my nose, eyes stinging with fresh tears. I liked Marco. He was the first person since Ming that I'd liked this way. I exhaled, and the wobble inside me settled. "I have a bad habit of going along with things that aren't right for me, and I'm just trying to do the things a person would do if they loved themselves as much as they loved other people, I guess." The word love nearly lifted Marco's eyebrows off his face. "I know you think I couldn't keep things open, but to be honest, I'd be willing to try. In a general sense, I mean. But anyway, I don't think that's what this is about—" His expression turned inquisitive as I said this. "People in open relationships have primary partners and stuff. I think primary, or primacy, is the word for me here. I want primacy, I guess."

"More strings."

"Yeah," I said. "More strings."

Marco sighed, but looked satisfied with the resolution we'd come to, one that left his ego intact. He slid his hand into mine and squeezed. Our hands retreated to either side of our border. I was alone again, but I felt okay. I picked up my book and continued to read. The words moved into me without struggle.

When I got home, there was a bar of expensive chocolate on the dining table. Rob had left a note saying well done, written in green highlighter on an A4 piece of paper. I dropped my keys onto the note and texted him to say thank you. When I opened up my phone, I saw that I'd been tagged in photos from the show. I sent them to Rob, and to Sarah, and then to my parents, and on a whim uploaded one to social media. Mum responded saying she was proud of me.

I wondered what she was proud of. Her genes, maybe. I wondered what I was proud of. Walking down a runway felt meaningless, and yet it felt like all that mattered; an escape from the norm. I slid under my duvet. I fell asleep, but floated on the surface of unconsciousness. I woke up a couple of hours later and read a text from Rob sent an hour before.

Hot stuff! Coming home soon.

I hadn't heard him come back, but he would have got home already. I lay down and shut my eyes, drifting back into sleep.

★ ★ ★

The sound of the doorbell woke me up. I checked my phone. Another two hours had passed. The buzz was continuous, and I could feel it in the innermost chamber of my ear. I pulled on my bathrobe and walked out of my bedroom. Rob's door was open. I popped in. His bed was made. Empty. Is it Rob ringing? Why would it have taken him so long to get home? Panic punctured through the rattling doorbell, a primordial instinct that something was wrong, something I felt at the top of my spine. I called out his name. There was no response. The buzzing continued. Dread swallowed my body.

I walked through the living room and into the hallway we shared with the downstairs flat. I moved down the stairs. The buzzer was still going, now matched by a knocking on the front door that was forceful and loud. As I reached for the handle, our downstairs neighbor peeked into the hallway. Her blonde hair was in a tall bun atop her head. Tiredness drained the color from her face. I pulled the door open.

Outside stood two policewomen. The one by the buzzer withdrew her hand, suspended in midair from the knocking. Their faces wore a stony seriousness, and this drowned out traces of what lay beneath.

"Sorry to wake you," the policewoman said. "Does Robert Gray live here?"

"Yes?"

She let out a breath. Not a sigh, but audible and sharp.

"Can we please come in?"

I led them up towards the flat. My hands began to shake.

19

Roller Coasters

My mother loved roller coasters. It's why I deem riding them to be a hot-girl activity, like eating Doritos in a bikini or walking on a treadmill.

She liked ones with sudden drops. There was a theme park in a shopping mall in Kuala Lumpur, and the roller coaster had orange tracks that snaked around the vast ninth floor. She kept a small album of photos of us on rides, most of them on that particular roller coaster. My dad was never in the photos because he waited for us at the end, either holding a processed bratwurst in a synthetic-tasting bun, doused in lines of ketchup, mustard and cheap relish, or cheering at us like one of those inflatable tube men outside American supermarkets.

Whenever the steel caterpillar plunged down the rails, the air moved so fast around me that I thought I'd suffocate. After the first nosedive I could feel myself breathe again, and I could calm down and enjoy the curves and the loops and the velocity, and by the time we got to the camera I'd be laughing ear to ear. I always gave in when my mother wanted to go for another ride, because I only remembered that kind of breathlessness whenever I felt it again.

Sarah calls me in the morning, after Alissa has gone to work. We haven't spoken since the last time I saw her, and I know she wouldn't call unless it was something bad. I feel the same breathlessness when she tells me that Rob was hit by a car and died on impact. She sounds so tired; the usual sharpness to her voice has wilted. A tear fights its way out of my eyes, but all that remains after is dry panic. My knees lower into the small space between my bed and my wardrobe.

"When did it happen?" I ask.

"Yesterday."

"Is Tom still in the flat?"

"Yes," she says. "I don't know if he's staying, though. It's only been a day."

She answers my questions like she's answered them many times before. Not irritably, but worn. I wonder how far down the list I am. I wonder how they decided who'd call me.

"Where is he now?"

"He's out for a walk," she says. "We've been calling his friends all morning. He needed a break. He had to tell Rob's family."

"Are you okay?"

"No, I'm not, but we have to tell people." Sarah's voice cracks.

"Should I tell Cass?" I ask.

"Yeah," she says. "Maybe. We haven't told her yet. It's hard to keep track of who to call." I hear her breaths rasp from the receiver, sending chills down my neck. "Are you going to come back to London, Ming?"

"I'm not sure yet."

She pauses again.

"Okay, then," she says. "Speak soon."

I barely say bye before she hangs up. I get up and pace around the few square feet of floor space in my room. Then around the living room. Then around Alissa's huge room that she pays for with her Blackstone money. I lie on her bed and try to force more tears. Nothing comes, but a force sucks my insides towards my stomach like planets caught in a black hole. I stand up and walk to the bathroom. I sit on the shut toilet with my feet on the seat. The floor is lava. I stare at the window by the stand-in bath. The larger pane is frosted, but the one right above it isn't. I can see a dirty panel of red brick through the glass.

I call my Dad and Cindy. They put me on speakerphone. Crickets chirp in the background. They must be sitting on the balcony. I say hello. My voice is weak. A pebble drawn out to sea.

"We've just finished dinner, Ming," my dad says. "We ordered it to the house with an app."

"Have you heard of it, Ming?" Cindy says. "It's called Food-something. Aiyah, what is it called again, John?"

"I'll have to check my phone. How do I exit the call to check?"

"Don't worry," I say. "Please, let's just chat."

"Have you got something similar in New York?" Cindy asks.

"Yes, and in London. It's been around for years."

"Adoi," she says. "Malaysia is always so far behind."

"You guys have had it for years, too."

"How are you?" my dad asks.

"My friend." I stop myself to take another breath. "Tom's best friend, Rob. He died last night."

Cindy gasps. "How?"

"Do you want to come home, Ming?" my dad asks.

I pause. I breathe slow breaths. The word home still tears me open. I begin to feel angry, because asking me to come home is as dumb as it is well-meaning. I wonder why I called them. A desire to feel close to somebody. But their voices further the distance between me and my world.

"Ming?"

"I can't, Dad. You know that."

The bargaining begins. It's the same as always. We can pick you up from the airport! No. You don't have to leave the house! I don't care. Airport security won't even notice. I don't know if that's true. Alamak, I'm booking a ticket right now! Please, Cindy, stop it.

I wait until the irritation boils off into sadness.

"Are you going to go to London?" my dad asks.

"I don't know."

"Have you spoken to Tom?"

"No."

"Who told you, then?"

"Sarah."

"Tom's other ex-girlfriend?"

"Yes."

Cindy gasps again. I think she's so lost in the web of coming-outs that she believes this to be a revelation.

"You should be in London," my dad says. "I'll send you some money for the flight."

"I don't know, Dad."

"Ming."

"We'll speak soon."

I hang up. It's still morning. I get up and sit on the living-room couch and I flick through my contacts.

There are people I think Tom and Sarah might forget. I call them. I tell them what happened to Rob. They ask questions about Tom, and I repeat the things that Sarah told me. After each call I lie down and shut my eyes for a while. I leave Cass until last because I know it'll be the hardest. She cries the most. The sound of her tears opens a lever inside me. I cry for a short while, and I finally feel worthy of a heart. She tells me I can stay with her if I come back to London. I tell her I'm not sure what I'm going to do.

★ ★ ★

The day has vanished. I'm waiting for Alissa to come home. It's five in the afternoon. I haven't eaten today. Food is my greatest pleasure, and indulging in it feels wrong. I don't know when Alissa will be back because she works Blackstone hours. I put on my mother's fur coat, soft and beautiful and illicit. I only wear it at home because I don't need to give people another reason to egg me. I climb out onto the fire escape outside my bedroom window, the metal wet with melted snow, and look over the dumpsters in the Chinatown alleyway. I've always wondered if I'd be surprised if I saw an arm hanging out of one.

I light the cigarette. Quick and deep inhalations until it's gone. I drop the end of the cigarette through the gaps in the fire escape, even though I have an ashtray. It lands on the stairs two floors below. They'll probably never know it was me. If they ever come out, I plan to look up and pretend-shout at the culprit. Excuse me, sir! Just what is your problem! Oh my god. New York men! Am I right, ladies?

I go back inside and pace the length of our living room. I lie facedown on the Moroccan rug. It's pink. I hate it, but Alissa spends her money how she likes. The toll of the day sits on my joints as my body presses against the plush wool. I fall asleep and wake up when Alissa comes in.

"Are you okay?" she asks.

She's wearing her gray suit. The trousers sit high up her waist; her blow-dried hair flows past her shoulders. She holds a box of sushi. I recognize the pink plastic. It's from the place up the road where mopey staff wear hats in the same magenta that say Ichi, Ni, San, Sushi. I rub my eyes, push myself off the floor and sit cross-legged on the blue couch against the wall.

"What time is it?" I ask.

"Nine."

"You're back early."

"Why were you sleeping on the carpet?"

"Rob died."

Panic sweeps across her face.

"Who's Rob?" she asks.

"Tom's best friend."

She runs towards the couch, breaking our sacred rule of no shoes in the house, taking rapid but tiny steps in her heels, the points banging against the wood until they reach the rug. Her shoes mash subway dirt into the pink wool. She sits next to me, leaving the sushi on her lap. There are tears in her eyes as she moves to hug me. She squeezes me like a ketchup bottle. The box of sushi knocks to the floor. I am jealous of her capacity for feeling. She lets go of me and holds my hands.

"Ming, I'm so sorry," she says. "Was he the transphobic one?"

"He wasn't transphobic."

"But he hated your play?"

"That's not what transphobic is."

She nods and looks towards the carpet for a moment. I look down, too. The sushi's a little shaken, but still in the box. The slivers of unagi have shifted off-center, and the fried-onion topping has fallen off the rolls.

"Have you spoken to Tom?" she asks.

"No."

"Are you going to?"

"I don't know if he wants to hear from me."

She cups my face with her dirty subway hands. I almost gasp.

"What can I do?" she asks.

"What?"

"How can I be here for you?"

She rubs her thumb across my knuckles, as if to smooth the bumpy bone. I want to throw the sushi at the wall.

"I'm fine," I say.

"Your friend just died."

"I know, but I'm going to be okay."

"Have you eaten?"

"I haven't," I say. "I think I'm going to go to bed."

I pick up the box of sushi and place it back onto her lap. I need to lock myself away. I walk towards my room, shutting the door behind me. As I lie facedown on my pillow, my struggle to grieve weighs on me. It's like wading through a vat of molasses. I don't know what to do. I need someone to look at, to give me instruction rather than sympathy. But nobody in New York knows Rob. Knew Rob. There's nobody to confirm the reality of the loss. Nobody can tell me how to feel.

I turn my head away from the pillow and stare at the long damp stain on the wall. It stretches from floor to ceiling. The muscles in my neck stiffen as the minutes crawl on. I hear Alissa open and close the front door of our apartment. It opens again a minute later. She knocks on my bedroom door.

"Ming," she says, her voice muffled by the wood. "I ordered some takeout for you. It's Malaysian food."

I roll off the bed and open the door. We stand facing each other. She's left a paper box at my feet. She steps back a meter, as if I'd bite. I don't realize how hungry I am until the scent of lemongrass and chili twirls up from the box. I pick it up and carry it to my bed. My door stays open. Alissa walks in and sits on the corner of my mattress.

"Thank you," I say.

"Don't worry about it."

I open the box. There are two pieces of roti canai set next to a mound of beef rendang, brown and sticky. I take a piece of roti and use it to pinch a chunk of the beef. I put it into my mouth. Each chew is strained, like my jaw is heavy. I swallow and Alissa nods. As the lump of meat and dough trails down my esophagus, I begin to cry. I put eyes into my palms, and the maroon oils from the rendang transfer from my finger to my forehead. I convulse. Alissa swoops in to hold me, and when I stop crying she runs to get a damp cloth from the kitchen. The soles of her bare feet are dirty. She comes back and wipes my face.

"It's really late," I say. "You should go to bed."

"Are you sure?"

"I'll be okay. I'll finish the food. I promise."

She hugs me again and leaves my room. I do as I said I would, tasting my tears as I eat. I set the box next to my bed and wipe my hands on my bedsheet. I fall asleep again.

It's chilly outside the next morning, so I put on the fur coat and climb onto the fire escape for another cigarette. I unlock my phone and look through old photos. Most of mine with Rob are from before I transitioned. I have selfies from a night around graduation. Our eyes were droopy from the drugs. We thought it was hilarious. I wish I had more pictures with him, but it's the price I've paid for being a cunt.

I climb back into my bedroom and fall asleep again until I hear a knock on my door.

"Ming," Alissa says, "I'm heading off to work, but I'll be back in the evening, okay?"

I roll onto my back and stare at the ceiling light.

"Okay," I say.

"Love you."

When I hear Alissa leave the house, I pull myself out of bed and pace the living room again. I can't think of anyone else to call. A stream of notifications from Dad and Cindy floods into my phone. Cindy asking if I have eaten. My dad telling me to check my account. They message me separately, but I know they're sitting next to each other.

I get my stuff ready to go to the Upper West Side for my class. A guest speaker is coming in for the morning, a playwright from Chile. I sit on the subway. A man at the opposite side of the car keeps staring at me. His eyes dart away whenever I turn to him. His hair is slicked back and he stands like an action figure, pretending that his arms are too big to put neatly at his sides.

The train jerks and he trips a little, and when he turns his eyes back to me, he looks embarrassed.

I go back to the pictures of Rob on my phone. I hold it so that other people in the carriage can't see. When I look back up, the suited man is gone. I want to show someone the pictures. I send ten of them to Dad and Cindy. I send Cass a picture of us with him.

As I step out of the station at 116th Street, I hear someone call my name. I turn around. Bunting is a few steps behind me. She hugs me. I don't move in time, and so she holds me with my arms lying flat against my sides. She doesn't notice. We walk towards our class.

"I went on a date last night," she says. "He was such a fucking tech bro. You know, like, one of those guys who goes to Yale then moves to a loft in Williamsburg."

"We're literally at Columbia."

"It's different. Anyway, I let him pay for dinner."

She turns, and then her eyes inspect me as we walk.

"Are you okay?" she asks, her face strewn with sympathy and disgust. "You look terrible."

I wonder if it would be weird for me to say nothing about Rob. I decide it would be pretty fucking weird. I take a deep breath.

"My friend died yesterday. Or the night before yesterday, I think. I found out yesterday."

I pace a couple of steps ahead of Bunting before realizing she's not walking with me.

"Why are you here?" she asks.

"I didn't know what to do."

"Were you close?"

Not for a while.

"Sort of."

"You should go home, Ming." She grips my upper arm. "No,

seriously, I'll tell Pam everything. She'll understand. You remember they were fine with what happened with Deandra?"

"Her mum died."

"There's no hierarchy of loss, Ming. Do you need me to
come with you?"

I shake my head.

"Okay. Well, go home. Call me if you need anything. Please.
Love you."

Does she? Does anyone in New York, except Alissa? Bunting
hugs me again and squeezes my hand before walking away. She
turns back as she opens the department doors. Her expression
is unsure, like she's leaving a shih tzu tied to a fire hydrant. She
vanishes into the building.

I close my eyes and stand still. She's wrong, I think. There
is a hierarchy of loss. I know I'm not supposed to dismiss the
death of someone's pet, but it's never the same as losing a family
member. Losing an ex-boyfriend's best friend is not the same
as losing a sister. Rob dying is not as serious as me losing my
mother. Rob to me is not the same as Rob to Tom, or Rob to
his family. His massive, grieving family.

I walk back in the direction of the subway and take slow steps
down the stairs. I stop before I push through the turnstile. My
brain pings and my lungs seize. I catch a citrusy, earthy smell.
It's Rob's smell. His cologne. My head spins round. I take one
step back, another to the side, and then another to the other
side. The whiff is gone.

A woman entering the turnstile next to me looks at me with
concern. I put my head down.

"Fucking move," says a middle-aged man behind me.

"Sorry."

I push back out of the turnstile and run upstairs and onto
the street, at a loss for what I should do. Rob always wore the
same cologne, and he wore a lot of it. The only other people
whose smell I can recognize are Tom and Cass. After Tom and I

broke up, I kept a bottle of his cologne in my room in London. I used to spray it around. It stopped the memories from smashing in whenever I smelled something similar around people at parties, which for a while I needed. This is the first time I've smelled Rob; a thunderbolt of him, and then of Tom, because to be with Tom, you also had to be with Rob, and when I lost Tom, I lost Rob, too.

There's a department store not far from the station. I walk there through the crowds, launching into a short jog with every couple of steps I take. I enter through the automatic doors. Sales associates stand across the wide room like chess pieces in black blazers, guarding branded racks of products.

I have a vague memory of Rob's cologne being Armani, and so I hone in on the assistant standing by the Armani rack, a Latina woman whose blue contacts lock on to me from across the room. Her skin is caked with foundation, making her impervious to the draining force of department store light, the kind of white gleam that makes people's skin look so bad they fill their bags with shit they don't need.

"Can I help you, ma'am?" she asks.

"Could I try a spritz of that one, please?"

"That's a nice accent," she says as she spritzes a paper stick. "Are you Australian?"

"Thank you," I say. "I'm British."

I inhale the perfume strip. It's not right. I ask her to spritz another. I clench the strips that I think smell close to the real thing in my left hand. By the time I've done my rounds, I have ten of them, and I sniff each of them again and again. None of them triggers the memory, and I forget which was which. I see the look on the sales assistant's face. Her wide smile has tightened. She looks pissed off at the freeloading tranny responsible for the carpal-tunnel on her spritzing finger. I point to a bottle and ask to buy it. Her mouth relaxes. I swipe my card and she places the bottle that doesn't smell like Rob into a paper bag. I should've called Tom to ask. Tom would have known.

When I walk through the front door of my flat, I sit at the kitchen counter and call Henry. We started fucking a couple of months ago, and have since developed a reliable rhythm. He's a bit older. He told me his parents named him Henry because his grandpa loved Henry Ford. His last name is Hoover, and when I showed him pictures of Henry the Hoover on my phone, he just said, ah! Okay! Cool!

"Can you come over?" I ask.

"Now?" he asks, his voice bright.

"Yes."

"Sure. My audition got canceled."

"Cool."

I wait for Henry. I turn up the thermostat and change into a miniskirt and silk halter-neck. He buzzes up to my apartment. I open the door for him. He kisses me. He wears his usual nice clothes; tailored trousers ending just above the ankle, bright socks, Doc Martens, a well-constructed jacket with clean lines. I get scared when straight-identifying men dress well. I like to say it's because they're more likely to be sociopaths, but deep down I fear well-groomed men because I fear their judgment. As I walk back towards the sofa, he rushes up to me and grabs my waist. I squirm out of his grip. He slaps my ass.

"You're looking hot," he says. "I'm gonna take a leak."

Henry vanishes into the bathroom. I like that he calls me hot. Men only started calling me hot after I transitioned, and I consider this a small victory in my transformation from an unhappy boy to an aberrant woman. I prefer hot to beautiful. Beautiful is sad. It reminds me of the way Tom said it, and how that changed after I went on hormones, or when he told me that my hair was growing fast. Beautiful means joy and loss. Beau-

tiful sliced a wound in us, as I knew it would, and each time
Tom said it, he scratched the scab. Hot is good. Hot means hot.

I get the paper bag I left on the kitchen counter and sit on
the couch. Henry comes out of the bathroom. He wipes his
wet hands on his trousers.

"I got you something," I say. "It's cologne."

He opens the bag and takes it out of the box.

"What are you trying to say?"

"It's a long story, but you can have it."

"I came empty-handed," he says. "Guess I'll have to make
it up to you."

I hate that I find him saying shit like this sexy, especially
because it reminds me that Henry has none of the sparkle of
someone who could ever become famous. He sidles up to me
on the couch and kisses me. He undoes the strings of my halter
neck. Henry licks my nipples and cups my breasts. The curves
of his hands are generous, as if my boobs are bigger than they
are. I imagine this is for him as much as it is for me.

He takes off my tights and flips my skirt up like an umbrella
in a storm. His teeth graze my hip as he bites my panties, drag-
ging them off my thighs like a dog. He runs his rough hands
along my shaved legs. He kisses the thin line of scab from when
I cut myself shaving my asshole. His hand creeps up my torso
to my neck. I shake my head and his hand retreats. He presses
his dick against the bone of my hip. He goes down on me. He
fucks me on the couch with my skirt on. He finishes in the
condom, rolls it off and ties a knot in it, holding it between two
fingers as he lies with his back on the pink rug. He's sweaty.

"You're so fucking hot," he says.

I twist my body to lie on the couch. Both of us are winded,
inhaling and exhaling heavy breaths. I wonder if sleeping with
men like Henry is my own sonata in the Great Regression.

"I found out a friend of mine died yesterday," I say.

"Woah," he says, leaning up and resting the weight of his torso on his elbows. "Are you okay?"

"I think I'm fine," I say. "I mean, no, I'm not really fine. No-body in New York knew him. He was best friends with my ex."

"Shit. I'm sorry."

"It's fine. It's just weird being away from home."

I'm scared to look at Henry. We don't have conversations like this. Henry wants sexy and easy and fun, and that's what I try to give him. Telling Henry feels futile. I look up at the ceiling. Our landlord painted the walls gray, but the ceiling is white. He must've done it himself. He's a cheapskate. Rich enough to own an apartment like this, but too stingy to pay a fucking painter. Whenever I focus on it, I can see the ridges where the two colors meet, tiny flecks of gray colonize the ceiling like stars.

I turn to Henry, expecting him to look uncomfortable, but he's relaxed onto the carpet, staring towards the ceiling, too, maybe at the same dots of paint.

"My friend Carl died last year," he says.

"How?"

"Overdose."

I'm unsure of what to say. Maybe the discomfort I thought he'd feel is my own. I sit up on the sofa and cross my legs. My eyes go to my feet. I know that the reason I told Henry about Rob wasn't because I wanted him to know, but because I wanted him to do or say something. I know it's unfair to demand what I can't give.

"Can I ask how it happened?" he asks.

I look at him. He's still staring at the ceiling.

"He was hit by a car."

"Was it a hit-and-run?"

"No."

"Are you going back to London?"

I don't say anything. He looks at me.

"I booked flights home when it happened," he says. "I used up the little bit I had saved to fly back to Ohio. I didn't know if anyone needed me, but I knew it was something I should try to move heaven and earth for."

"I'm just scared of fucking up. More than I have already."

"I getcha. Death makes room for fear and regret like that."

He pushes himself up from the carpet and sits on the sofa. He puts his arm around me. His other hand holds the condom, his cum pooled in the tip of the loose latex.

"You gonna be okay?" he asks.

I nod and hug him back. He smells of nothing. He gets up to put his clothes on. I take the condom out of his hand and throw it into the kitchen bin, hiding it beneath the takeaway boxes from the night before. I pick up the paper bag next to the couch.

"Don't forget the cologne," I say.

He takes it from me and says thank you with a lift of the bag and a wan smile. I let him out of the apartment. It's just past four p.m. I stare at my phone. I have an email from Pam saying I can take the time off that I need, but to keep her updated. Alissa has messaged, apologizing because she's going to be home late tonight. There's another one from Cindy and several from Dad. A litany from people I haven't spoken to for years. One from Cass. Another from Lisa, and I can't bring myself to read it in full. There's a new one from Henry saying that he's there if I need to talk.

I record a voice memo to Tom on my phone. It's in my corner shop voice, spoken with the resonance in my mouth. Men tend to speak from their chest and throat, and that's where they feel the vibrations. For women, the palate of the mouth tends to vibrate instead. Sometimes I slip out of it, but at other times it's consistent.

I listen to it over and then delete it. The words feel paper-thin. I'm sorry? I can't believe it. I'm thinking of you? My thumb circles above the call button like a vulture. I call Cass instead. She picks up on the third ring.

"Are you okay?" she asks. "I'm still in shock."

"I think I want to come home."

20
Guest

I have a row of three seats to myself on the plane. I lie across them like a beached whale. I choose a film, *Chicken Run*, and cry when the chickens escape. There's nothing else I want to watch. I rummage through my bag to find my notebook. I try to write down memories of Rob. It's early in the morning.

My memories are low resolution, my mind struggling to fill the gaps between the pictures on my phone. Parties and festivals. All they show is a cross-section in time, but my recall feels muddy, and without definition the memories are meaningless. Obviously, the dinner party, the one thing I want to forget, is still crisp. It was the last time I saw Rob, and I can remember every word of what he said to me.

The party was at Lisa's flat in Angel, right before Sarah and Lisa split. We were in the stupidly big living room with a very high ceiling. Three other people we knew from university were there. Tom didn't come, but Rob did. It was a weeknight, so he arrived in his corporate clothes with a bottle of wine. It was a few months after Tom and I broke up. Soho Theatre had agreed to show *Thin Frames*. I hadn't seen him in a while, but I thought everything was fine. I was busy writing, and I'd moved into the spare room in a crumbling house in Clapton with a few randoms from university. Rob hadn't responded to my texts. How are you? Would love to see you soon! Have you listened to that podcast about the crypto scam lady? I'd assumed it was Rob being bad with his phone.

"Rob!" I said. "How are you?"

"Ming."

He walked past me and said hello to everyone else. The way he said my name sucked the air out of my chest, like he was reciting it from a register. It was a lighter flame straight to the gooch. My whole body pinched, and I realized that I was in the shit. I drank my wine and made conversation with one of Lisa's friends, a boy called Jamie in a fisherman's jumper. He worked in marketing but also did stand-up. No questions about myself, just a monologue about wild swimming in the Thames, all while looking over my shoulder.

Lisa called us to sit down at the dining table with benches built into the corner of the living room. The woman sitting next to me was called Flavia. I'd met her once, but before I transitioned. I hadn't forgotten her. She wore a beret atop her golden hair. She introduced herself again. I couldn't decide if this was rude or weird or a version of considerate. She was doing her master's at LAMDA. She asked me if I was an actor, something only actors did.

"Not really," I laughed. "I mainly write."

Rob's glare burned into me from the other end of the table, as if I'd said a slur. I shifted in my seat, noticing the hardness of the wooden chair on the bones in my bum. Lisa placed a large filo pie in the center of the table.

"Spanakopita!"

The hungry audience clapped. She scooped up sections and put them into our bowls. Lisa hadn't drained the wilted spinach, and so it swam in a pool of its own juices with the clumps of vegan feta. The leeched chlorophyll soaked and stained the thin layers of pastry.

Amelia, a girl with a button nose and red hair, sat across from me. She told me about her internships at new-media publications, and about an article she'd written about a pop star doing a collab with a hologram of Karl Marx. Flavia, who looked down at her plate while Amelia spoke, interrupted her to ask me a question.

"You said that you write, Ming," Flavia said. "What sorts of things?"

"Plays. I take other theater jobs, too. Whatever I can, really."

"Amazing. Have you written anything recently?"

"Yeah, I've written a new play. It's on for four nights in a couple of months. At Soho Theatre."

"Oh my god, Ming," Amelia said. "That's incredible."

"Have you finished casting?" Flavia asked.

"Yeah. Lisa's helped out with it. The casting, I mean, and all the other stuff."

The table was divided into two halves of heads down, heads up. Sarah and Rob looked at their plates. Lisa's head tilted on the fence; she looked at me, the tension in her face making her eyebrows wobble.

"Cheers to that." Amelia brought her glass to the center of the table. It clinked against mine, then Flavia's and Jamie's, Lisa's and, last of all, Sarah's, which she held up but not out. Amelia had to stretch to reach it. Rob was unwavering and kept on eating.

"Rob!" Amelia said.

"Nah," he said.

"Oh, come on," she said.

"I'm all right."

Sarah touched her arm, and at that moment Amelia seemed to have understood how little she knew. She retreated back into her soggy spanakopita.

"What's the play about?" Jamie asked.

"Her relationship with Tom," Rob said, his head still towards his plate, one elbow now on the table. "It's fucked up."

"Rob," Lisa said. "Tom said he was fine with it."

He looked directly at her and dropped the handle of his fork onto the plate. I felt the clang in my neck.

"For fuck's sake, Lisa." He turned to Sarah. "You don't believe this, do you? You know that Tom says he's fine with shit when he isn't." Rob looked at me. "You know him just as well as me—that's how you can write a play about him, spin your relationship into something to make a quick buck."

"This isn't exactly a moneymaker," I said. "It's a play."

"That's fucking worse."

I took a deep breath.

"Look, Rob, you don't know our relationship and that's fine, but this isn't about you. You have to back off, okay?"

"Like fuck, I don't," Rob said, leaning back onto the bench. "Just because you're trans doesn't give you a free pass, all right? Like you can do whatever you want and fold it into your journey or whatever."

"Oh, fuck off. Nobody's saying me being trans gives me a free pass."

"You fucking act like it." He pointed at me. "Psychotic, narcissistic behavior."

"Rob." Sarah's voice grew stern.

"That's a bit transphobic, isn't it?" Amelia ventured.

It wasn't transphobic, but the table fell into deep stillness. A blue, pink and white bear had walked into the room, ready to maul.

"I have the right to turn trauma into art," I muttered, the words feeling emptier out loud than in my head.

"Oh, come on, that's so pretentious." Rob laughed and rolled his eyes. "You think you're some fucking Sally Rooney, do you?"

"Is Sally Rooney trans?" Jamie asked.

Everyone fell silent. Rob looked at me with a hatred so sharp it sundered me. Guts on the table. People poked at their food. He turned to Lisa again.

"And you, Lisa," he said, "you're just a foot soldier in all of this. Do you realize that? And what fucking for?" He pointed at me. "For her?"

Sarah lifted a finger.

"Don't speak—"

"Don't speak to me like that, Rob," Lisa said, her voice steely. "Not in my own fucking house. On what planet do you, like, accept an invite to dinner just so you can yell at the fucking host?"

The room fell silent again. I excused myself, taking my glass of wine with me. I walked up the stairs to the bathroom, sat on the toilet seat and drank the tart white. Rob must have hated me, and if Rob hated me, it probably meant that Tom did, too.

I didn't question that hate could ever be in the vocabulary Tom and I would use to speak about one another. It was my fault. I hadn't questioned whether Tom would still like me if he couldn't love me. And because of that I'd assumed, or willed myself to believe, that Tom and I had stopped speaking because we were both busy. I got up and flushed the toilet. I looked at my face and body in the mirror. The shadows in my bedroom deceived me into seeing curves, but the white light of Lisa's bathroom flushed these out. I was straight as a board, and no length of hair could disguise the point of my chin.

When I walked back downstairs, Sarah and Lisa weren't

looking at each other. Rob was gone, and everyone pretended
that he hadn't been there at all.

I arrive early, before the morning rush. The Tube takes me
in a straight line to Cass's house. As I step out of the station, I
inhale the exhaust fumes that litter Holloway Road. The pol-
lution hovers at eye level, weighed down by the overcast sky.
The gloom is suffocating.

London is an enclosed, messy web of buildings. When I walk
down a street in Manhattan, the sky fills the space between the
buildings, and the flatness of the terrain ahead of me makes the
blue look infinite, even through winter. It's something I like
about New York, something that helps me feel like I've moved
on to something better. Oh my god! You still live in London?
You must be so stuck! How sad! But as I stand in London again,
I know that I miss it, even as I watch a young man piss on the
window of a Tesco Metro.

I use my phone to direct me to Cass's address. My wheelie
suitcase knocks against the uneven pavement. I arrive at the
terraced house a couple of streets back from the main road,
and ring the doorbell for Flat Three. Cass comes to the door
for me and embraces me. Her hair is wet. She smells the same.
She's wearing sheer green tights and a Burberry checked miniskirt we once found in a charity shop. She's one of few people I
know who still dress like themselves at work. Parliament hasn't
claimed her. She takes me upstairs and shows me around the
flat. Her living room bursts with plants. Cass, like many women
our age, thinks fingering soil and watering shit will bring her
peace. She flattens the creases on her made bed. Incense sticks,
no clothes behind the door or on the floor, the curtains of the
sash window already drawn.

"How are you feeling?" she asks, standing by the doorframe.

"Tired." I sit down on the bed. "I didn't really sleep on the
plane."

"Take a nap. I'm about to head to work."

I get up to unzip my suitcase and give her the bottle of Absolut Peach that I bought for her at duty-free. It was a fucking weird choice. Seven hundred and fifty milliliters of inappropriateness sit heavy in my arms. She takes it from me with tentative hands, holding the bottle in her arms like a child. She starts to laugh. I laugh, too.

"I wanted to get you something," I say. "I panicked."

"No, it's very sweet, thank you so much. It's just, you know."

"I know."

I feel at ease. I take my pajamas from the suitcase and change into them as Cass eats breakfast in the kitchen. I draw her curtains and crawl onto the right side of her bed, by the window. I know that Cass sleeps on the left. She pops in to say goodbye before going to work. I pretend to be asleep.

"Try to call Tom today, okay?" she says. "Love you. I'll leave the spare keys here."

I fall into a dreamless sleep. When I wake up at twelve, I shower, then watch television as I comb my wet hair.

Cass is tidy, but she's still not clean. I put on a skirt, a pair of tights and a jumper. I find some oven cleaner beneath her sink and look up tutorials on how to clean an oven. I destroy grime with soap and steel wool. I run a damp cloth along the dusty skirting. I don't go into her flatmate's room, but I vacuum the carpet in Cass's. When I run my fingers along the carpet, there are strands of hair buried in the beige. I pull them out and throw them away. I buy lilies from the florist on the corner of her road and cut the fibrous stems. Domesticity consumes me in a way that would feel unnatural in my own home. I stop short of doing Cass's laundry. She wouldn't like me touching her underwear.

I put on a coat and find an Asian supermarket on Holloway Road, where I buy ingredients to cook her and her flatmate dinner. On my way back there's a man leaning against a railing outside a building. He says hello to me. I look down and pick up my pace. He laughs. I never know if they know, but I don't think it matters. Those looks come from a place of either hate or lust, and I've learned that those things often aren't far apart.

I take everything out of the bags and start chopping and mixing. I find a blender in the cupboard and throw in the dried chilies, fresh chilies, shallots, galangal; the ingredients for Nyonya chicken curry, which my mother used to make. It's Cindy's recipe. She has no idea what my mother's recipe tasted like, but my mother never taught me, and to me it tastes the same. Cindy would never tell me exact measurements, and so I learned to eyeball everything. How much of this? Just a little, ah. How much coconut milk? Let it glug for a while, lah. Do I use a whole chicken? Aiyah! Hard to say—if you use a kampung chicken, then a whole chicken maybe is okay, if hormone chicken then maybe less. How much less? Adoi, don't use hormone chicken—you want to die, is it?

Cass texts to say her flatmate isn't going to be in. I warn her that I'm cooking a chicken curry and she tells me that it sounds delicious. She's back at six thirty. She looks at me with a blank expression as she walks through the living-room door. I stir the pot on the stove as I crane my neck to look back at her.

"What the hell," she says. "It looks so clean."

"I cleaned."

"Thank you. You didn't have to. You shouldn't have."

"I made dinner."

Cass walks over to the pot as I move to the couch. She opens the lid. Her nose hoovers the steam coming out of it. She pauses. I am nervous. Cass was a fussy eater in the sense that for years she didn't eat. She once had a huge list of things she said she was allergic to. Before I left for New York I noticed her ordering things with chili, garlic and dairy, things she'd once said were on the list.

"This smells beautiful," she says, taking a ladle from a stand.

She takes some rice from the pot and drowns it in red curry before trying a bite. "Is there coconut in this?"

"Yeah, lots of coconut milk."

She pauses for a moment above the pot.

"Delicious."

I relax back onto the couch. She sits next to me cross-legged with a bowl in hand, mixing all of the curry with the rice. She takes big mouthfuls, but the rhythm of her chomping jaw is slow.

"Lisa says you haven't responded to her texts," she says, her eyes on the red pool in her bowl, cutting a bit of chicken thigh off the bone with her fork and knife. "She wants to see you while you're back."

"I haven't looked at my phone today."

"I guessed as much." She swallows a mouthful of food and looks at me. "You should try to see people while you're here."

"I know."

"Did you call Tom?"

"How was work?"

"Did you call Tom?"

"No."

She shifts her lips to the right side of her face. Calling Tom seems like something I have to do, but neither of us has explained why. She cuts up another bite of food.

"The first time you speak to him can't be at the funeral," she says.

"If I'm even allowed to go to that."

"You should call him."

"I don't know what to say, Cass."

I get up and walk to the kitchen. I haven't eaten for most of the day. I cover a pasta bowl with white rice, and place the curry in the center like the flag of Japan. I pick at a bit of chicken with my fingers to taste it. I shouldn't have left it on the heat for so long, or I should have used more dark meat. The bit of breast in my mouth is stringy and dry. I suck my fingers clean and get a fork and spoon from the drawer. As I walk back to the couch, Cass looks at my cutlery and laughs.

"What is it?" I ask.

"I'm just remembering how much you used to tell me off for eating Asian food with a fork and knife," she says. "I'll go and get a spoon."

She gets up, and as she does, I feel a twinge in my chest. It's something I told her at university. In the house where we lived. Where Rob visited. Grief makes dominoes of thoughts, the line of a spiral all leading back to the same thing. Rob's dead. I take a deep breath and count to ten. When Cass returns, she sits down on the couch.

"You know, I fancied him so much." She moves the food around in her bowl. "Do you remember that house party right before we graduated?"

"The one where he apologized to you?"

"Yeah," she says. "I remember feeling so vindicated. But I also felt super sad. I remember looking at how Rob was with you and Tom. He'd hold you both and kiss you. I felt so stupid and jealous. I don't know what of. The intimacy, I guess. My eating got so bad around that time."

Something in my body seizes. I know that Cass and I use the language of therapy. It's so important to allow yourself to sit in these emotions, babe. I think you might be anxiously attached. Don't pathologize your feelings—it's totally normal. You are valid and entitled to them! Both of us avoid talking about our shit in plain sentences. When I speak to Cass I say things like: How are you feeling? How is your therapist? Is it a constructive relationship? We don't talk about eating, even if it's something we observe. Any permutation of the word eat has always felt like a live mine.

"I used to really blame myself because he didn't want to be with me." Cass moves the food around in her bowl some more. "The more he pulled away, the worse I felt and the worse it got. Not that I'm saying if he'd wanted to be with me then it all would've been fine, because when my feelings for him went away I still felt like shit. But it took me a long time to stop hating him."

I set my bowl down on the coffee table and sit closer to her. She puts her head on my shoulder. I put my arm around her and rub my thumb over her wrist.

"I've been thinking about how I don't really know how to grieve." She sits back up. "I don't really know what I was to Rob. Whether I still count as a friend, or something more or less. It's bringing up all these bad things I used to feel about myself. Like, how I used to feel a bit not enough for him. Now it's like I'm not good enough to grieve. Does that make sense?"

"Yeah, totally." I pause. "Bunting said that there's no hierarchy of grief. I think you just have to allow yourself to feel how you feel. I don't know if defining the relationship to legitimize things helps."

Those words feel true to say to Cass. They feel false when I transpose them onto myself.

"You're right," she says. "I still can't believe you're friends with someone called Bunting."

"Seriously."

We laugh, both playing with bits of chicken with our cutlery. Cass spoons some rice, soaked red with curry, into her mouth.

"I don't really know how to deal with the fact that Rob died while hating me."

Cass swallows her food and looks at me. She is expressionless for a moment.

"I'm sure he didn't," she says.

"You have to say that, but it's possible, right?" I pause; she doesn't say anything. "Like, it's totally possible for someone to die while hating someone else. He was perfectly entitled to hate me."

"Your history's more complicated."

"I shouldn't have written the play."

Cass keeps quiet, and after a while she takes both of the bowls to the kitchen.

"I'll do the washing-up," I say.

"No, it's fine. I'd like to."

I fiddle with the TV remote and try to find a movie for us to watch. I give up, and the TV starts to play a trailer for a reality show about houses. The loud American voice is fuzzy in the TV speakers. I turn the volume off. A drone camera swerves round palatial homes embedded in forest and desert landscapes.

"The play's not an easy one," Cass says with her back to me, speaking over the sound of the tap. "I think it made sense to do it, and it was exciting because it did well, but I also understand why Tom changed his mind about it. And I can sort of get why Rob would see Tom's pain and react that way."

I don't say anything. Deep down, I've always known that people—even Cass—had mixed feelings about *Thin Frames*, even if they supported me at the time. I walk up to the sink with a tea towel and start drying things.

"You're going to get mad at me for saying it again"—she hands me some cutlery—"and I can't pretend to know what Rob would've wanted, but I just really think you should call Tom."

I dry the cutlery and put it back into the right drawers. I ladle the curry into Tupperwares with rice. I choose the wrong ones. It's too late when I realize the red will stain the plastic containers.

"You should take these into work for lunch," I say.

Cass comes up behind me and hugs me. We sit down and watch the show with the big houses. My jet lag starts to creep up on me, and not long after, I am sleepy again. I change into my pajamas and go to bed. I wake up before Cass but fall back asleep, and when I wake up again, she is gone. I walk around her flat and stretch my back. My muscles and joints crack and roll. I sit on the couch and yawn. I find my phone. A stream of messages. I respond to them one by one. I tell Lisa that I love her.

As I walk around the room, I scroll to Tom's name in my contacts and, without thinking, I dial him. My heart begins to race. He picks up just as I think to hang up.

"Tom," I say in my corner shop voice. "Hi."

"Ming."

The line is fuzzy, but the sound of my name in his mouth lowers me towards the old voice.

"I'm sorry it's taken so long," I say.

There's silence on the line.

"It's been days, Ming."

"I know, I'm sorry." I pause, shifting on the couch. "I didn't know if you wanted to speak to me. Sarah called me and said you were out for a walk when she told me. I'm not blaming her, but I took it as a hint. I really wanted to speak to you. I just didn't know what to do, you know. Are you still at the flat?"

"Our landlord is letting us—me—surrender the lease. I'm back with my parents. Where are you?"

"I'm in London."

"Where?"

"At Cass's house."

More silence on the line.

"Okay," he says.

"Are you feeling okay?"

He huffs. I imagine him taking the phone away from his face and looking off into the distance.

"No," he says. "He's dead."

"I know," I say. "I'm so sorry, Tom. I'm so sorry. I'm so sorry."

He begins to cry. There are only a few times I remember him crying. When he came back from his work party and told me about Jason. When I broke up with him. Each of those times, the way he cried was locked with restraint, and each tumult that emerged from his diaphragm was tight. This crying is unmitigated, and I hear its force in the cracking of the receiver, which, unable to process the decibels, splits the ends of his sobs into white noise.

I start crying, too. It's a reminder of the part of me that used Tom as a guide for what emotions were right. A perpetual voice of reason, the center of gravity through which I could measure my own unreasonableness. He guides me again, and I stop when he stops.

"Are you alone?" I ask.

"My parents are here. Sarah's in and out. I haven't seen many others. I've been bad at picking up my phone."

"Me too."

"I know this sounds pathetic, but I thought you'd call to ask to stay with me."

Something precious inside me breaks. I don't know what to say. We haven't spoken to one another for a year, but reciting this fact feels cruel. To both of us.

"It's not something I could've asked," I say.

"I know. But I really thought you would."

I bite my lip.

"Part of me feels stupid for flying back to London at all."

"You can stay in the spare room, if you like. My parents would be happy to see you."

"Are you sure you want me to stay?"

"Yes."

"Are you sure?"

"Please."

I bite my lip harder.

"Okay," I say. "I'll tell Cass."

"Okay."

I listen to him breathe through the phone. Tom has always been a heavy breather. Sometimes when I woke up at night, I would listen to the air coming in and out of his chest at a steady pace. I'd focus on the sound, the steady rhythm, a metronome of wind, flesh and bone, rocking me to sleep.

21
Buoy

I buy Tom's parents flowers and a small box of truffles. When I get to the checkout counter I panic and run back to pick up a good bottle of Riesling.

On the train I worry about the excess, and so I tuck into the truffles and eat the entire box. I hide the Riesling in my bag. The sugar and motion and nerves make me nauseous, and when I arrive at the station, I throw up into an open skip. I wash my mouth out with my bottle of water. I hold my phone camera to my face to check for bits of vomit and chocolate in my teeth. A family of four cross the street to walk on the other side. I don't blame them. I collect myself and walk towards his house. I can get there with my eyes closed.

He opens the door after I knock, holding its edge with his hand. Tom looks shocked, like he's spotted me through gaps in the crowd outside M&M's World in Leicester Square. For a moment I question whether we spoke on the phone at all.

"Tom?"

He stares at me. He's wearing a tracksuit, and I realize how much I've dressed up. Beneath my coat is a floor-length prairie dress. It's the height of winter. I packed my suitcase in New York too quickly. His eyes move over me and onto my bag. There are long, sparse hairs on his chin. I know it's a week's worth of growth. He looks like he streams *Fortnite* from his bedroom.

"You're here," he says.

He slips his fingers beneath the handle of my bag. I let go of it. He pulls it inside the house and looks at me again.

"Sorry," he says. "I'm sorry, I'm—I don't know—hi."

"Hi."

We stand at the border between his house and the street, inside and outside, safe and unsafe.

"Please," he says. "Please, come in."

He waves me into his home, the place where I lived for six months and where our collapse began. Everything is the same. The things I expected to stay the same, at least. The dark, creaky floors. The way it smells like potpourri, even though there isn't any. Copies of the *New Statesman* and *Waitrose Food* magazines on the sideboard by the stairs. The uninterrupted line of sight from the hallway to the garden.

Tom takes me through to the kitchen.

"Can I get you anything?" he asks.

"Water, please."

I sit on one of the high chairs by the kitchen island. I run my fingers along the smooth wood, and my nails along the scratches. It surprises me that I don't recognize a single one. It tangles my brain that I can't tell which are new or old, which ones were made before me, or during me or after me; and then I realize that hardly any would've been made during me, because I really didn't live here for long at all. If their lives in the house were a day, then my time there was mere minutes, like a visit from a milkman, a Jehovah's Witness, or a hot young trans woman selling flower subscriptions. Tom moves to the cabinet

above the sink where they keep chopping boards and weigh-
ing scales, and pulls it open to reveal shelves of empty glasses.

"You moved the glasses," I say.

"Oh," Tom says as he pulls the tap. "My parents did. It made
more sense to have them above the sink, I guess."

"Where are they?"

"They went for a walk."

He places the clear glass in front of me, setting it on a bump
in the wood. The surface line quivers. I sip the water and look
out into the long, narrow garden. There's new outdoor furniture on the patio. Rough black metal curved and welded into
chairs and a table.

"I wanted to ask about the funeral," I say.

He leans forward and puts his elbows on the countertop.

"It's in Manchester. In two days. You should be there."

"Are you saying anything?"

He looks out into the garden.

"Yeah."

"Is it hard? Figuring out what to say?"

"I guess," he says. "But I have to do it, don't I?"

I want to hold him, but find myself rooted to the chair. A
hug from me could be a violation. I don't know what it means
to touch someone when I know their body so well, whether it
worsens the intrusion.

"I'm excited to see your parents."

I'm not. I'm terrified. He turns towards me.

"They'll be back in a couple of hours," he says. "I asked them
to be out of the house."

"Why?"

"I was scared of seeing you. It's been a really long time,
Ming."

The hollowness in my stomach expands. My organs twist.

"What were you scared of?" I ask.

"I don't even know." His head plunges towards the wood,

atop his laced fingers. "Everything. I knew that I wanted you here, and that it made sense for you to come, but I don't know why, Ming." He keeps his head pressed onto his fingers. "There's so much we haven't spoken about. There's so much I've been angry about, but I just really wanted you here."

Relief and guilt sweep towards me in a wave. I get up from the chair and approach him. I place my hand on his back, and as I lean down he comes back up and hugs me, pressing my body close. The familiarity of his frame pains me, and this makes me wonder how familiar my own body is to him. I know this is the kind of narcissistic shit that Rob accused me of. I lift my arms around his back and hold his neck.

"I'm really, really sorry, Tom," I say.

"For what?"

"Everything."

Janice and Morris arrive as I'm unpacking my bags in the spare room. The sun has nearly set. Tom and I haven't talked about how long I'll stay, but I haven't booked a flight back to New York yet. I descend the stairs, gifts in arms, my feet slowing as I approach the bottom. I haven't seen them since the week before Tom and I broke up. Part of me wanted to text Janice after the breakup, but I didn't, and she didn't, and after the dinner party with Rob I assumed it was because Janice and Morris also hated me.

"Ming," Janice says. She takes me into her arms, the wine and flowers between us. Her tangle of hair grazes my cheek. She lets go of me and pushes my hair behind my ears, the thing I stopped doing when I grew conscious of the angularity of my jaw. She holds her fingers on the side of my face and chin. "You're looking so beautiful."

I mouth the words thank you as I hand her the presents. She beams.

"I like your hair," I say.

She fiddles with her wiry locks. They're shorter. And gray. The change exaggerates the lapse in time between past and present.

"I decided to stop dyeing it," she says. "I think there comes a time when you have to stop fighting upward."

Morris hugs me. We move back into the kitchen and Janice sits down where I sat earlier. From the cabinet, Morris takes two glasses and fills them up, passing one to Janice and holding one towards me. When he sees that I already have a glass, he smiles and his hand retreats, keeping it for himself. He tips some water into his mouth. We all sit around the countertop.

"Right," Janice says. "Have you two thought of what you'd like to do for dinner?"

"No," I say, and look towards Tom, who stands at the border of the hallway and kitchen.

"I can cook," Tom says. "Or we could?" he asks me.

I nod.

"That would be nice, wouldn't it?" Janice says to Morris.

"Very nice," he says.

"We can walk to Tesco," Tom says.

I go back upstairs to get my coat. I stare out of the window of the guest room. The view is basically the same as the view from Tom's. It's a little alienating. I remember looking at the same backs of houses and gardens, the same yellow windows of light puncturing the darkness, so often when Tom and I were together.

I think about what Janice said about fighting upward. Am I fighting upward? Transitioning feels like submitting to the forces I long resisted. Letting the flood take me. Sometimes, though, it feels like the opposite. Like I'm suspended by hooks rather than in water. My body on display for doctors and surgeons and for people with opinions not worth sharing but that they share anyway. We should think about how to optimize your breast growth. Have you considered getting a brow lift, too? Is she, like, going to go all the way? Is that a girl? Do you think she's got a dick? It's a new uphill fight.

I put on my coat and go back downstairs. Tom holds the door open for me again, with a few carrier bags scrunched up in his hand. We set off into the darkness, walking towards the big Tesco ten minutes away. We walk in silence. I know if we talk too much it'll feel like we're simulating our old life together. The sounds of our feet on the pavement, and my panting from struggling to keep up with his determined walk, start to get to me.

"Are you modeling now?" I ask. "I saw a picture from that show. Where did that come from?"

He keeps his head turned to face in front of him, angled downward.

"I did that show, yeah."

"What was it like?"

"Really crazy, from start to finish. Rob came with me to the casting," he says, tilting his head away from the pavement. "It was obviously exciting, but I felt kind of uncomfortable for a lot of it. I'm not sure if it was because of all the fuss with the makeup and clothes and stuff, or because of all the attention."

"People would kill for that experience," I say. "I'm jealous. You know, I saw those pictures of you and felt really bad. I don't think I ever told you that you were beautiful. Or said it enough."

I'm about to jaywalk when he holds his arm out to block my chest. A car swerves past us at the junction. The car behind it honks. We walk across the street as their rear lights shoot down the road.

"You were always the beautiful one," he says with a laugh. It's a soft laugh, hardly more than an exhalation, like a quarter of a cough, but it's the first since I arrived.

"Less and less. Did your boyfriend get you into it?"

"It was Marco's idea, yeah. But he's not my boyfriend."

"Is he not?"

"No."

"What is he, then?"

Tom doesn't respond. I don't push it. We arrive at the doors of the big supermarket. Tom goes to get a trolley. The eyes of the guard by the door linger on me for too long. I wait by the racks of flowers.

I've seen pictures of Marco. I made leaps in logic, assumptions from a comment on a picture. He's hot. Marco. A photographer. On a deep dive of his life, I found pictures of him in drag. In the pictures he wore a slinky dress with no attempt to cover the musculature of his arms, the inverted triangle of his shoulders and waist, the hair on his chest, or the longer ones that radiated from his armpits like flames. His merit wasn't in how little people noticed him but in how much they did.

I remember feeling jealous when I saw those pictures of Marco, and how much that confused me. His drag was different to what I did in *Death's a Drag*, or what I do now. A disguise that slowly transformed from an evening costume to my everyday life. A way of dressing and being to soothe an internal dissonance. Maybe it's subversive, too, but I still can't shake the desire to reach Hertfordshire-Sunday-roast-and-berry-picking normality. It's pathetic.

Tom returns with a trolley and the guard looks away from me. We stalk the aisles.

"What do you think we should cook?" he asks.

I think of suggesting char kuey teow, but venturing into the past with Tom feels dangerous. Here's the dish you loved when we were together. Open wide, you little bitch! Some memories harden into land mines. I don't know where the pressure points are.

"Pasta," I say.

Tom leads us through the aisles. He drifts from shelf to shelf, knowing where to find the anchovies, dried pasta, tomatoes, prawns. I go to the wine aisle and pick up a discounted cork-top. It feels like a good one, even if we don't need it. I find Tom waiting by the till. I insist on paying, and the woman manning the checkout counter stares at both of us. She's interested, like she's wondering what the sad, handsome man in the tracksuit is doing with the demure tranny, and why the tranny is willing to pick up the bill. My guess, if I were her, would be that Tom's my brother and that I have a sugar daddy. A sugar daddy who's a Tory MP and lobbies for Big Pharma and makes me dress like Maria von Trapp. Why else would I be wearing this? Tom measures the weight of each bag and gives me the lighter one.

We set off for home. I notice the mustard glow of the street-lights more on the walk back. The radiuses of their halos stretch into the night sky.

"I quit my job when I found out Rob had died," Tom says, his voice deadpan. "Handed in my notice, I mean."

I instinctively clench my teeth, but his eyes are fixed on the road ahead. Quitting a job at the height of grief is rash. Tom isn't a rash person. He makes his bed every morning. He brushes his teeth after nights out.

"Why did you quit?" I ask.

"I don't know. It never really fit me, did it? I think everyone could see it but me. Rob and I had talked it through a lot, and he'd said a few things that sunk in. When he died, I knew it for sure. I get the next week off fully paid, and they've let me stop working early. I've saved quite a lot, anyway."

"You've always been good at saving. Do you know what you're going to do?"

"Maybe I'll get more modeling jobs to tide things over," Tom says. "And I'm going to chat to the people at the pub down the road. They're hiring."

"Okay."

We continue at pace. I remember googling Tom once when I was in New York. The picture of him smiling on the company's website came up. I convinced myself that it'd got better

for him, but without reason. He always hated it. It never fitted with his worldview, even though he refused to see it. I'm
not sure modeling does, either, but I suppose quick fixes don't
exist. I want to hold his hand, because I think that's what he
needs, but his fingers are wrapped around the red plastic handle of the carrier bag.

At the traffic light near Tom's house, my left bicep aches. I
swap the bag to my right hand, and it knocks against the one
Tom is holding. He passes it to his other hand. We cross and
climb the steps to his door. He pauses as he twists his key, turning his face towards me.

"I've been really stuck, Ming. It's like something's happened
to me over the last six months." He pushes the door open and
holds it there with his foot, looking back at me. "The first six
months after we broke up felt like I was moving on autopilot,
and life and work just flew by, but then the six months after
that was harder. And now Rob is dead. I have no idea what to
do, and I just feel really stuck."

He pauses for a moment, then walks in, straight through to
the kitchen. I stand stunned at the entrance, my hand stopping
the door just before it hits the frame. I follow him in and gently
close the door behind me. We wave to his parents in the sitting
room. We start taking things out of the bags and move pots and
pans out of the cupboard to cook. Could you please boil some
water? Chop some garlic. That parsley is off. There's some cooking wine in the fridge. Thirty seconds on each side, please. Drain
them. Did you reserve some of the pasta water? How much salt
did you put in the pasta water? The pasta's quite salty, don't you
think? I don't have words to say, and so I follow his instructions
and respond only to his questions.

The prawns steal the white of the onions, and the onions steal
the translucence of the prawns. The anchovies and tomatoes
dissolve into the pan. The bubbling starch in the pasta water
melds the ingredients into a thick emulsion. I set some places

around the table as he calls Janice and Morris for dinner. I ask
them what they'd like, open the Riesling, and pour us all a glass
as they take their seats. We allow a gentle clink between our
glasses, the stems loose in our fingers. There's silence as forks
dive and spin through the pasta.

"How are your dad and Cindy, Ming?" Janice asks.

I clear my throat.

"They're good. My dad's still working. Cindy's been trav-
eling a bit."

"Have they visited you in New York?"

"Cindy has." The thought of her weekend visit makes me
smile. "I'm not sure if Dad will."

"How is it over there?" Morris asks.

"It's been good," I say. "Lots of writing. Lots of interesting
people from around the world."

"That sounds great," Morris says.

"How's the garden?"

"Lots of it is gone now," Morris says. "But we've planted a
few new things."

I twirl my fork in the pasta until the beige strands mummify
the steel points. I look up to Janice, and she smiles at me as she
takes a sip of wine from the tall glass. Awkwardness consumes
the space between us, replacing the intimacy we've forgotten.
Tom doesn't look up from his plate. I want to ask questions,
but I don't know what. Asking a therapist how business is going
feels inappropriate. Asking a teacher if this school year is much
different from the last feels inane.

"Have you been coping with the news?" I ask.

"You mean Rob?" Janice asks.

"Yeah," I say. "Sorry. I've been struggling to find the words
to talk about it."

"I don't have words, either," Janice says. She pauses, elbows
on the table, entwining her fingers in the way she likes to do.
"It's funny, isn't it? I counsel people through grief and yet I feel

so helpless. It's a reminder of how difficult things are for my clients. Rob spent so much time in this house. Just like you. He didn't live here, obviously, but I think of the times he'd pop round and we'd eat dinner together. That includes you, of course. When you were living here, I mean, and after. I'm sure it was no more than a few handfuls of times, but the memories have expanded in my head and now they feel like it was every week. And then, as a mother."

Janice glances at Tom, who no longer hovers over his plate, but sits with his eyes towards the corridor. Morris's shoulders are scrunched towards his neck; he holds his forehead in one hand. Janice's pleading eyes rest on me. My arms and legs feel coiled in the miasma. My mouth feels wetter than usual, and I think of Rob not as a man who hated me but as a part of my life who will never return. I feel at once weak and responsible. I shut my eyes through the tears, trying to silence myself. Morris's rough hand squeezes my arm through my dress sleeve. Janice holds my other hand from across the table. Tom leans over from his side of the table to hold me, and Morris's hand moves to my shoulder. I cry on Tom, and wafts of his smell fight their way through the piling mucus in my nostrils.

"The pasta's already too salty," he says, and I laugh into him. When we pull away, I use my napkin to wipe my wet face.

"I'm sorry," I say.

"It's a relief it's not one of us for once," Morris says.

We laugh again. After dinner we clear up the plates. I help wash up, and then say good-night and ascend the stairs towards my room. I fiddle with creams and toothpaste and hormones until I'm ready for bed.

I crawl under the duvet and fall asleep. I wake up just past midnight. I fell asleep too early. My body thinks it's taken a nap. Fucking jet lag. I feel parched and heavy. I get up to go to the bathroom and drink a glass of water. I stand on the landing, and follow my instinct towards Tom's door. I tap it twice with my knuckles.

"Come in," he says.

He looks surprised to see me, and he sits upright in bed. He's holding a book. His bedside lamp is on.

"I just woke up," I say.

"I've been sleeping badly, too," he says. "Come in."

I cross the threshold into the room I once shared with him. I look around and notice that everything is the same. The same posters, same furniture. The only things missing are the pictures of us he once had, and the canvas of a mangosteen I painted for him. I wonder where they all are; maybe collecting dust in the eaves in his parents' room upstairs. I sit at the foot of his bed, and he observes me from the other corner.

"That thing you said by the door, about feeling stuck," I say. "I've felt that, too, you know. It's like there was the play, and then I moved to New York, and now it's as if things are catching up to me."

Tom stares out of the window. The blinds are down. He takes a deep breath. I wonder what emotion he is trying to temper, which of anger, despair and grief he's fighting hardest. He sets the book down and stretches his eyebrows with his thumb and forefinger, smoothing the tension in their furrow. His eyes move towards the floorboards, inspecting the dark stain of the skirting. It's like when we stood in the doorway when I arrived, two like poles, as if the slightest movement will send the other off course.

"I watched *Thin Frames*," he says. "On the second or third night of its showing. I didn't tell anyone about it. It felt like a sick joke."

My heart drops. My head falls with shame, which in itself is shameful, because if I feel worse knowing he saw it, then I must've really fucked up.

"Why did you write it?" he asks.

I inhale to say something, but he moves to speak again.

"You said you wanted to help trans people, or couples going through what we went through," he says. "You said that thing about having more art by trans people. Rob thought it wasn't to do with any of that, and when he came out of that dinner with you, he was sure of it. And even though I don't know what was said that night, I agreed, and I didn't need to hear it from you, but now I think I want to."

I feel stripped bare. Tom holds a dossier of my shittiness. I bring my legs onto the bed and sit cross-legged.

"I told Rob that I wanted to turn trauma into art. It was similar to what I said to you."

"Art," Tom says, his voice dispassionate.

"I know," I say. "I think I believed it at the time, but when I retrace my steps or whatever, I think I wanted to turn it into an achievement. To prove that it wasn't for nothing."

"What does that mean?" he asks. "That you wanted to prove it wasn't for nothing?"

"Transitioning, breaking up. Everything, you know. I felt so worthless." I avert my gaze and stare out of the window. "I wanted to feel like I was worth something."

I stretch my legs out across the white bedspread before pulling them back under me again.

"I feel like you stole something from me," Tom says.

I shift my jaw to one side. Stole sounds serious. It adds weight. Barnacles to a hull. I might've done something bad, but I don't know what I took that he doesn't still have. My eyes are back on him. He looks out of the window.

"What did I steal?" I ask.

"I don't know. My memories, I guess. My chance to talk about it. My privacy. My dignity." He looks at me again. "You used me."

I sigh.

"I'm not blaming you," I say. "But I just wish you'd said something."

"Would you have listened?"

"Yes," I say, resentment slicked over my voice.

Tom relaxes again, and with a long exhalation he moves us away from the precipice of tit for tat.

"I don't think I completely understood it when you asked," he says. "It took a while to feel the hurt. Not just from *Thin Frames*, but it's like the play opened the floodgates for all the other stuff. The breakup. And I didn't know how to talk about it. There was this discord, I guess. You being the Ming I wanted caused you pain, and I get that, but I think losing that Ming caused me more pain than I wanted to admit." Tom's features sit heavy on his face, his jaw slackened, as if they bear the weight of the words he's speaking. "I wanted it to be simple, but it was more complicated than just growing apart. The clothes and boobs and pronouns and the nose didn't matter on their own, but together they felt like the world, and that was easy to know and feel but harder to explain why. That's the crux of it, I guess. I'm not mad at you for transitioning. That's not what I'm saying, but to use me for a play on top of that was wrong."

I twist my body and place my back against the headboard, looking straight ahead. My neck tingles with the heat of his eyes.

"I've been thinking that it's like you left all the bad stuff with me," he says. "All the things you ditched to go from Ming to Ming. To be happy, I guess."

"I don't think that's how anxiety works." I meet his stare. "I'm not skipping down Fifth Avenue singing 'It's A Wonderful Trans Life,' Tom."

Tom sighs. I slump down and lie on his bed. I stare at the cracks in the ceiling, black hairs on a white canvas.

"I'm sorry that you felt used," I say. "I'm sorry that I used you, rather. I think, deep down, I always thought you'd be fine. That of the two of us, you were going to come out on top, you know."

"Come out on top? How?"

"Finding love again is going to be easy for you, despite whatever happened with Marco. Men who want to fuck me are scared of that fact. Sometimes I think that I transitioned into loneliness, and I wonder if I'd have been better off denying myself what I wanted if it meant not being alone. I can't even go home, Tom. You know that." My eyes well, the bridge of my nose pinches. "You don't know how badly I want to go home, to just be with my dad, or to watch TV with Cindy. My dad tries to talk about the future. Like, where he'll live, but I shut it down. I can't even face it. I'm not going to have all the things that are easy for everyone else. The things that matter."

Tom and I lie like split bowling pins, and the tension seizing us relaxes. We've tired ourselves out. My arms are straight down my sides, but Tom holds his hands over his stomach, his elbows wide, the point of one touching my arm.

"Me and Marco aren't together. I really wanted to be with him, but he didn't want to be my boyfriend. I thought I loved him, but now I'm not so sure."

"Why not?"

"I can't see us ever needing each other. Or him needing me," he says. "And it's funny that you say that about loneliness. I think about being lonely a lot. Sometimes I think there's something wrong with me. I only seem to be able to love people who need me. My parents. You. Rob, even."

"Rob?"

"He didn't talk to anyone else like he spoke to me. I think he would've just bottled stuff up otherwise. And I thought you needed me, too, and when you didn't, things changed and we fell out of love."

My heart pounds. Tom feels so far away. I remember how much I used to like lying on him, how much I liked listening

to the murmurs of his stomach. But on his bed my body is cold.
Everything feels still except my beating heart.

"The times I thought you loved me most were when I thought
you needed me most," he says. "It's like I don't know the difference between someone needing me and me loving them."

"I don't think that's pathological, Tom. It's okay to need people, and it's nice to be needed. It all sounds human to me. Loving someone who needs you is safer, isn't it? It's like entrusting
someone with an organ, a part of yourself, you know."

"Showing your belly, I guess."

"Like when a cat lies on its back?" I ask. "I like that."

I shiver, and I slip beneath his covers for warmth. He joins
me, and we lie on our sides facing towards one another.

"You didn't have to choose loneliness," he says.

"Tom."

His fingers slip in between mine. It's a sorry. The heat of his
hand warms the rest of my body.

"I feel so scared," he says. "About Rob, I mean. Life without him."

"I miss him. I've missed him for a while."

I look into Tom's sad eyes.

He squeezes my hand, and he moves his arm across my waist.
We lie in silence.

"I think in some ways I still need you," I say.

He smiles a flat smile, digesting my words. I turn around so
that he can spoon me. He strokes my back.

"I think I still need you, too," he says.

He holds me close. I shut my eyes. We could be anywhere.
My second-year bedroom. My house in Kuala Lumpur. His
third-year attic. The flat we once shared. My mind clicks our
bodies through these scenes like a stereoscope.

Tom plays with the fabric of my pajamas. I open my eyes and
watch his hand as it moves up the buttons. My heart thumps. He
pushes a button out of its loop and my chest feels like it's cav-

ing in. His warm hand moves towards my nipple. He caresses it. This desire is unwieldy and cryptic, tainted with an existential rift. All I can think about is how much I still want Tom to love my body, the one I can finally love but worry I've ruined. He moves closer to me and kisses my neck. I turn around. He kisses my lips. I kiss him back.

He undoes all my buttons. I slip out of the sleeves, and he takes off his T-shirt and boxers. He's thinner, but more defined. The lines and shadows around his muscles have grown crisper. He licks my ear, the way he used to, running it along the edges before plunging it inside, flooding me with warm familiarity. He holds my breasts and kisses them. His hands find their way around my waist, and he takes me into his mouth. He rubs my nipple with his thumb. My body is limp. I am overwhelmed, but I receive the warmth of his wet tongue.

"Can I fuck you?" he asks. "I can do it."

"Tom?"

"I'm hard, I can do it."

I nod. He gets some lube and tries to push himself into me. He can't get in. I put a pillow beneath the small of my back, and he presses into the gap between my cheeks. He kisses me as he moves in and out.

"You're so beautiful," he says.

He smiles at me. Beautiful still feels sad. Beautiful still hurts, but I kiss him again and stroke his hair. He moans and shuts his eyes. A tear rolls down the side of my face. He slows, and his thrusts become stilted and weak.

"I can do it," he says, "I can do it. I just need a second."

He gives a few more sad, slow pumps.

"Tom. Please, stop."

"I can do it."

He pulls out of me, his body still over mine. He strokes himself. I bend my knees and rest my feet on the sheet.

"Tom."

"Please."

"Tom," I plead.

He looks at me. I sit up, take the pillow from under me and place it on my lap. He stares down at his soft dick. He cries. I hug him. His tears sting my neck like salt on a slug. I take him back beneath the covers and cuddle him. He cries until he falls asleep.

I stay awake for longer. I'm glued to his body. I realize that a small part of me hoped Tom and I would go back to the way we were before, as if all he needed was time until the laws of attraction could bend enough to accommodate me. But they didn't, and they never would have, and even though he doesn't say it, I know that Tom hoped for the same. I don't want to let go of him. And although the room feels submerged in grief, and the bed and lamps and books and bodies float weightless underwater, his body is an oxygen tank, a life raft, a buoy.

22
Trees

Tom's knees bounce across from me in the taxi. One knee touches my own, and so the vibrations from his rattling leg move into mine. Sarah sits next to me. They're both in suits. His parents have driven up separately. They said they'd keep their distance today. Not that Tom has asked them to.

"It starts in twenty minutes?" Tom asks.

"We'll be there in ten," Sarah says. "We have time."

I pinch the hem of my black wool dress. It's ridden up my thighs in the taxi. I'm worried it's too short. I bought it right before I left New York. At the shop I tried to remember what people wore at my mother's funeral, but my mind came up blank. At each corner of life I am reminded of the ways in which I haven't collected the things I need. Wedding clothes. Office clothes. Death clothes. It's like learning my mother tongue in later life. Whenever I think of this, the stupid takes I've read on the internet murmur in the back of my mind. Dress? A dress?!

Oh my god, of course the trans woman wants to wear a black dress. Narcissist. Worrying about clothes even at a funeral! I bet it's made of latex. That's what they think being a woman is!

I bought a black dress. There are times and places where all I want is to speak the language of femininity well enough that I can disappear. Airport security. Bathrooms. Funerals. The reality is that most men at funerals wear black suits, and most women wear black non-suits, and I had nothing to wear. I hadn't planned on someone dying. The simplest thing was a black dress.

I'm nervous. Tom, Sarah and I all look out of separate windows. The air in the cab is warm and stuffy. I haven't been to a funeral since my mother's. One of the only things I remember is my father crying during his eulogy. He sobbed through his words, and at one point he stopped speaking. His cries suffocated the church. Nobody moved to the altar to help him, but a friend of my mother's who sat next to us grabbed my hand. She was the same woman who gave me a rickety birdcage after the funeral. It was a square block, and its bars looked like satay sticks. It had two tiny brown birds in it. She told me to pull the door open, and the two birds flew into the air.

The taxi rolls further into suburbia. Terraced houses separate into semidetached houses, and sometimes split further into fully detached houses. Gardens grow more expansive. Sarah's and Tom's eyes still lie fixed on opposite windows. They've both visited Rob at his family home. I wonder if this is the last time they'll do it.

Tom pulls worn pieces of paper from his pocket, stapled at the top corner. The creases are wide and the corners scrunched. He mouths the words to himself. I try to decipher them from the movement of his lips. He wouldn't read it out to me when I asked him if he wanted to rehearse it.

Sarah holds my hand. I turn to her.

He'll be okay, she mouths.

She squeezes my hand tight. The back wheel hits a pothole,

which untethers our grip. Tom folds the piece of paper and puts it back into his pocket. He looks up at both of us, the color washed from his face.

"I don't think I can speak," he croaks.

"You can, Tom," Sarah says.

"What if I can't get through it?"

"Then I'll read it out for you," she says. "Or Ming can."

"Okay," he says. "I've had to scrap a bunch of it."

Tom takes the papers out of his pocket again and shows them to us. A full page has loops of black biro through it.

"Why?" Sarah asks.

"I read this thing once, about the self being a center of narrative gravity. It means that rather than being an actual physical thing, the self is just a collection of narratives we tell about ourselves and each other." Tom's eyes well. "I thought it was a nice idea, because I thought that if we kept talking about Rob, then he could live for as long as we do."

Sarah and I fall silent, and Tom returns to the window. I grew up with people who spoke with caution about the dead, as if doing so would reanimate the grief. Maybe that's the wrong thing to do, but now I wonder if it's more painful for a thread of someone to remain than for them to leave altogether.

"That's really beautiful, Tom," Sarah says.

"Why'd you scrap it?" I ask.

"Rob would say it's fucking pretentious."

Sarah cackles, and Tom laughs, and soon all three of us are laughing. We roll in the back of the cab. I laugh beyond the joke, hard enough that the muscles in my stomach ache. It feels both different and the same as the crying from the days before; the body takes release where it can. The taxi driver looks at us through the rearview mirror, and I can see the outer corner of his eyes pinch with a smile. We sigh in unison, and our chuckles punctuate the fresh silence. The taxi slows towards a redbrick church.

"We're here," the taxi driver says. "You lot take care."

As we step out of the taxi, the other cabs arrive, too. Cass steps out of one and waves. Lisa steps out of another and makes a beeline for Sarah; they embrace. Lisa lets go, turning towards me. I haven't seen her since we wrapped up *Thin Frames*, and although I know why, all that distance feels pointless and stupid. We hug for what feels like a long time, squeezing one another close.

"I'm sorry," I say softly into her ear.

"It's okay," Lisa says. "I'm sorry, too."

She doesn't have anything to be sorry for, but I guess we're all just holding on to shit that we need to let go of. It's also just really nice to hug her.

The gravel crunches under our shoes as we walk towards the church doors. The inner walls are white and tall. There's a stained-glass mural of Jesus at the far end of the church. Among the people still trickling in, a red-faced older woman with blonde highlights stands in the middle of the aisle. She turns to us. Sarah speeds up towards her, and the woman takes Sarah in her arms, holds her face in her hands. Rob's mother. Rob had her nose. Sarah hugs an older man by the front pew. Rob's father. My heart stops when Sarah hugs a boy who looks just like Rob, one of his two brothers. I follow Tom towards them. Sarah separates from Rob's other brother and wipes a tear from her own eye. She looks towards the casket at the front of the church and her head swings back around, her eyes landing on me. It's a look of disbelief. I shake my head. I can't believe it, either. Rob's mother puts her hand on Sarah's arm, directing her to sit a couple of pews behind the family.

Tom hugs Rob's mother. Her face contorts at his touch. Rob's dad stands up to hug Tom, too. I don't know why I'm watching so closely, but I can't look away. When Tom moves away from them to sit, I walk to the back of the church towards Lisa,

Cass and Tom's parents, but someone grips my hand from behind. It's Tom.

"Please," he says.

I let Tom lead me into one of the front pews. Sarah and I flank him. People I don't recognize fill the rest of the row and the ones behind me.

Chords boom from an organ. I fiddle with the glossy order of service on my lap. I look towards Rob's casket again. It's shut. I didn't realize that I would never see Rob's face again. I don't know if this is normal. My mother had an open casket.

Panic thrums inside me as a priest takes to the lectern. He says a few words about Rob. I hear the faint outline of achievements and a life history, but the words begin to lose meaning, blurring in their shape and definition the longer I stare at the closed box. There's an easel next to it, holding a framed black-and-white picture of a smiling Rob. All I can think about is how pictures don't capture the depth of a face. If the camera is too close, then it makes a person's nose look bigger, and flash rubs out contours and lines. I don't know if I have any videos of Rob, and I can't remember the color of his eyes. I know they were brown, but I can't remember if they were dark or if they were a bit green. I can't tell from the picture. I want to take my phone out to look, but everyone would probably think I was live streaming the funeral. After *Thin Frames*, people expect that kind of shit from me.

Everyone shifts and stands up. I stand up with them. The lyrics to "Jerusalem" are on the second page of the service booklet. I find myself falling behind. I'm fearful people will notice my voice singing out of time, and so I lip-synch the words instead.

The priest returns to the lectern after we stop singing.

"I would like to invite Rob's father, Peter, to say a few words," the priest says.

Peter goes up to the front. His voice is warm and rough. He thanks us all, and says a few things about Rob. He jokes about

Rob's appetite. He starts crying when he talks about Rob's unbounded potential, and the way that he always gave. As he speaks, I imagine Rob's smile, and then I imagine dying young. I imagine being hit by a car. Being in a crashing plane. Falling off a balcony. I'm sitting in the same room as his body, but I can't fully comprehend that this is what's happened to Rob. Dying young.

Peter tells a story about Rob at school, and my heart pounds. I can't focus. I know Tom is next. When Peter leaves the lectern, Rob's brothers run up to hug him. The priest returns to raise us from our seats for another hymn. I lip-synch the words again. We sit back down.

"I would now like to invite Rob's best friend, Tom, to say a few words of remembrance," the priest says.

Tom shifts in his seat and walks to the front. Sarah reaches across the empty space to hold my hand. He takes the piece of paper from his pocket and unfolds it. My face feels hot. I watch everyone watch Tom. He clears his throat and looks out into the audience.

"The greatest thing about Rob was his generosity. He was generous with his time." Tom hiccups. "A few months ago he dropped everything to join me on a trip that I was nervous about. I think other people would've waited to be invited, or felt awkward, but Rob just knew when I needed him, sometimes before I did."

It's the first I've heard of the trip. I feel a small pang of guilt for the things I've missed.

"Maybe Rob just loved a holiday," Tom says to a softly chuckling audience. "But he also just loved being with people."

Tom tells us about how they met. The Flying Lotus gig. He explains that Rob was much better at him at DJing, that everyone probably would've preferred Rob to play alone, but that Rob always insisted on being a duo, swapping out every couple of tracks to let Tom fumble on the decks. Tom tells us about their camping trip to Scotland, where everything went wrong, and they looked so unprepared that another group of hikers called the mountain rescue on them. I've heard this story before, but I laugh with everyone else. It was one story in a chain. I remember details Tom omits, like how Rob had forgotten to pack a sleeping bag. How Tom hadn't been able to poo all week.

"He made me feel like my time and presence had value. It sounds simple, but it meant the world." Tom pauses. "It all sounds simple, which is why I think the biggest struggle in thinking of what to say today comes from the fact that so many of my favorite memories of Rob feel banal when I say them out loud. They're little things that fill the day, things that become special because you do them with someone you love."

Tom lists some of these things. Foot rubs on the couch. Sharing music with each other. A walk through the botanical gardens on a winter day. These pinch my heart. They're things I was there for, even if I'm not there in Tom's mind.

"Even just living with him. I feel so lucky to have lived with him. Those places always felt like home, but at some point Rob started to feel like home as well."

Sarah's crying beside me. I'm not sure I've ever seen her cry. Her chin is down and her mouth is open; she's shaking. I hold her hand.

"I feel lost at how to fill the time he gave me." Tom wipes tears from his eyes with the knuckle of his thumb. "I don't know what replaces that feeling of home."

Tom stops speaking, and his body looks tense. It's more than a pause. I look at Sarah, who now looks at me, her tears stalling, her face consumed with worry. Tom takes a deep breath through his nose, shuddering against his rustling snot. The room is silent, but someone in the opposite pew lets out a sob. Tom exhales. He speaks again.

"But I've been thinking about how the trunks of trees bend and curve when they grow next to each other. Their leaves twist to accommodate each other. Their closeness reads on the shape of them, and you can infer the shape of one from the shape of another. When you know someone and you grow together, your shape and form become theirs. And so even though Rob is gone, and there'll never be another Rob, another friend I've known as well or as closely, the impression his life left on me will always be there, and in that sense we haven't lost him at all."

Tom looks towards the casket and then back at the pews. I look at Sarah. We smile at each other through wet eyes.

"Thank you," Tom says.

Tom steps away from the lectern. He returns to me, and I hold his hand.

The wake is at Rob's family's house, a ten-minute walk away. We hold back until all of Rob's friends have assembled to walk in one group. We float between each other. People come up to Tom to tell him his speech was beautiful, because it was just that. My heart thickens each time someone says it.

At Rob's house, people crowd the center of the beige living room. The gray furniture inside has migrated to the edges. Tom is enveloped by older people. I spot Janice and Morris standing close in a corner of the room. I stand with Cass and Lisa by the adjoining kitchen. I shift my weight from foot to foot. Cass runs her fingers along the fibers of her black silk bag. Lisa adjusts the black clip holding her hair back.

"I'm so proud of Tom," Cass says.

"Me too," Lisa says. "I was kind of floored by it. He's so eloquent."

"Rob would've loved it," Cass says.

I nod. Cass and Lisa make conversation with the people who flit in and out of our small circle. I pretend to listen, but have to ask people to repeat what they've said when they get to a question. An hour passes. I go upstairs to pee, trying not to look at the mountain of family photos along the stairwell. I sit on the

loo and take my phone out of my bag. Rob's eyes were dark
brown. I go back downstairs.

The heat of mourning bodies warms the room, and my dress
collar tightens around my neck. I hold my coat in my arms.
My eyes move to the windowpanes. Across the room, Rob's
dad unfastens two latches and pulls the sash open. The bodies
standing between me and the window absorb the breeze before it reaches me.

"Oh my god." Lisa elbows Cass. "Do you guys, like, remember that night we went to watch Rob and Tom play at that club,
and the toilets broke?"

"There was sewage leaking from the ceiling," Cass laughs.

I force a smile.

"Yeah."

My breaths become labored, and the bodies in the room
multiply. The radiator's behind my legs. I can't bear the heat.

"Hey," I say. "I'm just going to go outside for a minute."

"Do you want us to come with you?" Cass asks.

"I'm fine. Don't worry."

I shuffle past the people until I reach the front door. The
biting air meets me outside. I don't put my coat on. My heels
clack on the driveway, and I wipe a bead of sweat from my forehead. The sun has dropped; the sky is a medium blue. I stand
and breathe until my lungs expand towards my stomach. I walk
round the side of the house.

Rob's mum leans on the wall next to a drainpipe. She turns.

"I'm so sorry," I say. "I just came outside for some air."

"No, please. I don't know what I'm doing here, really. I
should go back in."

She stays still, and my body moves next to hers against the
wall.

"I'm so sorry for your loss," I say.

"Thank you," she says. "Are you Ming?"

I nod.

"Rob was so fond of you. Of all of you."

I take in her words.

"Have you ever lost anyone?" she asks, before shaking her head. "I'm sorry, what a question. What am I like."

"No, it's fine. I lost my mother."

"Oh, you poor thing."

She places her hand on my arm. The cold of her fingers feels precise, like I could draw the detail of her fingerprint if I shut my eyes. She looks younger than Dad and Cindy. The sun has ravaged my dad's skin, but she looks more youthful than him beyond that.

"And Rob, of course," I say.

"Rob," she says. Her tone is deliberate and yearnful. "Nothing prepares you for losing a child, does it? And as a parent, you just wish it was you. I never thought I'd outlive any of my children. Maybe that's naive when you have three. Had three. But you poor thing. Your mother. And now Rob. It's not fair, is it?"

She rubs my arm, and although her fingers are cold, I feel her warmth. I can hardly understand why parents would take a bullet for one child. I can't fathom doing it for three. I wonder what it does to a person to love their place midway up a tree trunk, in the line of a swinging axe. Rob's mum probably doesn't know anything but caring for people, valuing others more than herself, so much so that even at her son's funeral she's comforting me over my mother who died a decade ago. I pick stray threads of wool from the bodice of my dress. All I can give her is a sad smile.

"Right," she says. "I'd best go back in." She pulls the hem of her own dress down and dusts nothing from the front of the fabric. "Tom said your cabs will be here not too long. You take care. Don't be a stranger, okay? You're welcome here whenever you like."

She shuts her eyes for a moment, and then lets out a breath. After stepping away from the wall, she turns back to me.

"And take care of Tom. Such a lovely boy."

I smile at her again, the woman I only met today; the woman who raised Rob. After she vanishes round the corner, I walk along the length of the house until the chill settles beneath my skin. I go back inside, into the room full of people. My legs take me upstairs. I look for Rob's bedroom. I know I shouldn't be in here, but walk up to one bedside table and see a pre-transition photo of me and him and Sarah and Tom. It's from a disposable camera. We're on the couch together in the living room of their third-year house. Lisa took it.

There are two sets of built-in wardrobes along one wall of the room. I hold the picture frame in hand and walk over to one. When I pull the knobs, I recognize some of his old shirts from university. I hold the sleeve of one. It's soft in its age. The print is wild brush-marks in different hues of blue. I sit down with my legs together, my bum on the back of my heels, and then I crawl into the base of the wardrobe and shut the doors behind me, my back along the wall, still holding the picture frame. Sleeves and hems weigh on my head. I dip my chin forward so they fall to the back of my neck. I can just about make out our faces in the photo. I don't really know what it means that I'm in it. Isn't this a nice photo of us? It'd be much nicer if Ming wasn't in it, though, right?

I shut my eyes. I want time to pass, or no time to pass at all, to be stuck in the eye of a black hole. I hear muffled footsteps near the door.

"Ming?" Tom says.

I don't say anything. He leaves. I cry a little. Maybe Rob would feel differently because Tom and I are together. Not together, together, but still together. He might not hate me if he were alive, but his death is also what fixed things. There's pain in that irony. I'm glad I'm in the photo.

I hear footsteps again. I can see Tom's legs through the downward slants of the shutters. I can see scuff marks on his shoes.

He didn't polish them. The doors open, but the shirts and jackets and trousers above me block him out. There's a small scuffle of the metal hangers on the metal bar. And then he parts the clothes to uncover my face. He's holding my jacket over one of his arms. His jacket is already on. He smiles at me, and then he kneels. He crawls into the wardrobe with me, and so I scrunch my legs even further towards my chest. He pulls the doors shut, but they don't close because there's not enough room for both of us. His legs poke out of the wardrobe's borders. He doesn't say how he found me here. He doesn't have to.

We sit in silence, no noise but our breaths. Our legs gently rest on one another's. Time stops for a little while. I could stay here forever, even though I know we can't. I hold Tom's hand. It's so warm. We sit for a while longer, and then my hungry stomach rumbles, breaking the quiet. Tom lets out a breathy laugh, which I follow. He squeezes my hand then slowly lets go. He taps open the door with his knee, gets up and reaches for my hand, pulling me out of the wardrobe. I put the picture frame back on the bedside table. He hands me my jacket and leads me down the stairs.

"It's nearly five," he says. "The taxi company called. They'll be here soon."

We say our goodbyes in whispers, and Rob's friends from London move out of the room. The remaining attendees diffuse into the empty space. I push my arms through my coat sleeves and walk outside. Tom's parents are getting into their car. I turn back and can see Tom through the window, hugging Rob's mum goodbye. Taxis are parked in a row outside the house. People hop in. I wait until Tom and Sarah emerge through the front door.

"Ready?" I ask.

Sarah puts her arm around my waist, and I reach out behind me to hold Tom's hand. We climb into the last taxi. It feels emptier than when we arrived.

"I keep saying it, Tom, but I loved that thing about the trees," Sarah says.

"I liked the tree thing a lot," I say.

"Thanks, guys."

We sit in comfortable silence until the taxi draws up to the station. We get out, and I go into a shop to buy packs of beer and sweets for the journey, while Tom and Sarah float towards the train. I find them at a seat of four. They smile at the treats in my arms.

"It's been a long day," I say.

We crack the cans open and sip them as people take their seats. The train slowly pulls out of the station, gliding towards London. The city evaporates into green pastures, and the hard lines relax into the curves of rolling hills. We open our second cans. My eyes meet Tom's. We stare at each other.

"Are we going to be okay?" Tom asks.

I don't know what he means. There is a universe of ways in which I, and Tom, and Tom and I, feel delicate.

"I think so," I say.

He nods and turns his head towards the window.

"Maybe we should write a play together," he says.

"Fuck off."

Sarah laughs, and Tom does, too. His eyes sparkle.

We both take sips out of our cans. I stare at the beautiful boy in front of me, who stares at the grass fields out of the window. I scroll through the news on my phone, miserable enough for me to lock it soon after. I look at Sarah, and at Cass and Lisa, and the others further down the aisle. A carriage of important people. People important to me.

I look at Tom, the boy whom I've always loved; a boy, a buoy. I reach across the table to hold his hand. I rub my thumb along the flesh below his index finger. When we were lying on his bed, Tom said he carried all the bad stuff I left behind. Maybe he was right, and that's exactly what he did for all those years, long before he even realized he was doing it. Maybe that's what people are supposed to do, sponge out the bad, wring out the suffering as much as we can, even if it stains our hearts and hands.

Epilogue
Teething

I wake up at Henry's. His double bed is pressed up against the corner of his room. There's nothing on his walls besides an Aphex Twin poster. It's *Selected Ambient Works 85–92*, an old album but not an old poster. I try not to imagine him googling and purchasing it online, because when I do, I'm on the crest of an ick. The same kind of ick I get when I imagine him double-knotting his shoelaces, screaming at a jump scare or being harnessed to a skydiving instructor. I know this is unfair of me, but I've seen him do one of those things and that's more than enough.

I sniff the pillow. Henry changes his bedsheets every week, which is more than I do. Today I've woken up so close to the wall that my thighs are against it. My knees are touching the blinds that come down to just above the mattress. He drapes his hand on my thigh. I feel the fabric of his boxers against the back of my hip. He sleeps with underwear on. I sleep naked.

He kisses my shoulder once, then places his forehead against

the back of my hair. When I started sleeping with Henry, I
didn't know much about him. I never asked because I thought
he'd like to keep his life and me apart. When I got home from
London, things changed. I asked questions. He asked questions.
He wanted to know about Rob and Tom. He listened when
I told him that I missed them both. He hugged me as I cried.

He tells me about things he's done. I once asked him about
the first trans person he ever slept with. The first trans woman?
Huh. What a question! Promise you won't judge me? She was
a sex worker. I paid her. It was when I first moved here five
years ago. I didn't really know about the apps or how to meet
one. She wouldn't kiss me. I was like, aw, man! I mean, don't
get me wrong, I get why she didn't. I thought I was all horned
up, but I think I just wanted someone to kiss me.

The woman's name was Angela. I tried to look her up on
escorting websites, but there were thousands of Angelas and I
didn't have a last name. I haven't asked where they had sex, but
I imagine a dingy hotel room with white lighting and green
walls. Whenever I think of her, I hope that she's doing okay,
though part of me knows that the odds are stacked against her,
and in a way that they aren't for me. I'm still fond of Henry.
It's not shiny, sparkly stuff. Maybe it's mental gymnastics, or
my own weakness, but Henry's showing me his belly, as Tom
would say. I appreciate that.

He stretches his arms above him and yawns, and I watch him
through a slit in my eyes so narrow I imagine he thinks I'm
still asleep. I smile as if I'm dreaming of something lovely. It's
a late start for both of us this morning. He's not going to au-
ditions because of lockdown. Money's a worry for Henry, but
he's holding up.

I roll onto my back and allow my eyes to open towards the
ceiling. He's staring at me. I can feel it. I turn to my right and
smile back at him. Sometimes I get anxious about Henry. He's
been with lots of women, and I worry that once the world

opens back up he'll realize it's probably easier to date someone who isn't trans.

We kiss each other good morning and cuddle. We play with each other in bed. I get up. He watches me as I walk out of his room and towards his shower. His rich flatmate is a persona non grata because he fled to the Hamptons for lockdown, but we are privately happy because I can walk around the apartment naked. The look on Henry's face is so stupid and it makes me feel special. I shower, get out, then dry myself. When I walk into Henry's room, I see that he's fallen asleep again. I put my clothes on and kiss him on the cheek. He stirs.

"See ya tomorrow?" he asks.

I kiss him again. I start the walk home from Henry's to mine. It's a long stroll over the Brooklyn Bridge, but there's no real way to fill my days otherwise and so I like it. The streets are desolate. It feels like end times.

I don't have plans for today, but I want some time alone. Time at home will still mean time alone, because Alissa works round the clock from her bedroom. The more I learn about her job, the more confused I am. I've long suspected that jobs like Alissa's and Tom's old one do nothing, and the fact that she's so busy when the world is shut down seems to prove it. There's a list of words and phrases I'm not allowed to use. They make her see red. Fabricated. Wealth extraction. Moving money in circles and taking a cut. Oh my god, Ming! You just don't understand anything about the economy. Look, I'm as liberal as it gets, but you need to wake up to how the world works! One more fucking word and you're off my Office subscription. Go write in your fucking Google Doc! The last one stung more than I would've expected. She resents my and Henry's interpretation of lockdown compliance, but I don't say anything because we're all going through our own shit, and also her hair's looking really thin.

I go into our building and climb up the stairs. I open the

door and can hear Alissa in her room. She sounds angry, and so I know she's speaking to herself rather than anyone she works with. I put my bag on my bed and lie down. I want to speak to Tom. We've been teething. We work best in person. We always have. I don't think he hates me anymore. There's a lot of love there. I love that.

Sometimes Tom and I text. Long texts. Small talk feels too impersonal, but long messages are hard to sustain. We haven't got into a flow of speaking round the clock, but he's in my thoughts all the time. I'm rooting for him. Not in a way that's patronizing, or as if I'm doing super well, but I'd let a lot of my own life go to shit if it meant he'd be okay.

I check my phone and see that Tom's sent me a message.

Hey. I'm about to go out for a walk. Do you want to speak on the phone? We could video call.

My heart races. We haven't spoken on the phone since I left London.

Yes! Give me ten minutes.

I don't need ten minutes, but for some reason a phone call with him makes me nervous. It's giddiness. It doesn't make sense. It's not romantic, and it's not being in love. That's long over for me and Tom, but in some ways I feel like I'm going on a date. I pace the small strip of floor at the end of my bed. Are my clothes dirty? I take off yesterday's clothes and put on a demure blouse. What if he asks for a tour? I chuck some things into the wardrobe. The strap of a top, a wayward tendril, hangs out. I open the door again, throw it in and slam the wardrobe shut. I hear Alissa grunt through our shared wall. Please stop slamming things! Some of us have jobs!

Last night's wine sucked the moisture out of my skin. I run to the bathroom and wash my face. I scrub the dirt away. I towel my face and slather Alissa's expensive moisturizer over my forehead and cheeks. No fucking difference. When I return to my room, my ten minutes are up. I sit in the middle of my bed. My spine is straight and my phone is in front of me. I call Tom.

"Hello!" I say.

"Hello!"

He's walking. A clear sky is above him. Trees dance along the borders of my screen. I think it's Brockwell Park. He looks handsome. He's clean-shaven. No more peach fuzz. Thank fuck.

"What have you been up to?" I ask.

He takes his eyes off the screen to look at the road above it. He lowers the phone slightly. He's still beautiful from this angle. I'd look like Miss Piggy.

"I've just been at home. I haven't really been doing anything."

"How are you for money?"

I wince at my directness, but it's always been my way with Tom. He doesn't react to the inappropriateness of the question.

"I'm not spending anything, and I got in with that pub a couple of weeks before the cutoff for furlough."

"That's good."

I round my spine. My shoulders relax.

"How is it over there?" he asks.

"Slow. This play I wrote was supposed to go into production, but I'm not really sure what's going to happen. I even got excited and did these sketches of the poster. Wait, I'll send you one."

I text it to Tom. I sidle up on the bed so that my back is against the wall. Tom's camera blurs and freezes as he goes to check the picture. After a couple of seconds his face unblurs and he looks down at the camera.

"It looks cool," he says. "What's it about?"

"Trans people with dementia."

"That sounds really depressing."

"Thank you," I say. "You're the first person to say that. It's really fucking depressing."

Tom laughs.

"Have you been up to much else?" he asks.

"Not really." I look towards my wardrobe. I think of Henry. "I've just been working on my own stuff. I'm writing a screen-play, too."

Tom sits down on a bench. He's holding the phone by his thigh. I'm still looking up at him.

He turns and smiles at someone. His head follows them as they walk past him. His eyes linger on them before turning back to me. I expect he's about to say something important, but then he asks me if I've watched anything good. We exchange lists of television shows and movies and comment on each of them. There's a lull in conversation. He looks ahead of him.

"I've been finding it all pretty hard, Ming. I've been seeing lots of Sarah, though. Just outside and stuff. Cass also got in touch. Is it weird that I get a bit nervous when people ask me to do things?"

"I don't think it's weird," I say. "You should try to see her, though."

The thought of Cass and Tom hanging out one-on-one warms me. She asked me last week if it'd be strange to message him. Shyness is a thorn in the British psyche. It's agonizing.

"I guess I didn't realize until a couple of weeks ago how I don't actually speak to that many people," he says. "Speak-speak, I mean."

"You can call me whenever, you know."

"Thanks," he says. "I'll do it more." He smiles at the camera, and then the smile disappears and he looks down to his side. He furrows his brow. "I want to talk to Rob a lot. There was a night a couple of days ago when I knelt by my bed with my hands clasped and I just started speaking to him."

"What?" I let out a nervous laugh. "Like, prayed?"

"Yeah, isn't that weird?" He sends a nervous laugh back. "I just really wanted to talk to him, and that was my only reference point for speaking to someone that's not here anymore. At first I sat cross-legged on my bed like I was meditating." He does a quick look-around, then stretches his arm away from himself and brings his legs up onto the bench to show me. I giggle. "But it didn't feel real enough. So I got my phone to ring his old number because I thought I could leave him a voice mail, but then I thought how much it'd hurt to hear his voice like that, or, worse, that it'd been disconnected. I couldn't press the call button." He looks away from the camera. "And so I went back to what came to my mind first and just knelt on the floor with my elbows on the bed and told him how much I missed him and wished he was here, even if he'd hate the world right now. I told him about how you came to stay. And how me and Sarah had been spending a lot of time together. I told him about quitting my job, and the pub, and about how Sophia said modeling's going to pick up. It just felt really good, Ming. It's stupid, though, right?" He lifts his phone upward so that I have a more direct view of his face, and even through the grainy video I can see the slight rise of his eyebrows. "It sounds really crazy."

"It's not crazy at all."

I try to make sure that my face is as earnest as I feel. Tom is so kind. He gets up from the bench and starts to walk again.

"How's Alissa?"

I look at my wardrobe, knowing she's just behind it on the other side of the wall.

"She's working all the time." I keep my voice low. "She works from home now. She's been a bit of a nightmare."

"What's she like?"

I hunch over my hips a little. I can feel a smile creep onto my face, the gossipy kind. Tom has the same one.

"She gets off the phone from a meeting and just screams. Like, not even cries, just a really guttural scream. Once, the internet went down and she started banging her fists on her wall. It's weird."

Tom laughs.

"Were people like that at your old job?" I ask.

"No, but maybe if they weren't in the office. Is she all right to you?"

"Yeah, she's fine. Like, she's obviously embarrassed about the fist-banging, and she knows this shit wouldn't fly with anyone else." My mind goes to Henry again, and I wonder if I should tell Tom about him. "But I've been out of the house a lot, which is probably better for both of us."

"Doing what? School?"

"I'm sort of seeing someone new."

Tom's face wears a sudden attentiveness.

"Who are they?"

"He's this actor. We were sleeping together for a while, but I always got major chaser vibes from him. Not that that's always a bad thing, you know, but he's been really good since I got back from London."

"I'm happy for you, Ming."

I believe him, even though it's hard to read excitement and sincerity over the phone, even if on video. Tom seems distracted by his walk. He's out of the park and back on the street. He checks his right and left before crossing the road. I hear the sound of a truck driving past. Tom turns left into a quieter street.

"What's he like?" he asks.

"He's really kind. He's from Ohio. He asks a lot of questions about you."

Tom's face brightens. He smiles widely, and I can see more of the roof of his mouth.

"He does?"

"Yeah. Not in a bad way. He's just interested."

My stomach dances; it's the odd mixing of Tom and Henry. It's a version of happiness. Being happy about Henry; being happy I can tell Tom about him; being happy Tom's happy for me.

"Have you spoken to Marco at all?"

Tom shrugs.

"I haven't. He sent me a message last week, but I don't think I'm ready to see him again." He zips up the jacket he's wearing with his free hand. "I'm just happy being alone for the moment."

"I'm happy for you."

I hope he believes it.

Tom stops walking and leans back on something. I can see the familiar red brick of his family's house behind him.

"Mum keeps asking after you. We've been cooking loads from that cookbook you got. We say it's like you're here."

"Really?"

"Yeah."

My insides ripen, and I feel unnervingly close to crying. Tom gives me an update on his parents. I tell him about how Cindy got her eye-bags surgically removed, which seemed pointless to me because she's always wearing sunglasses, anyway. Tom laughs.

"I've been wanting to do something a bit more creative," Tom says. "Now that I have a bit more time, I guess."

"Like what?"

"I bought some new decks. And I've been doing some writing."

"Have you?"

He nods. He looks away from the camera again, as if observing something across the street. We both stay silent. The idea of him writing warms me, even if it's about me. It's not like I have a leg to stand on, anyway.

"I don't know if it's any good, though."

"I'm sure it is." We fall into a brief silence. "I can read it if you want?"

"Can you?"

"Of course. I'll be critical if you'd like me to be, but I'd also just love to see what you've written. What is it about?"

"You'll see," he says with a smirk.

For a moment I am taken by how much can be said in a look, a smile, a smirk. I could be writing about you! Payback time, you bitch! How does it feel? Just kidding—talk about narcissism! And the prerequisite to all of this seems to be history, even if some stretches are beautiful and others are torrid and ugly. It's time I spent with Tom; time I wouldn't and couldn't have spent with anyone else.

"I'd better head back inside. Dad wants help with the garden," he says. "It's been really nice talking to you, Ming. I'll send you the stuff. Let's have another call to talk about it. And to catch up again."

"Yeah, of course."

It's time for us to say goodbye, but neither of us does it.

"You're smiling," he says.

I am confused for a moment, and then I understand.

"I'm smiling. You're smiling."

"I'm smiling."

★ ★ ★ ★ ★

Acknowledgments

Mum, Emma-Jane and Claire.

Monica MacSwan, Lesley Thorne, Jazz Adamson and the team at Aitken Alexander.

Bobby Mostyn-Owen, Louis Patel and Milly Reid at Doubleday and Grace Towery at Hanover Square Press.

All my friends and party girls, but especially Aisha Hassan, Daisy Schofield, Jay Crosbie, Leo Sands, Ciara Nugent, Elaine Zhao, Amy Hawkins, Jess Franklin, Mollie Wintle, Faith Waddell, Fin Taylor, Jo Marshall, Joe Goodman, Amber Chang, Jonny Dillon, Molly Flood, Laura Inge, Lauren Chaplin, Nina, Jones, Tayiab Ramzan, Camille Standen, Zander Spiller, Isobel Cockerell, Franklin Dawson, Linda Chen, Awut Atak, Leo Benedict, Billy Gore, Michael Kirreh, Freddie Carter, Shan Li Ng, Katrina Ibrahim, Makissa Smeeton and Kevin Chang.